TRIPLE M MURDER

A JACK CALLOWAY THRILLER

By

Carmen Cady

Happy Reading
Carmen Cady

Printed in the United States of America

First Printing, 2021

ISBN 978-1-7360075-0-1

Cady Publishing, LLC

Website: https://carmencady.com/

Edited by DeeAnna Galbraith
Book Cover Design by VCBOOKCOVERS.COM

For The Many Who Supported My Journey

TABLE OF CONTENTS

TRIPLE M MURDER

A JACK CALLOWAY THRILLER

CHAPTER 1

JACK CALLOWAY

ONE HUNDRED AND TWENTY-EIGHT. That's how many concrete blocks shape the ceiling of this cell. I have counted them five times over the past two days. My gaze lingers on a drop of water sweating from the wall. The air is stifling—muggy. Like a boa constrictor wrapping around me, it strangles my lungs, squeezing the life out of me.

On my back, with my arms folded behind my head, I count the concrete blocks again. One. Two. Three… Another bead of water drips down the wall and catches my gaze. My thoughts drift and I recount the events of the last two months. What did I miss? This question fuels and invigorates me. To solve this question means my freedom.

I replay the night I flew home from San Francisco. It started with a call. A call that changed everything.

I avoid day flights. Airports are full of frenzied activities. Demands blasting overhead, hired drivers waving signs, a cacophony of passenger carts parting the crowds, babies crying, and gate areas spilling over with passengers. It's a sea of pacing and bustling or yawning over the long day's travel or elation of recognizing your loved one. Emotions in an airport are edgy and impatient. So, I prefer night flights—less noise and congestion. And it's night.

The airport is calm this evening. I'm standing in line at the security gate, scanning the area. Only a few people are ahead of me.

A security officer sitting at the podium doesn't greet passengers but with his hands outstretched, waits for their ID. He inspects their license, then his screen, and back to the passengers. Dark circles and bloodshot eyes express his fatigue. I hand him my ID. He takes his time reviewing my information, longer than the other passengers, and I wonder if there's something more, something I don't know, he's considering. With a nearly imperceptible shrug of his shoulders, I'm allowed to advance through the gate.

My walk through the terminal is steady and casual. The news is running on several televisions, which I ignore until a bold caption reads, "The City Can Rest Tonight." I stop and read the closed caption, "Police arrested the San Francisco Strangler."

I've spent the last two days here, comparing the criminal profile I created a year ago for the San Francisco police department to recent evidence—another dead body. Confident they had the right guy; they arrested him this morning. When the criminal in a case is arrested, I breathe easier knowing the families will find justice and can move on with their lives.

Now, I'm on my way home to Seattle.

I walk into my apartment at 2:30 a.m. With a loud meow of indignation, Jasper, my cat, is there to greet me, circling my legs. Angling for me to pet him, I pick him up and give him a good scratching behind the ears, "Hey there buddy, miss me?" Purrs roll through his body. Work often takes me away, but he's never completely alone because my housekeeper, Maria, cares for him while I'm away.

I've gotten little sleep over the past few days and I'm longing to shut out the world for a few hours. My legs drag me to the bedroom closet. I put my shoes away and strip down. Heaviness rests upon my eyelids and I fall into bed saying good night to Jasper and drift off to sleep until a persistent vibration gnaws me to consciousness.

I gasp for air to catch my breath. I sweep the room with my eyes and find my bearings. *Home.* I reach for the nightstand and pick up the phone. "Calloway." There's a familiar, gravelly voice on the other end of the line, Chief John Phipps of the Seattle Police Department, otherwise known as the Seattle PD.

"Jack, Chief John Phipps here. We have a case. We could use your expertise."

The air in my room has changed and I can feel heat rising underneath my skin. "What time is it?"

"It's 7:30 a.m. If I remember right, you like to work at night? Was hoping to catch you before you call it a day… or night."

I had slept for four hours, but it felt like five minutes. "Yeah, normally. I had a case that didn't rest." I swing my legs over the edge of the bed, my slippers waiting. I step into them and walk to the bathroom.

"Homicide, rape, or arson?" I ask as I reach for a towel to wipe the sweat off my face. I was having the same nightmare. The one I've been having for years. The one I can't seem to get beyond.

After a long pause, as if weighing the pros and cons of answering my question, the chief's reply comes across strained. "You'll want to see for yourself." I hear shuffling of paper and a few taps to flesh it out like the matter is settled, a sign he's satisfied with his answer. Chief John Phipps likes things organized and tidy, his desk, his department, his cases, and his life. I can relate, but I gather from his response; this case is anything but tidy.

I turn, lean on the counter, and run my fingers through my hair. His response irritates me. "I need a little more than that."

Phipps's voice is low, like he's worried someone will overhear. "It's a strong possibility we've got a serial killer."

"How many bodies?" I ask.

"This makes three."

"And you're just bringing me in now?"

There is a long pause before he answers. "Budget issues."

My thoughts take me to the San Francisco case. The SFPD lost momentum in their investigation because the press leaked information, causing the perp to go underground for the next six months. Any spin the press makes can either help or hurt an investigation. "What does the press know?"

Phipps sighs. "Not a lot. We're doing our best to contain it, for now."

"Good. Give me a heads up before you put out a statement."

There are certain things I prefer to know before I agree to a consultation. If multiple agencies are involved, it's almost not worth taking on. The red tape is daunting and too many egos get involved. Headaches I don't want. "Are there other agencies involved?"

"Not yet, we'd like to keep it that way."

"Where do you need me to go?"

"Seward Park. Detective Halstead and Officer Dunn are at the scene now. Dunn was the first to arrive. His team secured the crime scene and Halstead was called in. The CSI unit should be there."

The Criminal Scene Investigation, known as the CSI, is the Seattle PD's division of forensics. I glance again at the mirror and decide shaving can wait. "Carla's team?" My gaze turns to the counter, and a lump forms in my throat. My thoughts briefly drift to the case Carla Briggs and I worked three years ago.

"Yeah, Detective Halstead called her team in for forensics. Halstead's lead detective. And you can't miss the crime scene."

Crime scenes leave clues. The nature and character of the criminal is determined based on patterns, behaviors, and methods found at the crime scene. That's where I come in. Jack Calloway–Criminal Profiler and Private Investigator.

Occasionally, I work for police departments by developing criminal profiles. I also provide services to non-law enforcement agencies. Missing persons, infidelity, robbery, vandalism, cases where the police run into dead ends or situations where individuals don't want to involve the police.

Already, I wasn't off to a great start. I should've asked about the lead detective before agreeing. Ed Halstead and I have a history. "Does Ed know you're bringing me in?"

The chief pauses long enough for me to know it's been discussed, and a decision was made. "He knows."

"Give me an hour." The call ends and I take a deep breath, exhaling slowly.

I glance at myself in the mirror. My hair is disheveled, caused by the same nightmare and the same fight I always have. My fingers won't be enough to style my hair. I retrieve a comb from the drawer, reshaping the waves of my black hair.

Dark shadows hold my sunken eyes into place. I don't tan, but on my better days, my skin is more like white satin. Right now, it's a flat eggshell white. The fact that I haven't eaten in a couple of days, or slept, shows. If I had followed my gut, I might've gotten more sleep. Not that I need a lot of sleep. I don't.

I was chasing a dead-end lead before I got called to San Francisco. I was running down a small-time outfit, who had pickpocketed the wrong person. A junkie who I sometimes use for information steered me to Adam Young. And although I could usually trust the information I got on the street, my gut cautioned me this time. At the very least, I should have hired someone else to follow up, rather than spend twenty-four hours following this kid.

I frown at myself in the mirror. I look like I'm wasting away. A shower, nourishment, and donning a high-end outfit will cure all of my afflictions.

I like to take pride in my appearance. I prefer designer clothes, tailored to fit, and the accessories to match. Right now, I look like I had been lost in the woods for a week.

I take a quick shower and get dressed. The first forty-eight hours in a case like this are critical. The chances of solving a homicide are cut in half if a viable lead isn't found. Sleep takes a backseat. It will be another long day.

I gulp down a breakfast drink, grab my keys, and head into the elevator reaching the main floor.

My office is in the same building as my apartment. I don't have time to stop and leave a note for Shannon Tieg, my receptionist slash assistant, but I can check in with her later. I enter the garage, jump into my Porsche, and take off toward Seward Park.

***

Seward Park, located at the Southeast end of Seattle, is on a peninsula. Hundreds of acres of forested land surrounded by Lake Washington. It is an outdoor playground, extremely popular during warmer weather.

As I pull into the entrance, flashing lights draw my attention. A combination of police cars and barricades block the area. I pull forward and bring my window down. A woman in uniform stops me. She squares her shoulders and leans toward my vehicle, and with an authoritative voice states, "Sir, you need to turn around, the park is closed today."

As if distracted by my presence, she studies me. I naturally draw women in, and I used to take full advantage of their blind attraction. Anymore, I ignore the bait, unless it serves me.

Her posture relaxes and her gaze softens. She lifts her chin slightly, exposing her neck. The vein, dark and slightly protruding, pulsates, pulling me in. Her badge reads, "Officer Sanders".

Officer Sanders is plain looking, not unattractive, but not memorable either. Her frame is stocky. She has short brown hair and soft facial features. The muscles in her jaw are tense and I can tell, by the pulse in her vein, she's nervous. Her youth and nervousness inform me she is new to law enforcement. No training prepares you for murder.

I clear my throat. She slightly jumps as if coming out of a daze, shaking her head. "I'm a consultant for Seattle PD." I pull out my ID. She glances at it. Her lips purse. She sighs, steps back, and radios for approval. She watches me as she waits for the answer. With a slight upturn of her lips, she murmurs, "They're expecting you. Follow Seward Park Road to the second parking lot, you'll see the command center and check-in there."

As dawn breaks, the park becomes a silhouette of itself. I drive to the lot and park. It's cloudy now, but in Seattle, it rains while the sun shines. I reach into my glove box, take out a pair of sunglasses, and stuff them into my jacket pocket. With long, confident strides, I walk toward a white canvas tent—the command center. The central point where decisions get made on how a crime scene is processed, how evidence will be collected and cataloged, and where anyone who enters the crime scene needs to sign-in. Men and women are bustling about. Some in uniforms and others in street clothes. Contentment and delight surges within. I'm in my element.

A tall blonde, blue-eyed woman in a periwinkle-colored pantsuit spots me. A white blouse opens just enough to highlight her cleavage. A holster and badge firmly secured on narrow hips. Hips I know well.

I nod. "Ms. Briggs. "What do we have?"

She steps toward me. "Calloway," she retorts with a curt nod, offering a firm handshake. She turns back to the makeshift tent and reaches for a bag containing latex gloves and booties. With a furrowed brow and precise movements, she hands me the bag. "Put these on." Our fingers briefly collide and a jolt of electricity passes through me. Her touch loosens three years of regret I've locked away.

Carla pulls back, averts her gaze, and her cheeks flush. I slip into the protective gear while she grabs another pair of gloves and booties and slips those on. Clearing her throat, she commands, "follow me." Behind that confident voice, she's flustered. My insides warm and the word "beautiful" slips through my lips. Thankfully, not loud enough for her to hear.

Carla Briggs is an excellent forensic investigator. For several years, she worked as a detective for the Seattle PD. She's one of the few CSI's who carries a badge. After she completed her master's degree in Forensic Science, she promoted to lead the CSI unit. That was shortly after we solved a serial rapist case three years ago.

Carla's laser-focused determination serves her when canvassing a crime scene and analyzing evidence. She finds nuances in the details. Things others miss. She has damn good instincts and a sharp mind. When we worked together, she prepared early, stayed late, and anticipated the next steps. Working with her was invigorating, and it was easy to trust her judgment. I can't say that for most people, alive or otherwise. We haven't been in contact since that rape case and the icy reception speaks volumes.

We walk along a well-worn dirt trail for about twenty yards. The trail is peppered with the remnants of autumn, weathered by the winter months—trampled maple leaves and rust-pine needles. The fir trees remain statuesque and the air is pine-scent infused. Another month or so and the Madrones will have flowering buds.

We approach an area marked off with crime scene tape. I raise the tape and forge through the inner perimeter of the crime scene, careful to stay within the entry points. The area is active with detectives and investigators in Tyvek suits. Small yellow cones are placed next to potential evidence as a photographer takes pictures. A sketch artist is capturing the body.

Outdoor crime scenes are delicate, especially in populated areas. Weather is an issue, and these investigators will work quickly to avoid the damage the promising rain will cause.

I assess the area. My senses take it all in. I can capture smells imperceptible to others and notice visual details that aren't obvious. Especially missing details. I can hear words at a whisper a quarter of a mile away. These abilities are unknown to most, but they are a few of the reasons I'm highly sought as an investigator.

The medical examiner hasn't arrived yet. My focus is drawn to the body, fifteen feet away, partially hidden within the carefree landscape. The body is prone—the head peering to the left, eyes open. A mop of short brown hair drapes the face. The victim's red dress is hiked up around her midriff, legs exposed to the elements. The dress has patches of mud stains and tears along the hemline. The feet are tied by an abraded, white nylon rope. On the right side, leaves lightly cover part of her body. I notice red, abraded skin on the left wrist. My mind churns on what I'm seeing—detailing, like a shopping list, *partially covered, face left, feet bound, no shoes, abrasions on wrists*. I search for other marks.

Interrupted by fragrances dancing all around, layer upon layer, I smell a trace of rose and musk. A familiar smell, yet I can't place it. There is a pungent and musty odor that provokes an image of dampness. Something else—medicated. Another layer slams my nose and taste buds alike—copper and iron. *Hmmm...* reminds me of a dinner I had recently. Another odor pulls at me and lingers in places only an animal would notice.

I continue to look for patterns, things out of place. Often serial killers have signatures, a way to identify or mark their work. It's too early to know what that is, but noticing what I can may lead to something relevant.

I complete my initial survey and turn to Sergeant Briggs, who is standing solidly, focusing her gaze on the crime scene. My body leans in with a desire to erase all distance. Jerking back, I avert my gaze.

The medical examiner arrives and begins her initial examination. She turns the body over. Bluish-purple bruises cover the back of her arms, legs, and buttocks. They are a clear sign she died hours earlier and left laying on her back. Face muscles, fingers, and toes are stiff—a sign of rigor gradually coursing through the body. "Anything you can tell us at this point?" Carla asks.

The woman crouching over the body tilts her head. "Appears to be female, early to mid-twenties, considering temperatures she's been dead anywhere between five to seven hours. No significant blood loss here. The ligature marks around her neck could mean she was strangled to death. That won't be clear until the autopsy."

Carla stands silently as the medical team bags the body. My chest tightens in the silence and I clasp my hands together to stop my need to touch and explore Carla's skin.

We return to the trail and stand just outside the inner perimeter. I look at the people milling around. "Who found the body?"

Arms folded, she nods toward the command center. "A jogger, around 5:00 a.m., Detective Dunn did the interview."

"What do we know about the jogger?"

"Single, white male lives nearby. He's an engineer. Jogs here daily."

"How did he stumble across the body? It's not like it's right on the trail and it's dark. Did he see or hear anything?" My gaze darts to Detective Dunn, and I can feel my jaw muscle tighten. It's not uncommon for serial killers to be a bystander at the crime scene.

"His dog was unleashed and took off. He followed the barking. When he caught up to it, his dog was next to the body."

Carla gazes at where the body had been. I could tell that even though she was responding to my questions, she was processing the crime scene in her mind. "That's when he called the police."

The moment fills with silence. Carla looks up. "Why, what are you thinking?"

"I'm thinking I'll want to re-interview him, get a sense of the guy." Pivoting toward the crime scene, I lead the conversation elsewhere. "The leaves scattered over the body look like the killer was attempting to hide it."

"He could have been in the process of disposing of the body and was interrupted by the dog?" Carla points out.

I muse on this for a moment. "That could mean the killer left in a hurry and unexpectedly leaving something undone, missing, perhaps visible." On instinct, both Carla and I scan the periphery of the crime scene.

"Chief Phipps thinks this may be a serial killing. Why?"

I hear footsteps approaching. I turn around to find Detective Ed Halstead standing next to us with his chest puffed out, his shoulders square, and a wide stance. Carla takes a couple of steps back and her posture stiffens. She avoids eye contact with us both. His presence adds another layer to the already felt tension. Carla and Ed's divorce was final three years ago.

Facing me with an intense, fevered stare, Detective Halstead answers my question. "This is the third murder victim we've found in three months. All have had their feet and wrists bound. The bodies' discarded face down. White nylon rope was found at each crime scene." He looks disapprovingly between Carla and me, and continues, "all in their early to mid-twenties. The first two were raped. Different causes of death."

"What were the causes?"

Ed's answer is coated with anger. "Throat slashed and head trauma."

It's no secret Detective Halstead doesn't like my presence. A few years ago, I was asked to consult on a murder case he was working on. He vocalized his dissent with his sergeant, especially when I disagreed with his assessment of the evidence. Ed was new to his position and eager to prove himself. When command assigns an outside consultant to a case, it can feel like a slap to the face. Unfortunately, his reluctance to take advice and his insistence on being right led to a waste of department resources.

Detective Halstead stands three inches shorter than me at 6'0, broad-shouldered and muscular, with a military haircut, high and tight. Put a few beers in him and I have known him to get aggressive.

I tip my head. "Detective." If he understood what I could do to him with one hand, he'd be less cocky.

I notice Carla wringing her fingers as he continues, "The other victims had unexplainable puncture wounds on their necks and wrists older than the abrasions found on their wrists and feet."

I raise my eyebrows in piqued interest. "What are you saying?"

His voice is low-pitched, and he's shaking his head, "It's as if different forms of torture took place over several weeks. We're not sure what to think." Detective Halstead looks at Carla, his face briefly showing a pained expression. With a heavy sigh, his gaze lands on the ground.

Carla revealed more than I wanted to know about Halstead. After he came back from his last deployment, he wasn't the same person. The war men fight when they return home is often more difficult than combat itself. Over the years, I've seen too many lose themselves to alcohol, pills, and suicide.

Six months after they separated, Carla and I dated. It was an intense five months. Our attraction was primal, and we didn't hide it well. Her smooth and silky voice captured my attention. The way she walked was an invitation. Her laugh was intoxicating. Her touch tugged and begged me to follow. Her mind was a playground of savvy intellect. We couldn't deny the chemistry and we didn't. She consumed me like none other. When I wasn't with her, I thought about her.

My feelings for her are unsettling. I've always preferred to be unattached—a brief sexual encounter, an evening, perhaps a night. Nothing more. It's safer and easier. So, my attraction, no, my need, for Carla took me by surprise.

During those months of working closely, there was something more between us. I came to respect her and I couldn't let her go. I should have stuck to my protocol the first night we were together. When Halstead came across Carla and I groping each other in the parking lot at the lab, it was the intervention I needed.

After that, Carla needed time to sort through things. A month later, when she had left me a message I didn't return, she came to my apartment. And even though I had company, I buzzed her up. When the elevator doors opened, there was no mistaking another woman was in my apartment. Carla didn't leave the elevator and the relaxed, casual manner she'd exhibited when the doors opened, abruptly changed. I stood there, with my shirt off, looking back over my shoulder, coyly saying "I'll be right there." When my eyes met hers, I could see the pain and the tears forming as the doors shut. If my heart could have sunk, it would have. I wanted to go after her, but there was no way I could. I wouldn't let myself. I belong to the shadows. To live a life barren and alone. And over the years, I've mourned the loss of too many. I had to let her go.

As I stand near her, I want to put my arms around her, but the pull has more to do with numbing my guilt and filling the emptiness I've carried these past three years. The palpable silence between us echoes sadness, betrayal, and anger. The depth of our connection was undeniable, but unrealistic. I shove aside my feelings and turn my focus to the crime in front of me.

I continue my questions. "Any of the victims reported missing?"

"Yes. All three had been missing anywhere from four to six weeks. The medical examiner's reports suggest varying timelines between the torture, death, and disposal of the bodies," Halstead says.

Torture doesn't surprise me in these cases. Serial killers find gratification in humiliating their victims, and the gratification is often sexual. "What's the evidence showing torture?"

"Several burn marks were found on their legs—made when the victims were alive. There are cuts on their torso. The size and shape of the cuts come from something like an assisted opening knife. The forensics reports concluded they were gagged and malnourished."

Detective Halstead's radio interrupts the conversation and he answers. "Didn't take long for the news to show up," he says to the person on the other end of the radio. "No, I'll deal with it. Be there shortly." Ending his call, he looks back to us and says, "I've gotta go take care of this."

I step forward to stop him, "Wait. We want to keep this locked down. Give them only a little information. We don't know yet what this killer is about."

He pivots toward me, squaring his shoulders, fists flexing, "Are you trying to tell me how to do my job, Calloway?"

I match his stance and firmly state, "Protecting the integrity of the crime scene, that's part of my job."

Ed's jaw muscles twitch. "Know your place, Jack. I'm the lead and if I want, I can remove you."
He lets out a breath and turns toward Carla. "I'll see you later at my office. We can go over what we have."

"Okay, Ed." She says.

My skin begins to tingle, and my eyes feel like sandpaper. I pull out my sunglasses. I turn to Carla and clear my throat. "How long before your team processes today's evidence?"

"Some reports will be ready this afternoon."

I look at my watch. It's 9:00 a.m. already. I soften my gaze as our eyes lock. "His issues can't get in front of this case. Is he going to be a problem?"

She frowns and looks away for a moment, then waves it off, "I'll handle it."

"All right, I'll see you at the South Precinct this afternoon." The smile on my face probably looks more like a grimace.

She nods and walks away.

CHAPTER 2

Jack Calloway

THE SUN PEEKS THROUGH THE trees, warming the ground. My quick steps to the car cut through the steam rising from the pavement. As I approach my car, I am glad for the reprieve I'll have from the tinted windows. Daytime investigation can be a drag for a vampire. We can function, but our senses are dampened. Still, our senses—hearing, eyesight, and strength are better than a human's.

I pull my phone from my jacket and listen to my two messages. The first message is from Shannon notifying me she printed Mrs. Winters pictures and will be in the office at nine. The last, a message from Simon Johnson. This time, I hope he has the information I need.

I start my car and head back. It's ten a.m. when I walk into my office building. My business is on the main floor of a high-rise building. The front entrance of the building opens to an atrium. Marbled flooring, chandeliers, sturdy pillars, and walls adorned with artwork, create an elegant feel. My office space has a reception area, a file room, and a separate office for my desk and computer. My office isn't large, but it does the job.

Four business offices, including mine, are on the main floor. Across the atrium from my office, next to the elevators is the law offices of Boyd, Leighton, and Zirkle, and down the left corridor, Metz & Solis, Realty, and Hopper and Fitz, C.P.A.'s lease spaces. An office for my building security manager is located in that corridor too. The right corridor leads to restrooms and an office space where computer servers, security equipment, and electrical systems are housed.

When I walk into my office, Shannon is in the file room. I'm old school and like to keep a file on my clients, at least with basic information. She greets me bright-eyed and eager, "Hey boss! You have a few messages, bills, and a letter. I placed them on your desk." I glance to the corner where the coffee pot is half empty and understand why her speech is rapid.

When I first came across Shannon, she was living on the streets. I was working on a case involving a breach of secured data. The investigation led me to her. She had hacked into my client's computer systems and extracted their client's personal identification information. I gave her a get-out-of-jail card. It wasn't free. The agreement we made was work for me or go to jail. She was eighteen, living in and out of shelters, with no real guidance. A computer whiz and an excellent pickpocket. That was five years ago. Now she works for me part-time and attends school pursuing a degree in forensic science.

"Good morning. How's my favorite girl?"

She smiles and hands me Mrs. Winters' pictures. "Thanks. Call her and set up an appointment for Monday." Shannon nods, returns to her desk, and begins typing.

The pictures in my hand are of Mrs. Winters' cheating husband. Infidelity cases aren't my favorite, but they're easy money and having these pictures means I can close the case.

Mrs. Winters is a woman in her early forties and had suspected her husband of having an affair. A year of working late, an increase in "work" travel, and various excuses to get out of social events, made her question his faithfulness, especially when she found a receipt for a diamond necklace she never received.

Mrs. Winters will inherit her grandmother's estate, which is worth twenty million. If she can find evidence her husband is having an affair, their prenuptial agreement will be nullified, saving her a quarter of the inheritance. Mr. Winters is the CEO of a multi-million-dollar pharmaceutical company. With no infidelity on Mrs. Winters' part, she will get an equal portion of their estate in the divorce.

I've been following Mr. Winters for the past two months. Surveillance can be tedious and involves a lot of waiting. Through my resourcefulness, hypnotic eyes, and rhythmic words, I compelled his secretary and got his full schedule. Dinner reservations, work meetings, trips, tee times—I had access to it all. The waiting was minimized. I watched him at dinner multiple times with various women, often kissing and holding hands. A few times, he checked into a hotel and didn't check out until the next day. The front desk employee readily offered me his room number. Securing a room next to his, I recorded his conversations. It may surprise Mrs. Winters to know that Mr. Winters uses an escort service regularly. One woman, Stephanie, whom he met several times, works for Mr. Winters' company as the Senior Director of Public Relations. She's in her early thirties and based on a recorded conversation, she believes Mr. Winters is leaving his wife.

It is my policy to always get half of my fee up front and make a second copy of any evidence I find. Between the pictures and audio feed, Mrs. Winters has everything she needs. I'll meet with her, show her the evidence, and once she pays me the remainder of my fee, I'll hand them over.

"We have a new case," I say to Shannon. "Possible serial killer. Seattle PD contacted me this morning. I'm just returning from the crime scene."

A gleam in Shannon's eyes sparks, her eyebrows perk, and the corner of her lips turn upward. "Finally, a murder investigation close to home. What research do you need me to do?"

"None, yet. I'm going to the precinct this afternoon to review what they have. I'll fill you in on Monday."

"I have class Monday morning."

I respond, walking to my office. "Okay, then we'll go through the case in the afternoon. Schedule Mrs. Winters for the afternoon, too."

I shut the door and pick up my messages. Another message from Simon Johnson. I pick up my cell phone and text him "I'll meet you tonight at the Shipwreck. Eight p.m.".

I read through my emails, replying to requests for services. I like to screen potential clients before I take them on. Many people want revenge or to blackmail someone. I'm careful about those. I want to know how the information I find will be used. The first time I meet with them, I affix my gaze on them, and in a melodious tone I ask for their motive—I compel the truth. I prefer cases where my services lead to justice, closure, or some realized greater purpose. Not cases that take other people down, unless it's truly deserved.

Rummaging through paperwork and bills, I find an unopened letter. No return address, just my name. I pull the letter out.

"Sieh hin, sieh her! der Mond-scheint hell.
Wir und die Todten reiten schnell."

From my military time in Germany, I know the words are German, but something else tugs at my heart. The tug lingers like a warning. I grab the letter and walk out of my office. "Who dropped this off?"

Shannon pulls her gaze away from the computer, looking at me, "It was under the door when I got here this morning."

I put the letter into my jacket pocket. "If anything else comes without a return address, let me know right away."

She rubs the back of her neck as she yawns. "Gaawd it, boss."

"Late night studying?"

"Yeah, for quarter exams. But," she nearly bounces out of her chair and a wide grin covers the bottom of her face, "I have a date tonight."

I clap my eyes shut as if the action alone will make the statement go away. I know there's a better way to respond than how I am going to, but instinctually, I go into father mode, imagining a bat in my hands when he arrives. She must see the conflict on my face because she tells me about him.

"I met him at school. He's an English major. He works part time. His name is Brad. He lives in Ballard with a male roommate." As if those facts would satisfy me.

"What's his last name and where's he taking you on this date?" Nope, not satisfied at all.

"Jenkins. We're gonna hang out, get something to eat, walk around."

I step back and cross my arms. "I think I should meet him first. Make sure he's okay."

Shannon jumps out of her chair, hands on her hips, and her voice elevates. "Jack, I'm twenty-four years old…"

"Exactly," I interrupt. "In my da…" I trip over my words. "A man should have a respectable and clear plan in place for his date. He should pick her up and make sure she gets home, safely." I run my hands through my hair. They land on the back of my neck. "Hanging out isn't a clear plan."

She takes a deep breath and releases it. She responds calmly, softening her voice. "I don't even know if I like him. When I figure that out, you'll be the first to meet him. I promise."

My gaze locks onto her. Her offer of reassurance soothes my angst. "All right." I put my hands in my pockets, still not liking it. "If there are any problems, you call me."

Pointedly, Shannon says, "Okay. Settle down. I know how to take care of myself." She pulls out a desk drawer, withdraws a file, and sits back down.

I turn to leave. "I'm heading upstairs if you need me."

I probably didn't handle that well; I say to myself. *Brad Jenkins.* I file the name away, knowing I'll investigate later.

I walk to the elevators across from my office, past the main lobby waiting area. I face three elevators. Two of them are for the tenants in the building, and the third is a private elevator that goes directly to my apartment. It's accessible by digital print only.

I enter and on the way up I reflect on the words in the letter. I try to place them. No way was the letter meant for someone else. There's no mistaking my office. To the left of the door, in large lettering reads… Jack Calloway, Private Investigator and Criminal Profiler. Yeah. The letter was meant for me.

The doors open, and I step inside my apartment. My living area takes half of the top floor. The other half is my pool and gym area. When I was growing up, swimming was not only a reprieve from the southern sun but a way to clear my head. It's as if with each lap, the world and all its concerns fade away. I try to get a swim in each day. With Jasper on my heels, we head down the dimly lit corridor, passing a painting of my parents.

My father, a tall and slender man, was a well-respected and prominent figure in Georgia. He owned a large plantation. At one point, he was elected to the Senate. My parents' deaths had been difficult for me. A fire claimed their lives.

I pass more artwork—Jean-Francois and a self-portrait. At the end of the corridor, I slide open the doors where Jasper and I enter the pool area. The pool stretches eighty-two feet and has five lanes. Beyond the pool, at the end of the room, is a changing room, shower, and a fully equipped gym. The picture window reveals the Cascade Mountains soaring in the distance. My shoulders relax, and a calmness washes over me as I stroll toward the changing room. Like Pavlov's dog, the water beckons. I change quickly and ease into the pool. Jasper sits on the edge, swatting at the water. I'll spend the next hour here, escaping.

When finished, I rinse off and wrap a towel around my waist. Jasper and I head back to the apartment and into my bedroom. My closet is a masterpiece of luxury. Fine fabrics, in a palette of colors, and a buffet of styles for all seasons and occasions. I quickly dress, style my hair, and give a last nod of approval at my reflection.

The view from my penthouse apartment is spectacular. The specialized windows repel U.V. light, allowing me to comfortably enjoy the breathtaking view during the day. The snow-covered Olympic mountains embrace the horizon as West Seattle huddles below. Mount Rainier's commanding presence backdrops south

Seattle. The Emerald City illuminates all around and it stirs something within me.

Next to the kitchen is a secured room, accessible only by security code and a retina scanner. It's my private office and includes security monitors for the entire building. An exit door opens to stairs descending to the parking garage. A leather couch faces a bookcase and TV. And there's a small kitchen, which prompts my stomach's growl. I open the refrigerator door. This refrigerator, unlike the one in my main living area, contains all the nourishment I need. I grab three IV bags of human blood, gulping down one after the other. It warms my insides as it glides from my throat to my stomach. My body fires up like a jump-start to an engine.

Blood, there's no way around it. I need it for strength, energy, healing, and mental clarity. I can go a couple of days without drinking it and not experience any side effects. There was a time when the sight or odor of blood would kick-in an instinct to kill. In my first few decades of being a vampire, the bloodlust was uncontrollable. I didn't know it could be controlled. The bloodlust that plagues most new vampires becomes manageable with time and discipline.

When you've spent decades killing people, well, that's a situation I don't want to find myself in again. There's a blood mix, a serum called Vita-Life that tempers bloodlust for those that struggle. I take it. Not because I struggle, but because I agreed to.

Today, accessing blood is easier thanks to a vampire-owned blood bank called the World Hematology Center, serving both human and vampire populations.

Unless there's agreement, vampires don't drink from humans. It's highly frowned upon and can be subject to punishment.

Even so, the beat of blood pumping in and out of a heart and the babbling brook of blood cells running through veins calls to us. Restraint comes with practice. And I've had a lot of practice.

The taste of blood lingers in my mouth and I savor it. I notice an increase in taste sensations, different from what I'm used to, but I don't think much of it. If a vampire drinks from a human, sometimes the blood can initiate expression of the human's temperament, but only briefly, and it's more like a vague impression that comes through. With blood bags, that doesn't happen.

My senses shift. They alert me the earth is warming underneath the sun's power. If I leave now, I can get to the precinct by one p.m. I draw a breath, tuck away any feelings I have for Carla, and head down the stairs.

CHAPTER 3

Carla Briggs

CARLA BRIGGS WALKED INTO HER office building and went directly to the evidence lab's bathroom. She stood in front of the mirror thinking how unlucky she was working with the two men she could avoid for the rest of her life. Given her work, she knew that would be next to impossible, but a girl could hope.

The blinding florescent lights pierced her eyes. "Wow, these lights illuminate the maps on my face," She said out loud. Carla had been on the job seven hours and it was nowhere close to quitting time. She reached into her cosmetic bag, rifling around to find her lip gloss. After applying the gloss, she rubbed her lips together.

She kept a cosmetic bag in her car because she never knew how long or where her job would take her. It had all the basics—lip gloss, gum, toothpaste, toothbrush, eyeliner, mascara, a comb, and a hair tie. Carla pulled out a comb and ran it through her hair. An internal debate clattered in her mind. Leave it up or put it down.

Her mind aimlessly wandered, imagining Calloway's dreamy whisper in her ear, "Beautiful." He would say as he tucked a strand of hair behind her ear. Carla sighed deeply, stared at herself in the mirror, and said, "snap out of it."

She picked up a hair tie. "Hair up it is." Pulling her blonde hair back, she twisted the hair tie around it. Next, she brushed her teeth. The repetitive motions of her toothbrush lulled her mind back to Jack Calloway. When she saw him at the crime scene, her heart skipped a beat. She stood, breath held. It was infuriating to Carla that after all these years, and the tears she shed over Jack, he still had that effect on her.

Jack was seduction. Greek gods had nothing on him. Tall, black hair, and deep blue brooding eyes. She'd get lost in those eyes. It was like staring into the deep end of a pool when the sun was shining—dark, mysterious, with shimmering shadows. High cheekbones and a chiseled jaw gave him a rugged look. At the same time, his face expressed a youthful appearance—No laugh lines or crows' feet. Unmistakable wisdom, more than age and experience, emanated from his eyes. His smile was warm and alluring.

Jack's tailored shirts molded to his sculpted body. He glided as he moved. Jack had a tempered strength and confidence about him, like a steel structure framing a building. Perfect. That's what he was.

Many men in law enforcement, appearing reserved and controlled, are a dam ready to explode. With Jack, it was hard to tell if he was holding something in or keeping something out. That can be part of the gig, too. Something Carla knew too well. Her father, a police chief in her hometown, was unreachable at times.

Carla didn't know something was missing until Jack Calloway entered her life. He made her feel alive. Her insides would melt at the sound of his voice. He was attentive and caring. He took her breath away. And he was a gentleman. The few times when they went out, he arranged for a car to pick them up. He had opened the door, extended his hand, and kissed the back of hers. It was like something out of a 19th-century novel. It made her feel cherished.

But he could be aloof, mysterious, and calculating. Uncannily, she sensed he understood the predators he profiled beyond his training. Often, he was a step ahead, and many in law enforcement lauded his work.

In the bedroom, he was passionate and tender, caressing her body as he explored her. He would cradle her in his arms after they made love. He could be greedy and animalistic too. His eyes would darken and something behind them would flicker, like a spark igniting a flame. A low growl would purr through his chest and his movements were swift and decisive, taking control of her body.

Carla scowled in the mirror when she remembered she was only a meaningless affair to him, one in a long line of women. That had hurt, but she had since moved on. Her life was full—she managed the CSI unit, traveled around the country as a forensics trainer, and was dating someone new. Ted. For the past two months, she and Ted were spending more time together. She'd moved on. Hadn't she? Her determination turned into doubt.

She shut off the water, hastily cleaned up, and zipped up her cosmetic bag. As she walked out of the bathroom, she chastised her trailing thoughts.

Passing the lab where her team evaluated evidence, she poked her head in and announced, "I'm heading over to the South Precinct, forward any reports from this morning's homicide to Detective Ed Halstead."

Amy Dupont, her point person for fingerprint analysis, lifted her gaze from her microscope to find Carla's, and stared her down, eyebrows raised. Amy, colleague and best friend extraordinaire, brought Carla tissues and ice cream while she picked up the pieces of her broken marriage. Amy pushed Carla to take a chance, "Enough blubbering and get out there," Amy told her.

Carla's phone pinged as she walked out of the building. With a reluctant reach, she looked to see who it was. Amy. "Call me later with the goods," the text read and Carla chuckled. Carla knew when Amy found out that Jack Calloway was on this case, she'd be on Carla's doorstep, with tissues, ice cream, and a gun.

***

Jack Calloway

If you didn't know the South Precinct building was a police department, you might mistake it for a library. Nestled in a park-like landscape, with a view of a baseball field, it embodied the feel of a quaint community. However, a killer is on the loose and there's nothing quaint about that. Inside the precinct, the air feels pressurized, like a rubber band pulled beyond its elasticity.

A smile greets me as I check in at the counter. Despite the bulletproof glass that stands between me and a receptionist, the reception area matches the outside. Bright colors and fluorescent lights make the space open and airy.

The precinct reminds me of a community center I had visited several years ago when I was hired for a missing person's case, for a child who was last seen at a local community center.

Community. Exactly what the police are trying to portray. Except their world is governed by a unique set of codes and they are held to a higher standard. It's a world the average person doesn't have access to.

I show the officer my ID. She hands me a visitor's badge and buzzes me inside. I'm escorted to a conference room. Before I reach the door, I peek through the window. The conference room is rectangular and a long table seating up to twelve occupies the center of the room. A large projection screen plasters one wall at the end of the room. A sink, counter, and refrigerator are at the opposite end.

As I enter the room, my senses are heightened. Carla is sitting at the head of the table, reading a document she's holding in one hand while the other is rubbing the back of her neck. That one slight gesture says enough about how she's feeling. Detective Halstead methodically pins photographs and sketches on a corkboard that covers three panels of the wall next to the conference table. His eyebrows crease downward, focusing on the mission at hand.

You could hear a pin drop as I walk into the room. Immediately, I assess the crime wall. The evidence of the three murders are presented chronologically, while next to the board is a map with push pins. I assume where the murders took place, or where the bodies were found. I clear my throat to speak. I hear the increase of Halstead's pulse and he jerks his head around, push pin in hand.

"Detective. Sergeant." I look back and forth. "Walk me through this." I nod in the wall's direction. Halstead's eyes follow my nod and he points at the evidence, giving me a rundown of timelines and findings. His tone, matter of fact, is like a narrator of a wildlife documentary. Carla adds depth to the discussion, peppering in forensic findings.

"The victims don't seem to know each other. They are in the same age bracket, but as you can see, we have a brunette and two blondes. Their hair lengths are varied. As are their heights." Halstead reports.

"What about occupations, any connections there?" I ask.

Halstead continues, "A student, a bartender, and a secretary. They didn't cross paths. In talking with friends and families, we think they met the killer through a dating website called Match, Meet, & Mingle. The first two went on dates and didn't return. We're not sure about our recent victim, Kelly Whitfield, but we think we'll find the same."

I'm not satisfied with his explanation. "They could've crossed paths at a bar."

Hands at his sides, Halstead's fingers flex. His stance becomes rigid and I note a spike in his heartbeat. He snaps back, "They had a date, didn't return."

"And what have the *dates* said?" I toss back at him. "The website could be a commonality. Have you interviewed all the men, the victims dated through the dating website, not just the men from the night they disappeared?" By asking this, I'm insulting his abilities as a detective. He's withholding information pertinent to my profile and I need to push him.

"What I'm trying to get at is victimology. For instance, are they extroverts, or introverts? Do they frequent the same bars, have drug problems, go to the same school, nail salon, or the same church?"

Halstead's gaze remains flat. "Similarities are dating sites and bars near each of the victim's homes. All victims were new to the area, less than two years. Deaths are about one month apart."

Halstead points to the wall. "We've identified these men, Billy McCord, Terry Leland, and Aaron Diggs. And Aaron's wife, June Diggs. Per witness statements, Billy, through Match, Meet, & Mingle, went on dates with our first two victims, Tori Henly and April Thompson. Aaron Diggs had an affair with Tori Henly. His wife, June Diggs, and Aaron were out of the country at the time of the murder. Their alibis checked out, but we haven't completely ruled them out. April worked for Terry Leland, who has a history of domestic assault, and we're looking into our third victim, Kelly Whitfield, but it looks like she worked for Terry Leland too."

"What about the computers or phones used to access the dating site or call the victims? Any digital footprints tying a suspect to these crimes?"

Halsted's shoulders drop, and he swallows hard. He looks at the crime scene photos and back at me. "We don't have that information. We tried to follow the digital address to a physical location but found it was rerouted through a proxy server, or they used a burner phone. Dead ends so far."

The air is thick with tension between Ed and I and Carla must've noticed it. Her brow furrows as she rises from her chair with an icy gaze, staring us both down. Her gaze speaks volumes. This isn't about her. She clears her throat, redirecting our energy.

I make a mental note to have Shannon follow up on the IP addresses. Her computer hacking skills would put any professional to shame. "I'll want the IP addresses. I can have Shannon trace them."

Halstead shifts his stance toward the photos, "You have access to all the records on these cases, in electronic format—who we've interviewed, witnesses, family, boyfriends, and others. The logon information is in that file."

"What do you know about the UNSUB? Other than, he's finding the victims through a dating site?" I ask. "Are the bars random or do they mean something? This one's in Queen Anne, the other one's in Ravenna."

"The bars are within a mile of their homes."

I pause in thought. "Most likely the victim was familiar with the bar. Familiarization would help her feel comfortable, especially if it's the first date. It could also mean the UNSUB was watching the victims, knew where they liked to go."

"From what we gathered, they'd been to those bars recently, but not frequently."

"The first murder, that you know of, was in December?" I ask.

Ed answers, "Yes, December, January, and now February."

I face Carla. "Earlier it was mentioned the scarring on the victim's bodies pointed to different patterns of torture, and based on the healing of those scars, the injuries were weeks apart." I point to the wall, "Show me."

Carla walks to the first victim's picture on the wall. "Here," she points. "On the inside thigh of the first victim are these two puncture wounds. On the second victim, similar puncture wounds, but on the left wrist. They are the same size and width apart. These occurred at about two weeks before the abrasions on the wrists, feet, and arms. The abrasions occurred within the last week of the victim's life. We found vaginal scarring, consistent within the victim's last week of life." She slides over to the second victim and points, "The same pattern here."

I study the photos and look at the marks and abrasions, my gaze landing on the puncture wounds. "The wounds on our third victim from this morning seem consistent with this pattern."

The animal surges inside, scratching to get out. In my mouth, a faint throbbing begins. If I had much of a pulse, it'd be pounding. I avert my eyes and tamp down my instinctive reactions, not wanting to give anything away about what I'm thinking *or feeling.*

Carla responds. "Yes, so far, it's consistent."

"Can we assume she lived near Seward Park?" I ask.

Halstead's gruff voice cuts in. "No, because the manner of death is inconsistent in each case."

"How so?"

He stands closer to the pictures and points, "Look here, the first victim's hands are tied, she was found in a dumpster with her throat slashed, wholly nude. The second victim," he points to her head, "Cause of death is blunt force trauma. She was left in an alleyway with only a shirt on. And the third is death by asphyxiation, per the preliminary report."

"Meaning, their actual deaths happened elsewhere," I say.

"There's a lack of blood at the disposal site in each case," Carla says.

I look toward Carla as she continues. "All the bodies were exposed at disposal and treated like trash. We found ejaculate on the first victim, and a partial fingerprint on the second victim."

Carla shifts her attention. Our gaze meets briefly for the first time this afternoon. I want to hold on, but she looks away. "The planning and organizing required to arrange a date, let alone the patience to understand the victim's habits, is in sharp contrast to the disposal."

"Agreed," I say, satisfied with her deduction. I go quiet, but my mind is stirred. The puncture wounds mimic a vampire's bite, but killing humans isn't commonplace. It's a thought I won't share here, but a line of inquiry I'll take up with Simon Johnson. My gaze returns to the evidence on the wall. "Any thoughts this could be two killers?"

Carla returns to the table. Her fingers dance across a laptop keyboard. "I've read cases involving two serial killers. Typically, one is a dominant player and the other, having learned helplessness from being victimized, becomes a submissive player. The submissive is psychologically dependent on the dominant. The torture and the killing become a way to please the dominant and avert further abuse."

Halstead pinches the bridge of his nose. A thickened air presses down. "I don't like it, but it's possible." He pauses. "Do you have enough information for a preliminary profile?"

I shrug. "Rough at this point. The evidence points to two different styles. Could be one person, but it may be more. Either way, I'd say the age range of the killer, or killers are eighteen to thirty-five. If there are two, the older one is in their mid-thirties, the younger eighteen to twenty-five. They're targeting women from twenty to twenty-five. No preference is known at this time, but he's finding them on a dating site. By the shoe print impression, at least one of them is around 185lbs. One of them may work, while the other hunts. And that's if there are two. There's sophistication and planning involved. One of them is probably college-educated."

"Did any of these men's dating profiles identify where they work?" I ask.

"Nothing specific," Ed replies.

"My guess is the younger one makes the dating profile. Either one meets the victims at the bar, somewhere the victim knows. Given the pattern, I'd say there's already another victim."

I look back at the photos and continue, "I'd scour the dating sites and surveil the bars in the areas the victims were found." I pivot, shifting my stance, reaching for the file on the table. I flip through the pages, passing names and addresses of people interviewed. I find the IP addresses and send a text to Shannon. An uncomfortable silence hangs in the air.

Satisfied, I close the file. "I'll look at all of it, the interview statements, cross-reference the victims, and I'll reach out to the suspects. If something comes up before we meet again, I'll get ahold of you. You have the same phone numbers?"

A curt under-tone sharpens Ed's voice. "Yeah, hasn't changed."

I glance at Carla, catching her eye. She nods. A conversation of emotions passes through me. I rub my forehead and force away the whirlwind of emotions welling inside. "Do you need me for anything else?"

She holds my gaze, bitterness flaring in her eyes. She shakes her head, "No, that's all."

At six foot three, my shoulders cave and I shrink in size as the energy of her words slam into me.

I straighten my posture. "Ed, you mind if I go to the morgue and check-in on the autopsy? Dr. Patterson and I have worked together in the past. We have a good rapport."

Ed nods. "No, go ahead. I'll check with Ron tomorrow."

I walk out of the precinct and get into my car. I shake my head and declare... *let her go.*

Unfortunately, the morgue is in the same building as Carla's office. With any luck, I won't run into her again.

CHAPTER 4

Jack Calloway

DOCTOR RON PATTERSON, THE CHIEF Medical Examiner for the Seattle PD, and otherwise known as Doc, runs his operation like nuns in a catholic school except he's a bit quirky. He wears polka-dotted bow ties and his hair is disheveled. Sometimes his social skills are lacking, but he's kind and highly intelligent. He was a medical officer in the Gulf war. And he should be near retirement. However, with all the energy and the love of life he has, I don't think he'll quit soon.

I approach the double glass doors of the lab building. Inside, a receptionist behind a glass window greets me and checks my identification and authorization. The stairway to the morgue is to the left of the lab. Not wanting to be noticed by anyone in the lab, I hurry down the stairs. My movements are swift and most humans would only catch me as a blur in their peripheral vision.

A security guard is sitting at his desk talking on his cell phone. The tight face muscles, restricted voice, and words escaping through clenched teeth suggest he's in a tense conversation. Once he sees me, he quickly gets off his call. I hand him my credentials. Satisfied, he pushes a button underneath his desk, and the doors to the morgue automatically slide open.

The exam room is long and narrow. Rows of labeled drawers and cabinets line a wall the length of the room. Three examination tables are positioned symmetrically in the center. There are sinks and surgical equipment on the opposite long wall. At the end of the room is a desk where a computer sits. Dr. Patterson calls this exam room his "office." It's really a human butcher shop with similar tools. He has an actual office, but I don't think he spends much time in it. The "freezer" is located adjacent to, and accessible by, the exam room.

To a vampire, the many faces of death reflect life. For most humans, the smell of formalin and dying flesh curls the stomach, but even to a vampire, there isn't anything appetizing here.

When I enter, I see Dr. Patterson with a magnifying glass. He is examining the finger of a corpse. He looks up and with a gleam in his eye, cheerily greets me. "Jack, my boy, what brings you to my office?" Doc and I go way back. In the 1970s we met at Joe Crandon's wedding, a mutual friend of ours. Joe's grandfather is Ron's great uncle. Ron also served as a board member for the World Hematology Center some years back. He talked me into being a member. For me, that was short-lived—politics.

"Hey, Doc. You have a body, Kelly Whitfield, came in this morning from Seward Park. I'm on the case. Have you examined it?"

Doc whimsically replies, "Haven't got to it yet, young man, but we can go take a look-see right now. Let me get her." He hands over his current exam to his technician.

Walking into the next room, Doc disappears into the freezer. It's called the freezer, but the room is only slightly cool. The freezers remind me of the ice lockers we had on the plantation where I grew up. When the iceman with his horse and cart came up the road, the air was filled with a buzzing excitement. It meant cool, sweet tea in the summers. At least until the ice melted. In those days, making ice last was a losing battle.

The sound of clanging metal and loose wheels clacking grabs my attention as Doc wheels in a gurney with the body wrapped tightly in a blue body bag. Doc whistles a tune I think is from a child's film I saw at a drive-in in the 1980s. A movie I was talked into taking Nick Crandon, my godson.

I join Doc, viewing the body under the bright lights. Scissors break the seal of the bag and it folds away from the body, exposing it. The clicking sounds and flashes of light from Doc's camera begin the examination. He sets the camera down, studies the clothing, and scribbles notes.

Next, he removes the clothes. Section by section, Doc pokes, prods, and measures the stiff body. He pulls down the magnifying glass strapped to his head to examine the hands, searching the nails, the palm, and the back of the hand. Like a palm reader, he takes his time. An eerie silence fills the air.

I, too, make my observations; like a student, following Doc's motions. My eyes are all I need. I can see the layers of broken skin, the small tears in the nails, and the layers of bruising impressed by fingers around Kelly Whitfield's neck. I didn't need a magnifying glass to know the pain and terror she experienced before her death.

The air feels tight in my chest as Doc examines her neck, his focus on the two puncture wounds. Quiet, he stalls as if questioning himself, searching for an alternative answer. Slowly, he lifts his gaze to meet mine. An inquisitive scowl forms on his face.

"That's what I'm thinking too, Doc, but I don't want to believe it," I say, agreeing with his silent assessment. "The two other victims had the same patterns, except the punctures were on the wrist or leg."

He looks straight ahead, pensively for a moment, then turns to me, "Yep, skippy... I remember those." A deep sigh escapes. "But didn't put it together until now." He paces. "If it's a vampire, why does he, or she, stop feeding weeks before the torture and killing of these girls?" He scratches his head.

"Maybe there's more than one killer?" I say flatly.

Doc turns, walks to his computer, and sits. With a wave of his hand he says, "Jacky ol' boy, I must get to work. You'll get my report." He hesitates briefly. "Official and unofficial in a few days. You may go."

"Thanks, old man." I leave him to it. Doc will be up half the night continuing with the autopsy and conversing with the body. He'll get answers quickly. He understands what's at stake if it involves a vampire. It could set us back a century. A heaviness presses on my shoulders. I hope to find some answers at the Shipwreck tonight.

A wave of energy flushes through my body and my senses heighten. I look at my watch. The day is waning. I turn and, in a blur, reach the top of the stairs. Just as I exit the morgue, a familiar sound, melodic, and soft reaches my ears. My insides flutter and I freeze. Even though I know there isn't another way out of the building behind me, I look anyway and step back. *Carla.*

"These flowers are beautiful; you didn't have to." I hear her say. "Thanks for bringing me food. It's been a long day." I hear the puckering sound of lips touching. My muscles tense and I can feel heat flashing through my body as my nostrils flare. My stomach turns and my hands ball into a fist. I tell my feet to stay, holding myself back. I draw in a breath and flex my fingers. Internal dialogue fills my head, *calm down, let it go, it's not your place, walk away. Did*

I think she wouldn't move on? Of course she would. Just because you haven't...

My thoughts are interrupted. Carla emerges into the hallway with her *friend*. I adjust my jacket, straighten my shoulders, and with all the swagger I have, stroll down the hall toward them. I nod. "Sergeant. We can catch up later." I smile and Carla stops mid-stride, her head jerks around, and with a hitched breath, stands as I continue past her, exiting the building. I get into my car and say out loud, "I guess I'm not that lucky."

I pull out of the parking lot and glance at the clock on the navigation panel. It's three-thirty p.m. It's a good time to interview the jogger who found the body, and I'm close to his workplace. I pull out the lists of addresses and head in that direction.

The building I enter is four stories of concrete and glass. A security officer stands near the front desk. He has a towering presence, his stance firm, and arms crossed. I glance at him and walk up to the desk. The receptionist is talking into a headset. She smiles and raises a finger to signal "one minute."

"Hello, how can I help you?"

I flash her my standard issued Seattle PD badge. "I'm here to see Steve Reneger." She makes a call and before long a dark-haired, tall man wearing glasses approaches.

He extends his hand. "Jack, is it? I'm Steve. What can I do for you?"

"Is there somewhere we can have a private conversation?" We go into a small conference room near the reception area. I question him about that morning, and he gives a step-by-step accounting of events. Nothing he says deviates from what he told the police, and I don't sense he's lying. Nor is he a vampire.

A little disappointed, I leave and head home.

CHAPTER 5

Jack Calloway

I CHARGE TO THE SHIPWRECK driving my red Porsche 911. The car matches my mood tonight—raw, edgy, and fast. I want to be noticed, and this car turns heads.

I step out of my car and a warmth soothes my insides. I've got a lot of memories here. When I first came to Seattle in the sixties, I found myself holed up at the Shipwreck. Joe Crandon would chat with me from time to time. Joe owned the Shipwreck.

Joe was a burly man, with a handlebar mustache, warm smile, and a full beard. Friendly to everyone if you kept to the rules. His bite *was* tougher than his growl. He was a shifter—a were-person, or Were, as they prefer. The Shipwreck was a neutral place for all. No Killing. No Fangs. No claws. And if you broke the rules… well, be thankful Joe gave a stern talking to, first.

After a few months of watching me try to drown myself with alcohol and waste nights with random women, Joe sat at my table. And we talked. He was easy to talk to and even though our species rarely get along; I felt comfortable with him. After that, he became like a brother. I was the best man at his wedding and I'm his son's Godfather. It was an unusual relationship for a were-person and vampire, but he saw me as a member of his family.

I was wrecked with anger and guilt because I'd lost so many people. I wanted justice and closure. He encouraged me to take those feelings, along with my "special" abilities, and use it for some good. I'd earned a law degree in 1862, but it wasn't useful in 1965. I got a degree in criminology and joined the Behavioral Science Unit with the Federal Bureau of Investigation in the seventies.

Posted outside the wooden doors of the Shipwreck are two security guards, Stan and Jim. "Hello, boys," I say. I step inside and scan the environment. When vampires and were-persons are in the same place, it's always good to know who you're dealing with. Conversations can get heated. Thankfully, the Shipwreck is large enough to provide space between the groups.

The room is naturally broken up into sections by six floor-to-ceiling beams. The L-shaped bar easily sits twenty people. They organize tables seating up to four people throughout the room. Two pool tables are in the back, with a pinball machine and dart games in the corner. And pull tabs are affixed to the wall. A group of humans sits near the center. A few Weres are playing pool. Two vampires sit at the end of the bar. In a few more hours, this place will be full.

Nick is behind the bar. He looks up and greets me with a big smile, waving me over. Nick is formidable himself. Tall, muscular, and with a booming voice, you can't miss him. And I've seen his teeth. This dog can be vicious. I found that out when I mercilessly teased him about a girl he liked when he was sixteen. He wasn't in control of his shifting, and I had to pin him on the floor. He's in his forties now.

He challenges me with a smirk. "Hey pops, what brings you in?" He thinks making jabs about my age will rattle me.

"You do know I died; a lot younger than you are right now? And I'm aging far better than you."

"Yeah, but you're slower than you used to be." He turns around, grabs a bottle of scotch, and pours me a drink.

"Wiser, that's all." He sets the drink in front of me and starts wiping down the counter.

"Nick, any new vampires in the last few months?"

"A few, here and there. Passing through mostly. Why?"

I throw back the scotch; the smoothness slides down my throat. A server approaches the bar with an order. Nick grabs two glasses and fills them with beer, topped off with foam, handing them to her. He picks up the scotch bottle. "Want another one?"

"I'll just take a beer. I've had nothing to eat."

He gives me a quizzical look, knowing any amount of alcohol I ingest only gives me a light buzz. And that's not dependent on whether or not I eat. He shakes his head. "See, even your humor is tired."

Alcohol is my medicine. It doesn't get me drunk, but it keeps the anxiety attacks at bay. Something I discovered long ago.

Not letting his comment distract me from my line of questioning, I say, "I'm working a case. It might involve a vampire. Someone who doesn't adhere to the mandates."

"A couple of members with the Vampire Sovereign League were in here last week, playing pool. They seemed harmless. More talk, less walk."

The Vampire Sovereign League or VSL is an organization fighting against the directive to coexist peacefully with humans. They were strong in numbers in the 19th century, but over time most vampires saw the benefits of adhering to the mandates set by the Dracul's. I was, unknowingly, a league member.

The VSL doesn't have any regard for life. We took what we wanted. Killing. Raping. Torturing. We were the things people feared in the middle of the night. The lifestyle was never in my constitution, but I didn't know a thing about being a vampire because the vampire who turned me didn't stick around. When I stumbled into a nest of vampires in New Orleans in the eighteen-sixties, I wanted to be a part of them. Terrorizing humans became a way of life.

When I came to Seattle, I was lost and racked with grief. What I knew was I didn't want to return to the life I lived at the turn of the century. The VSL believes vampires are at the top of the food chain. Vampires should be feared and revered. The only value humans have are as slaves and nourishment. When I was turned, I didn't know about the Dracul or the Ascenders.

In the mid-19th century, the Dracul was formed by twelve of the oldest vampires, who represented the largest vampire families. They allied, and they call all who follow Ascenders. In the early 1900s, I killed all those in my nest connected with the VSL and cut all ties with them. Even so, the Dracul never really accepted me. After helping on a case with the Guard, a supernatural law enforcement agency, some years back, two Dracul had warmed up to me. They never encouraged my membership, but if they had, I wouldn't have joined. By not having allegiances to one group or another, I remain available to work with them all.

"Do me a favor and keep your eyes and ears open. Let me know if something seems suspicious or you remember anything else." I look up to see Simon Johnson walking my way.

I extend my hand. He takes it, holding it in a firm grip. "Good to see you, Jack."

Simon Johnson is a captain in the Guard. The Guard manages and monitors supernatural activity. Its purpose is to ensure peaceful coexistence with humans, without most humans knowing about our existence.

The Dracul and the Lycaon created the Guard. The Lycaon is the equivalent of the Dracul for the Were community. And Simon is the head of the Guard's vampire division.

Simon is one of the few vampires I trust, and he's a good contact when a case takes a supernatural turn.

I point to the bar. "Simon. Grab a drink. It's on me." I wink at Nick.

"He means it's on the house." Nick rolls his eyes. "What are you drinking, Simon?"

"Thanks, a beer is all."

Nick hands Simon a beer and I point to a table in the corner. "Let's move our conversation."

On our way, a group of young ladies holler and whistle as we walk by. "They're starting early," says Simon.

"Yeah. Looks like a birthday celebration." I smile, raise my beer in a toast, and nod their way. My eyes dilate. "They may need someone to watch after them tonight."

Simon frowns a look of disapproval, telling me he can see the yellow highlights around my pupils.

He shakes his head. "I'm on the clock."

It's a good excuse. He's still licking his wounds from getting his heart broken two years ago. I shrug and tip my head toward him. "Your loss. My gain." We reach our table and sit.

"Fun, that's all you seem to have, Jack. You ever interested in something permanent?" Simon pauses, "What happened to that detective, a couple of years ago?"

I glance at the girls over my shoulder, then back around to face Simon. "What about her?"

"You were… different about her. Seemed like it was more than a sexual conquest."

I shift in my seat and look away. "If I was interested in settling down, which I'm not, it isn't possible with a human. Look at how it turned out for you." I say, knowing it is a cheap shot. I lean back and shrug. "It was fun while it lasted. That's all it was."

Simon's eyes narrow. "Try not to break any hearts tonight."

Not wanting to think about Carla, I let myself get distracted by the light hum of activity. The break of billiard balls, dropping into the pocket, and laughter from a joke that was told.

My fingers tap on the table. I interrupt the silence. "You have some information?"

Since my death, I've been eager to find the monster who killed my family, the vampire who turned me. It happened over a hundred and fifty years ago, but I remember the night like it was yesterday. He made me watch as he killed my daughter, raped my wife, and hear my parents' cries for help, trapped in a burning house. He growled in laughter as my wife screamed in terror. I have few details about him—the coarseness of his voice or the scent covering his clothes, a combination of wood smoke, musk, and rose. I'd recognize him by his height and the color of his hair. But that's all.

Simon belongs to one of the oldest vampire families. Through his connections, I hoped he'd have information about this vampire. From time to time, I ask him to check with his father. In the early 20th century, I thought I saw the man I was hunting. It was my chance to avenge my family's death, so I thought. I'd mistaken another man for the monster. If I'm among the living, I'll keep searching.

Simon clears his throat, "As my father has said, it's unusual for a vampire to be on its own without a clan or nest. Typically, someone in the Ascender community would know about them if that's the case. It's not something that can stay quiet for more than a few decades. You know as well as I do if you turn an insane person, vampirism only heightens the insanity. An insane vampire would have the most difficulty assimilating into any society. My father has known of such vampires but believes none of them are walking this earth anymore."

I take a drink of my beer. "Any different news other than what you and I know already?" My voice is brusque.

"Yes. He'll take the question to the Dracul council next month."

I chuckle. "That's a first. After all these years, I must be on his good side."

"Or, after fifty years, he's tired of hearing about it." Simon presses his lips together in a bitter smile. "Sorry Jack, wish I had more."

"Hey, I appreciate you checking for me. Scanning the environment, I notice the bar has more patrons. The noise will make it difficult for anyone with supernatural hearing to home in on a distant conversation. "I need to run something else by you." I take another sip, "I'm working a homicide case for Seattle PD. Looks like a serial killer. Preliminary forensics is pointing to a vampire, but it's not conclusive."

Simon sits up straight. He has a commanding presence even when sitting down. He's stocky, medium-built, and a couple of inches shorter than me. His hair is brown and his beard has reddish hues. His arms are tattooed from his wrists to his shoulders. I've never understood why a vampire would want tattoos for eternity.

Originally, Simon's family is from Scotland. He's older than me, but we look the same age. Older in the sense that he was created before me. His strength and speed outpace my own. He has eyes like a hawk. And when we're not competing, he is a formidable ally and friend.

He leans in closer, his eyebrows raised in piqued curiosity. "What are the specifics?"

"Three female victims, early twenties, each have puncture wounds, different places: femoral artery, the wrist, and the carotid artery, respectively. Some discrepancies in timelines." I sigh heavily and lean back. Voices behind me, loud and daring, erupt. I can sense they aren't close, but I look toward the bar, anyway. I catch the eye of a woman and I drink her in. She winks at me. I smile and watch her as she sensually glides her way back to her table. There's a lot on display—long legs, skirt just low enough to let the imagination run, brown hair pinned up, with whisks of hair falling around her face. Her neck is slender, delicate, and inviting. Simon interrupts my wandering ways by clearing his throat.

I turn back and continue, "The puncture wounds were made two weeks before other abrasions. The actual killing doesn't appear to be by the vampire, if it's a vampire, unless he or she likes to keep their victims around for several weeks. They found human DNA on two of the bodies."

Simon shakes his head, "Vampires rarely play with their food for more than a couple of days."

"Exactly. And the bodies aren't drained of blood. They're mutilated, burned, strangled, sliced. It doesn't fit for a vampire."

"But the puncture wounds do?" He asks.

"Maybe. It could be someone mimicking. Have you come across anything similar?"

Simon gives a quick nod. "There's been an uptick in vampire-to-human casualties. We've been working to track the vampire or vampires. We have undercover Guards active within the VSL. They haven't taken responsibility for these killings. In the past twenty years, there hasn't been any new movements against humans, more talk than anything else."

Puzzled by this information, I ask, "Have these casualties been unusual in any way? Apart from vampires killing humans?"

"Not really, other than the frequency. Most vampires have access to blood supplies. There's no need to attack humans." He sighs. "There was one victim. We found a poem written in German by her bedside. Unusual because she didn't speak German. She wasn't even of German heritage. It was a poem by August Graf Von Platen."

My thoughts drift to the letter I received earlier that day. "German?" I ask. "Can you send it to me along with your case notes?"

Simon asks skeptically, "Does it mean something?"

"Maybe. I'm not sure."

Simon's leg shakes. His eyes narrow. "A couple of weeks ago we found evidence that a vampire may have compelled a human delivery driver to steal blood from the blood bank. We've just started our investigation. I have little on it."

"You think there's a connection?"

"Unusual events, sure, but connected, I don't see it."

A bar server approaches the table and sits a shot of whisky in front of me. "Courtesy of her." He points at the brunette with long legs sitting at the birthday table. She'd written her phone number on the napkin.

I lift the glass in her direction, then turn to Simon. "And that's my cue. Send what you have. I'll keep you in the loop." I get up, shake his hand, and say my goodbyes. I walk over to her table, smiling. "Hello, ladies."

It didn't take long before Riley, the long-legged brunette, with an inviting neck, was in my car heading to my place. She had a bit too much to drink, which will work to my advantage. She'll easily forget this night, with a bit of compelling. She'll be a pleasant distraction.

In the elevator, riding up to my apartment, I pin her against the wall, her left leg around my waist. The scent of her Apricot shampoo fills my senses. My lips crash into hers. Her hands are tearing at my shirt. She breaks away panting, our eyes meet. She licks her lips and smirks.

The elevator opens, I pick her up and take her to my bedroom. She greedily unbuttons my shirt and kisses my neck. I toss her on my bed, remove her shirt, and unclasp her bra. With a swift motion, I remove my clothes. I lean down, kneel on the bed, and run my hand up her thigh. I reach to her waist, pull off the few remaining clothes she's wearing, and bring her to me. A low growl leaves my throat. My lips find her mouth. She claws at my back and her kisses are frantic. I'm so lost in the rhythm I don't realize her mouth is on my neck until I feel her teeth. For an undisciplined vampire, this simple act could bring out an uncontrollable animal. The feeling is intoxicating. My teeth extend and a blindness falls over me as the animal takes control. I'm not myself—I am more. Which pulls me in further. I reach heights only fresh blood can take me.

As I'm enjoying my release, I realize I'm ravaging her neck. My teeth are sunk in and her warmness flows down my throat. I catch myself, release my teeth, and pull back onto my knees.

She's not moving. I panic. "Wake up. Wake up." I reach for her wrist. Her pulse, it's faint, but beating. Her lips are blue. I need to get blood into her.

In a blur, I grab three O–negative bags out of the refrigerator. Next, I move to the closet and grab a medic bag. I've got a field blood transfusion kit, something all vampires should have. During the war, I learned how to prep one.

I rush back to the bedroom. I place a protective cover between Riley's arm and her body, use disinfectant wipes, sterilize the skin, find the vein, and insert the needle. Next, I spike the saline, prime it, and attach the lines to the saline and blood. For the next couple of hours, two, three-hundred ml units of blood are pumped into her. Color returns to her lips and her racing heart slows down. I sigh. *Close call.*

I slip on underwear and a robe. I hear Riley shift and turn in her direction. She's conscious and her eyes are open, when she sees me her eyes widen in panic. To ease her distress, I compel her into believing she's enjoying a spa treatment. When she walks out of this building, she'll feel light-headed and confused and will go straight to the hospital. I erase any memory of me or this experience.

I check her heart and pulse rate. She's alive enough to stay alive. I remove the needle and seal the insertion marks on her hand

and neck by placing a couple of drops of my blood on the wounds. It will speed up the regenerative process in her body.

She stands shakily. I hold her up to steady her, and she gets dressed. I call her an Uber and go with her down to the lobby. I tell the Uber driver to take her to the nearest hospital. Riley says, "How did you know I wasn't feeling good?" I smile and say goodbye.

Relief washes over me. If she had died, I would've been in serious trouble. I lost control without realizing it. I haven't killed a human since I was in WWII. War is a good place for a vampire. It's easy to hide who you are on the battlefield, but even there, I was in control.

The last time I lost control was shortly after I killed my nest in 1901. The Vita-Life serum wasn't developed until the 1960s, so I had to learn through sheer grit and determination, how to control myself. I've never needed to take it, but for newly turned vampires, it's required. I started taking it in the early 80s, to reassure the Dracul I would not reawaken any bloodlust while working for them. They didn't want the liability, and they didn't trust me. Still don't.

Losing control tonight concerns me. I've prided myself on the ability to contain the animal within and to blend into the human world. I've also worked hard to distance myself from my past destruction. Tonight wasn't a reflection of who I'd become, but who I used to be.

There's only one person I can talk to about what happened tonight. Nick. If other vampires have found themselves recently in similar situations, he'll know. The Shipwreck is full of secrets. Quiet discussion among friends. Gossip and rumors circulate. Mostly, it stays in the tavern, but to those who keep their ears open, they can learn much.

In my bedroom, bandages and tubes are strewn on the floor, and empty blood bags lay on the table. The protective covering I used under Riley's arm is splattered with blood. I strip the bed and use a solution of hydrogen peroxide to wash away any areas of blood and throw the covering away. I quickly pick up, removing any indications of tonight's disaster. Once done, I head to the pool to clear my head. I put in fifty laps, take a shower, and collapse into bed.

Before I drift off to sleep, my thoughts return to the case. This killer, whoever it is, is on the verge of killing again. I need to work fast.

CHAPTER 6

Jack Calloway

FOR THE PAST TEN YEARS, I've been a consultant for the Seattle PD, and mostly have an established professional relationship throughout. At least to the extent I get access to their portal when working a case. But my relationship with them didn't start on a positive foot. Years ago, I was hired by a husband who became a suspect in his wife's murder case. Besides the wife's homicide, the Seattle PD pinned two other murders on the husband. He wasn't guilty. Chief John Phipps, who was a Captain placed Detective Ed Halstead as lead investigator.

The case came to me through Nick Crandon. The husband's wife was half Were, and the husband suspected his wife was murdered by her half-brother's family. Were-people belong to a pack or extended family. The leader of the pack is called the Alpha and traditionally, the lineage for Alphas followed males. Now, women can be the Alphas and the title would have fallen to the wife. The half-brother, mother, and other members weren't happy with this change. But rather than go the traditional route of challenging for the Alpha title, they killed her and framed the husband. He wasn't Were, and they didn't like that either. As humans say, two birds, one stone.

Over the weekend, I'd logged into the Seattle PD portal and reviewed Ed's case files. I'd displayed evidence photos of each victim, in chronological order, victim one through three. I printed out witness statements and read through them. In doing so, I learned about our victims. Each had developed profiles on the Match, Meet, & Mingle dating website in the last six months. I looked through their profiles for similarities. None of them were married, they didn't have any children; they were minimally educated, and all were new to the area. Each of them had moved here within the last two years. But they were vastly different in other ways—hair color, height, interests. One loved horseback riding. Another scrapbooking and another had a love of learning foreign languages.

The first victim, Tori Henley, was a secretary at a law firm. Her best friend revealed she was secretly involved with one of the partners, Aaron Diggs. He was married. Eventually, she ended it. She started dating again, and Aaron didn't take it well. She was out to dinner with her new friend when Aaron showed and threatened her date. A case note confirmed Aaron Diggs was out of the country with his wife when Tori was killed. The police investigation, including phone and computer records, didn't uncover any nefarious plans between Aaron, his wife, and Tori.

The second victim, April Thompson, lived with her older sister. She was a student. I recognized her picture but couldn't place her face until I read her sister's name, Katie Thompson. I knew instantly.

I met Katie at a fundraiser for the Greater Seattle Area Theater Arts Council. A yearly fundraiser that brings the who's who of Seattle together. It was the second community event I attended where Katie was the event coordinator. She was a dirty blonde with long legs, voluminous breasts, and brown eyes. We flirted, I got her number, and the next night we had drinks and ended up in her bed.

Katie had a picture of her and her sister in the living room. Katie's parents had recently died in a car accident and April was going to live with her. To lose her parents and her sister will be tough and an ache pulls in my chest thinking about it.

I read the police interviews of the suspects. Billy McCord dated victim one, Tori, and victim two, April, through Match, Meet, & Mingle. Kelly Whitfield, victim three; and victim two, April, both worked at the same restaurant, different times, but the same manager, Terry Leland.

I read the statements from each. Billy went on a date with Tori, three times, and April, once. Billy was on another date when April was killed. The police haven't been able to locate the "date." However, text messages and an eyewitness corroborate his story.

An ex-employee of Terry Leland informed investigators Terry favored the younger female employees. He made sexual advances, cornering them in his office, or his car. He'd threaten to fire them if they didn't comply. Terry also had a criminal record—A domestic violence charge seven years ago. An all-around pillar of the community. I have no respect for men like this.

I stand and stretch my legs, rolling my head shoulder to shoulder, and rub the muscles to get the kinks out. I've been sitting in my office for the past six hours, studying reports on computer screens, and going over the evidence again and again. It stares back at me—all the pieces, like an incomplete jigsaw puzzle. I've studied the colors, shapes, and patterns, putting together the structure, and filling in details. Like a composer weaving the sweet simplicities of life through the dark and the vile, hoping to shed some light, and bring the dead back to life.

An email file arrives from Simon and I open it. It's a summary of his case notes on the recent vampire-to-human deaths the Guard is investigating and the poem he found at one of the crime scenes. I pull out the anonymous letter left at my office.

At the end of WWII, I was briefly stationed in the Rhineland where I learned some German. I translate what I can of the letter. "Look, look, the moon shines bright. We the dead ride fast." I search on the computer for the origin. These are the words of Gottfried Burger's Ballad, a German composer.

Next, I translate a portion of the poem "… Oh, whose pain means life, whose life means pain, may feel again what I have felt before…" I'm not sure what it means, if anything.

I study the handwriting of each, noting some similarities, but not enough to be sure. I'll ask Carla to run an analysis of the handwriting, comparing the two.

I read Simon's case notes on the women who died at the hands of a vampire in the past four months. My gaze lands on a name. Nicole Leedy, age thirty, and a registered nurse. My throat tightens and a sudden coldness hits my core. I continue to read. *Nicole Leedy*. She was found dead, two months ago, in her house. She was drained of blood. No witnesses, and there wasn't enough evidence to generate any leads.

I knew Nicole. The last time I saw her was five years ago. Nicole had been the nurse on duty when a victim, related to a case I was working, came into the hospital. Nicole agreed to meet for coffee. She was full of energy and sass, with a daring smile. Her hair was strawberry blonde and in the sun it lit up with gold highlights. Her tongue playfully twirled the straw of the iced coffee she was drinking. She meant it as a tease and it worked. One thing led to another, and we ended up at her place.

Seattle isn't a small city. And, well, people die. They die from many things, including murder. But to know two people who were murdered in the last two months? It's an odd coincidence, even for a vampire. I compared Simon's cases with the Seattle PD cases. The causes of death are different, as are the crime scenes. They don't appear to be related.

A knock on my door interrupts my thoughts. "Come in," I call out, shifting in my chair to straighten my posture. The door cracks open and Shannon pops her head in.

"Is this a good time to go over the case?" Her voice is hesitant and timid. Shannon can be distant and short when something is bothering her, but not timid. She's been quiet today. I can't blame her if she's avoiding me. After the way I grilled her about her date, I'd avoid me too.

"Sure, come on in." To reassure her, I won't interview her about her date like he's a suspect, I smile and wave her in. She steps inside, shuts the door, and takes a seat in front of me.

For the next forty-five minutes, we go over the evidence, but I don't include Simon's case notes. Shannon doesn't know I'm a vampire, and I'd like to keep it that way. The more humans brought into that world, the more dangerous it becomes.

She reads the evidence and scribbles on a notepad. After about fifteen minutes, I ask her questions and test her knowledge. I want her to develop her reasoning skills and draw logical conclusions. I ask her questions about the position of the bodies, blood loss found, type of death, and place of death.

Back and forth we volley, question and answer, as she paces around the room. She stops mid-pace and mid-sentence, mouth falling open. She looks up at me with widening eyes and says, "Two killers, it's got to be two killers." I didn't reply to that statement, not right away anyway. "What's your reasoning." Barely catching her breath, she fires out in rapid speech, dissecting the evidence, pointing to two killers.

"Your analysis is good." I pick up the reports on my desk and continue, "Put a little more thought into the composition of the killers—who are they, what do they do, how do they find these victims, and how are they different from one another." I stuff the papers into a file folder and set it on my desk. "You can tell me what you come up with tomorrow." Shannon jots down the questions I threw at her. I put my feet up on my desk. "Any luck tracking down the digital footprints?"

"I'm getting there. It's a little challenging because they're using a VPN routing through multiple servers. It's sending the trace around the country. I've broken through two false pathways but don't have a location yet."

Right then, the phone rings, and my email pings with a message. Shannon answers the phone and places the call on hold, "Dr. Patterson."

"I'll take it." Shannon pivots, turning away from me, and exits my office, closing the door.

I put the phone on speaker, "Doc, what's the word?"

"The official report, I just emailed you. My call is the unofficial part."

I open my email and attachment. "Okay, I got your report."

"There are two different and distinct patterns of injuries. The timelines and methods strongly suggest it involves different people. I evaluated and remeasured the puncture wounds. If they are teeth, which I believe they are, it's the same person." Doc pauses and sighs. "However, the evidence doesn't point to a vampire killing those girls."

"That begs the question, how are the two UNSUBs connected?" My stomach turns as I ask the question. To discuss a vampire as the unidentified subject, or an UNSUB brings a chilling reality. I sigh, pressing my lips together.

I hear Doc letting out a breath. "I'll leave that for you to solve, Jacko. You'll want to consider letting the Dracul know about this. It could be bigger than you think."

I lean back in my chair and shake my head "No, isn't at that level."

I could hear Doc's pulse speed up. "Jack, if this continues…"

I interrupt him. "If it does, I'll reach out. I've already alerted Simon Johnson."

"Good. Let me know if you need anything else. And don't be a stranger."

I hang up and look at my computer screen, glossing over the report he sent me. It confirms two individuals are involved, and a vampire is the same in all three cases. I take it all in, not liking where the evidence is going. I must bring Simon up to speed. I'm not interested in having the Guard involved, but I might not have a choice.

I glance at my watch. The phone intercom buzzes and Shannon announces Mrs. Winters is here. I open my door and welcome her into my office. She sits down and I hand her the pictures. As she goes through them, relief crosses her face. We talk a little. She looks up and smiles. Then reaches in her purse for her wallet and hands me fifteen-hundred in cash. I wish her the best and walk her out. Case closed.

I print off the poem and grab the letter. I open my door, turn off the lights, and stop in front of Shannon's desk. She twirls a finger in her hair, a habit she has when she's anxious. She looks up through the corner of her eye, eyebrow raised, waiting for me to say something.

I try to act indifferent, putting my hands in my pockets. "How was your date on Friday?"

She sighs loudly with an ugh. but answers me anyway. "It went well. We met yesterday afternoon too." She says with a smile and a dreamy look in her eyes.

"When are you going to introduce me?"

Her gaze falls to the desk and her lips press into a thin line. "Not yet, but soon." Once those words leave her mouth, her eyes squint and her shoulders tense. She's preparing for my bite.

Instead, I shrug. "Okay. I'm ready when you are. I'm heading over to the Seattle PD evidence lab and won't be back today. If you need anything, call."

With a look of surprise and probably a bit of relief, she nods and I turn and walk out the door. I give myself a congratulatory pat on the back for handling that well.

The traffic can be monstrous when leaving downtown Seattle. Timing is everything and mine's not great today. Forty minutes later, I arrive at the evidence lab. I exit my car and approach the building. Only eight steps between me and the door. I reach the top and a tall, olive-skinned woman with shoulder-length curly black hair greets me. The scowl on her face says a lot.

"Amy, nice to see you too. Lovely day, isn't it?" I look to the sky and back to her. Maybe talking about the weather will lighten her mood.

"Jack." She stands, one hand on her hip, the other points at me. "Carla's in a good place. She's moved on. She has someone new in her life. Don't screw it up for her."

She must've seen me get out of my car to be so quick on my heels. The corner of my lips turn upward as I answer in a smooth voice. "I wouldn't dream of it. Glad she's happy."

Amy never did like me, even when things were good between me and Carla. What I don't need right now is Carla's best friend scolding me. It's been three years. Everyone's moved on.

She holds her position for a moment more, eyeing me like she's peering into my soul, mining for the truth. Then she turns around and walks back inside the building. *Well, that was fun*, I say to myself and follow her inside.

Carla should be happy. She's an incredible woman. I would do anything to see to her happiness, including walking away from her three years ago. I've justified my actions several times by telling myself ending things between us was for the best.

I walk to the lab and stand at the door's entrance. I'm not a large person, but the top of the door frame is only a few inches above my head, and I take up most of the space. I spot Carla standing over a microscope. She wears a white lab coat, her hair is pinned up, and she's wearing glasses. Mesmerized, I'm fascinated watching her. Now and again, she moves away from the microscope to type something into the computer. A few moments later, I'm interrupted by the sound of someone clearing their throat. I turn to find Amy standing behind. *Great.* I step aside and let her through. I make my way to Carla and stand on the opposite side of the table.

Carla looks up, her body tensed, and she takes a step back. Her eyes grow wide in surprise. "Jack. What are you doing here?"

I walk over, reach into my jacket pocket, and pull out the poem and the letter. "I… ah," My words have a hard time forming. "Have these… need an analysis done on the handwriting." I hand them to her.

She hesitates and reaches for the envelope, undoing the clasp. "Where'd they come from?" She pulls out the letter and the poem, glossing over them.

"One is from a case a friend of mine is working and the other was sent to me."

"Is this German? Are these related to our case?" She turns them over to read what's written on the back.

I nod. "Yeah, it's German. I'm following a hunch." Rather than continue to look at her, I shift my gaze to skim the lab. My scan stops on the roses on her desk. I glance back at her. A ping of regret rents space in my chest.

Our gazes meet. "Have you come up with anything else on the case?" She asks.

I look away briefly, studying the floor. "A few things, still looking into them."

Carla sets the letter next to the computer on the table. The computer is the only thing between us. "All right, I'll get these looked at." Her feet shuffle, switching her weight to her left leg. "When are we going to get together? I mean… us, Ed, for the case." She stumbles over her words and her face turns a shade of pink.

"Ah, how about we meet up at Ed's precinct on Thursday, about 2 p.m.?"

She opens her calendar on the computer. I can see *dinner w/ Ted @ Lark* written for Wednesday at six p.m. I scowl and flex my fingers. Carla types in our meeting. "Okay, Thursday works."

My eyes fix onto hers. I hold them, not letting her look away. All sounds fade away like echoes in a tunnel. I'm drawing her in, pulling at her soul. I hear her breath catch. Her hand reaches toward her neck and pulls slightly at her collar. Her lips tremble and I'm drawn in, leaning toward her.

A voice pierces the moment. Jolted. I snap to and release all ties. I quickly avert my eyes, pivot, and walk out of the lab, slamming the door shut. The force surprises me, and I look back to make sure the door is intact. It is.

Emotions long-forgotten stir inside, and I don't like it. I'm stirred in other places too and shift a bit as I walk. I swear under my breath. I reach my car, jump in, and speed away.

CHAPTER 7

Victim

THE WOMAN REALIZED IT DIDN'T matter anymore. She wouldn't escape this hell. She tried to focus on anything else, other than the pain and fear. If she didn't, she knew her mind would break.

In and out of consciousness, she clung to memories of the past. Childhood memories of her sister arguing over paint color for their shared bedroom. After a week of bribes—bribes to do each other's chores, bribes to do the other's homework for a month, and threatening to tell Mom and Dad what they surely knew would get the other in trouble, they settled on the color peach. She lingered on the awful taste of her grandmother's fruitcake she received this past Christmas, wishing she hadn't thrown it in the garbage.

Why hadn't she listened to her dad? She thought he was too overprotective about her moving to a big city by herself or because she was online dating. Something she wished her mother hadn't told him. Had the woman listened to his warnings, maybe she wouldn't be chained to the basement wall knowing she would soon die.

The woman didn't know how long she'd been his captive. Her days and nights were mixed up. Initially, she paid attention to how many times he fed her, but it wasn't long before she felt drugged and time slipped away. Drugged by what, the woman wasn't sure.

For the first few hours of her imprisonment, maybe days, when she could, the woman screamed, but no one came to her rescue. Her voice was no longer hoarse. And once she stopped struggling, her wrists and ankles weren't as sore. She'd fought against the iron shackles binding her, tugging and pulling to get free. It didn't take the woman long to understand he enjoyed her fear and struggle.

The woman heard a door close, and the sound of stairs snapping from the weight of each step. She willed her body to calm, but it trembled. She no longer had control over her body, and the sense of powerlessness made her mad.

In the last effort of defiance, she refused to make eye contact with him, turning away as he got close. The sound of his laughter made her shoulders sink. Her head jerked up, meeting his gaze. How could this man, who was polite and charming on their date, and who is now casually dressed as if he's going to the store, be such a vile and cruel monster?

To give him easy access to what he wanted, when he brought the woman here, he stripped her clothes and dressed her in a short sleeve t-shirt. He'd rendered her powerless to do anything about it.

A wooden chair scraped across the concrete floor, and he set it next to her. She'd been through this before and knew what was next. He hoisted her drained body onto the chair. Rather than push his hands away, LeighAnne spread her legs. She didn't have the energy to do anything else. She disliked hearing his voice, but if she had to hear it, accolades were better than punishments. He gave her a 'good girl' nod and smiled.

His eyes dilated and turned a reddish hue. His teeth elongated, like tiny daggers protruding from his mouth. He settled in on his knees and sunk his teeth into her inner thigh. LeighAnne winced at the pain and turned her head away as he drank her blood.

The mere image of it made her stomach churn. Tears welled in her eyes and streamed down her face.

When he was finished, he wiped his mouth with the back of his hand. He grabbed her face, forcing her to look at him. His face took on sharper features, his cheekbones, around his eyes, and his jaw. The edges were defined. His face was so close to LeighAnne's, she could smell her blood.

"My pet," he purred. "I'm done with you."

Her eyes widen in fear as she stared at her death in his eyes. Tears continued to stream down her face. She wouldn't beg, she was past that now.

He stood, pulled out a key from his pocket, and begun unshackling her. One by one, LeighAnne's extremities were freed. She remained slumped in the chair. He walked to the bed, grabbed some clothes, and began dressing her.

She mumbled, "Where are we going?" She knew it was a stupid question, but the rational part of her mind sought for something concrete to hold on to.

"Somewhere, you'll enjoy more."

Once dressed, he bound her mouth, her hands, and carried her upstairs. When he carried LeighAnne outside, cool damp air brushed along her arms. Other than the faint sound of a few cars strolling along, it was quiet. She could barely open her eyes, and what little she saw was fuzzy, but before her vision went dark, she saw enough to know it was nighttime. What day, or week, was of no consequence, but at least she'd have another memory to block out this nightmare.

And with that, he placed LeighAnne into a small area that held her body in a fetal position. Something above her closed, encapsulating her, and within a few moments, she heard what sounded like a car door shut. Then she felt the vibration of rolling tires. Her thoughts raced to what the end would be. Would it be painful? Would it be quick? Would my family find me? Tears streamed again, and she wondered what she did to deserve this fate.

CHAPTER 8

Jack Calloway

THE COOLNESS OF THE WATER rushes over me with each stroke. After an intense weight training session, the water's invigorating. The last lap of a hundred, I touch the pool's wall and grab the ledge. Holding onto it, I scan the room and spot Jasper sitting on a windowsill. I leap out of the pool. Heightened sight and sound aren't the only advantages of being a vampire. Accelerated speed and herculean strength can create the illusion we fly. We can't. Well, not most of us.

I turn on the shower and step in, letting the hot water roll down my body. My arm extends, bracing the wall. I rest my head onto a forearm, letting the water soothe my neck. My mind wanders to the woman with delicious curves I devoured in my bed last night.

I linger in the shower a bit longer, thinking about the dream I woke to this morning. The sounds of my wife's laughter when she teased me about my tie collection. She used to say I was obsessed with ties like women are with ribbons for their dresses.

My dream went from playfulness to terror when tears, screams, and pleas for help sputtered from her mouth as she was ravaged by a monster. In my dream, I ran after her voice. I kept ending in the same place, unable to reach her.

I miss Caroline, and my heart aches thinking about her death. It shattered a light in my soul that day. She was smart, playful, and innocent. Always ready to help others who were facing misfortunes. My family had wealth and privilege, and she made sure that privilege wasn't wasted.

I turn off the water and reach for a towel. I wrap the towel around my waist, walk to the apartment, Jasper in tow, and into my office. I open the refrigerator, staring inside. What to eat? I've arranged my blood bags by blood type. A's on the first shelf, AB's on the second, and O's on the bottom.

Today, I will settle on A-negative. I take three, leave the office, and go to the kitchen, grabbing a glass out of the cupboard. Jasper jumps up on the kitchen counter. "You know you aren't supposed to be up here," I scold, but not well because I'm scratching him behind his ears as I do. I get a purr of approval.

I finish my breakfast and head to my closet to get dressed. I pull grays and blacks together and grab a silver-banded watch. I still have a tie collection, but watches are functional in my line of work, and ties are a choking hazard. After completing my grooming rituals, I take a last look in the mirror and smile in approval. I grab my keys, tell Jasper to be a good boy, and leave.

Today, I'm interviewing the identified suspects and I drive South to Leland's House of Pancakes, where I hope to find Terry Leland. It's located in a town called Burien and when I arrive at my destination, the building reminds me of a fifty's diner. Orange, yellow, and blue paint adorn the exterior and outline gravel-like walls, with large windows.

I enter the building through the glass door. It's a small restaurant that probably seats around seventy-five people. It's Tuesday mid-morning and by appearances, whatever breakfast crowd they had, if they had one, has thinned. I show the hostess my card. "I'm looking for Terry Leland."

Before long, a burly, bald man saunters out from the kitchen. His button-up shirt is stretched around his middle and a cigarette is tucked behind his ear. "I'm Terry, how can I help you?"

I pull out another card and hand it to him. "I've some questions about two employees who used to work here. Do you mind if we talk in private?"

He frowns as he reads my card and he rubs the back of his neck. "Sure. Let's go to my office."

Leland's office is small and barely accommodates two people. If it wasn't for the clutter, maybe three people. Stacks of paper strewn about overtake his desk. The file cabinet has papers sticking out of the drawers. An empty, scrunched up bag of chips lays next to the garbage can on the floor.

Leland sits in a chair behind a desk and gestures for me to have a seat. The only chair available is orange and plastic. Terry folds his arms. "So, what can I do for you?"

"I've been hired to look into the death of April Thompson and Kelly Whitfield. I understand they both worked for you?"

I watch his reactions for any tells that expose the truth. Tells like averting his eyes, touching his face, or a racing heart rate. He leans back in his chair. "I don't know nothin' about murder." Once these words are out, his gaze diverts slightly behind me. I follow it to a coat rack in the corner.

"I'm not suggesting you do. I'm here to find out more about them, like their background. Can you tell me what kind of employees they were?"

"You're a private investigator, huh? For whom?"

"I can't tell you who hired me, but yes, I'm a private investigator. For my own company." I didn't want him to know the

Seattle PD hired me. People are less forthcoming with the police than they are with private investigators.

He pauses and tugs at his shirt collar. A sign of nervousness. "Well, Kelly, she, ah... worked here for about three months. She worked evenings in the bar."

I want him to be at ease, so I lean back in my chair and drop my arms to my side. "What kind of employee was she?"

"She was all right, I guess. Made it to work on time." His eyebrows slope downward into a frown. "She had a bit of an attitude problem. Thought she was better than everyone. I don't want to speak ill of the dead, but that mouth of hers probably got her killed."

"Are you saying she had it coming?"

"What? Ah... No... No." He stammers. "Nobody deserves that. I'm just saying she was too big for her britches. Thought she could do whatever she wanted. Rules didn't apply to her." A mischievous grin reaches the corner of his lips. He leans in and his eye twinkles. "You know. Women. Sometimes they don't listen and you gotta put them in their place. Show 'em who's boss." He smacks the top of the desk with a hand.

"And did you, show Kelly who's boss?"

"Damn right I did. I told her if she didn't follow my rules, she needn't come back."

"Rules. like you show me yours, I'll show you mine, kind of rules?" It was a question either he would brag about or get defensive. Either way, I needed little more from him. And I couldn't stop myself. Predators like him are the worst kind.

"Listen, mister, I don't know what you're getting at, but this is a legitimate business. I treat all my employees fairly and within the law."

I smile and lean in. "Mr. Leland. I meant no offense. I was only suggesting that sometimes putting a woman in her place comes with benefits."

A boisterous laugh filled the small space. "Not even that would have calmed the bitch down. Not that I'm saying anything happened."

I laugh. "I know what you mean." And I did. Just not in the way he might be thinking. "When was the last time you saw Kelly?"

"About three weeks ago. She came by to pick up her last paycheck."

I nod in acknowledgment. I only had one more question. "And what about April Thompson? When was the last time you saw her?"

He rubs his head. "Probably three months ago. She didn't work here that long. Hard to find good employees in this business."

He stands, signaling he's done with the conversation. "I need to get back to work."

I extend my hand to shake his. "I appreciate your time."

Before leaving his office, I glance at the coat rack again and see, underneath the straps of a white apron, a woman's red silk scarf. When I asked him about Kelly's death, he glanced at the coat rack. Something about it pulled his attention.

I find the restroom, not because I need to use it, but because the state of the restroom could provide insights into Leland's habits.

The men's bathroom has two stalls and a urinal. The urinal has a slight crack on the edge and is marked with yellow splotches. The floor is swept, but visibly the corners are filled with dirt. The walls are streaked with something faint as if whatever it was, was wiped away. The garbage is overfilled with paper towels. The sight of the place makes me reach for the soap and wash my hands.

I leave the building and get into my car. Leland is arrogant and chauvinistic, I'll give him that. What's clear? He's hiding something, but he's not a vampire and he's not organized. Terry Leland wouldn't be able to cover up a murder, let alone a series of them. He's guilty, but not of murder.

I head toward Pioneer Square in downtown Seattle to the Law offices of Jameson, Nichols, and Diggs. Their office is near the courthouse. Shannon found Aaron Digg's schedule and on Tuesdays, he should be in his office. I park in the parking garage and walk to an elevator.

The elevator doors open once I reach the 7th floor. The office I'm walking toward is near the elevators. Inside, a large window frames the reception desk, overlooking downtown. The words Jameson, Nichols, and Diggs jut out from the face of the desk in bold letters. Brown leather, dark woods, and sharp lines fill the space. It's formal, stuffy, and lacking personality.

I hand my card to the receptionist and ask for Aaron Diggs. She asks if I have an appointment and of course I don't, but she calls him to see if he's available. She shows me to his office, opens the door, and hands Digg's my card. A tall, slender man greets me. "Come in, have a seat."

I sit in a large brown leather chair. "Thank you, Mr. Diggs. I'm here on the behalf of Tori Henley. I would like to ask you some questions."

His voice is steady, with no inflection. "Anything I can do to help. I'm assuming you're here about her murder. Or are you here about something else?"

Aaron Diggs is weathered-looking. The file said he's thirty-six, but the fine lines around his eyes and his lightly peppered hair make him seem older. He wears a tan suit that looks, based on how the suit fits his shoulders, tailored, with a tan, black, and white striped tie.

I read he's been a partner for about five years. An ambitious goal to attain so young. I remember when I started a law practice after the war in 1866. Before the conflict, I received a law degree from Yale University. When I returned home, I was eager to begin my practice. Six months later, my family was killed.

I glance around and notice how strategic and functional the office is. The items he uses daily are within reach, but organized. I skim the bookshelf behind him. A library of law books organized by size is within his reach. He has awards positioned at eye level so that anyone who walks in can spot those immediately. A few photos and other mementos are placed around his office. Even those are functional, as if to say, "Look at me."

"Yes, I'm investigating her murder. I understand she worked here?"

He straightens his tie. "She did." His voice and movements are controlled, and his eyes don't waver from mine, but his face betrays him. His skin appears grayish and the dark circles under his eyes point to a lack of sleep.

His eyes soften and tears well. "I'm sorry. It's been difficult. It's all been difficult."

I'm surprised by the emotion and it makes me uncomfortable—suffocated. I need distance and shift the conversation to facts. "How long did she work here?"

He opens a desk drawer and retrieves a tissue, dabbing his eyes. "About two years. She was my secretary for eighteen months."

"Eighteen months. Not two years?"

"Yes, well, after eighteen months she went to work for another partner."

Of course, I knew there was a breakup, but I wanted to get his version and perception of their relationship. "Was there a performance issue?"

He clasps his hands and rests them on the desk. "Not really. She was a good worker. Punctual. Smart. Everyone liked her."

"But..."

His posture straightens and his gaze falls to the floor before returning to mine. "We were involved for about six months. It ended. Another opening came up, and she transferred."

"I see." I flip through my notes. I knew what I wanted to ask but didn't want to appear eager. "I have here, from a friend of Tori's," I look up at him, and then back to my notes, "who said you didn't handle the breakup well. Says, you stormed into a restaurant and threatened a boyfriend."

The muscles in his jaw tensed and his lips pursed. He frowns and in a quick, stern voice, he says, "It wasn't like that."

I lean back into my chair. "What was it like, Mr. Diggs?"

"I'm married. Separated now." He shrugs and nods at me with a grimace. "We kept seeing each other, occasionally, after it was over. She said it wasn't fair for her to wait around for me, she should be dating."

"And you didn't like that?"

"What choice did I have? I couldn't easily leave my wife. I was angry. She was flaunting it in my face. He'd come to the office to pick her up for lunch. Send her flowers."

"Mr. Diggs, when's the last time you saw Tori?"

"She didn't show up for work for about a week, and then I was told she'd been killed. That was about two months ago." His eyes gloss over with tears. "I'd gotten back from the Bahamas and had a voicemail from the police." He places his hands to his forehead and shakes his head. He's visibly distraught, but he is a lawyer, and acting is part of the gig.

I stand to leave. "Thank you, Mr. Diggs. I don't have any other questions and I appreciate your time."

He comes around his desk and shakes my hand. "I hope they find the bastard. She was a beautiful person who had so much life in her."

I smile, nod, and see my way out.

On the way to my car, I reflect on the interview. A murder. A jealous lover. Does he have a motive? Yes. Intent? Possibly. Opportunity—he was out of the country. What about the other victims?

I shake my head. There aren't any connections between Aaron Diggs and the other victims. What about the man Tori was dating? I don't remember seeing much about him in the case notes, other than the timeline fits when Billy dated her.

I get into my car and look at the time, three-thirty p.m. One more interview and I can call it a day.

CHAPTER 9

Jack Calloway

LATER THAT EVENING, I ARRIVE at the address I found in April Thompson's file for her sister's address. When I knew her before, she had lived in an apartment in Northgate. I sit in my car near Green Lake park staring at a pale green, craftsman style house. It's not quite dark, but lights illuminate the inside. I wonder if she's married. I look at the address in the file again to make sure I'm at the right place.

I walk up three concrete steps and knock on the door. A tall, strawberry blonde opens the door. It takes a second before her eyes go wide in recognition and her lips curl into a smile.

She wipes her hands on a towel and looks around behind me. "Jack. What are you doing here?"

I smile and hand her my card. "Katie. I'm sorry to pop in like this. I'm here on business, working with the Seattle PD."

Katie stands in the doorway, unmoving. She isn't wearing any makeup. Her eyes are red and puffy, and her hair is matted in places. Her appearance tells me she's not coping well.

"Oh. Come in."

I close the door behind me and scan the room. Reds, browns, and golds warm the living room. Soft lighting fills corners. Wood floors stretch to the dining area, but when I look closer, I see papers scattered across the dining room table, empty food cartons in the living room, and clothes strewn about.

She follows my eyes. "Sorry, I…" Her gaze falls to the floor and her shoulders sink. "Can I get you anything to drink, Jack?"

"No, thank you. You have nothing to be sorry for." I reach out to touch her arm. "I can only imagine how difficult it's been. Do you have anyone to help you?"

"No, I'm fine. I'm just, well…." Tears stream and I pull her into me. She's sobs, racked with grief. I pick her up and set her on the couch. She's light, lighter than I remember, and seemingly frail.

I cover her with a blanket and smooth her hair. "It's going to be okay. Let's get some food into you."

Over the next two hours, I get her to eat some soup and take a shower. Katie has been off work since her sister's murder, and she's been alone. I talk her into calling her best friend and having her stay for a few days. I wait until her friend arrives before I begin my questions.

"Katie, I need to ask you some questions about April." She nods at me and I continue. "Do you know Billy McCord?"

With her gaze on the floor, she answers softly, "April had a date once with a Billy McCord. They met through a dating website. Only one date though, it didn't go anywhere after that." She pauses, then continues. "The last guy she went out with, I guess they hit it off. They went out a few times." She hesitates and looks at me. "I thought he came on too strong. Sending her flowers, professing his love. He wanted to be with her all the time. It wasn't right, but she wouldn't listen. I think she liked the attention. His name was Jim. Evans, I think was his last name."

I jot his name onto my notepad. "Did you ever meet this Jim?"

With a slight shake of her head, she answers, "No. I only know that he worked for some department store as a manager. I'm sorry, I don't know what store." She put her face in her hands and sobs.

I stand to leave, grabbing the jacket I'd discarded when I first arrived. "It's okay. It's not important."

She reaches for my hand. "You'll find out who took April's life. Won't you?"

I smile. "I'll do everything I can." I squeeze her hand to reassure her. "I'll check in on you in a few days."

I get back into the car and look for Jim Evans in the file. That name came up before when the Seattle PD interviewed Katie, but there wasn't a lot about him. They couldn't find his profile on Match, Meet, & Mingle. I'll have Shannon dig into this.

I sigh deeply. I know the ache of losing someone you love. Grief affects people in different ways, and as an investigator, you never know what you'll walk into. Anger. Denial. Avoidance. Tears. Often you're faced with all those emotions. Interviewing family members isn't the fun part, but it's necessary.

I have one more interview to do. Billy McCord and he's not been easy to find. Right now, though, I need to head home. Ever since San Francisco, my days and nights have been switched around. Tonight, with any luck, maybe sleep will descend upon me by four a.m.

CHAPTER 10

Jack Calloway

BEFORE INTERVIEWING KATIE THOMPSON, I went to Billy McCord's work. Tracking Billy McCord has taken me to several places. The thought of Katie and the pain she's going through tugs. I know all too well how loss can leave an emptiness that's difficult to fill.

Billy works for an auto body shop in Greenwood. Unfortunately for me, it was his day off. However, his boss told me Billy keeps his head down, stays out of trouble, and focuses on his work. He'd had no problems with Billy, and his detail work is exceptional.

This afternoon, I went to Billy's house. He wasn't home, but I met an older brother, who Billy lives with. His brother, Earl, was about my height and fair-skinned. He had rings on several of his fingers along with a nose and lip piercing. And if all that didn't impress, he had a tattoo on his forehand which captured my attention. It was a pentagram and in the center was a dragon head. The letters S.C.S.T.C. were in between the points of the stars.

I asked for Billy and showed him my card. Earl ranted on about how laws and institutions cripple individual freedoms, the government shouldn't regulate autonomy, and how he has a right to choose his destiny. I had no right to interfere.

It was a familiar rant. One I heard more than a century ago. Only this wasn't the musings of rebellious vampires. Because of my experience, I understood his angst. So, I joined in. We discussed self-governance, the over-reaching hand of the government, and how hierarchies cripple self-expression.

It's not that I've got an opinion on those things, one way or the other, but to understand and agree with what he was ranting about got him to relax enough to tell me where Billy would be tonight.

Once I left Billy's house, I called Shannon and tasked her to research the dragon symbol. It thrilled her to get in on the detective action.

A few hours later, I pull into the parking garage of my building and head to the main floor. I step out of the elevator and walk across the lobby toward my office.

A woman's voice calls out my name, "Mr. Calloway." I turn toward the familiar voice and see my building manager, Meghan Williams, walking hurriedly to catch me.

"Ms. Williams. How are you today?" Meghan has been working for me over the past five years. She manages the tenants and any building issues that arise, including security. To bring someone into my circle, I need to know everything I can. I spent six months vetting Meghan. She's ex-military—Army. She served for six years and earned several distinguished marksmanship awards. She returned to school and received a bachelor's degree in Psychology. I brought her in when she graduated.

She's an only child, both parents deceased. Her father was an alcoholic and died when she was eighteen. Managing her father's alcoholism was her first training in detection and concealment. She has a strong sense of justice and the ability to act accordingly. That's important to me, even though sometimes justice doesn't always fit into the law. She's one of three people who has access to my apartment. The others are Nick and Simon.

"Good sir. I wanted to apprise you of a concern I'm handling."

"Let's go to my office." I open the door and we walk in. I smile at Shannon, who's standing at the printer.

Shannon turns back to what she's doing and says, "I found the information you wanted when you're ready."

Once in my office, Meghan says, "I found something on our video feed that I don't like. I'm not sure it's anything. I wanted to know if you had noticed anything missing, or different, in your apartment in the last week?"

"I haven't, no. What's this about?"

"I was reviewing video from last week. During the time frame when you were out of town, I found blips in the recording, like signal interference. I've given Paul Crandon, and ComNet a call. Neither has gotten back to me. I wanted to make sure it wasn't an outside signal issue before I jumped to any conclusions. But I'd like to check your apartment."

"I'll be gone for the next few hours. You can go up then."

She nodded and left my office. I thought about what she said, and about the past week. Had anything been out of place? No, not anything that stood out. If someone had been in my apartment at the very least, I would've smelled them. I'm pulled out of my thoughts with the sound of my cell phone ringing.

I see the name of the caller and slide the green arrow to the right. "Simon." It's the middle of the afternoon and although we both would rather be in a darkened room tucked away, our jobs often require a delay in resting. Fortunately, like many vampires, Simon can tolerate the sun.

"Jack. How are things?"

"Moving along. You?"

"Yeah. A couple of things. Two human women are missing in North Seattle. They've been missing for about two weeks. One woman lives with her parents, got into a fight with them, and took off. The other left to go on a date and never returned."

There's only one reason Simon would readily offer this information. "Match, Meet, & Mingle date?"

"That's correct," he says.

"Do you know who he is?"

"I understand the Seattle PD North is checking on a couple of leads."

"I have a meeting at the precinct tomorrow. I'll follow up with them," I say.

"Something else." I hear him take a deep breath.

The ability to breathe is a remnant of our former selves. Though it's unnecessary, it connects us to what we once were—human. We also have a heartbeat. A slow one—one beat per minute or thereabout. "I mentioned to you before about the delivery driver at the blood bank. I didn't mention we found him dead, and we recently discovered someone has tampered with some deliveries. In one of our cases, a Vamp lost control and killed a woman. His normal blood deliveries contain the Vita-Life. When we analyzed the blood in his last delivery, it wasn't the Vita-Life mix," he says.

I grow quiet and think about how I lost control with Riley. "Do you think it's connected to these cases?"

"I don't know, but we're investigating that theory."

I can't tell Simon about Riley. Not yet. I don't want to give any reason for the Dracul to sideline me, perhaps even permanently. But the thought of all of it makes me frown. "Our cases could be connected."

"We'll see where our leads take us. Keep me informed on what you find. If they're connected, we could have a political nightmare. It could become a shit show fast. I've got to give NISCU a heads up on the possible connection." Simon says.

NISCU is the National Inter-Species Crime Unit. It's a shadow operation that's been around for about forty years. Only a select few know of its existence. Colonel Jeffrey Gregg spearheaded it. He was the Secretary of Homeland Security at the start of the NISCU. Homeland has authority over the division. Currently, Ann Rimes holds the Secretary position. The division's board members include Homeland, FBI, Military, an Ascender representative, and a member from the Lycaon.

I worked for the FBI Behavioral Sciences Unit when discussions were underway on forming NISCU. Though I spent more of my time with humans, I'd successfully navigated both worlds, supernatural and human. My inherent vampiric abilities allowed me to swiftly identify and aid in capturing serial criminals. I became renowned in the law enforcement community. The Dracul asked me to be a consultant and representative for both communities to aid in the NISCU formation.

I was reluctant. I'd been working as a "human" and didn't want my identity revealed. Doing so was a risk to my life, but they took precautions to protect everyone's anonymity, and they earmarked the unit classified.

Over the next two years, I worked to get the NISCU up and running. I wasn't the only vampire either, Simon was there too. It was a lot of work and it wasn't smooth. Distrust was a hurdle we had to overcome. It was a challenge to find a pathway through all those bureaucracies. In the end, we did it. It wasn't perfect and continues to develop over the years. Although many of the original members are retired or have passed, I'm still involved, if only distantly.

My involvement in the formation helped improve my relationship with the Dracul, at least with one member, Simon's father, Aron Johnson. He fought for my involvement in the program, and the Dracul took a chance. It helped that Simon was on the project. Someone to keep close watch over me.

I continued my involvement as a member of the tactical advisory board. However, about twenty years ago, I had a falling out with the supervisor of criminal investigations and one of their west coast lead investigators. We strongly disagreed on the tactical approach to dealing with a rogue Were pack. His distrust of vampires was obvious, and he didn't respect my experience with were-people. It created a divide that had the potential to explode. I chose to step away. That supervisor is now the chair of the tactical advisory board. The lead at that time, Adam Jacobs, is now the Associate Director of Criminal Investigations.

I roll my eyes and glance away, "That's all we need is the Torpedo involved in this." That's my nickname for that asshat Jacobs. His approach to operations is to shoot first, ask questions later.

"If they get involved, he most likely won't be the one on the ground," Simon says.

"Yeah, well, he won't be far away from it either. And he'll have the ear of Seattle PD Chief and the Dracul." I tap my fingers on the desk. My insides prickle at the thought of Adam Jacobs. "I'll check in with you in a couple of days."

I hang up and scroll through my emails. I read the who and subject line and decide whether to open or delete. A credit card statement. An email from Jennifer Shultz with "Confidential" in the subject line, I don't open.

A light rapping on my door interrupts and I close my email. My door opens slightly, and Shannon pops her head in.

I wave her in. "What do you have on the symbol?"

Shannon had printed off several depictions of the symbol with its mythologies and uses. She hands those to me. "The symbol is often used by satanic groups. The initials stand for the Seattle Chapter of the Satanic Temple Church."

I study what she gave me as she explains the different mythologies related to the dragon head and the pentagram. I'm familiar with many pagan and supernatural beliefs. Their images rarely mean what humans make them out to be.

"From what I read, the Seattle chapter isn't worshipping evil or dark forces. They reject the notion of the supernatural and hierarchal systems. They meet on Wednesdays. Tonight."

I learned about their meeting from Earl McCord when he told me where Billy would be. "I'm going tonight. A suspect is a member. I'm going to question him and find out about this organization."

Her voice turns indignant. "I don't think you can just show up. You have to be invited."

I grin. "Lucky me. They've invited me."

With a honeyed voice trying to butter me up, she bats her eyelids and replies, "Oh, in that case, can I come with you?"

"No, and your wiles won't work on me, young lady. In all seriousness, I don't know enough about this yet."

Her hands go to her hips. Her reply is a matter of fact, "Isn't that what the job is? Investigate? Ask questions? If I'm going to get good, I need to experience all of it. Not just researching and studying your notes."

She's frustrated with me. Enthusiastic to learn the craft and I keep wanting to protect her. "You're right, and you will, but not on this one, kiddo."

Shannon glares at me. "How will anyone take me seriously in this profession if you treat me like a kid? I'd been taking care of myself way before you came along."

I sigh. I know she's right. "How 'bout I get you a summer internship with the forensic team at the Seattle PD? Between my work and that, you'll get a good foundation. Then you can go out on a case."

Her eyes narrow. "While I'm there, who are you gonna find to help you?"

I smile and wink. "I've been taking care of myself long before you came around."

Shannon laughs, waves me off with her hand, and walks out of my office. She's right though, I need to expose her to the field. However, this isn't your everyday case, not that any serial criminal case is, but most don't involve the supernatural or cross-species elements. I need to keep her at arms-length on this one. Offering to arrange an internship with Carla's team should satisfy her curiosity. And keep her far away.

CHAPTER 11

Jack Calloway

SURPRISINGLY, THE TEMPLE IS AN AMERICAN gothic-style white building. The lawn is lush, as are the trees that surround the property. It's provincial looking, like something straight out of the 1600s. It's reminiscent of a structure the Quakers or Puritans would build. The building is L-shaped. I'm guessing the L was an add-on. A semi-wraparound porch, held up by five pillars, greets the front of the building. A large arched window sets under a pitched roof.

I wanted to blend in, so I drove a Dodge Ram truck, and wore dark jeans and a black hoodie. In my research, I found other chapters using a Ram as part of their symbology. Maybe my truck would help me play the part.

Billy's brother, Earl, stands on the porch and when he spots me, waves me over. He introduces me to Billy, and we go inside. Billy is about twenty-two, not tall, and although he's wearing loose clothes, I can tell he has some muscle to him. I'm interested in what this is all about, so I'll wait until it's over to question Billy.

Inside, the walls are paneled with wood. Tapestries are draped around the room with the pentagram and dragon symbols. The words "live in freedom, and autonomy" are on banners behind a podium. The podium stands before thirty blue, cloth-covered chairs placed in five rows. A candelabra with lit red and black candles stands to the right side. To the left side, a step below the podium are three chairs where a woman and two men sit in black robes.

The woman starts the meeting by calling all members to state their tenets aloud, which are hanging on the wall, placed easily to read. I stumble through words, sincerely trying, but finding there's a constriction in the back of my throat. It's a familiar taste of righteousness, a righteousness that can lead men to do unspeakable acts.

In an attempt to welcome, they encourage guests to state their names, which I do. Next, one man goes to the podium and talks about "a life free of worship." What they don't realize is by not worshipping something, they're still idolizing an idea, thus worshipping it. So, rather than listen to words blind men speak, I listen for other things. Sounds. Heartbeats. Breaths. What else happens here, I wonder. Does anyone seem nervous?

I watch Billy, who is sitting in front of me, and by the look on his face, he isn't listening either. His gaze darts. His foot is nervously shaking.

Near the end, they perform another ceremony. Each member removes a leather bracelet from their arm and places it into a metal bowl that's passed around. When the bowl finds its way to me, I peer inside and study the bracelets. It's a half-inch wide. A metal clasp that looks more like a shackle, anchors it together. The bracelet has the church's initials on it. I listen to the words from the man at the podium. "This act serves as a reminder to each of us, of our commitment to break the shackles of oppression caused by a society full of rules-an oppression that enslaves the mind."

Except for Billy's nervousness, overall, it looks aboveboard. The service ends and when I catch up to Billy, he's outside smoking a cigarette.

I lean against the porch pillar. "That was a good meeting tonight,"

Billy shrugs. His focus is on his feet. "Yeah, I guess so."

I reach into my pocket and hand him my card. "I met your brother earlier today at your house. I've got a couple of questions for you. Hoping you can clear up some things."

He takes the card and falters back, just slightly. Most people wouldn't have observed the change in his position. I do.

He looks at me. "Ah… sure… what about?"

"I understand you know Tori Henley and April Thompson. How did you come by that?"

Billy looks around. He puts his hands in his pockets and bites at his bottom lip. *Nervous. Hiding something*, I think to myself.

He stammers. "We…, I don't really know them. I… went on a date once or twice. They were both stuck-up. Acted like they were better than me. Like they could do better. So, it didn't go anywhere." He crosses his arms.

"Do you know a Kelly Whitfield?"

He reaches for the back of his neck. "Yeah, my cousin. Can't stand her. Why?" His voice is sharp and quick. "What are all these questions for? I did nothing to them. I already talked to the police about that." So far, he's kept his eyes averted.

I straighten my posture, shrug my shoulders, and open my arms, palms up. "Hey, man. I don't work for the police. I'm just trying to find answers on who'd want them dead. Any ideas on that?"

"No, I don't. As I said, they were full of themselves and I had little to do with my cousin."

"Where were you on Thursday night?" I ask, thinking about our Seward Park victim.

He flips his cigarette butt into the grass. I watch its arc. I turn to him. He clears his throat and grabs at his shirt. "I was on a date. We went to the movies. Theater on Capitol Hill."

"The entire night?"

He shakes his head. "Look, I already talked to the police about this. I got nothing more to say." He hurries to his car and takes off. I watch his car as it leaves. I wonder if those tires are a match to the partial found at Kelly Whitfield's crime scene.

He's hiding something, and his attitude toward the women raises my suspicions. He had motive, opportunity, and intent.

I get into my car and wait. Once everyone's gone, I grab a pair of gloves, a small plastic bag, and retrieve the cigarette butt. With any luck, forensics will find a match.

CHAPTER 12

Jack Calloway

WHEN I ARRIVE AT THE South Precinct, the clouds burn away, letting the sun's rays break free, if only for a moment before the drizzle begins again.

I enter the station, check-in, and I'm escorted to the conference room. As I walk by the modern office spaces—Few walls and lots of glass, projecting transparency, detectives gather. Before they see me, I hear someone getting razzed about some bet they lost. The laughing and teasing stops once they spot me. Law enforcement is a tight group and they don't let just anyone in. And even though I've consulted for this police department for many years, I'm still an outsider and not privy to their inner workings. I understand and appreciate their protectiveness.

When I reach the conference room, it's empty. I go inside, sit at the head of the table, and reach into my jacket. I pull out my phone and scroll through my messages. An echo of female voices reaches me, as does the smell of coconut and lime hitting my nose. It's Carla's lotion.

Carla walks in and I lift my gaze, nod, say hello, and refocus my attention on my emails, blocking all sensations. I will not let my emotions or misguided judgment influence me. Strictly professional. Nothing more.

She sets papers on the table and sits down. "Hello, Jack," she says. And minutes tick by in strained silence.

She speaks, then stops. "I…" She twists at her fingers. "Jack, what happened to you the other day at the lab?"

I raise my head and place my phone on the table. "When?" Acting nonchalantly, as if this is news to me, even though I know exactly what she's talking about.

"When you stomped out of my office, slamming the door." Her voice was low, but her words were sharp.

With a slight wave of my hand, I reply, "Oh. That. Nothing. Something I forgot to do."

Carla folds her arms. "It didn't seem like nothing."

Ed saunters in. I'm glad to see him because his presence ends this conversation. Ed holds a coffee in one hand and sits directly across from Carla, near the crime wall. "Where are we at?" He says roughly to me. His eyes narrow. I'm not sure if his gaze is daring me or if he overheard Carla's conversation.

I stand to face the whiteboard behind me and grab a black marker. I draw a line down the center and list the identifiers, characteristics, and M. O.'s of two UNSUBs, knowing that one of them, no matter what the list is, won't be caught by humans.

"One." I begin. "Is organized, methodical. He probably studies his victims. He knows their habits. Where they go. Where they live. What they like. He uses the information to gain access to them. He gets off on the hunt. It's a cat-and-mouse game for him. If there's sexual motivation, it's in the build-up, before the kidnapping. It's about power and control. Once he has the victim, the excitement wanes. He gets off more on creating terror than harming them. He uses an instrument to provoke fear, inserting it into the body, probably as a punishment, for not doing what he says." *The instrument is his teeth.* I think before continuing. "Internally, having power over someone reduces his inadequacy or impotence. Someone in his life made him feel small and powerless. He's older, more experienced. He's practiced, doesn't leave a trace of who he is. He uses the second UNSUB to cover his tracks."

I start writing in the empty column. "The second UNSUB is disorganized. Not a lot of thought goes into what he's doing. I believe he gets the victim from the first UNSUB. He finds sexual gratification in torturing. The torture itself arouses him. And that gives him a sense of power and invincibility. However, the position he leaves the bodies in suggests he's ashamed. He probably had someone in his life who berated him. He never felt good enough. Someone may have shamed him sexually while he was developing, maybe around age nine or ten. I'm guessing a mother figure. Each victim was killed differently suggesting he's interested in the dying process itself and killing humans is new for him. He probably started out killing animals, watching them die. Since he isn't very savvy, I'd say he's a loner and maybe still lives at home with a parent. He's probably under twenty-five, maybe even late teens. He may work, part time, somewhere he has access to supplies—tape and rope."

Carla interjects, her voice toneless. "We've analyzed a partial shoe print, partial fingerprint, fibers, skin cells, blood, stomach contents, soil, and hair. We have a trace of DNA from the ejaculate found on the first and third victims, it's the same DNA, but no match found yet in the database. We have a match on the rope fibers taken at each crime scene. It links the cases to the same killer."

"You say," Ed points to me, "he's disorganized. Well, he's organized enough to cover his tracks." Ed scoffs out loud, his sarcasm apparent. Ed looks to Carla and asks, "Were you able to make out other identifiers on the rope, like the manufacturer or fiber type?"

My jaw clenches. A warm feeling floods into my hands. I could grab him and pin him to the wall. Instead, I release my fists and interrupt, cutting him off. "Disorganized doesn't mean dumb. I guarantee he'll make a mistake. They always do."

Carla clears her throat, breaking the tension between Ed and me. We glare at each other.

Not willing to play Ed's game, I break eye contact. "There was a pungent, musty smell on victim number three. Maybe killed in a basement or somewhere damp."

Carla responds to Ed's question. "Not yet," She stares at both of us. "We're still working on a manufacturer."

I take a breath and reach for my notes on the table. "I interviewed these suspects." I step to our crime wall and point at Aaron Diggs, Terry Leland, and Billy McCord.

I turn to Ed and Carla. "Aaron has a motive. He's organized, and his occupation gives him the advantage of skirting the law. He seemed genuinely distraught about Tori's murder, though. Terry is guilty of being a pig. If there's a motive, it would be revenge and power. He could have the opportunity and intent. He worked with two of the victims. Doesn't respect women and makes sexual advances to his staff. I understand if the women reject him, he threatens their job. He's disorganized. His office and bathroom are a mess. He's arrogant and entitled. I'd watch him. Billy's connected to all three victims. He was nervous and hiding something. He has a negative perception about the victims, I'd say he's dealing with inferiority."

I reach into my jacket. "Oh. And this," I hand the plastic bag with the cigarette butt to Carla. "That's Billy's." She takes the bag and Ed's eyebrows furrow. "Billy's involved in the Seattle Chapter of the Satanic Temple Church. That's where I found him last night."

Ed's posture stiffens and his head jerks. "A cult?"

I nod. "I attended a meeting last night. By all appearances, it seemed harmless."

A slight smile creeps over Carla's mouth. Maybe she's impressed by my actions. My boldness. Or maybe she's thinking about Ted. I clench my teeth at the thought.

Ed, on the other hand, is rubbing his temples. I know what he's thinking. Maybe these victims are connected to the temple or part of some sacrifice. "The evidence doesn't lead me to think a cult is involved but you shouldn't rule it out."

I scan the crime wall. More names and information have been added over the last week. Another name stands out, Jim Evans.

Jim Evans met April through the Match, Meet, & Mingle dating site. The name Jamison Evansfield is connected to Tori, and connected to Kelly, is an Evan Emerson. *Too easy. What are the odds,* I think? I point to their names. "What about these guys from Match, Meet, & Mingle? They stand out."

Ed leans back in his chair. His elbow rests on the arms, his hands clasp. "They do. That's what we thought too, but we've run into some walls. They took their profiles down and the company is fighting us on accessing their information. We're still waiting on a search warrant. It's probably not their actual names."

"It's doubtful. Might be one person." I turn to Carla. "No forensic evidence on these guys?"

She shakes her head. "Not yet."

"One other thing you'll want to look at is Billy's tires. See if the partial tire print matches," I say.

Ed stands and starts pacing. He rubs the back of his neck. "This case gets more complicated the more we dig into it." He pauses and continues pacing. A minute of silence goes by. "Okay, we have a cult, Billy McCord, Jim Evans or whatever alias he is using, and possibly Terry Leland as strong suspects. It's a start." He looks at Carla. "Maybe you'll find a match to the cigarette butt and the crime scenes. I'll inform my team of what we have so far. Hopefully, we can catch them before anyone else dies."

Ed didn't know a quarter of how complicated this case is. I shake my head. "Based on the timelines, I'm not sure we'll find either of them in time."

"Either of who?" Ed asks.

"The two young women reported missing a little over a week ago. I understand one didn't come home after a date."

Ed's head jerks toward me. He frowns and barks. "Where d'you get that info?"

He's ticked off that I know something he doesn't. Not my fault that Seattle PD has communication problems. I ignore his question on how I know and answer, "North Seattle." I wasn't about to tell Ed where I got that information. From a group, he knows nothing about. Vampires, no less.

Ed turns away, presses his lips before he replies. "I'll give the North Precinct a call and get the details."

As far as I can tell, this conversation is done and I'm ready to escape. Space is closing in on me and I've had my fill. I move to the door. "Anything else you need from me?"

"I'll let you know if anything pertinent arises," Ed says.

I tip my chin and reach for the door. "I'll be going then."

As I step out of the room, Carla's voice ripples through the air. "Jack, wait, I'll walk out with you." My stride hesitates slightly, and she catches up to me.

We walk side by side through the corridors of the precinct. She buzzes us out and we enter the lobby. She softly touches my arm. This action stops me from taking another step. "Jack, I know you well enough to know whatever it is you said you forgot the other day at the lab, wasn't something you forgot." Her voice is sharp, letting me know I've been caught.

This time I'm caught in her gaze. "Carla, I…" My words stumble. The warmth of her hand reaches my chest. The smell of her lotion dances with my senses. My body tingles. I hold myself back from caressing her cheek. She licks her lips and I'm taken back to how soft and tender her kisses are. It's all I can do to restrain myself.

I step away. "I don't want to have this conversation." I pull on my sunglasses before I walk outside. I need to put distance between us, but she's right there on my heels. Cornered between her and my car, I'm stuck. Her heartbeat speeds up with her nervousness.

I grab her, pulling her in, and gently cup her face with my hands, leaning in to kiss her. Her lips are tender and soft. She doesn't resist, but neither does she reciprocate. Instead, she places her hand on my chest, pushes us apart, and steps back. My hands drop to my side. "I'm going to go," she says and walks away.

I straighten my shoulders and shift my feet. To push away my desire, my lips press together, and my jaw muscles twitch. I sigh.

I jerk around, pull the keys out of my pocket, and get into my car to leave. I don't look back. Instead, I yell in frustration.

CHAPTER 13

Jack Calloway

I'M SEARCHING, IT'S DARK. THE clouds give way to a starlit sky. The pitter-patter of rain ceases and the moon is like a lamppost, illuminating my path. Water fills the ruts in the road and it slows my walking as my boots sink into the ground. The moon shines through a lattice of leaves and the tall, shadowed pines stretch up like arrows into the sky. Getting lost in these woods is easy.

This is my home. Three hundred acres in Wilkes County, Georgia. Although surrounded by these woods, we have one of the largest plantations in the state. This place is as familiar to me as the back of my hand. As a boy, it was a playground of wonders, feeding my imagination and longing for adventures. I couldn't wait to experience the world, and this road was just the beginning. The world opened up around the time I was born. By horse, paddleboat, or rail, the world was just a step away. And yet, here, right now, I feel like I am grasping onto something I don't want to let go of.

I'm distant and removed from a place I am so familiar with. A place where I know the road that leads to the church, where to find relief from the southern sun in the stream nearby, and where the trees open to a lush field for a picnic. But now all of those things seem out of reach.

In the distance, I hear a faint sound, like a child's cry—*Julia*. The beating of my heart reverberates throughout my body. *How I long to hear that sound again.* What sound escapes next spikes my blood pressure. A blood-curdling scream echoes through the trees.

Panic sets in as images of what-could-be flash through my mind. "Caroline." I am propelled forward as if I have wings. Uncertain where my family is, I look all around. Another sound draws me out. A growl, deep, as if it's warning me to stay away. My mind tries to discern the potential dangers. Screeches echo around me, like an owl vying for its prey.

Slowly and cautiously, I reach into my jacket and find my gun is missing. *It's strange I would be out here without a gun.* I desperately call out, "Caroline. Julia." Only howling returns my call. The desire to flee wells up, but I push on, moving forward with false bravado. Perspiration slicks my hands and my legs are shaky.

Walking hastily around the bend in the road, I freeze at the scene in front of me. A broken-up carriage, doors ripped off, wheels missing, and the horses are nowhere to be seen. I rush toward the heap, desperately searching through the wreckage for my family. The carriage is ravaged as if a tornado twisted its way through. I scan the area. Nothing else seems disturbed—the trees are still standing. There's a tightness in my chest and my stomach churns, "Where are they?" I say pleading to myself.

A strange mist gradually swirls. Scents of rose and musk fill the air, and the mist becomes thicker. It reduces my vision. My limbs are weighted, and my eyes grow heavy. A whisper beckons in a language I don't understand, "Komm Zu Mir." It's soothing and I am pulled in. Heeding the sounds, my feet carry me. I'm not moving on my own accord and I try to stop. Using the heels of my boots, I dig in. I slip and stumble to the ground, losing my spectacles. I don't need them to see what's in front of me. A sudden coldness hits my core and I'm jolted out of my haze. Shakily, I rise on my hands and knees. I pause to refocus my breath hitches and my body trembles.

Bolting to my feet, I back away, only to trip and stumble to the ground once more. Bile rises in my throat and I'm unable to hold it back. Strewn on the ground is a man's body, at least what's left of it. The chest is shredded as if racked by claws. The leg, from the knee down, is gone. The flesh on its neck is torn away. Blood oozes onto the ground. As my gaze expands, I stand among the wreckage of broken and torn bodies, blood pooling and seeping into the ground.

I spin around, trying to spot all danger, and I'm momentarily distracted by a faint cry in the distance. The sound of my heartbeat thrashes in my ear and increased stamina moves my muscles, I turn to run, but my feet are stuck. Shallow, fast breaths pass through me as fear grips my torso. "Where do you think you are going?" A deep voice rises from the mist and floats upon the air. I cannot see who the voice belongs to. With a shaky voice, I try to get the words out, "I... I... need some help, my family, I think they're in danger." A form begins to swirl and take shape out of the mist from beyond the trees. A man. He appears large and tall. His steps are unusually quick as he moves toward me. Closer and closer he gets. His eyes glow a crimson red. There's something feral behind them. His teeth are deformed, jagged like stalagmites protruding in a cavern. Like a moth to a flame, I'm drawn in. In a growl, he responds, "Yes, I will help you." I form another sentence, but the man is swiftly upon me. My airway is cut off and I feel a sharp pain in my neck.

My head is spinning as thoughts scramble to understand what is happening. Mustering up a strength I do not recognize, I break through his gaze and strike him square in the chin. "I will not let you do this again," I voice forcefully. I grab his throat and with the strength of ten men, hurl him toward a tree. The force causes the tree to waver, but it does not deter him. With the speed of a gale wind, he picks me up, slamming me down. "You will always be mine," the menacing rings in my ears. Once again, I'm choked and slipping away. Something faint and distant begins vibrating. Repetitive, the sound becomes clearer and more intrusive. I jolt straight up, awake, and my chest is pounding. Electricity zings through my heart. My throat is constricted and sweat pools around my forehead. I'm paralyzed with fear and the walls are closing in. I work to slow my breath and tell myself *I'm okay*. Anxiety is gripping me. After what feels like ten minutes, my muscles start to relax and I'm able to move. The bed covers are strewn half onto the floor. "Damn it, another nightmare," I say out loud. And another anxiety attack.

CHAPTER 14

Jack Calloway

IT'S BEEN TWO WEEKS SINCE I've worked on the Seattle PD case and put distance between Carla and me. However, she hasn't been far from my mind. Three years ago, I pushed away all feelings and thoughts I had about Carla by diving deep into my work. I spent a few months in San Francisco working on a missing person case. Then, I flew to Boston to work on a high-profile case involving a mass murderer. I had little downtime to think about anything else. And when I did, I found someone to pass the time with. Any thoughts about Carla, I pushed away.

Now, lying in my bed, Carla lingers in my mind. Another woman won't distract my thoughts anymore. And worse, I've lost interest. Last night was proof of that. When I met Geneva, a sexy red-headed vampire for drinks, I had no interest in participating in our usual tryst. Whenever she comes into town, we always make time for each other.

Over the decades, we've spent a few nights together. Sex with a vampire is unapologetic. It can be rough and sensual. And vampires can blood share which heightens the sexual experience. We don't tire easily, and we don't have to be careful with one another. Geneva is an all-around good time with no strings, but unlike most other times, I couldn't go home with her. We've known each other long enough to understand each other's moods. And she asked why I was distant.

I ended up pouring my dead heart out about Carla. It was embarrassing, but once I started, I couldn't hold back. And that's not good because I need to keep my feelings close and my guard up. It's too dangerous otherwise.

Anyway, there I was, an old vampire, talking about love. Something rare to find, let alone keep.

Geneva doesn't pull any punches, and I reflect on our conversation. "Who says it can't work between a vampire and a human? Many vampires have had humans as drudges or have sex agreements with them. I've heard, although rare, vampires and humans can even procreate." An anomaly I know to be true.

"I don't want her as a drudge. I don't want to control her. I respect her. She's intelligent, savvy, good at her job, and beautiful. Her world is whole and I don't want to destroy any of that. You know what our world is like? Dangerous, brutal, and animalistic." I stirred the straw in my drink as I responded.

"That's not our world anymore. The Dracul has done an effective job of providing us structure and meaning beyond killing for our survival. We've assimilated into human society. Many of us have human friends. So no, that's not our world today." She tried to tempt me with a smile and a swirling of a maraschino cherry between her lips. It didn't work.

"Well, it's the one I see, and I can't let my feelings put her in danger."

Geneva's voice purred. "It sounds too late for that." She winked at me. "Jackie, you haven't had a thing for someone since the twenties. The fact that you're spun about this, means something."

"Yeah, and look how that turned out."

Geneva was referring to Ester. Ester and I met in New

York City in the early twenties. She had been a vampire since the beginning of the century. We passed each other walking in opposite directions. Intrigued, we both turned around and stood facing one another. We didn't move for the longest time as we drank each other in.

She was cute with green, cat-like eyes, a button nose, and rosy cheeks. The length of her dark hair was cut just under her ears and she wore it in a bob. The top of her head reached just to my collarbone. That evening, she wore a large-brim hat shading her eyes. I found that peculiar because it was dark.

I soon discovered she was an excellent pickpocket. After the night we shared, I had to track her down the next day because she and my wallet were gone. She laughed and told me it was her plan all along, to lure me in. I found her in the exact spot we'd met the day before.

We were inseparable. I was alive again for the first time since someone had turned me. A couple of years later when I came home, I found her decapitated. The place was trashed, and her blood was everywhere. I had my first anxiety attack. Known then as psychasthenia.

My shoulders shrink and my chest is heavy with the memory. Lost in time, I linger a moment longer. I see once more the word *Blutrache* written in Ester's blood on the wall. Blood Revenge. At the time, I thought the VSL had acted against me for what I did in New Orleans. In the context of what's happening today, the word slices into me. Another German reference.

I sit on the edge of the bed, putting my feet into my slippers, absorbing Geneva's words. I kick around the idea of calling Carla. What would I say? Volleying it back and forth in my mind, I remember the handwriting analysis. I could stop by the lab to inquire about the results and casually ask her to lunch. Not planned, of course. A gesture of an apology for how I treated her. An apology for how I handled our conversation and the kiss.

I get out of bed and open the sliding glass door to the balcony. Sitting outside, the expanse of the city captures me. It's vibrant, not with color because it's cloudy and gray today, but with the activity of a city. There's a buzz in the air.

The sound of raucous mewing bangs in my ears and I turn to find Jasper on the other side of the closed French door. "Are you hungry, bud?" I call out.

I get out of my chair and go inside to the kitchen. I open the cupboard and reach for the cat food. The cupboard is nearly empty. On a mini whiteboard, I scribble a note for the housekeeper, Mrs. Sanchez, to pick up cat food. She comes during the week to clean the house, run errands for me, and look in on Jasper. I'm her only client and I pay her well, but it's the weekend and she won't get the message until Monday.

Today, I'm meeting Shannon and her new guy for coffee. She left me a message on Thursday and asked if I'd meet them. I'm glad she did. I didn't want to have to bug her anymore or stalk him any longer.

Time to get ready. I head for the shower. Once finished, I get dressed. Jasper has dragged his toy into the closet where I'm standing. He wants to play, and I oblige, twirling a feather attached to a string and stick through the apartment. A vampire and a cat playing. It's comical and unusual. The phone interrupts our play.

"Jack," Simon says, "We've got a dead human with vampire marks." He stops and I wait for him to continue. The pause is long. "I thought you might be interested in the crime scene."

His voice is toneless and matter of fact. He provides no more details, but I know he wouldn't invite me to a Guard investigation if he didn't think I would be of value. I tell him sure and walk to the table to grab a pen. "Where do I go?"

I hear the hesitation in his breathing. Maybe he's distracted. "Capitol Hill. In the alley. Two buildings away from the Shipwreck,"

There's an edge to his voice. Did I hear him right?

Even after Joe died, the shipwreck maintained it's no harm policy. On the front door and throughout the bar, the policy is stated. It's a known fact, and it's observed. If a vampire broke that rule, it won't go unnoticed.

"Is the body in Were territory?" I ask.

Two buildings north of the Shipwreck is Were territory. Both Weres and humans live and work in that area, but we vampires know how territorial dogs are. We don't hang around there too often. The Lycaon and the Dracul have worked to keep the peace between us. Although it's not a vampire-to-were-person killing, the Guard will want to keep this quiet.

"The body is lying right next to it. You'll see when you get here," he says.

"Does Nick know?"

"He knows," Simon says in a sharp tone.

"Okay, okay, don't get your knickers in a knot. I'll be there in an hour."

I hang up. The Guard doesn't request my help, but there was a strain in Simon's voice which tells me he's holding something back. Whatever it is, must be related to the Seattle PD case. Why else would he call?

I grab a jacket that's hanging on the back of a dining room chair and take the elevator to the main lobby. Shannon and I agreed to meet for coffee near the office, just on the other side of the building. The doorman, Hal Davis, opens the outside door to greet me.

Hal has worked for me for about ten years. A few years ago, his mother began having dementia. It had gotten so bad she needed around-the-clock care. Hal and his family couldn't afford it. And he was missing quite of bit of work to care of her. When I found out why he was missing work, I paid for his mother to be in a care facility.

It wasn't easy for him to accept, and he kept telling me to take it out of his paycheck. I finally convinced him to let it go. It was a win-win. Now, I can count on his loyalty and discretion. That's worth the price I paid.

I step onto the sidewalk. My building is in Belltown, an area of Seattle that is filled with pricey high-rise apartments, nightclubs, Indie boutiques, galleries, and cafes, making it a trendy and hip place to be. Over the years, I've tried to stay relevant with the times. It's a long way from the country boy I once was.

When I get to Starbucks, Shannon and Brad are already there, sitting at a table. They both appear on edge by the way Shannon's foot is shaking. Brad's posture is stiff, and his pulse is above resting. Shannon quickly stands when she sees me.

"Hi, Jack." She turns to her friend. "This is Brad Jensen." He stands and shakes my hand. His grip is firm, but his palms are clammy.

"Hello, sir, nice to meet you. Can I get you a coffee?"

I glance at their table. They had gotten their coffees already. "No, thank you."

The truth is, I don't drink coffee. I find it bitter and rancid. "Sit, let's all sit down." I point to the chairs, "I only have about fifteen minutes and I want to learn all I can."

Relief and horror flash in Shannon's eyes. I wink at her. "What? I'm not that bad. Give me a break."

I turn to Brad. "You raise 'em and this is how they treat you," I smirk at Shannon and she rolls her eyes.

We engage in small talk and I watch Brad, what he says and how he says it. He's respectful, but something seems off. His eyes have a flash of emptiness from time to time and some of his movements are jerky, like he has a tic.

I checked into his background and found no red flags. He grew up near Portland on a farm. His parents are still together and he's the oldest of three. He played football in high school. Got good grades and doesn't have a criminal record. But right now, he doesn't seem natural. Maybe it's nerves.

I'll keep an eye on him. Maybe it's nothing. I don't really have a right to be overprotective, but since I took Shannon in, I have a sense of responsibility. I wonder what my daughter would've been like had she'd gotten to live.

I peer at my watch. It's time to go, so I excuse myself, stand, and shake his hand. I bring Shannon in for a hug and whisper, "Be safe." I leave the coffee shop, walking hurriedly back to the building to get one of my vehicles. Hal gets the door once more for me and I tell him to have a good day.

By the time I get to the Shipwreck, it's eleven a.m. and the parking lot is empty. Not surprising for the time of day. Like many taverns, the night hours are when it's most active.

I get out and walk behind the building to the alley. It's big enough for a freight truck to pass through. There are dumpsters, periodically placed by the buildings. The road itself, angles away from the buildings, inverting to a center point—to drain water away.

Two bulky vampires search the alley, another two are crouching over a body, and a female vampire drapes caution tape around the scene. Simon's next to his vehicle on the phone, pacing. A combination of eavesdropping and reading his lips tells me he's speaking with his father, Aron Johnson.

Aron is a Dracul residing in the Seattle area. As one of the oldest families, his authority covers the governance of the States west of the Rockies. Two other members are located in the United States. The other Dracul's are scattered all over the world, with authority in their respective geographical areas. Aron is one of the few leaders who tolerate me. He's been generous, inviting me to his home a few times over the decades.

I walk toward the scene and move through an invisible force. It's what I imagine walking through a multi-layered spider web would be like. It's a protective field that repels and detracts outside interest in the area. A rare ability only a few vampires have. Others may exhibit extra strength, levitation, or the ability to transform appearances.

As I get closer to the body, I'm hit by the smell of rose and musk. Struck by the past, I'm taken back to when these scents were common in men's aftershave. The body is prone and I'm not able to see the victim's face.

The crouching vampire looks back at me. He rears up and stands in front of me with his large muscular arms crossed. His lip curls into a sneer and his incisors extend. "You don't belong here, traitor," he barks.

Meet Jarvis Fisher. A Romanian vampire. At six-foot-five, he lords over me by two inches. He's adept at warfare and has engaged in many battles over the last three hundred years. Years ago, he got into a scrap with a were-person who nearly took his life. The tip of his right ear is missing.

I'm a traitor because of my affiliation with the VSL over a century ago. Some can't let that go, and for them, I'll never be welcomed as an Ascender. I step forward and my incisors extend. This gets the others' attention and they crowd around. In a low growl, I say, "Simon called me here."

His hand reaches my chest and with force, he pushes me. I don't move. "I don't care who called you," he says.

Simon, who's Jarvis's boss, quickly walks to us. "Jarvis. Back away. Jack stays."

Jarvis steps back and mumbles disapproval. I turn to Jarvis and nod toward the body. "The victim. What have you found?"

Jarvis is silent. He doesn't look at me, and it takes Simon's intervention again to get him to respond. "If you don't want to cooperate on my case, I'll remove you." The other Guards have already gone back to what they were doing.

Jarvis looks down and then back to me. "She's been drained. Her neck is shredded. Bite marks on her thigh too." He says in his husky, Balkan voice. "Nick said she was at the Shipwreck last night around ten."

"You know who it is then?" Jarvis took a couple of steps away from the body. As he did, the victim came into my view. On the inside of her wrist was a heart tattoo. A tattoo I was familiar with. I take a deep breath, hoping it's not the same one. My nose picks up her scent—a hint of apricots. I was wrapped in that scent a month ago between my sheets. I look at him and my eyes enlarge. Simon, noticing my look of recognition, quickly intervenes.

"Riley Jackson," Simon says. I turn to him as he says her name. If I weren't already pale, the color would've drained from my face. My chest tingles and a pounding in my ears grows louder. I look away and gasp for air. I'm stuck and another anxiety attack is building.

Simon clears his throat, snapping me out of my daze. He barks, "Jack, I need your eyes on something I have in my truck." He points toward his truck. I follow him while I rub my chest and take slow breaths. No wonder he said little on the phone.

When we get to his truck, I murmur. "Damn it," louder than I intend. "I was at the Shipwreck last night with Geneva." I drop my head in thought. Partly in disbelief. My mind is grasping. I can't put it together. "I left about nine-thirty. I didn't see Riley. I would've noticed her if she was there."

Simon grabs my arm and his words are abrasive. "Jack, what the fuck. You look like you're ready to bolt."

We square off, staring at each other. A low growl reverberates in my chest. Part warning and part soothing my anxiety. I glance away. "No, no. I'm good." I jerk my arm away from his grasp.

"Well, then stop bringing attention to yourself."

I nod. I'm uncomfortable. Caged in. I need his scrutiny off me before I suffocate. "Do you smell rose and musk on her?"

Simon's eyes dilate while he opens his senses. In a low voice he replies, "Yeah, I do. What about it?"

"It was a common scent in men's cologne, but it hasn't been used in that way in over a hundred years." My gaze falls. "I've recently come across that same smell. The Seattle PD case I'm working—It was faint at the Seward park crime scene."

Simon's eyes widen and he lets out a deep sigh. A frown descends upon his face.

"And," I stop, uncertain of the next statement. Do I tell him? An uneasiness squeezes my throat. "On my wife. The same scent."

Simon scans the crime scene, and his gaze lingers. He blinks. His eyes processing information, placing the pieces. He reaches inside his truck and pulls out a postcard. It's in a clear plastic bag. He hands it to me. I stare at the picture, flip the card over, and read, *Graveyard under the Snow by Caspar David Friedrich.* "Where did you find this?"

"It was lying on top of the body." His eyes squint as if it hurts. "It's a *German* painter." He emphasizes the word German, "And I found this." He reaches back into his vehicle and pulls out another evidence bag. "I grabbed this. Not sure what it means."

Inside the clear, plastic bag is a white handkerchief with the initials W.T. embroidered. I stop breathing and squeeze the bag.

Simon clears his throat, pulling me back to the present. I stare at him and utter, "William Thomas." My throat is dry, stifling my voice. "It's my name." Simon has only known me by Jack Calloway.

"What do you mean your name?"

"It's my given name. William Thomas. I'm William Thomas Jr. But this," I hand the bag back to Simon. "My wife made this for my father, William Thomas Sr."

Simon frowns, takes a step back, and snaps his gaze to Riley's body. He stands square with his arms crossed. Quiet. He looks at me with probing eyes.

"I didn't do this, Simon."

A serious expression sets on his face. He nods and paces. "So, what is it then, a setup? Who would be behind something this elaborate?" He throws up his hands as he speaks. I understand his caution. If I were him, I'm not sure I would believe it either, but he knows me. Surely, he can see this isn't me.

My hands reach back to cradle my head. "I don't have answers. I'm not sure what any of it means."

I watch as they bag Riley's body. My chest floods with emotions. I'm confused. Pissed. Heartbroken. My teeth dig into my lip.

"There's something else," I say, my gaze shifting to Simon. "The vampire who lost control and killed the human... "Riley." I stop. My body rebels against what I'm about to say. My throat constricts. I'm lightheaded. I don't know what these next words will do to me, but if I don't tell him and he finds out about it, he'll feel betrayed. It'll look like I'm hiding something. "That happened to me that night with Riley," I mumble the words and stare at the ground.

Simon's eyes grow wide. "Obviously, I didn't kill her." I pace and tell him the details of that evening. "Then I called for an Uber and sent her to the hospital."

"Jack. Dammit." His hands ball in fists at his sides. He snaps the muscles in his jaw, flexing. "I don't know how I can ignore this?"

He shakes his head. "This doesn't look good. And the Dracul, given your past…" He didn't finish his sentence. He didn't have to. I know the repercussions. I know how it looks.

"You think I don't know that." My voice is shaky. "This isn't me, Simon," I say, hoping the truth of those words reaches his ears.

Simon's shoulders loosen. He stands squarely in front of me and says matter-of-factly. "I don't know how long I can keep this quiet."

"Look, I don't want you to do anything illegal, but if you could buy me a little time… I've got some leads on this case. I'll get to the bottom of it."

Simon's gaze cuts back to the body bag. "I'll do what I can. You might have a week, maybe two, before this trail points to you. Then, it's out of my hands."

The muscles in my body relax. For the moment I'm out of danger, even if the clock is ticking, I've bought myself some time. "Any chance you can send the body to Ron Patterson? He's performed the autopsies on the other victims."

"Yeah, we'll send the body that way." A pained look crosses Simon's face. "I reached out last week to NISCU. They are aware you're working on this case." He points to the crime scene. "After this, they'll probably send someone out."

We both grow quiet, thinking about the ramifications—how this looks and where it could go. "Jack, it could be a better play for you to be open about all this to NISCU. They'll pull you off the case, but they'd clear your name faster if you're implicated."

I cross my arms. "Exactly. Which is why I don't want to say anything until I must." My voice tightens. "If… I'm connected, I've got the best chance at closing this case. If this has anything to do with my wife. I need to know."

Simon nods but looks away. He knows what that means to me. I've been searching for information about the vampire who killed my wife for over a century. I don't know if the rose and musk smell is connected, but I've got to find out.

I consider whether to bring up Ester's death and decide against it. I've shared too much as it is. It'll only corroborate any belief that I'm a prime suspect. I need to find out how and why the killer is targeting me. And fast.

I pull out my keys and my gaze meets Simon's. "I appreciate whatever you can do. I'll keep in touch." I turn and walk to my car. The Guard loads the body into a vehicle, and I hear Simon give directions to take the body to the Seattle PD morgue.

I think about Carla. As I do, fear stirs my insides.

CHAPTER 15

UNSUB

HUMANS—OBLIVIOUS. EACH IN THEIR world, milling around like ants. Not aware of the dangers near them. Snakes. Bats. Beetles. Waiting patiently to strike their prey. A meal, that's all they are— Easy.

I'm like a cat, hunkered down, ready to pounce. Invisible, I move through the crowd following them. It's a popular place for Friday night. Lovers and friends scurry about.

It's a clear night. Thankfully. I'd rather be anywhere than this dreary place, with all its rain. She stops, taking delight in the ornamental glass that highlights the garden—the oranges, blues, and reds peppered throughout. Their unusual shapes bursting out, grabbing attention. Hidden, I watch her. She checks behind her, feeling me as my energy brushes against her. She takes up a conversation with the boy standing next to her. A boy. I furrow my brow and shake my head. After nearly two hundred years, all humans seem like children.

They slowly walk along the paths, making their way through the crowds, stopping from time to time, pointing at things, chatting incessantly. Their laughter fills the air, unaware of the cruelty around. One selfish act is all it takes to ruin it all.

They continue through the park, arriving at a pavilion. Once inside, a shrug of shoulders, pointing at the choices, smiles, and a "whatever you want," takes up five minutes. Their indecisiveness and fake politeness as they figure out what they want to eat are wasteful.

I lean against the wall and watch across the pavilion as they eat. My hat shades my eyes, but my eyesight is sharp. I study her. Movements. Facial expressions. Body language. She hesitates, shoulders straightening, and looks around, scanning the crowd. Searching. She senses me even though she cannot find me. I know she understands what it takes to survive. Not finding me, she returns to her conversation.

Anyone who's connected to Jack Calloway, I'm interested. It's taken decades to find him, and when I did, my life found purpose once again.

Hmm... the boy. If I can get five minutes with him, I can use my powers. What fun I'll have. A memory of watching marionettes at play invades my mind. It's captivating, the power a puppeteer has. A giddiness fills my chest. Let see, where? I look around. The restroom. They'll get up, and one or the other will need to use the restroom. I watch as excitement fills my bones.

The boy's attractive. Tall. His hair, blond. Part of it is pulled back in a ponytail high on the back of his head into a top knot. The rest of his hair falls, shoulder-length. He has high cheekbones and a smile that lights up his face. If he knew the dangers ahead of him, he wouldn't smile so brightly.

Eventually, they both rise from their chairs, clearing their trays from the table. Eyes searching for the restroom. Finding it, he heads in my direction. I can't hide my smile. Humans are so predictable.

I wait inside the restroom and make eye contact with anyone who enters. I give a verbal command and they promptly turn around and exit.

The boy enters. "Excuse me, sir," I say to him. He looks up, and that is all I need. I'm swift upon him. His arm raises in defense, pushing against my chest as he tries to block my embrace. He struggles as I drag him back against the closed door, blocking the entrance. My eyes latch on to his and I soothe his fear, "You are safe and relaxed. I'm your friend and you are glad to see me," I tell him. He drops his arms to his sides, surrendering to my will. "You will follow any direction I give. You will listen to me and do as I say." He nods in acknowledgment. I take his wrist in my hand, bring it up to my mouth, and bite down, drawing his blood. Not taking too much, just enough to connect. I'll have access to him night and day, no matter the distance. I slip out, none the wiser.

The small taste of blood invokes a hunger and my stomach aches. I look around, as a hawk does when it scans the fields for vermin. I contemplate a quick draw as an appetizer in the alley, or the shadows. The animal stirs.

At home, a feast waits for me. I can take my time, savoring every drop, taking pleasure in the frightened eyes staring back at me. The control I have over life and death is as sweet as a peach cobbler.

Pie, I muse, not something I'd the luxury of when I was human. I had to scrape by, finding odd jobs to provide for my wife and son. Our home, located on a Savannah riverbank, was swept away in a flood. It took the bit of nothing we had. Our clothes ragged and our hair disheveled. We looked homeless because we were, begging for food. Poverty took my wife as I watched her die of cholera, helpless to do anything about it.

Those well-to-do folks in suits and petticoats didn't so much as look at us, let alone help. Men. With their propriety, entitlement, and self-importance. They look at you as if you aren't anything but an animal, only fit for outside. Devoid of any humanity. As if you don't exist.

Over the years, I've enjoyed my life as a vampire—the death, destruction, blood, watching terror fill my victim's eyes. The thought makes me smile. That terror invokes an excitement within me. The power I have, no one can take from me anymore.

A long exhale leaves my lips as I stare off into nothing. With a slight turn of my body, I decide to flee; to where dinner awaits at home.

It takes no time to get to my house in the Queen Anne District. It's nestled between two three-story homes across from a park. It doesn't draw attention. An older home, in the early 1920s. One story with a large basement.

I close the basement door and descend the stairs. To my right and towards the back is the laundry area. But where I want to go is in the opposite direction. I follow the concrete wall, rounding the corner, a small light illuminates the space. A bed and a partial bathroom fill part of the room. The bathroom is unkempt but serves its purpose.

On the other side of the bed, on the concrete wall, are chains attached to iron bolts. A wide-eyed, trembling woman is bound. She drops to the floor and crawls to the corner. She shakes, trying to shrink away from me.

I laugh at the pathetic display. So easy. "You cannot get away from me, sunshine. You're mine as long as I want you. And if you want to live, you better do everything I say to keep my interests."

She shakes, tears rolling down her cheeks. "Please, don't hurt me. I'll do whatever you want."

I take a step toward her. "This is true, you will do exactly what I want."

My incisors extend, a growl escapes, and I lunge at her. She struggles as I pin her down. They always struggle. That's the fun part. My teeth sink into her neck and she screams out. Eventually, she stops struggling, but I only drink to the point of weakness. I'll keep this one a while longer.

Satisfied with dinner, I head back upstairs and notice the clock reads 12:01 a.m. I step outside for some fresh air. Beyond the trees, stars pop against the night sky. The air is crisp and a light breeze dances on my skin. Night, like an oasis in the desert, is invigorating. I sit on the ledge of the porch and look out at the park across the way. My eyes cut through the thickness of the dark. I see movements from those that think they're hidden. Teenagers. I wonder if they know a monster's watching them. I could stomp out their puny lives. It would be nothing to me.

I turn my attention back to my problem. The stupid boy is getting sloppy and putting my plan at risk. I give him simple tasks. Torture and kill. He's a liability I must dispose of soon. And now I've someone who fits better with my plan. I'm so close to the sweet taste of revenge.

I'll take from William Thomas what he took from me on that fated day. The day my life ended. My boy dying at his hands while he laughed at my son, gasping for air. He wasn't even remorseful.

If I must, I'll torment his offspring for eternity. He'll know my pain, my rage, my loneliness. I'll make his son pay for his mistakes.

I lick my lips, savoring the lingering taste of her blood. She'll serve me another week, then I'll dump her. Getting Brad prepared for this excites me. And speaking of Brad, it's time for a visit. I take off on foot, letting my speed carry me away.

I reach Brad's apartment complex and slip inside. It's magical really, being able to alter mechanical systems. Not that I could bring down a power grid, I don't have that ability, but I can make small changes—stop an internal time clock or alter video images. All I need are my thoughts. This ability has proved useful at keeping my identity hidden.

I watch Brad sleep. Poor wretch. It's not his fault he's another casualty of Jack's misfortune. Wrong place, wrong time, but the right time for me. I can't help smiling.

I lean down and hover over Brad's ear, reinforcing my earlier commands. "You will obey only my commands." I continue to speak my demands, commanding what he'll do to the women I bring him, how to torture them—sexually and physically, and ultimately kill them. "To keep her happy, you must hurt her."

The last command I give Brad is, "Bring Shannon to me."

Now I'm off to visit James. Then I'll focus on my next move, my next meal, and exposing Jack. My plan will work. I won't falter.

CHAPTER 16

Jack Calloway

I WIDEN MY EYES TO release the strain from staring at video footage. I roll my head, shoulder to shoulder, to loosen the tightness, and stand to stretch my legs. A courier delivered the mysterious letter to Hal, and he slipped it under my door. I found out the courier company didn't know the origin of the letter. I wasn't the only one who thought this was odd, but despite their searching, they found nothing.

I've scanned the dates and times Meghan, my building manager, alerted me to. The only explanation on how my father's handkerchief ended up at a crime scene was someone broke into my apartment. I kept it in a drawer with all my other pocket squares, which are colorful and made from silk. A white cotton square would have stood out—it's the only one with our initials. It was a Christmas present for my father. Caroline had finished the stitching a week before. He didn't get it, and it was one of the few items I escaped with. When I got home the other day, I looked, and it was gone.

Simon called earlier to tell me the surveillance cameras at the Shipwreck recorded Riley talking to a man, but the camera didn't capture his face. Some vampires can alter appearances and create illusions. For those, it would be easy to go undetected by projecting different images or even altering the video and audio. I've only known of one vampire who could alter images and he told me to do so, was as simple as a thought or a command. It's a rare gift. And one I hope we're not dealing with. The thought causes an unshakeable unease in my stomach.

Simon put Nick on the scent trail and the trace led him to the Shipwreck. Simon said, "there's something else. We found your business card in her apartment." At that moment, I went still. It was like I was skating on thin ice, and the ice broke through.

I don't recall giving her my business card. That doesn't mean she couldn't get it elsewhere. Either she got it after we met or before. It's the *before* that has me most concerned. Too many pieces aren't fitting. Not in a way that makes me look innocent.

I close my eyes, trying to recapture who was at the bar that night. The killer had been there. I search my mind, but I don't see him. The bar is usually full on Friday nights, but last Friday was St. Patrick's Day, any supernatural of Irish descent was celebrating, and the night started early for many. I got there at about seven-thirty and I didn't see Riley.

The German references can't be mere coincidences either, and the scent of rose and musk isn't something I'll ever forget. It's etched into my senses. The cut is as deep as the pain and guilt I've got over losing my family. Now, there's my father's handkerchief at the murder scene. And when did Riley get my business card? None of this can be a coincidence.

I switch a light on the bookcase near the mini-bar. I need a distraction and the burn of scotch in my throat is inviting. I grab a glass, plop two ice cubes into it, and pour scotch from the crystal decanter. The crystal captures the light and a tiny rainbow bursts through it. I take a drink and savor the smooth, warm burn coating my insides. I pull my phone out of my pocket, open a music app, and choose a playlist. The speakers softly pour music throughout my office.

Music, another distraction, but it, unfortunately, becomes the background to my thoughts. I'm distracted by the emotion and fervor moving through the air and the impact it has on my senses. Beethoven's Symphony No. 5, and I'm listening to my wife play once again. My chest fills with warmth as I think of her. It isn't long before agony seeps in too. For our anniversary in 1861, I gifted her sheet music for Moonlight Sonata. Less than a year later, I left for the war.

Lost in thought, I'm watching Caroline in our sitting room, playing the piano. The sun's rays are highlighting the golden strands in her hair. The music is melodic, demanding-a journey into emotional depths I'd never plunged. I stood in the doorway, mesmerized. It wasn't a sound I'd heard before. Her body moved with every note. I stood there silently, watching in awe. She was my lighthouse.

I learned later Brahms composed the piece Caroline played. Arnold Wainwright, who lived near us, gave her the sheet music. His family had immigrated from the Rhineland to Georgia in the early 1800s.

While at war, Mr. Wainwright was helpful to my wife and family. She paid him for the upkeep of our buildings around the plantation. I felt obliged to him for taking care of my family. Once I returned, I didn't get to thank him because he never came around again.

I sigh, releasing old memories. I look at the glass in my hand, rattling the ice. I finish the drink with a gulp and set the glass down. I turn to the bookcase. Books, mementos, and antiques line the walls.

A portrait of Caroline and Julia, when Julia was a one-year-old, stares at me.

I open the hidden safe in the bookcase. I still have a few items of Caroline's. A picture, our wedding rings, and her book of German poems. It had been a gift and even though she didn't know the language, reading the words gave her a sort of peace I didn't understand.

Among the keepsakes of a life I once lived, are passports, currency, and another identity should I need. I've changed my identity twice since I've turned. I've remained a Calloway, but have created variations of that identity. I ran a paper press as Andrew Calloway before WWII.

I'm purposeful in my movements. I run my hand along the edge to find a switch and press it. The panel rotates, displaying an array of weapons. A sword, a Colt 1851 from the Civil War, a Colt rifle, and a semi-automatic handgun. More memories. A single lifetime is full of them, but three can be overwhelming. Thinking about them isn't something I indulge in. Too much pain can paralyze. I close the panel, locking them away once more.

My attention shifts to the present. I hear a long buzz followed by a quick buzz. The elevator intercom is signaling I have a visitor. I don't have many of those, not unexpected anyway. I walk over to the intercom and look at the image displayed through the camera. When I see who it is, my breath hitches, and a rock forms in my stomach. It's Carla. She buzzes again. My movements are slow. I enter a code, allowing her to proceed to my apartment. The memory of her last visit floods and guilt squeezes my chest.

I close the office door and the automation of clicks ripples securing the door. My feet feel heavy with each step as I cross the foyer. I cross my arms and begin tapping my left fingers on my right forearm. The door parts and time inches by slowly.

Carla stands, her posture relaxed. At least one of us is comfortable. I can't resist, and my gaze surveys her body. She's wearing black jeans and a floral black and white blouse. It contrasts and highlights her facial features, and her blue eyes envelop me. Her lips are plump and inviting. Her hair's up granting me access to her neck and I'm seduced, licking my lips. A diamond pendant lies slightly below her throat. I'm lost in her presence.

Time stills, and neither of us moves. Her gaze moves from my eyes to my torso and doesn't leave. A draft of air reaches my skin and I realize I'm not wearing a shirt.

Just as the elevator doors close, I stop the door with my foot. "Would you like to come in?" I wave her inside and my stomach flutters.

She has a file in her left hand. Waving it, she says, "Sure, I have these for you."

I walk toward the kitchen. "Can I get you something to drink, wine perhaps?" She nods. "Red, that's what you like, right?" There's a shirt on the back of the chair I grab and pull on. The soles of her shoes shifting on the tile tell me she's close behind.

She sits at the kitchen bar. I reach for a bottle of wine, find the corkscrew, and with a pop pull it out. My back to her, I can sense her piercing gaze. I pour her a drink and place it in front of her. I step away, putting space between us, and lean on the opposite counter near the refrigerator.

She opens the folder. "This is the handwriting analysis result." She pulls out a piece of paper and pushes it toward me. "The lettering is a match. Same paper too. You're not having a drink?"

I reach for the paper. "I had one earlier." I read the summary and study the chart. "You came all the way here to tell me this?" My eyebrows arch and a slight grin forms on my lips. "I mean, you could have called instead," I say, looking down at my shirt and pretend to brush something off. I need to push away the tightness in my chest and release the churning in my stomach. And the ache in my groin.

"Well." She shifts in her seat, "It seemed like it was important and I hadn't heard from you." Her gaze skims the room as she fiddles with her necklace. "I was in the neighborhood." Her voice presses and elevates. She pauses then demands, "If it has something to do with our case, I want to know."

I set the paper on the counter. "Work, right?" I run my hand through my hair, resting it on the back of my head. What do I say? I shift my stance. "The poem," I hesitate. "Was found at a different crime scene, unrelated to ours or at least until now unrelated, and the letter was anonymously left under my office door a few weeks ago." I walk out of the kitchen to the dining room and stare out across the bay.

In the window's reflection, I watch Carla. She stands and walks toward me. "How are these connected to our killer?"

I shrug. "That's what I'm trying to find out," I say just above a whisper.

Carla folds her arms, a sign she will not let this go. "Jack, what aren't you saying?"

I'm shaking my head back and forth ever so slightly. If only I could go into the litany of what I'm not saying. How I want to reach out and touch her. Take her to my bed and ravish her. How bad things happen to people close to me. How I'm trying to keep her safe. And how I'm a vampire whom she should avoid.

Instead, a heavy sigh escapes, and I turn to face her. I cross my arms in fear they'll reach for her. "The two marks on our victims' neck, legs, and wrist?" I raise as a question. "Those same marks were found on an unrelated homicide and a note was left in German at the crime scene." I turn and look away. "It's not good." My left hand reaches for my temple. I pace the length of the window, from the dining room, halfway to the living room. and back. "The killer, I believe, is the same in all cases, and may be the one who's leaving the notes."

Carla stares out the window, her eyebrows furrow. She's not focused on the beauty outside, she's lingering between time and space as her mind churns the information. I sense her pulse quicken as she fits pieces of the puzzle together.

She stands abruptly and moves closer to me. She's close enough that I feel the heat radiating off her body. Close enough that her smell ignites a fire within. I feel my eyes dilate and the animal stirs. I freeze. I try to step back, only there's no place to go because I'm against the window. She looks up at me with narrow eyes, brows inward, and her lips purse, like she's questioning me. She shakes her head and continues talking about the connections.

"He left that letter at your office." Does he know you? Or is it you're on the case?" She asks. I step to the side and put my hands into my pockets, leaning against the window. "I'm not sure, maybe both."

The soft palate of her neck moves as she swallows. I imagine my lips kissing her neck and as I do; she reaches for her throat. She steps back. Her body angles away and her gaze drops to the floor. "Do you know these women?

She meets my gaze, and I stare back. I know the real question she's asking. Did I sleep with them? "No… And yes."

She quickly looks away, shaking her head. Her question rips through me like lightning tears through the sky. Danger, fear, and awe wrapped in one bolt of electricity. My muscles twitch with an impulse to move. I'm uncomfortable but remain still, readying myself to face the truth head-on.

"Yes," I say as matter of fact. "I know April Thompson's sister and the woman in another case." I pause. "And another woman murdered on Friday. I know her too."

Carla's shoulders slump and a pained expression crosses her face. I'm unable to meet her eyes. I twist my torso, wringing out the guilt in my chest.

She steps back, reaching for her wine, and takes a drink. I want to reach out and provide her some sort of comfort. "Do you know German?" She asks.

I press my lips and nod. "A bit."

"This makes you a suspect."

The muscles in my jaw flex. She's right more than she knows, but I cough out, "How about I'm not, and we go from there."

Carla pushes her shoulders back. Her lips tight, and determination pushes her forward. "Okay, what do you know about this guy?"

In that question, I know she believes me. With her faith in me, the muscles in my body relax. My left hand reaches for the right shoulder blade muscle. "I don't know a lot at this point. I'm still putting the pieces together."

I study her, watching her movements. The corners of my lips curl up. "I'm relying on your team to come up with something we can go on. I don't know if he's targeting me, but if he is…" My voice trails off and I look away. "People close to me could be in danger."

"Does Ed know about this?"

The totality of what *this* means hits me and my shoulders cave in. "I'd rather Ed doesn't know, yet."

"Is that possible? Who's handling this other murder?"

I look away. It's an important question, but it's one I cannot answer truthfully. "There's a special task force handling it, and Seattle PD Headquarters is aware. Parts of the investigation are… classified." Our gazes meet. My soul's pierced by her stare. I can tell my answer raised more questions for her, but for now, she lets it go.

Carla's standing a few feet in front of me. A piece of hair has fallen out of her ponytail, landing near her face. Absentmindedly, I lift the hair and tuck it behind her ear. She gently grabs my hand when it grazes the bottom of her earlobe. Our gazes lock and I hear her pulse in my heart. The rhythm calls to me. Her lips part slightly. I think she's going to stop me, but her hand reaches for my jaw and her fingers glide along my jawline. Rather than lean into her touch, I grab her hand, pushing it away, and step to the side.

She frowns but isn't dissuaded by my reaction. "Why pull away?"

I throw my hands up and lean against the window panel. "Carla, this killer," I pause, "You may not be safe around me. It's probably best if you stay away."

"Is that what all this is about? You think I'm in danger? Jack, I can hold my own. You don't get to decide for me."

I cup her face, wanting to kiss her, but I hold back. "If something happened to you, I wouldn't forgive myself. It's better this way."

On the kitchen table, my phone buzzes. Our gazes hold one another longingly. I'm drawn in and it's tempting, but I release her and walk over to pick up the phone.

"Jack." Shannon's voice is trembling.

My chest tightens. "Shannon, what's wrong?"

Her breathing is fast. "Shannon," I demand.

Her voice quivers. "I don't know. It's Brad. He was acting weird."

"Where are you? I'll come get you." I look at Carla. She maintains eye contact, even though her expression appears pained. She swallows hard and looks away. I can only imagine what she's thinking after the conversation we had tonight, probably that I'm involved with Shannon. Which is the furthest from the truth. I don't want to think about it because when I do, trickles of self-loathing creep in. *I hurt her again.*

"I wouldn't go with him. He stormed off, leaving me stranded," Shannon says.

I hear sirens and background voices arguing through the phone. "Are you on foot? Where?"

"I'm in Ballard. The tavern on 24th and NW Market St."

I grab my jacket off the chair. "Stay there. I'm on my way."

In a jerking motion, Carla picks up her purse. Her lips thin into a hard line, and she briskly walks toward the elevator.

I step behind her. "Wait," I call out and reach for her, touching her shoulder. She slightly flinches away, repulsed by my touch. "I'll go down with you."

We enter the elevator. She stands in the opposite corner from me. Silence hangs in the air. My breath releases loudly in frustration. I stammer out, "Shannon, she's my receptionist." The look in her eye clues me in on how that explanation makes things worse. "She, I'm, putting her through college. She works for me part-time. I helped her get off the streets." I quickly list the facts of my relationship with Shannon. Carla glances at me, her eyes soften.

The corners of her lips raised into a slight smile. "Sounds like she's in trouble. It's good of you to be there."

Another moment of quiet passes. "I'm sorry." It slips out, not knowing what I'm sorry for exactly. Everything, maybe.

"No, it sounds like she's in trouble." She averts her gaze. "I'm the one who came over uninvited. I should've called."

I close the distance between us and touch her hand. "I'm glad you came." She doesn't pull back. She looks up at me and our eyes lock. Her hand reaches out to my chest. I caress her face. "You've always been beautiful to me." My voice is low and reassuring.

Her other hand rests on my arm. "What are you trying to protect me from?" I take a deep breath, breathing in everything that's her—hair, lotion, blood. Her blood.

Jarred, I pull back, dropping her hand and stepping away. "Me." The ding of the first-floor rings and the door opens.

She steps out of the elevator, taking her energy with her. She turns, and her gaze trails down my body. "That's too bad." She turns back and walks through the lobby door. By the time I reach the garage, I've locked away my feelings.

CHAPTER 17

Jack Calloway

THE UNDERGROUND GARAGE IN MY building is like any other concrete structure, except there are two separate areas. One public and the other private. I turn right from the elevator and approach a steel door. It's a secured entrance, accessible only by retina and fingerprint scanner. I bring my eye to it and place my index finger on the pad. Green lights flash and the door opens.

I've fifteen cars to choose from. Today, I walk to my jeep, open the door, and reach for the keys in the glove box. Another scanner verifies my identity before the garage door opens to the main garage, spilling me out onto the exit path.

I push away lingering thoughts of Carla and turn on the radio, but my thoughts betray me and wander back to her. I think about what Geneva said the other night, about vampire and human relationships. A picture of Riley's dead body flashes. There's a killer—a vampire and somehow, I'm connected. I must stay focused on stopping him because I can't let the people I love become victims of this monster.

I think about Shannon's trembling voice, and my chest tightens with worry. I glance at the clock. At this time of night, I should get to her in twenty minutes. I get onto Denny Way, head toward Elliott Ave W, and make my way to Shilshole Ave NW. I must've hit every green light because when I arrive at the tavern, it's taken only fifteen minutes.

The tavern's rooftop is missing a few shingles and duct tape holds a window together. A partly burned out neon sign flashes. All obvious signs of age and neglect.

I walk in and see Shannon sitting at the bar. I step over to her. "What happened?" She jumps back startled and looks up at me. There's fear in her eyes and tears well.

"We came here to eat and play pool. Everything seemed normal." She shakes her head. "He was polite, we were laughing and joking. Then something changed. I thought it was something I said. It's like he wasn't himself. He became mechanical in his movements and his words were flat. The way he looked at me… it's hard to describe, it's like he was looking through me."

"Then he insisted that we go to the shipyards on 54th street. I told him I didn't want to. He became angry, grabbed my arm, and told me to never question him. He started dragging me out of here. Surprise took me and didn't realize right away what he was doing. When I did, I practically had him on the ground and then a couple of guys stepped in between us." Shannon's body shivers. "He got up, sneered at me, and stormed out."

I put my arm around her and pull her into me. "I'm glad you called. Let's get you home." I take my jacket off and put it around her.

Shannon lives close by in a house I bought when I got her off the streets. We pull up to the house and park. I go ahead of her, unlock the door, and go inside. I turn on the lights and scan the area. Nothing's out of place. I search the rooms to make sure no one is there.

I wave her inside. "I'm going to search the outside, stay put."

Shannon's posture stiffens, and she looks behind her, her eyes darting. "What are you looking for?"

I smile at her. "Just making sure nothing's out of place." I step outside and close the door. I scan the street right and left. Quiet. Porch lights are on. No dogs are barking. All a good sign. I walk around the back and check the shed. Nothing of concern here either. I pull out my phone to call Nick's cousin, Paul Crandon. Paul owns a security company, installing security systems, and providing security personnel. His company installed the systems in my building.

"Paul, Jack Calloway here."

I've known Paul for many years, and he's always had a business-first mentality. Paul is a little rough around the edges, but damn good at what he does. Before starting his own business, he worked several years in the Secret Service. "Hey, Jack. Any more issues at your building? We've been working with Meghan and from our end, everything looks secure."

"No, it's not that, it's all working great."

He chuckles. "Well, then since you can handle your security, it's must be for someone else."

"I have a house in Fremont, and I need a security system installed right away. It's a top priority. Can you make that happen tomorrow?"

He clears his throat. "I can have someone out there first thing in the morning. Same set up as your place?"

"No, perimeter cameras and secure the entry points. Do you have someone on your team who can tail someone for me?"

"Sure. Let me look." I hear clicking sounds on a keyboard. "Isaac Bowers is available. Email me the information and we'll get on it."

"Great. Thanks."

I hang up, go inside, and sit down. Once inside, I open my phone to email Paul the details. Once I hit send, I say to Shannon, "I called to have a security system installed. They'll be here in the morning."

"Why do I need that? Are you going to track all my movements?" The look on her face could've sliced me in half.

I laugh. "I'm glad you're feeling better. No, I've been meaning to have it done. Now is as good a time as ever. It will make me feel better, that's all."

She rolls her eyes and huffs. She takes her shoes off and plops down on the couch. "You want something to drink?"

"No, I'm going to go. Everything looks good." I reach for the door, turn around, and say, "I'm glad you called. I'll see you tomorrow." I walk to my jeep, get in, and drive down a couple of houses. I make a U-turn and park on the opposite side where I have direct sight to Shannon's house. I crack open the window and wait.

In my email, I'd asked Paul to have a security detail at Shannon's house for the night. About an hour later, on Shannon's lawn, the streetlights reflect glowing eyes staring back at me. An oversized black dog walks across the lawn toward me. Another one stays put. He approaches me, stops, and our eyes lock in recognition. He nods and heads back to the house.

The security detail has arrived.

CHAPTER 18

Jack Calloway

"I CAN'T BELIEVE YOU HAVE me out here," I say as I pick up the engine block and place it into Nick's 1969 Chevelle. He's been talking about restoring this car for two years. He's finally getting around to it. "It's hot and my eyes are burning."

Nick scoffs from underneath the car. "The sun is not on you. Who else is strong enough to lift that thing?"

I pick up my beer and take a drink. "Plenty of other vampires. Flattery will get you nowhere."

I knock a screwdriver off the edge. Metal clangs underneath the hood in its descent. "Jesus," Nick says. "Quit your complaining. A bit of grease will not kill you. And watch what you're doing."

The inside door to the house opens. Emily, Nicks' daughter, pops her head into the garage. Her voice is shrill. "Dad. Philip took my tablet and won't give it back."

Emily's eyes light up. "Oh, hey Uncle Jack."

"How's my favorite girl?"

Nick rolls out from under the car. "Emily. I'm kind of busy right now. Where's your mother?"

A pfft escapes her lips and the door slams shut. I look at Nick and chuckle. All these years without a family of my own, I've been lucky to raise Nick and now I get to be around his children. The thought warms my insides.

Nick rolls back under the car and as if in tune with my thoughts says, "Ever think about having a family?"

I shift my stance. "No, and even if I did, not sure that's possible. Anyway, back to what we were talking about."

Nick is quiet, deciding whether he should push me further on the subject or let it go. He should drop it. He doesn't know I was married or had a child. Instead, he says, "It does seem strange considering how long it's been since you last lost control. What do you think it's about?"

"I don't know, but it can't happen again. Simon's looking into a case involving the blood bank. He thinks a delivery driver was under the control of a vampire. They found the driver dead. His neck snapped. Bite marks too."

A loud clanking noise interrupts me. Nick's pounding on something underneath. I wait for him to stop before I continue. "There are other human deaths, not related to my case, but I wonder if those vampires lost control too?"

"Something to do with the blood mix?" He asks.

I shrug. "You hear anything at the Shipwreck?"

"Some grumblings, but nothing concrete. Vampires aren't going to come out and talk about it considering it could kill them for doing so."

I take another drink of my beer. "Yeah, but if it's happening to several vampires, something bigger is going on."

More clanking sounds from underneath the car echo in the garage. When Nick's done banging around he asks, "What are you going to do about it?"

Nick rolls out from under the car and asks for a wrench. I hand it to him. "Until I know more, celibacy."

Nick laughs. "Well, I guess that's one way. Not sure how successful you'll be."

My phone rings and before I answer it I say, "I have no choice." I grab my cell phone.

"Jack." Barks a gruff voice.

"Ed."

"Got a call from the North Precinct. A woman at Swedish Medical Center in Ballard says she escaped a man who was trying to kill her. I'm told she was tortured. I'm on my way."

I look at my watch. It's two p.m. "I'll meet you there."

***

I arrive at the hospital. As the emergency room entrance opens, I'm hit with a lively scent of blood. I breathe deeply. The smell alone is intoxicating. A vampire can smell an open cut, oozing blood, a mile away. One of the many sensations we must learn to control.

A medical assistant sits behind a long desk. An outward-facing window reveals a lush garden. The ambient lights illuminate the wall behind her. If I didn't know this was a hospital, I might mistake it for a spa.

I scan the waiting area. It's not busy, only a few people are waiting. I check in with the receptionist and she opens the door, "Room ten."

I enter the emergency ward and the activity picks up. Nurses, doctors, and medical assistants are going from room to room. I approach the workstation and show my badge. On the other side of the nurse's station, Carla's talking to a doctor. I stop and all sounds fade away as I watch her. She's wearing slacks that hug her curves and a short sleeve blouse that accents the strength in her arms. Her hair is down. I'm lost in her mouth as I tune into her conversation. She's talking about the victim. She glances my way and our eyes meet for a moment until a nurse clears her throat. I'm drawn back to the desk in front of me. The nurse points toward room ten.

Ed's standing outside the room, talking to a female officer when I approach. "Jack Calloway, this is Detective Killian, the lead investigator." He looks at me and then back to the detective. "Jack's helping on my case." The detective nods and Ed turns to me. "This is the same as ours, except alive. The victim, LeighAnne Grigsby, is in her early twenties. She's been sexually assaulted. There are abrasions and puncture wounds. She escaped and ran into a diner off 24th street asking for help. Paramedics picked her up. The detective said we can ask her questions."

The three of us walk into the room. A young woman dressed in a hospital gown looks up at us. Her blonde hair is matted. There are lacerations on her right cheek, bruises on her arms and legs, and her wrists are raw and red.

Detective Killian walks to her. "These detectives are here to ask you some questions." The young woman nods and looks away. Shame fills her eyes.

There's a knock on the door and Carla walks in and looks at the victim. "Hello, sorry. I'm Sergeant Carla Briggs. I work in the forensic department of the Seattle Police Department." She points to us. "Is it okay if I join them?" Carla's voice is soothing, and it warms my chest. Her presence is nourishing. A machine's incessant beeping pulls me out of my trance. I look at the blonde woman in the bed. She nods at Carla and Detective Killian leaves.

Ed takes a step closer. "I know it's hard to talk about Miss and we wouldn't be here if it wasn't important. We need you to walk us through what happened from beginning to now."

Through tears, she recounted what she could. She had gone on a date with a man she met through Match, Meet, & Mingle. He was in his late twenties. His profile showed a picture of a man with brown hair, pale skin, and blue eyes. He was tall. And worked in healthcare. He was attractive and charming. She started to tear up at that point and needed a moment to compose herself. "I must've been mistaken because the guy who tied me up and did this to me, wasn't charming at all. He didn't even look like the same guy I met at the Shipwreck tavern."

I try to hold back any signs of recognition, so I look down.

Carla moves closer to the scared woman and holds her hand. "It's okay. Sometimes when things like this happen, our memories can get jumbled. That's normal."

The woman nods.

"Next thing I remember is waking up, my hands and feet bound, tape on my mouth, and he… he… was on top of me." She sobs as she speaks. "He told me if I didn't do what he said, he'd kill me. When I didn't obey, he burned my thighs. He laughed and told me next time I'd better listen or it'd get worse."

The woman trembles and Carla speaks softly to her. "You stayed alive. That's what's important."

Ed impatiently cuts in. "Do you remember anything about where you were?" Carla glares at him. I smile inwardly in satisfaction at the silent scolding he got.

"It was metal. I could hear boats. The restaurant I found, I think was by the water. I don't remember where. I was just focused on getting away."

"How did you get away?" Ed asks.

"I had to put a black dress on, which meant he had to untie me. He stood with a knife and watched me. He made me do it slowly, like I was putting on a show. "He..." She looks away. "He was doing things—touching himself."

The woman shuttered at the thought. "His phone rang. He answered and walked away from me. There was a large bolt cutter on the floor near the fridge. When he turned his back, he was distracted enough that I could grab it and hit him on the head. He stumbled and fell. I got out and started running."

Carla smiles and squeezes her hand. "What did he look like? Anything you can remember about him will help."

She peers at Carla. "A few inches taller than me, sandy brown hair, stocky build, brown eyes." She closes her eyes and shakes her head. "He had a swastika tattoo on his upper arm. He'd leave in the morning, at least I think it was morning, said he had to go to work and that he'd be thinking about me all day." Distraught, she buries her face in her hands.

"What about the room you were in? Can you describe anything about it?" Carla asks.

"A bed on the floor, a small refrigerator, and stove, a box of women's clothes. It smelled like, urine and waste."

A nurse enters the room. She gives a stern look to Ed and me. She smiles warmly at Ms. Grigsby. "Your parents are here. They are asking to see you."

Ed places his card on the table next to the bed. "If you can think of anything else, anytime, call."

Carla hands her a card. "Here, honey. Anytime." She smiles at LeighAnne Grigsby, turns toward Ed, and frowns.

We leave the emergency center and walk outside, standing on the sidewalk. Ed places his hands in his pocket. "Sounded like there were two different men."

I nod. "Near the diner on 24th are shipyards."

Ed scans the horizon. "There's a unit on the docks, searching now."

Carla asks, "Why did she go to the diner? Why not get help at the shipyards?"

"If you were being held at a shipyard, would you trust anyone there?" I say.

A call comes in on Ed's phone. He looks from Carla to me and answers. "You found what? Where? Okay, we're on our way." He ends the call. "They found where they think he kept Ms. Grigsby." He forwards us the address. "Let's go."

We part Ed, going in the opposite direction from where I parked. Carla is not far behind me. I stop and turn. Reason didn't communicate to my mouth in time before I ask, "You want to ride with me?"

Carla's phone chimes. She grabs it and reads her text. "My team's on the scene. Sure."

We arrive at the NorthStar Shipyards in Ballard. A ten-foot fence blocks the entrance where an officer stands. We check-in and park. It's an enormous property. A couple of docks jut out from the pier, men operate orange cranes lifting cargo on and off ships, and forklifts shuffle containers and drums of products around. They set a barricade to block the workers from entering the crime scene.

Ed arrived first and flags us over. There are containers piled onto containers and we pass rows of them until we reach five storage units at the end of the yard. Crime scene tape blocks off the area. A CSI van is parked nearby.

Carla walks to the van, puts on gloves and booties. She disappears into a storage unit. Fifteen minutes later, she comes out and tells me to put on PPE. "You're going to want to see this. It's the last unit on the end."

We walk past the first four units and arrive at the crime scene. We pass the white metal garage door and enter the unit through the side door. Once inside, I scan the area. A cracked wooden chair lies near the door. Next to it, a bolt cutter. At the end of the unit, there's a makeshift bed. A bucket of water sits in the corner. On the right side of the unit, on a small end table, a rusty Coleman stove sits, and next to it is a dishpan with a bowl and cup inside. On top of a mini-fridge, there's an open tube of A&D ointment. The medicated smell reaches my nose. I walk by a garbage can where a fish odor wafts. Inside, there's an open can of beans and tuna. In a large cardboard box is women's clothing.

An investigator sprays a coat of Luminol on the wall near the bed. Luminol is a reagent that highlights blood when none is physically seen. Blue splatter lights up, streaking the wall.

I walk out of the unit and make my way to the command post. Ed's standing there. "This is it," he says. "Where they were killed." I remove the protective gear.

Ed's chin juts out. "They've found strands of hair, different colors. Lifted some prints too."

I nod. "The break you needed." More like the break I was needing. The quicker Carla's team can get all this analyzed, the quicker my name can disappear from any suspicion. I glance around the yard and look inland, eyeing people. My gaze lands on parked cars, people on boats, the activity in the yard. I'm not sure exactly what I'm looking for. Anything connected. Maybe him. "With any luck, the DNA found here will match the evidence we have."

Carla walks to us. "They're going to finish and get this back to the lab for processing. We should have some results by tomorrow." She slips off the PPE. "What leads do you have so far?"

Ed shifts his stance, his body positions toward Carla. He points to the woman categorizing the collection bags. "Not a lot until these get processed. I'm going to access the surveillance footage. Maybe, our killer is on camera."

Ever since the victim mentioned meeting this guy at the Shipwreck, I've been uneasy. I also know I need to get ahead of this part of the investigation. It could be the key to all this, and the police will only get so far. I jump in. "I'll go to the Shipwreck. I've been there a few times. I can talk to the owner, see if they have cameras." I look at my watch, it's five p.m. Saturday. Nick should get there soon.

"I guess I'll go with you," Carla states firmly, looking at me. "I didn't have lunch. Do they have food?"

I stand there stiff, quiet. In my head, I'm trying to figure out a way around that. It's not a place I want her to go. Not a place I want to take her. I curse silently when I remember she rode with me. "Yeah, they do." I smile and think, at least she'll be safe with me.

Ed's stance is firm and his chest puffs out. He scowls at me, then at Carla. "You two rode together?"

Carla shrugs her shoulders, "Yeah, it was easier. You know how parking is around here." Her forefinger points and draws a circle in the air. She looks at me. "We better get going."

We walk to my car and I don't notice we're walking close until our hands brush. A jolt of electricity surges through me and I shift my stride away. I open the car door. She looks up at me and smiles.

"Milady, your chariot awaits," I say.

She laughs out loud. "Thank you, kind sir."

CHAPTER 19

Jack Calloway

ON THE WAY, WE TALK about the crime scene and compare mental notes. The air is filled with fervor. It's a dance of facts and suppositions, and leaps of logic. It's what we do well, together.

Carla grows quiet and stares out the window before asking, "Did everything turn out all right on Sunday night?" My face must've filled with confusion because she clarifies. "With Shannon?"

"Ah… yeah. She was having… boyfriend problems. I got her home and made sure she was okay. She's a good kid."

We pull into the Shipwreck. "So…" I begin to say, stop, and gather my thoughts before I proceed. I need to prepare her in a way that won't cause alarm. I never wanted to be in a position to compel her. To her I'm ordinary, a human, and I want to keep the monster and everything connected to it, away from her, but I can't guarantee what we will find inside. For everyone's safety, I must.

"Carla?" She turns to me and I gaze into her eyes, capturing her energy. "This tavern is like all other bars. You see everyday people here. Nothing will be out of the ordinary."

She nods. "Of course."

We walk in. Carla scans the area and points to a table toward the back-right corner, an area for Weres. I shake my head, take her hand, and guide her to a table in the left-back corner. "Better view," I tell her.

Before we get to the table, she squeezes my hand, a sign she needs my attention. I turn around to face her, not letting go of her hand. She speaks in a low voice. It's not loud in here, but even if it were, a whisper at this distance would be clear. "People are staring at us."

My eyes lift and scan the room. "Just a few people I know." It's odd for me to come here with a woman, let alone a human woman, and that doesn't go unrecognized.

We reach our table and sit. The server comes over and she smiles at Carla, but when her eyes cut to me, her gaze narrows. "Jack." It's Nick's aunt and her eyes are questioning my decision.

All supernaturals know when a human is present. It's an innate built-in survival instinct. They learn to be careful and cautious. I know she won't give anything away, but I reassure her anyway. "Jenny. This is Carla. She's a colleague of mine. Jenny's my Godson's aunt." Jenny's eyes remain wary, but they exchange pleasantries. She sets menus on the table and walks back to the bar.

Carla has a playful smirk on her face. "You seem to have a life I know nothing about. A Godson?"

I don't answer, other than a slight tilt of my head, and I change the subject. "Do you know what you want to order?"

Carla skims the menu. Based on today's special, I know what she'll order, but she looks over the menu, anyway.

When Carla was growing up, her father was the police chief of a small town in Oregon. He often worked long hours and days on end, leaving her and her younger brother to fend for themselves. For Carla, that meant looking after her father and brother. Her brother was a handful, and keeping tabs on him wasn't easy. However, the one meal they always seem to come together for was lunch on Sundays. It was church and lunch. They didn't always make it to church, but no matter where the other was, they found themselves home for lunch.

When she was a teen, there were only a handful of items Carla knew how to cook, outside of frozen meals. Spaghetti, peanut butter, and jelly, and BLT sandwiches. Her brother didn't like peanut butter, but they all agreed on BLTs. She told me lunch on Sundays were some of her best memories. Not having parents around isn't the best way to grow up, but Sundays made up for it.

Her mother had passed when she was ten years old and her father died when she was eighteen. After her father died, her brother got caught up in drugs and went to jail. Lunch ended.

The special today is BLT with fries. So, when Jenny returns, I order a scotch for me and the special for Carla.

That made Carla smile. "You're not eating?"

I shake my head. "Not hungry, had a big lunch."

We talk randomly, catching up—She and Amy went to the Bahamas last year. About her promotion at work and my case in San Francisco. I shouldn't have, but I asked, "And Ted?" She shrugs and says no more, but by the distant, empty look in her eyes, I assume there isn't much to say. Relief washes over me like I'd been holding my breath until now.

Jenny brings our order. I scan the bar for Nick and spot him. "That's the owner. You eat, I'll go talk to him."

Nick's wiping down the bar when I approach. "I must be unlucky, two times in one day." He chuckles.

I pull out a picture of our victim, handing it to him. "Well, I hadn't planned on it, but duty calls. He looks at the picture. "She met her date here," I said.

"When? Did she have a description?"

"Would've been on the 25th around eight p.m. The description was vague. In fact, there are two descriptions—one tall, brown hair, and with blue eyes and the other stocky, sandy brown hair, and with brown eyes."

He nods toward the seating area and hands the picture to me. "I remember her. She was talking to someone, a man. I don't remember how long they stayed or when they left. You can check the video footage."

I take a glance at Carla. "I think I will. Be right back."

On my way back to our table, a tall red-head, with deep green eyes cuts me off. She places her hand on my chest and steps closer. Her lips purse into a pout. "Jack, you didn't return my call last week. How unlike you."

She's right, it's not like me, but I've been distracted. I grab her hand, pull it away, and smile. "Selene, darling. I'm with a colleague and I'm working." I kiss the back of her hand. "If I get some free time, I'll return your call."

It's never a good thing to upset a female vampire, especially in a public setting. I don't need Carla witnessing something like that.

I steal a glance at Carla, and Selene follows my gaze. Selene purrs. "Your loss."

When I get back to the table, Carla looks away. Her brows pulling in and lips press. When she turns to me, her gaze flicks upward. "Another friend of yours?"

I don't want to lie, but I can't say the truth either. I'd sound like a mad man if I said I've been lost without you and unable to have any meaningful relationships. Not wanting anyone but you. So, I fill my time and loneliness with random women to ease the pain of not having you. Instead of that, I say, "Someone I've known for a while."

I clear my throat and change the subject. "The owner will let us look at the video footage. When you're done eating, he'll show you to the office."

I pivot away from her and take a few steps, stopping mid-stride, and turn to her. "If anyone bothers you, that guy right there," I point to Nick, "Will handle it."

Her eyes burn through me. She says pointedly, "What does he have, that my gun can't do?"

I glance around the room. A few Weres, vampires, and some humans. "Well, let's just say he knows how to handle this crowd."

Normally, she's right. She can handle herself, but here isn't normal and I'm not comfortable leaving her for too long.

I go into the office and sit at the computer. Nick comes in, he's drying his hands with a towel. A smirk unfolds on his face. "A colleague, huh? Is that Carla, Carla?"

My shoulders turn inward, and I glance at him. "Not by choice. I… compelled her. She thinks she's in an ordinary bar. Can you keep an eye on her while I do this?"

Nick shrugs. "Sure." Before he leaves, he adds, "You think it was a good idea bringing her here?"

The answer's obvious. I feel like there's a rock in the pit of my stomach and the tension in my muscles is screaming. "No, but I'm past that now."

I speed through the video dated March 25th, specifically reviewing times between seven and nine p.m. My vampire vision digests each frame. Our victim enters the bar at eight p.m., sits, and orders a drink. At eight oh five, she looks up and smiles. I can see she is talking to someone and by the build, a man, but next they disappear. Gone. The footage doesn't show them leave the table. One minute I see them and the next they're gone. I re-watch, looking at the timestamps. They are visible until eight-fifteen. The next time shown is eight thirty-four p.m. and the table is empty. Either the system went down or someone has tampered with the video.

Footsteps approach. They're not the silent steps of a killer or the sound of four paws pouncing. It's soft and purposeful. I don't have to see to know it's Carla.

She stands behind me. "Hey, find anything?" Her voice is soft and forgiving.

My head turns to look at her. My mind imagines grabbing her waist to pick her up, setting her down, with her straddling my lap. My eyes widen at the thought. I quickly turn to the computer. "About twenty minutes are missing from the feed. During the window, the victim said she met her date."

Carla reaches for her phone. "We need to secure this recording. I'll call Ed and have him get a warrant. My team can analyze it and see if we can determine where and how it was altered."

I hand her the name of Paul's security company. There's a door that leads outside and I point to it. She steps outside to call Ed. My eyes find the live video feed in the office corner, watching Carla outside. Not so much her, but her safety.

Nick walks in. My gaze remains on Carla. "There's missing footage and we're getting a warrant for the video. Can you call Paul and give him a heads up for me?"

Nick pulls out his phone. The outside door opens and Carla steps inside. "Ed's on it. Also, he said, they angled the camera at the shipyard in a way that didn't capture the storage shed. He'll get a warrant for that video too. The UNSUB has to be on it." Carla glances at Nick.

"Carla, this is Nick Crandon. He owns the bar." They smile at one another, exchanging 'hellos and nice to me yous.' He nudges me in the shoulder and grins.

Carla's watching our silent exchange. "Oh. You know each other."

I blurt out a "no." Nick calmly says, "Jack's godson." I glare at Nick. Carla eyes us both but doesn't ask.

An uncomfortable silence rents space. I stand and clear my throat. "I could use that drink I ordered." I turn to Carla. "Shall we sit at the bar and have a drink before we go?" She agrees and I open an arm, gesturing her toward the bar. "Ladies, first." I drink her in as she walks in front of me. The walk isn't far enough.

We reach the bar area and I see Simon. I touch Carla's arm. "Go ahead and find us a seat. I need to talk to him." I point to Simon.

Simon's with his brother Donovan. Donovan works closely with their father. If their father cannot attend to Dracul matters, Donovan steps in. One day, Donovan will replace his father. He's liked among the vampire communities. He's diplomatic, but his attitude can be haughty, especially with me.

I approach their table, glancing at each of them. "Simon. Donovan." Donovan barely looks at me and Simon meets me with a nod and a brief smile.

"Jack." Donovan raises his brow and nods toward the bar. "I saw you come out of Nick's office. That yours?" He refers to Carla.

I snap, "Work." Donovan's gaze expresses his disgust. I turn to Simon. "Speaking of work, you got a minute?"

Simon stands. "Let's go outside." To Donovan, he says, "I'll be right back."

Once outside, I speak in a low voice. "There was another victim today. She's alive. Escaped. Said she met him here on the 25th. I reviewed the video, and it's altered. A twenty-minute time window is missing."

His eyebrows knit together. "Is the UNSUB meeting them here?"

"Not sure," I say.

"Two weeks ago?" He questions, then an apologetic look crosses his face. "Were you at the Shipwreck that night?"

I should be mad at Simon for asking, but I know he's doing his job. I'm wrapped up in this somehow. "No, I was in Redmond with Geneva."

He looks away briefly. "I couldn't keep the handkerchief any longer, I had to enter it into evidence. The NISCU's involved." Regret fills his eyes.

"I understand. You've got a job to do. Hopefully, today's break will give us a solid lead."

Simon looks at the entrance. "You're with Carla? Does she know about this place?"

I shake my head. "No, she doesn't, and I'd liked to keep it that way. I better get back in there."

We go back inside and part ways. Next to Carla stands a dead man, running his finger along her arm. My jaw muscles tighten, and I clench my teeth when I hear, "My, you are lovely." He sits down next to her. Rage fills my head, and my fists clench. I rush over and throw him off the chair. I lose all composure. "Not yours," I growl.

Carla, wide-eyed, pulls back. Nick, out of his office, drops the box he's carrying and rushes over to step between me and this vampire.

Nick scowls and yells, "Jack. Get a hold of yourself."

Next, two firm hands grab my arms. Simon and Donovan are dragging me away. "Jack let's go to the office." On the way, I get a glimpse of myself in the bar mirrors. My eyes have turned red and my fangs are exposed. I hear Nick apologizing to the vampire. "Jack is having a bad day. This won't happen again."

"Dammit, Jack," Simon growls." Are you looking to get your fangs removed?" They release me once we are inside.

Donovan sneers. "That should have happened decades ago. He's a stain on our kind."

I turn to Donovan, growl, and bare my fangs. We are face to face. "Say it again and you'll wish you'd never met me."

Donovan exposes his fangs, steps back, and straightens his suit. "That's already the case, Jack."

Nick steps in. "Both of you knock it off or get out." He looks at me. "I called Carla an Uber. It will be here in two minutes. She didn't see… she saw you overreact, that's all. Get yourself composed, go out there, make up some excuse for why you suddenly need to go. And get out." He brushes his hands together like he's removing dirt from them.

I take several deep breaths before walking out to Carla. My head hangs low. "I'm sorry, I overreacted. I've been called away on another case. Nick contacted an Uber for you, it's almost here. I'll talk to you later."

She reaches for my hand, holding it tenderly. "Are you all right? I've never seen you get that upset. Did something happen?"

I brush the back of my hand along her cheek as I hold her gaze. "Yes." I turn and walk to the office, passing Nick. I murmur my thanks to him, exit through the back door, and get into my car.

When I saw his hands on her, rage and possession blinded me. I lost all reason and I would've killed that vampire. What's wrong with me? I've no claim to her. Yet, I acted like she was mine.

My behavior put everyone in jeopardy. And tonight showed me Carla would never be safe in my world. I wouldn't be able to protect her from others, let alone from myself.

CHAPTER 20

Ed Halstead

ED SAT IN THE RECEPTION area of Chief Phipps's office, arms crossed, and his leg bobbing up and down. He glanced at the clock. The time irritated him. They scheduled his meeting with the chief for nine a.m. and now, the small hand of the clock reads nine-twenty. He didn't like to wait, but he put a smile on his face when the secretary told him the chief was ready.

Ed walked into his boss's office. The office was polished—reflecting order, structure, and formality. *Too stuffy,* Ed thought. The chief looked at Ed and took his glasses off. Ed stood alert. "Chief."

Chief Phipps cleared his throat. "Have a seat Ed. How are you?"

Ed didn't like pleasantries either, not when there was work to be done, but supposed that diplomacy mattered in such positions. Internally, he scoffed at the idea. Back door deals in the name of diplomacy caused a lot of good men to lose their integrity. Deals made by men who didn't know a goddamn thing about what's real.

He knew what the chief wanted, a status report, and he would have preferred his boss started there. Ed tipped his head. "Good. What can I do for you, sir?"

The chief smiled. "Right to it, I see. Okay, status on the case. Washington D.C. has got involved and I'm getting pressured. This case has become a media circus. They're calling him the Triple M Killer. People want answers."

Ed grimaced at that title. "Triple M Killer?"

"Yeah. Like I said, a media circus."

"Excuse me sir for asking, but what's D.C. have to do with this?"

"Homeland's involved. It's still our jurisdiction, but they've sent someone. They'll be on the periphery for now."

Ed's back straightened, and he folded his arms. "Homeland?"

"That's all the information I can share. The rest is classified."

Ed raised his hands. "Classified. Come on, chief, that's bullshit. This is my case."

The chief's posture stiffened, and his voice was low when he sternly said, "It's still our case. Nothing's changed." His chest fell with an expulsion of air, and his shoulders relaxed. "We work it the same. Look at it as an extra pair of hands."

Ed nodded reluctantly. "Is that it?"

"For now."

Ed shifted his weight, leaning more on his left leg. The injury sustained to his lower back from his tour caused him problems. The nerves, feeling like fire and pressure, weakened his legs. "I'm headed to the evidence lab to review the forensics on our latest victim. We're close, Chief."

The chief nodded and smiled. "Good. You're dismissed."

"Yes sir, thank you." Ed walked out of his office.

The meeting left Ed with questions, and he was more irritated than when he went in. Now, he had to deal with some asshole from Homeland Security. *Why would Homeland be interested in this case? And what's the chief not saying?* He reasoned it's his case and if something more was going on, he should know about it. He shook his head. *Politicians.* When do their agendas benefit the actual work done?

Ed walked to the elevator. A tall man, in a dark gray suit, stood next to him. By the suit, Ed guessed the man was in law enforcement, and probably a Fed.

Both men got into the elevator. The awkward elevator silence hung in the air, but it wasn't the only thing in the air. The hairs on the back of Ed's neck tingled. Ed turned to face the man. "You got something to say to me. Or you just sizing me up? If you're wondering, I got no problem taking care of myself."

Ed's hands clasped in front of him and his stance didn't waver.

The man, not looking at Ed, said, "Ed Halstead, isn't it? You're handling the Triple M Killer case." He paused. "I've read."

"Look, I don't know who you are, other than some dressed up sniper in a suit, but unless you're assigned to my cases, it's none of your business who I am."

The elevator dinged and lit up, signaling their arrival to the lobby. The man, whoever he was, strolled away with a smirk on his face. Ed didn't appreciate the stare down he received from the man. But he could admit he may have overreacted.

Ed got in his car and drove through downtown toward the industrial area, to the evidence lab. He had seen little of Carla since their divorce. Now he saw her weekly.

He thought about the last two years of their marriage and wished he could have been the man she married. The man she needed. When he came home from his last tour, he was going through the motions of life while stuck in a tunnel. He'd witness his team blown away by a roadside bomb on a path he mapped out the night before. He had a hard time living after that. They called it Survivor's guilt, at least that's what he learned in the veteran's group he joined after their divorce. In her presence, he faced his failings.

Of all the people Ed got stuck working with, it had to be Jack Calloway. Just thinking about Jack made Ed's fist clench. Goddamn know it all. Sure, he's good at what he does, probably the top in his field, but something's off about him. Dark, brooding, like he's hiding something. Ed didn't trust him. Never had. Why the chief did, Ed would probably never know.

But the one thing Ed was sure of, Jack broke Carla's heart. He saw it on her face at the park a month ago. Jack's not the guy everyone thinks he is, and Ed didn't want to see Carla hurt.

Ed pulled into the lab parking lot, parked, and walked inside. The receptionist checked his badge. The clicking sound of the door unlatching let Ed through. The lab, housed in a building built in the early thirties, reminded Ed of the smells in his high school gym, with a splash of a pine-scented air freshener.

He walked through the corridor toward the lab, opened the door, and stepped in searching for Carla. His gaze met Amy's. She smiled, half-heartedly and said, "Carla's in her office."

Ed's chest tightened. Another misstep in his relationship with Carla. They were separated for almost six months and he was in denial, thinking it was temporary, that some way they'd figure it out. Who was he kidding? Their relationship was over the day he physically came back from Iraq. Emotionally, Ed hadn't returned until after their divorce.

After he saw Jack and Carla in the parking lot, hands all over each other, that's the day he came to. It was like a slap in the face. The guilt and anger he had been directing toward himself found a new target. That day, with his hands balled in fists and his head exploding with rage, his instincts took over. The enemy stood right in front of him, and this was his war.

Ed thought he had the advantage. With Jack's back to him, he could stealthily attack, knocking Jack out. He wouldn't know what hit him, but Jack must've anticipated Ed because Jack's hand took the brunt of the force. Ed hadn't seen him move, and it took little for Jack to render him helpless.

Surprisingly, Jack didn't hurt him, just held Ed back until he was calm enough to walk away. Looking back at it now, it filled Ed with pain and regret. Ed was the one who pushed Carla away, not the other way around.

Back then, pain strangled Ed and his lungs were drowning in grief. Rather than admit defeat, he wanted to get back at Carla. He got drunk, showed up at Amy's place, hurt and tearful, then made a pass at her. That's when she slapped him, and he came to again. Later, he apologized. It wasn't his finest hour.

Carla filed for divorce and Ed found his way to a veterans' group. Those men—that group saved him. He learned how to live again.

He returned a smile to Amy, turned, and walked down the corridor until he reached Carla's office. Her door ajar, he knocked, peeked his head in, and cleared his throat. "Sergeant Briggs. Is this a good time to go over your findings on our latest crime scene?"

Carla's office was large. Her desk took up half the wall, extended across the corner, and past the only window. The view from the window was uninteresting. Concrete, asphalt, and traffic.

Carla set her coffee down and stared at Ed with perplexity. "We're being formal? Well, then, yes detective, come on in. Shut the door and have a seat."

A deep weighted sigh escaped his lungs. "Well, I didn't want to assume."

Carla turned to her computer and started typing. She opened an on-screen file. "Here's what we found. Billy McCord's cigarette butt doesn't match the DNA found at any crime scene. And his tires aren't a match either. Forensically, he's not tied to any of it."

Carla continued. "The partial print found at the first crime scene matches prints found at the storage shed. The semen found on our recent victim, LeighAnne Grigsby, matches the semen found in victims one and three. Also, blood splatter matches on all the victims in the storage shed.

Ed's heartbeat quickened. "So, we have our guy?"

Carla shook her head. "We don't have a name, but the DNA profile is running through CODIS."

A burst of energy moved through his muscle like an inner excitement hard to contain. He stood and walked to the sink counter and back to the chair. The corners of his lips turned upwards. "Great work."

Carla looked at Ed and smiled. "I've got a great team." She turned back to her computer. "We found more. A hair at the storage unit didn't belong to any of our victims. We ran the DNA. It matched another homicide."

Carla pulled up the report. "A Riley Jackson was found dead in an alley on Capitol Hill. She had puncture marks on her neck. Items found at the crime scene included a handkerchief with the initials T.W. and…" She stopped mid-sentence. Her head pushed back, creating a distance between herself and the computer screen. Her gaze was unflinching as her mouth opened.

Ed cleared his throat. "And?"

"A… business card in her handbag."

Ed's impatience grew, and he frowned. "Okay, your reaction and what you read doesn't match."

She'd gone pale. "It was Jack Calloway's business card. She was killed near the Shipwreck tavern."

Ed didn't know what to make of her reaction. He decided not to ask. Yet. Give her a minute to collect herself. "Who filed the report?"

"The only signature I see is Chief John Phipps."

"The chief?" Ed thought that was odd. Maybe it had something to do with Homeland's involvement. "No precinct? No detective on the case?"

Carla shrugged. "None that I see." She scrolled through the report. "Ron Patterson performed the autopsy."

Ed folded his arms and watched Carla. Her gaze affixed to nothing, she appeared lost in thought. Now he was interested in Jack's connection with the victim and what Carla wasn't saying. So, he put it out there. "Jack Calloway's business card, huh? I wonder how he knows the victim?"

Carla didn't respond. Her gaze darted. Ed knew something wasn't right, even though he wasn't sure what it was. Carla stood and faltered, clumsily brushing against a stack of paper, and knocking over the pen holder. He reached out to steady her. "Carla. What's going on?"

She snapped a quick look at him. "I… I just remember I'm meeting someone for lunch in Bellevue. I'm going to be late."

She appeared nervous and her movements were jerky.

Ed pointed to the computer. "Are you sure? You don't look all right. Do you know something about this, about Jack's business card?"

His phone rang, but he continued to stare her down. He would not break contact until she answered him. The phone rang again, and she looked away.

The phone kept ringing. Ed took a deep breath and answered. "Okay, email me the UNSUB's name, contacts, known associations, and addresses. You and Roberts go to his workplace. I'll grab Calloway and we'll talk to relatives and friends. See if we can find this S.O.B."

Ed ended the call and shoved the phone in his pants pocket. He didn't miss the abrupt look Carla gave him when he mentioned Jack's name. He'd let it go for now. "The match came through. James Everly is the UNSUB's name."

She cocked her head. Her expression was blank, like she didn't know what it meant. "James Everly. The unknown suspect who altered his name with each victim he dated."

Relief washed across Carla's face and color returned to her cheeks. She looked at him and smiled.

"Are you sure you're okay?"

"Yeah, I'm sorry. I'm not feeling well and I'm going to be late if I don't get going." She walked over to the closet and grabbed her jacket. "I'll see you later."

Ed left the building and dialed Jack's number. "Jack, we got a DNA match. We have identified our UNSUB. James Everly. I'm heading over to his mother's house. Can you meet there? I'll text you the address."

He got into his car and drove toward White Center. A flutter in his stomach signaled him, an intuitive nudge, like an itch that must be scratched. His mind churned over Carla's reaction. Something about that report unnerved her. She knew something. Maybe about this Riley Jackson, or maybe something about Jack's involvement.

It's partly why he called Jack and invited him. Keep him close. Watch him. If Carla would not tell him, he'd find out on his own, even if it meant asking the elusive Jack Calloway.

CHAPTER 21

Ed Halstead

ED PULLED ONTO A LONG narrow street in a poorer section of the area. The houses reflected neglect. The vibrant colors that once lit up the neighborhood were dull and faded. Gang markings tagged houses, boarded windows attempted to keep out vagrants, and wooden porches crumbled. Cars hugged both sides and children played in the street. Up ahead, Jack's jeep was parked against the curb with just enough space for Ed to pull into.

Ed stepped out of his car, walked to Jack, and reached out to shake his hand. Together, they crossed the road. "Jack. Thanks for coming. Maybe he's here. At the very least, talking to his mother should help validate your profile."

They reached the sidewalk and stopped to scan the house. Jack casually stood. He was taller than Ed and although not big; he was lean and muscular. He might've held Ed down before, but since, Ed had been training. If it came to it, he could take him.

Jack's jaw flexed. "Have a problem with my profile, Halstead?" The edges of his lips curled upward into a smirk. "At least I get it right." He opened the gate.

Anger billowed in Ed's chest. He was sure Jack was referring to their first case together. Ed was a new detective, and his suspect profile didn't match Jack's. Ed had refused to budge, and it turned out Jack's profile was accurate and Ed wasted time and resources targeting the wrong person. It was a rookie mistake, one he'd never forgot. It helped him become the detective he was today. He wouldn't thank Jack for it, though. He might be good, but he's still a jackass, even if his teeth are so white and perfect. Jack's perfect teeth galled Ed, too.

They knocked on the faded wooden door. A cat sat in the window watching them. A woman with disheveled black hair, in her late forties, opened the door. She wore a halter top so low it was no doubt intended as a trap. She wore cropped pants that stopped just below the knee, and stilettos. Her lipstick was slightly smeared. In the background, a gruff male's voice demanded, "Who is it, Charlene?" By her appearance, she was entertaining.

She waved a hand. Her voice was tight when she spoke. "What, can't you see I'm busy? I don't want what you're selling." She shook her finger and started to close the door. Jack stamped his foot between the door and the casing.

Ed flashed his badge. "Ma'am. We're here to talk to you about your son, James. We're with the Seattle PD."

She opened the door and peered at Jack's foot. She caught his gaze and scowled. Jack smiled. Her body physically pulled toward him. Like a magnet was drawing her in. "I beg your pardon, ma'am," Jack said in a silvery voice. "We just need a minute of your time. We won't take long. May we come in and talk?"

Ed had noticed no accent in Jack's voice before, but his *ma'am* had a slight drawl to it — Southern and made him curious to know where Jack was from.

She straightened her shoulders and swiped her hand through her hair, and with a devil's smile said, "Sure, honey, come on in." She attempted to use a satin-laced voice, but it came out rough. If it wasn't for the thirty years of smoking, she might've had a pleasant voice.

What they stepped into as she closed the door behind them was an entirely different era. It was like they time-traveled to the 1970s. Wall-to-wall yellow shag carpet, an orange knapsack material surrounded the windows as curtains, and a green and gold floral print on a white fabric couch sat against the wall. Dark brown wood paneling lined the opposite wall. The house was lived in. The couch was well worn, the coffee table stained and scratched, and the carpet was singed in places. Probably cigarette burns.

Her rough voice interrupted Ed's thoughts. "Would you like something to drink officers?"

Ed shook his head and handed her his card. "Detective Halstead and no ma'am. Is your son here, we have some questions for him." Ed pointed to a picture of James on the wall.

A hand went to her hip. "Is he in trouble? What did that no-good son of mine do? He can't do nothin' right. I get so frustrated with him. Last week I sent him to the store to get me milk. He doesn't come back until the next day. I swear he's more and more like his daddy. His daddy wasn't no good either."

She went to the couch and sat. Her legs slightly parted. At one time she was probably a good-looking lady, but hard living had caught up with her. "Ma'am, does he live here?"

She reached for the pack of cigarettes on the end table. "He hasn't been around in a couple of days. He comes and goes. I don't know where he stays half the time. He works part-time at Harland's. You might find him there." She lit up and took a drag.

Jack walked over to the family photos, looking carefully at each one. He stood near the next room, Ed assumed was the kitchen. Jack glanced around, probably searching for the man who barked out earlier. Assessing the threat, if any.

"Does he have any close friends? A girlfriend?" Ed asked.

She scoffed, finding humor in the questions. "James? He can hardly carry a conversation. How would he get a girlfriend? You'd have to tell him what to do. He's useless." She took another drag. "When you find him, tell him his mama needs him to come home." The woman paused. Her face lit up as if a brilliant thought occurred to her. "Sometimes he hangs out at the community center. He plays video games there."

Jack moved toward Ed.

"Right now, we just need to ask him some questions. When you see him, please have him call? We'll be going," Ed said.

They walked down the steps and out to the sidewalk. Ed asked Jack, "Learn anything else from your perusal?"

There was no inflection in Jack's voice when he answered, "Fits my profile. He's a loner. It doesn't appear his mother's fond of him. If her words have any action behind them, she's at least emotionally abusive. Most parents make excuses for their kids, even if those excuses aren't plausible. A high school graduation picture places him about twenty."

Ed scanned the street, gazing at the houses, and wondered if any neighbors were watching. He shrugged. "With mother's like that, it's no wonder people turn out the way they do."

Jack jammed his hands into his jacket pockets. "What next?"

"I already put out a BOLO on him and my men are checking out his work."

Ed's phone rang, and he answered it. "Halstead. Yeah. Okay. Not in the last week? Okay. Thanks."

He ended the call and put the phone back into his pocket. "James hasn't shown up at work this week."

Jack scanned the neighborhood. "Let's check out the community center, maybe we'll find him there."

They parted ways and drove to the community center. A group of young men were outside playing basketball, and spectator eyes followed them as they walked from the parking lot to the entrance. Ed suspected they knew they were police. If any of them had outstanding criminal issues, they'd leave once he and Jack got inside.

They entered the office. Ed showed the staff James's picture, and the staff answered their questions. James hadn't been at the community center for at least four, maybe five days. They learned little else, except James played video games with Zach Yarborough, who was here today, in the game room which was down the hall and to the left.

There was only one young man in the game room, and Ed assumed it was Zach. Zach sat on one of two couches while he played a multiplayer game, His eyes were affixed to the large TV screen in front of him. He wore a headset, talking to someone on the other end.

Zach was a pudgy young man with short dirty blond hair. It was thick and sort of reminded Ed of a bird's nest. Jack tapped him on the shoulder and Zach lifted a finger, signaling them to wait. Ed pulled out his badge, stepped in front of him, and shook his head. Zach paused the game and his wide eyes darted between Jack and him.

Zach answered their questions. He'd last saw James a week ago at the center. He tried calling James since, with no answer. He's known James for nearly four years and about three months ago, James started acting differently. He explained what different meant.

Sometimes James wasn't himself, his eyes vacant, and he was coming to the center less often. When he attended, he talked about someone watching him.

"What do you mean vacant?" Jack asked.

"It's like something came over him and his eyes would glaze over. It was weird. We'd be playing, and he'd leave abruptly. Never saying why. He just got up and left."

"He said someone was watching him?" Ed asked.

Zach shrugged and threw his hands up. "Yeah. He seemed more nervous too."

They finished the interview and walked out of the building. They stopped at the end of the walkway before the parking lot.

Ed glanced at Jack. He was wearing his sunglasses, a signature style. Added to Jack's pretentious bastardness. "What do you make of James's behavior changing?"

"Hard to say. Could have an underlying mental health issue. Maybe drugs. Maybe the stress of killing people." Jack began walking toward his car. "I guess it doesn't matter at this point. We just need to get him off the streets."

Once they reached their cars, Ed said, "I'll check in with my guys in a bit and see what they're finding."

Jack opened his car door. "I'd like to go back to the storage unit. See if anything else stands out."

Ed nodded. "Oh, and Jack. The evidence on Billy McCord came in. It ruled him out."

"One down, two to go," he said and climbed into his Jeep.

"And there's one more thing," Ed said. "Who's Riley Jackson?"

Jack's movements stopped and in the reflection of his side mirror he said, "She was a friend." His expression didn't change. No slack in the shoulders; no sadness expressed over a friend dying. Jack turned over the ignition and drove away.

Ed decided he would find out what Jack was hiding. He'd make sure of it.

CHAPTER 22

Jack Calloway

JAMES EVERLY IS STILL MISSING. In the past three days, the Seattle PD has been watching his work, home, and community center. Nothing. He's one of three things—hiding, running, or dead. He's out there somewhere and I'm desperate to find him, if only to clear my name. Whoever's helping him won't make that easy.

I contemplate hiring out. When I can't be in two places at once, and I need someone followed, or an extra set of eyes for surveillance, I employ others. Right now, I'm balancing the risks against the benefits. It'd have to be the right person. Not the kids I find on the street looking to earn their next meal. They work great when I need a human followed, or a pocket picked. However, this is dangerous, requiring heightened senses, an ability to blend in and to see what's not there. Vampires aren't the most trustworthy, even if we are more civilized as a race now, we're still swayed to do what's in our own best interests. And Weres don't like vampires.

I bring a glass of blood to my mouth as I stare at West Seattle from my window. The metallic smell hits me, like the smell of aluminum seared by heat. The liquid smoothness glides down my throat. I savor the richness and it ignites my senses. My teeth extend and a low growl erupts from my chest.

The image staring back startles me and I turn away. My eyes return to the glass. I haven't had that type of visceral reaction to the taste of blood since… I set the glass down. Riley. And that worries me.

Jasper sits on the arm of the chair behind me. We look at each other. He meows and scampers away. He senses something's different. For the last few weeks, he's been timid around me. When I got home the other day, I called him, and he didn't come. Normally, he greets me at the door, or when I wake up, he's curled in a ball at the end of my bed. Lately, he's been avoiding me.

My cell phone on my kitchen counter rings. I pick it up, glancing at the name of the caller. It's Paul Crandon.

"Hey, Paul."

"Jack. I just got a call from the team assigned to your house in Fremont. There's been a break-in."

"A what? When?"

"Timestamp is nine p.m.," he says.

Quick movements reach for my jacket. I bark. "Where's Shannon?"

Paul's voice is calm and exact, making sure his words reach me. He probably senses a shift within me too. "I'm told she's on her way home now. We checked it all out. No one's there, but they broke the door casing."

I push the elevator button for the garage level. The doors close. "I'll call her right now. I'm on my way. Do you know who it was?"

"We got him on video."

"Send it to me." I end the call. There's a tightness in my chest and a wave of dread washes over me. I'm in the path of a tornado with no place to go. I breathe slowly in and out, willing the panic away.

When I get to her house, a stocky man is standing on the porch. His hair is long and unkempt, and there's a familiar smell of dog wafting off him. Vampires have an autonomic reaction to the smell of dogs—Weres included. He works for Paul and I'm reassured with his standing post.

I walk inside and find Shannon sitting at her kitchen table. She looks up at me with brows furrowed. Her wide eyes make it apparent the scowl is just a front. She's scared. Her heartbeat matches the fear.

When I talked to her on the phone, I explained someone broke into her home and the security staff I hired were at her house. I told her I was on my way, for her to go inside, and let them do their jobs.

I try to smooth her fear and irritation with a calm, "Hello, sunshine." But the words are strained through my anxiety and it comes out tight.

I sit next to her and pull up the video. We watch Brad, the same young man I met at the coffee shop weeks ago, break-in using a crowbar to pry open the door. We watch him roam from room to room. Not finding what he's looking for, I suspect Shannon, he leaves. Thankfully, Paul's team arrived by nine-thirty p.m., five minutes before Shannon got home.

It's apparent Shannon's no longer safe here and I decide she'll stay with me, at least until this gets solved. While watching Brad, I noticed a far-away look in his eyes and wonder if he too is tied into this mess.

Shannon has the heels of her palms pressed to her eyes. She trembles and shakes her head. She whispers, "Brad." It's a mixture of fear, disbelief, and guilt. I know what she's thinking. How did she miss it?

"Hey kiddo, this had nothing to do with you."

She's silent. I'm not sure she heard me, let alone if my words provided any reassurance. My need to fix this, change the comforting words into action. I need her attention. My tone turns curt. "When's the last time you've heard from Brad?"

She gazes at the floor, her lips pressed. Her voice is brittle when she speaks. "A couple of days ago, he called and asked me out. When I refused, he threatened me."

I stand up. My hands ball into fists. "You didn't tell me that. Exactly, what did he say?"

"That I told him, no, only to make him mad. I was teasing him, and he said he would punish me for it. Then he laughed and hung up."

"Pack a bag. You're staying with me."

I expect her to argue, to tell me how she can take care of herself, but she doesn't. She trembles when she stands.

I place my hands in my pockets and make a promise. "He won't hurt you. You'll be safe at my place."

While she packs, I email Meghan, my building manager, to arrange for Shannon to have access to my apartment. I need to take extra precautions and I email Paul to place a security detail on Shannon and one on Carla. I don't want Carla to know, and I request her detail stays in the shadows.

It's after eleven when we get to my place. Shannon has never been here. I show her around and get her set up in the guest room. I let her know she'll have access to the main entrance in the morning once Meghan gets her into the system.

After she goes to bed, I spend the next few hours in my office. My abnormal hours and the little need for sleep are enough to cause anyone to question who I am, or at least my sanity. Fortunately, Shannon's familiar with my odd hours.

I doze off, thinking about Carla, only to awake with a start by the ringing of my phone. Surprised I fell asleep, I sit up quickly and reach for my phone. I see Ed's name pop up and look at the time before I answer. It's three forty-five a.m. My days are getting mixed up and I struggle to realize it's Friday morning.

To wake a vampire from dead sleep can be a risk to life and limb, but in the life of a private investigator, I'm used to working all hours of the day and night. Doesn't mean I'm happy about it, and I snarl when I answer the phone. "I'm guessing this isn't a social call?"

"We have a body. I'll text you the address." The phone goes dead.

I blink a few times and rub the back of my neck. I fell asleep in my recliner and my neck muscles are objecting. I stand, stretch my legs, and look around. No empty blood bags in sight. None in the garbage. Shannon won't have access to this room, but I still want to be careful. Satisfied, I walk out of my office and make sure I hear the locks click when the door shuts.

My phone vibrates with a text message. The address. My stomach flips. I pull the address up on the map, hoping it is somewhere other than where I think. Something stabs my chest and my muscles tighten throughout my body.

By the time I get over to West Seattle, it's nearly five a.m. and the sunlight's highlighting the night sky. On a clear day, West Seattle has some of the best views of the city. Downtown Seattle is a majestic forest that rises out of concrete. A spring day, like today, can bring a mix of clouds, rain, and clear blue skies.

I make it past the police barricades on California Avenue and reach the parking lot at Hamilton Park. They have set the outer and inner crime scene perimeters. I spot the command post and walk to it. I overhear officers organizing a grid search pattern. Hamilton Park is a relatively small park, at least compared to Seward. Searching the park won't take nearly as long.

I look back toward Palm Avenue and the surrounding area. My eyes searching. Not for clues, but for a house. A tightness clutches at my chest as I look. Carla's house is right there. *Too close*, I think to myself. A quiet, but toneless voice interrupts my thoughts.

"That's what I thought too. A little too close to home."

I turn to find Carla. A slight smile hints at the corners of her mouth. Almost reassuring.

I reach for her and pull her into me, not thinking about where we are, only about my need to keep her safe. "Yeah, I don't like it."

She stiffens in my arms and I realize her discomfort. It's a professional faux pas at a crime scene, no less, in front of her staff and police officers. I silently curse at myself and quickly release her, pull at my collar, and put my hands in my pockets. "Are you all right?"

She steps back, looks at me, and nods. "Yes, I think so." Despite my misstep, her face is soft when she looks at me.

I look at the crime scene. Both anger and fear squeeze my throat, and I utter another promise. "I'll make sure you stay safe."

I spot Ed hurrying toward us. I take a couple of steps back. I already made Carla uncomfortable, and more fuel on the fire is not what's needed right now. "Jack. You're here. Grab PPE. The coroner's getting ready to take the body. I want you to get a look before that happens."

I follow Ed across the grassy area, along the cone-marked path. The evergreen trees greet us with new foliage as we make our way through the pine branches. We spill out into a small opening. The trees protect the space from dangerous elements. It's a hidden oasis. Or would be if there wasn't a corpse sprawled on the ground.

The coroner scowls at us, impatiently waiting for my perusal. I skim the area, taking it in, recording it to memory. My gaze lands on the body. It's different. This is different. The muscles in my face strain as I absorb what the scene is communicating.

I can feel Ed's steely gaze. It's unnerving and unusual. Like he's looking for something beyond my powers of observation.

Voices behind us interrupt my thoughts. The coroner's team is ready to transport the body. Ed and I step aside.

We walk to the command post, neither of us saying a word. At the parking lot, news teams have arrived and they're spilling out of their vehicles. Ed curses and takes off in their direction, waving another officer to go with him.

I stand near command and watch the officers and forensics work to search and memorialize the scene, taking pictures, and sketching their findings.

Carla approaches the command center and talks to a young man who is categorizing evidence. She discusses the process with him, giving him direction. There's something she doesn't like, but she's not stern in her approach, even though her stress and concern are apparent. It's not the crime scene itself that causes her concern, but how close it is to her house and what she knows.

However, she doesn't show it. She's patient and generous. It's a teaching moment, and she's a master at her craft. My insides warm watching her and she must've felt me staring because she glances over and our gazes meet.

She finishes her conversation and walks toward me; her stride purposeful and confident. She removes her gloves. With seriousness in her face and warmth in her eyes, she asks, "The body. What do you think?"

I shake my head. "It doesn't fit what we've seen so far. She was face up. Dirt and leaves covered her body. She wasn't exposed to the elements."

Carla agrees with a nod. "She was fully naked, and prelims suggest heavy blood loss."

"The cuts. The angle was different, like the perp is left-hand dominant. A right-handed person did the others." I pause. "What else do you know at this point?"

She points toward the west of the crime scene. "The grass is saturated with blood and we found a boot print next to it. The coroner said the time of death was between twelve and two a.m."

I fold my arms. "Who found the body?"

Carla points toward a house. "Neighbor said they heard crying and shouting in the park and called the police."

Carla's house, although close to the park, others are closer. They'd be in a better position to hear a commotion at the park. Still, fear rises from my chest to my throat and the next words I say are demanding. "Where were you?"

It was out before I could think about tactics and diplomacy. Internally, I cringe at my stupidity.

Carla steps back and folds her arms. "Where I was or wasn't, isn't the matter at hand. As I mentioned before, I can take care of myself."

What is it with the women in my life and this notion of how they can take care of themselves? I support a woman's need for independence, but the extent of not letting a man help them is beyond my comprehension.

My reply is strangled. "I... ah." My gaze shifts to the ground and I run my hand through my hair, stopping myself from saying anything further. I'll keep her safe, regardless. She doesn't need to know about the how's. "Considering my connection to this. I only want you to be safe," I say in a low voice.

I take a deep breath and exhale. Regroup and steer the conversation back to the crime scene. "From what the evidence suggests, the murder took place here. That's different from our other victims. Something's changed."

Carla shrugs. "We must look at everything we find today before we can make that determination."

"I don't like what it's saying so far."

Carla's eyes dart, scanning for what, I didn't know.

"What? Spit it out," I say.

Her shoulders deflate. "Ed knows about Riley."

I'm irritated with myself for placing her in the position of carrying my secrets, and guilty because I need her support. "I know, he talked to me about it."

Her eyebrows draw together. "I don't think he's letting that go. He's been asking me questions about you. Like how well I know you. Your background, history, and friends." Her eyes are fixed on Ed, who's walking toward us. "Since I know little, I have nothing to say, but once he gets something in his mind, he will not stop until he's satisfied."

I don't respond. It's all too close and too many things point my way. Now, more people are pulled into this. The NISCU's involved and add Brad to the mix, and it's a cluster.

When Ed reaches us, he doesn't discuss the crime scene or asks me about my impressions. It's odd because isn't that why I'm here? "Can we meet at the precinct this afternoon to debrief, say around one p.m.?" I'm included in that ask, but Ed speaks directly to Carla, not making eye contact with me.

I blurt out, "Works for me." Carla smiles at both of us and nods in agreement.

The walk to my car isn't long. I puzzle over Ed's behavior, not paying attention. When I look up and out, I see a large, muscular man in a sports jacket and jeans leaning on my car, his arms crossed. It's easy to spot a military man and a bureaucrat. And he's both. No doubt he's from the NISCU.

"I wondered how long it would take the Department of Homeland to beg me to come back to the unit?" I smile. "Twenty years. And they would send you of all people. Whose ass are you kissing now?" I stand with my arms crossed, waiting for Kerry LaMoine's response.

NISCU recruited Kerry from the Navy Seal Division twenty years ago. He had an exceptional skill set, but when it came to the supernatural world, he was a bit green. They knew he had a run-in with a couple of vampires that took most of his team out. They compelled those who survived. The only problem was Kerry's immune to a vampire's compulsion. He remembered everything and demanded answers. He got answers and was recruited.

All employees of the NISCU have some sort of knowledge of this world before joining. Once they join, they're sworn to secrecy. When I met him, he had to be in his late twenties. Now he's a lead agent covering the west coast.

He moves off my car, standing firm. "We won't be needing you back anytime soon, Jack, especially now that you're a suspect."

I scoff. "I may be many things, but a murderer isn't one of them."

Smug and full of himself, he says, "Not quite a confession, but close. At least we're on the same page. Murder."

As much as I'd like to knock that look off his face, I know it won't help. I maintain my composure. "Look at the evidence a little closer. Someone's trying to pin this on me. I'm not the UNSUB here."

He steps away from my vehicle. He walks past me toward the command center and says, "See you around, Jack."

I get into my car. *Crap.* I think. They're here. It's only a matter of time before I get hauled in and questioned, but not by humans, by the Guard. The Dracul does not look favorably on vampires who murder humans. I've got to get this solved and fast. I'm not ready to leave this world. My mission isn't complete. I need to find the vampire who took my family. That mission has kept me going. Despite the losses, I continue to endure.

Loss is a fact for a vampire, and they must learn to deal with it, or it will eat them alive. It's suffocating. The thought of avenging my family has propelled me. After that, I don't care what happens to me.

I search for Carla before leaving. She's walking away from Ed and Kerry. Her pace and the scowl on her face tell me she's angry.

Earlier, I'd noticed a were-person nearby. I assume he's Carla's detail and wonder if he saw what happened here.

Right now, I need to get home and make sure Shannon's okay.

CHAPTER 23

Jack Calloway

I STOPPED BY THE BAKERY to pick up Shannon's favorite breakfast—bagels and cream cheese. I thought Shannon would appreciate something to eat since my refrigerator had little in the way of human food. By the time I walk into the lobby, it's seven-thirty a.m.

Near the elevator, Simon is waiting for me. "What brings you by?" I open the keypad and scan my print. We both get into the elevator.

His posture is stiff, and his arms are by his sides. "NISCU is in town."

I nod. "Yeah, I just saw Kerry. I'm a suspect."

His brows draw together. He usually has a better poker face, but his worry is visible. "Jack, it'll get worse. The investigation on you is moving forward. It's out of my hands, but I'll do what I can to help uncover the truth."

As an investigator, Simon is by the book and as a member of one of the oldest families, he walks a tight line politically. For him to withhold evidence says a lot and I'm grateful for his friendship, but I don't say any of that I just smile and tell him I appreciate any help he can give.

We walk into my apartment deafened by music blasting throughout. Shannon found my logon and accessed my music account. Both Simon and I cover our ears at the raucous sound. We have two things not helping us right now—sensitive hearing and a refined taste for music that doesn't include screeching and growling.

I open my phone to find the app that controls my systems and turn off the music. Simon's hands fall away from his ears, but his eyebrows lift, silently asking what the hell? However, before I can answer, Shannon comes flying down the corridor from the swimming pool.

"Why d'you do that?" In a bikini, Shannon has too much skin visible as she barrels toward us. Simon's mouth opens as he looks at Shannon. Shannon abruptly stops and I hear an "Oh," escape from her mouth. A weird vibe hangs in the air between Simon and Shannon, it's like everything stopped at once. They remain still and stare at each other.

Before I can answer her question and put an end to their staring, Meghan's voice comes through the intercom. "Jack. Your security has arrived. We'll be up in about fifteen minutes."

"Okay. Thanks."

Too much is going on at once, and I've got an overwhelming need to flee. With all this activity, I'm sure Jasper's found a good place to hide too. I take a breath, flex my fingers, and bark, "Shannon cover yourself up. Simon, close your mouth." Shannon hurries through the living room to her bedroom. Simon's gaze follows.

He's still staring down the hall when he asks, "Since when do you have women stay the night?"

I scowl at this. "That's not a woman. I mean... she is obviously, but that's Shannon. I think our killer is trying to get to her. She's staying here so I can keep her safe. I've hired a security detail. As you heard, he'll be up in a minute."

His mouth agape. Again. "Shannon your assistant?" I nod. I see a flicker of fire in his eyes.

I try to keep my worlds separate. Simon and Shannon have talked on the phone before, but never in person. "Wipe the drool off your face. She's not available."

A few minutes later, Shannon comes out of her bedroom dressed, brushing her long, wet hair. I point to the table. "I brought breakfast for you."

Although Simon hasn't thought about anyone since his break-up, he isn't at a loss for words with women. I don't want him to have any of those types of feeling with Shannon, but it's obvious something's happening. He's wringing his hands and glances away whenever Shannon looks at him. This is a new side of Simon. I've seen reserved, contemplative, but not this.

Annoyed with what I'm witnessing, I cross my arms. "Why are you here again?"

He stammers, "Ah... I..." He stops, looks down, and timidly says. "The case."

"What about the case?" I say in part exasperation and part desperation. "This is taking too long. I have other things which require my attention, so spit it out."

The elevator doors open and in walks Meghan and company. Simon straightens and the muscle in his jaws lock. No doubt the smell of a Were reached him. "Jack, this is Adam Jacobs. He's with the security company you hired. Everything checks out."

Adam is probably in his early thirties. Sharp features. He's not tall, but he's thick like a Rottweiler. He has a two-inch scar across his left cheekbone.

"Thank you, Meghan. Is there anything else?"

Meghan opens the elevator and steps in. "Just have Shannon come to my office this morning and I'll get her security access in place." The doors close.

I introduce Adam to Simon and Shannon and give Adam a tour of the apartment. When we return to the kitchen area, Shannon's handing Simon a glass of water. Simon smiles at her and nods in appreciation. I had heard laughter, but now that I'm present, they're both quiet.

"Shannon, Adam is your security detail. He'll be around, but not in the way. He's going everywhere you go."

She starts to object, and I hold my hand up. She goes silent. "There's no budging on this one so, don't try." She glares at me and sits down with an expressive sigh.

Simon turns to her. "It isn't safe right now for anyone who's connected to Jack. If there was another way, I'm sure Jack would figure something else out. This is for the best."

In the acceptance of Simon's words, the tension in Shannon's face softens. She smiles at him.

My entire world is turning upside down, and I'm losing the control I'm used to having. "Well, this has been exciting. Simon, how about I walk you out?"

In the elevator Simon's quiet, but halfway down he turns to me. "You think you can keep her safe?" The worried look he had earlier, returns. "A were-person?" He frowns.

I straighten my back. I'm irritated, confused, and worried myself, but I don't let my voice expose any of that. "Yes, I do. I've spent the past fifty years with Weres. There's no problem."

"What if something happens to you, how are you going to keep her safe?"

I understand his concern. I could get locked up or worse, but my answer is simple. "If my money can't keep her safe with security, then you must. I can't let anyone hurt her. Sh… She's like a daughter to me."

He nods. "I'll make sure she stays safe. You have my word on that." More promises.

CHAPTER 24

Jack Calloway

AT TWELVE FORTY-FIVE P.M., I walk into the precinct, check-in, and go to the appointed conference room. As I walk down the hall, several heads turn my way and then return to their work. The precinct is quiet. No chatter, no jokes, just a focused intensity.

As I approach the conference room, I hear voices inside. I knock and walk-in. Seated around the table in discussion are Carla, Ed, John Phipps, and Kerry. The wall displaying our crime scenes color the room.

The chief's focus is on me. "Jack, good to see you. Come on in and join us. You know everyone I assume?" The chief's aware of my history with Homeland. He also understands the confidential nature of that involvement.

I catch Kerry's eye. The corners of his lips are turned upward in a smirk. I glare at him. "Yeah, I do."

The chief continues. "We're going over the case. Looks like it's taken a turn."

I raise my eyebrows, not sure what taken a turn means. "In what direction is that, sir?"

He barks in his gravelly voice. "The bullshit kind. The kind we don't like. When we're not sure and don't have answers."

I stand, facing the group. The pressure of everyone's eyes on me creates an uneasiness in my stomach. "Ed's team has done a great job. They're closing in on a prime suspect."

Ed clears his throat. "About that, Jack. I got a call from the East Precinct. James Everly was found dead. His body washed up on the shore last night."

My eyebrows furrow. "And?"

Carla stares at a report in front of her. "According to the coroner, the decomposition of the body places his death at least two days ago."

"What do you think that means, Jack?" Asks Kerry. He stands, putting his hands in his pockets.

A fury of annoyance balls my hands into fists. Glaring at Kerry, I ask, "And why are you here?"

The chief quietly observes me. Of course, the chief's aware I know exactly who Kerry is and who he works for, but I can't help myself. I'm irritated because he's accusing me of murder.

The chief speaks in a way one speaks to soothe an upset child. "As I explained to Ed, Kerry's assigned by Homeland in a joint effort between the Federal Bureau of Investigation and Homeland. He's an investigator, but Ed remains the lead on the case. Another set of eyes won't hurt."

Still standing, I lean against the wall, relax my arms, and clasp my hands in front of me. I need to watch myself and communicate to the chief, I'm not here to challenge. "Either we have a copycat, or we've been looking in the wrong direction. Neither seems logical. Too soon for a copycat and forensic evidence, along with witness photo identification, clearly points to James Everly."

Kerry looks directly at me. "Then there's something missing."

I shake my head. "Not based on my original theory. Two killers. My guess is one killer, took out James, and killed our latest victim."

Ed stares at me through hooded eyes. I get the feeling he's calculating the right time to accuse me of being the killer. He clears his throat and looks to the chief. "That fits with our working theory."

"What do we know about today's crime scene?" The chief asks.

Carla straightens and leans into type on her computer. Images project onto the wall. Carla dissects the evidence her team has uncovered. The body belongs to Emma Davis, who had recently graduated from Eastern Washington University and got her first teaching position in West Seattle. She moved to the area last summer. She and her best friend, Maggie, are roommates.

Emma created a dating profile on Match, Meet, & Mingle in January. Maggie said Emma hadn't been home since Saturday, since Emma's lunch date. Maggie wasn't able to get a hold of her and on Monday reported Emma missing.

Evidence of forced sexual intercourse and bruising on her face suggests she was raped and beaten. Abrasions on her hands and wrist suggest restraints. A knife was used to cut her neck, and because she sustained heavy blood loss, forensics reasons the killer had experience hunting. Enough blood soaked the scene to determine she died there.

"We're' still analyzing the blood and semen," Carla says.

I straighten and stand slightly forward. "What about any puncture wounds, like on the other victims?"

She shakes her head. "None."

Ed clears his throat. "Something has changed. And not just that James Everly was murdered." Ed stands up and goes to the crime wall. "The puncture marks were made at least a week before any other abrasions or lacerations were made on our other victims. Based on the evidence found and analyzed, James was sexually assaulting and torturing our victims, killing them in the storage shed, and dumping the body elsewhere."

"We've been assuming James picked up these women for another killer and tortured and killed them. What are we missing?" Ed asks.

"Outside of today's evidence, we don't have any proof that a second killer exists. That's circumspect at best. If he exists, we don't know who this guy is or what the motive is," Carla says.

By this time, I'd taken to pacing the width of the room, while listening to the discussion. "What if the killer found someone else to play his game? Think about it. James got sloppy at the end and Ed was closing in. I'm guessing the killer got rid of James and found someone else."

The room's quiet with speculation. The urgency of time, coupled with unanswered questions, provokes a sense of desperation. "The coroner found a piece of paper inside Emma Davis's mouth." Carla peers at me and hesitates. "Written on the paper was your name, Jack."

All eyes turn to me. The air is thick with silence, but emotions are cutting through it. The chief is the first to break the silence. "Jack?" His eyebrows lift, prompting for an explanation.

Ed jumps in. "It's not the first time his name has been intertwined with our victims. Riley Jackson had his business card at her apartment, and Jack dated April Thompson's sister Nicole."

Kerry's eyes meet mine. His gaze, like daggers, shreds me. He knows more. About Nicole Leedy. The handkerchief. The German. He wouldn't say any of that. Not here anyway.

I look at Carla. She also knows about the notes in German. I need to get in front of this. "Chief, I believe someone's trying to set me up. I'm not sure why."

Ed's voice is pressured when he barks, "He needs to be removed from this case, chief. Who knows how deep this is? Or even if he can be trusted. He could be the killer." Ed glances away as if he hadn't meant to say those words out loud.

The chief stands and paces the room twice before speaking. "I've known Jack for a long time. I know his work and his ethics. If you're going to make that kind of accusation, Ed, your evidence better not have holes. Until then, don't bring it up again." He stops, his gaze on me. "If you think you're a target, Jack, I've got to pull you off the case. We don't know enough about what's going on and your involvement could jeopardize lives."

I cross my arms and stand my ground. "I understand your position. However, I won't stop looking into this. You know that, right? I've got more at stake here and I don't trust Ed with my life." I stare at Ed.

The chief straightens his shoulders and scowling at me, says, "You're off this case."

Fed up with the accusations and my removal from this case, I walk out of the room, expecting Kerry to follow, but he doesn't. I'm not sure if that's good. I have a feeling it doesn't matter. I'm in deep and he's here to clean it up. I think about my whereabouts and alibis. Last night, I was at home. Shannon was there, but she wouldn't have known if I left. My security camera footage will hopefully provide me with a solid alibi.

I'd been at the bar right before Riley got there, and Nick's cameras had been altered that night. That isn't in my favor. I don't have any DNA tied to any of the crimes, but that proves nothing, not really. Vampire blood or prints don't register the same as humans. They're undetected by human equipment.

I decide to head to the morgue and get Doc to make impressions of my bite and measure my teeth. Never know what evidence may be the one that separates guilt from innocence.

Thirty minutes later, I arrive at the morgue and walk into Doc's office. A body is on the table and he and a technician are taking measurements. The scent in the air is an unpleasant mixture of blood and raw meat.

Doc looks up at me. His eyes flicker with excitement. "Jack. I wasn't expecting you. What brings you to the dungeon?" He chuckles. "Whatever it is, doesn't look good." My face must've given me away.

I grimace. "Doc, I need a favor."

He waves me to follow him. We leave the morgue, go into his office, and sit. Doc leans forward. "What's going on?"

I tell him all of it. About the Seattle PD victims, the Guard's victims, my connections to some of them, the letters, and notes in German, and the break-ins. I even tell him about losing control, about Ester, and my wife. I tell him about the theories I've got on the killers. We discuss the contamination at the blood bank and the other vampires who have lost control.

It was like a confessional. All the losses, the secrets, and the weight I'd carried, released. I needed someone to know. I came here to get help to prove my innocence, but it felt more like I'd been given my last rite, like I'm walking to my death.

Doc sits quietly, absorbing all of what I say. "It's a lot, and it sounds like someone's targeting you, but I haven't heard the favor you want."

"If this goes south, I want you to have impressions of my bite and measurements of my incisors. Perhaps it'll be evidence in my favor."

Doc jumps up. "Well, that's easy enough. Come with me." We go back to his lab and he tells his techs to take a break. Once they leave, Doc gets out the mold and other materials. I lay on the table while he goes to work on my mouth.

My phone rings, which makes me move. "Hold still," Doc says. "You're like a damn kid." He sighs. "The dead are much easier to work on."

Through a mouthful of molding material, I mumble. "I am dead."

He squints at me. "Well, you're the moving kind of dead, like a chicken with his head cut off. This needs to be exact. So focus."

When the molds set, he hands me a wet cloth to wipe my mouth and compares the impressions to the measurements taken from the victims. "Your overbite doesn't match, and I could argue that if you bit a human, your teeth would be a skosh shorter than whoever bit the victims."

My insides lift in relief. "That's good to hear, thanks."

"One last thing." I jump off the table. "Can you send these to Simon Johnson? Between you and him, they'll be in excellent hands."

We say our goodbyes and I leave the building. I scan the parking lot for Carla's car. Thinking about Ed's accusations, I wonder what she thinks. Does she still care, or will she want nothing to do with me?

I let out a weighted sigh. I need to see the people I care about in case I don't get another chance. I'm not giving up, but I've often seen the Dracul's quick hand of justice. Although I'm in their better graces, I've never been fully trusted. Even if I'm cleared on any charges of murder, I'd lost control on Riley. Once that's known, someone like me doesn't stand a chance.

After I went home and checked in with Shannon, at eight p.m., I found myself at the Shipwreck, sitting at the bar.

I overhear a shifter at a table behind me. "Then she busts my balls for not remembering our anniversary. I've been in the doghouse for a week." He laughs at the pun intended.

"Another refill, Jack?" Nick asks.

I nod. I watch him as he sets another shot in front of me. A guy at the end of the bar waves at Nick. He walks to the guy with a smile on his face and sets a beer in front of him. Nick's optimism makes for a good bartender. He's always had a cheerful disposition. I've enjoyed being a part of his life.

When he was seventeen, he and his buddies, all Weres, found themselves in trouble before the homecoming football game. They had been dared to spray paint over their opponent's hillside emblem, which overlooked the town.

The night before the game, they got drunk and made their way to the top of the hill. However, someone tipped off the school and informed the police. The kids were caught. They didn't get into any trouble, but if Nick's dad found out, he would've grounded Nick for the rest of the year. Their pack had rules about such things and breaking rules led to consequences.

Nick called me scared from the police station. My law enforcement connections paid off, but it'd be the only time I covered for him. I told him to remember that.

"You're unusually quiet tonight, Jack."

I gulp my drink. "I have a few things on my mind."

Nick pours me another shot. "The case or Carla?" He has a sympathetic look in his eyes.

"I suppose both."

"Want my advice?"

I shake my head. "Not particularly, but I'm sure that doesn't matter. You'll give it, anyway."

Nick laughs. "It goes with the job." He pauses and his smile leaves his face. He looks at me. "Don't wait any longer. You're miserable and have been for the past three years."

I said nothing immediately. He's right. I'd done everything I could to not be miserable, but she's never left me. "Thanks for that." I roll my eyes.

I sit there for another half an hour watching people spill in. It's Friday night and by nine it's becoming difficult to have a conversation without yelling. I take it as a sign it's time to go.

I'm not sure I ever enjoyed a room filled with conversations. Even before I turned, I preferred the sounds of the countryside, which demanded a certain stillness to be heard. The cicadas singing in the trees, coyotes howling, and the lightning bugs buzzing. And my wife playing the fortepiano.

I sigh deeply and become distracted by Nick's words, *don't wait any longer* as I settle my bill. I have little time. I decide to heed Nick's words and go to Carla's. At the very least, I can make sure she's safe. And I need to see her, if only for one last time.

CHAPTER 25

Jack Calloway

EARLIER, I'D TEXTED SIMON AND asked him to check in on Shannon this evening. I wasn't sure if I'd be home before midnight. And now, sitting in front of Carla's place, if I can help it, I won't go home at all.

I watch for ten minutes or so, not knowing if she's alone or not. I'm not sure how I'll react if she's entertaining a man. The living room light is on and I see a shadow cross the window. I listen in, projecting my senses inside. One heartbeat. One pulse.

I know I should've called. It's the polite thing to do, but tonight, I don't want to be rejected.

I text her I'm at her door and ascend the porch. I wait impatiently, holding myself back from breaking through the door. The porch light comes on and the door opens.

She dresses comfortably in a matching pink and white athletic outfit. I try not to stare, but she isn't wearing a bra and her shirt is molded to her breasts. I feel the tension heat in my groin.

I meet her gaze and lock on. I can feel her pulse race. I need to be sure of one thing before I make her mine tonight. Vampire or not, I'm a gentleman.

I step inside and close the door. I turn to her and move quickly to close the distance. She steps back until the couch stops her. There's nowhere else for her to go.

I pull her into me. My breath fast and shallow. "Where's Ted?"

She looks at me. "I… He's no… We're not." It's all I need to hear. My lips crash onto hers and I drink her in greedily like I've been without water for weeks. She responds just as thirsty, her tongue twisting with mine. My hands cup her ass and I pull her into me.

I lift her shirt over her head and begin kissing her throat while cupping her breast. She moans with pleasure. It's a sound I've longed to hear. I pick her up, throwing her legs around my waist, and take her to the bedroom.

I'm not gentle. I can't be. I've longed for this for years. I throw her on her back and tear off her clothes. Her nakedness causes me to growl.

I drop to my knees, straddling her. Hovering. She starts to say something, and I shake my head, taking her mouth into mine. I kiss her slowly at first, starting on her lips and moving down to her neck. I savor her neck as she moans and squirms beneath me.

My fangs stir, but I fight those back which amplifies my desire. My mouth inches down and I take my time. Carla's fingers grab at my hair and she cries out my name while her body shakes, tumbling down from ecstasy.

"Don't move," I say, standing up and admiring her body. I remove my clothes. Carla gasps in anticipation.

I grab her by the ankles and pull her to me. "I need you." My mouth reaches for hers, tenderly kissing her as we match our rhythms, her cries fuel my movements.

Her fingernails dig into my arms and our gazes meet. I don't let go. Sweat beads on my chest and I can feel her building. I whisper, "Not yet. Stay with me." Until we both cry out, trembling together.

I kiss her, taking her lips hostage before I roll off her onto my side. Quiet, except for our breathing, consciousness takes a moment to return.

I lay there with my eyes closed. I can feel her staring at me and I open my eyes and smile. "Hello." She meets my smile. "Not sure what I did to deserve that."

I reach my arm around her waist and pull her closer to me, kissing her mouth and then her neck. "I'll show you what you did."

We make love again. This time intimately. I take my time with her body, savoring every moment of her being. It might be the last chance I get.

When we're done, for the first time in a while, I relax enough to sleep. I pull her into me, my arm around her, and before I fall asleep, I whisper, "I've missed you."

It isn't the sun's light illuminating the space that wakes me. I slept through that, but it's the sound of my phone's incessant vibration jarring me from sleep.

I feel heat in my chest and open my eyes to find Carla wrapped in my arms. I move gingerly to not disturb her. I step out of bed, pull out my phone from my pants, and walk to the living room before answering.

"Hello."

Simon's voice booms. "Where are you?"

"Uh," I look at the clock. Nine a.m. "Why?"

"NISCU has a search warrant. They're almost to your place."

I drive a hand through my hair. "I'm not there. I'll give Meghan a call, make sure she lets them in. I'll have Shannon's security get her out of there."

"I'm in the lobby." The other end of the line goes quiet. "Simon?"

"I got her out already. I…" His voice fades.

My insides cringe at what he's not telling me. Before he explains, I say, "Not a conversation we have time for."

I get off the phone and call Meghan. NISCU's warrants look different, but I explain they're legit and to let them in my apartment.

When I hang up, I hear footsteps coming up behind me. "Sounds like you have something you need to take care of."

I reach out to pull her in and squeeze her tight. Her head fits nicely under my chin. My heart's in my stomach knowing I have to let her go.

I kiss the top of her head. "I do. I'm sorry. I'd planned to spend the morning with you."

We're both quiet as I get dressed. We kiss until we're gasping for air. My hands still needing her, caressing her skin as I hold her, perhaps for the last time.

Carla pulls away slightly and looks up at me. Her brows furrow. "Jack, I don't know what's going on, but I know something isn't right. Last night. All this. Are you going to fill me in?"

"I can't answer that right now, but when I can, I will. Don't worry." I kiss the top of her head again and release her.

I step through the front door and turn to face her. "Thank you for a wonderful evening, love." I wink at her. I have a smile on my face when I reach my car, but my heart's sinking. Time to face the music.

CHAPTER 26

Jack Calloway

AN HOUR LATER, I PARK near my building. I don't want to cause further suspicion or accidentally get myself killed, so rather than take the elevator directly from my parking garage to my apartment, I go through the building's main entrance. Hal greets me as I step inside. His eyes dart back and forth, nervously.

His voice is tense and shaking. "Sir. You've got guests in your apartment."

I scan the lobby, surprised there isn't a Guard officer or NISCU agent waiting for me. I suppose it's a sign they don't have enough evidence to arrest me. "I know Hal. Thank you. Could you ring Meghan for me and let her know I'm on my way to her office?" I walk off and turn to Hal and smile. "And don't worry. It's fine."

Meghan's office is on the main floor toward the back of the building. I walk down the left corridor, past the realtor and C.P.A. offices. I reach Meghan's door, knock, and step inside.

Meghan's sitting at her desk in a black leather chair. Her executive desk holds two computer monitors. On the opposite side of the room is a sixty-inch CCTV capturing the building's common spaces in real-time. Behind Meghan, on the wall, is a picture of her receiving a bronze star medal for her bravery in Iraq. A floral arrangement sits on her desk, a contrast to the rest of the office— black and gunmetal grays. The edges of the petals are tan and curling in. Hidden in here are two or three weapons, a request I approved.

"You gave them full access, correct?"

She stands, smoothing out her blazer. "Yes. Like you said. If I may, what's going on, sir?"

"I'm being accused of murder. In the meantime, until this gets solved, I may be unreachable for a few days."

Next, I give her instructions. "Nick Crandon has financial executorship of my estate, and Boyd, Leighton, and Zirkle have that paperwork, as do Hopper and Fitz. The C.P.A. will continue to pay the bills. Shannon must have a security detail and stay in my apartment until this clears. No exceptions to that."

Meghan nods. "Got it. I'm here to help in any way I can."

"I appreciate knowing I can count on you." A measure of relief washes across my shoulders.

Now that I've wrapped everything up, it's time to go upstairs. I assume Simon's in my apartment and call him, letting him know I'm on my way.

When I reach the top floor, the elevator doors open, and I'm greeted by blue lasers peppering across my chest. I follow the laser to the end of the barrel. The lasers are attached to an IM rifle, specifically used to immobilize the supernatural. Filled darts with a mixture of silver and clay won't kill a vampire, but it'll make one immobile. Two members of the Guard stand unwavering, ready to take me down.

I put my hands up in front, palms out, keeping my body relaxed, and my gaze scans the room. From where I'm standing, I've got a view into the kitchen, dining area, down the corridor to the pool, and a partial view of the living room. Kerry's distinct voice, smooth and deep, reaches my ears from inside my office. He's giving orders to someone.

I chuckle. "Boys, boys. You're the ones breaking into my apartment."

The lasers don't move. Simon walks out of the bedroom and our gazes meet briefly. His eyes are apologetic. I know he's doing his job, but I can't help the sense of betrayal stabbing me in the chest.

Their search is in progress. I hear sounds throughout the apartment, the pool room, the bathroom, and my bedroom. *My bedroom-Riley's blood.* The cleaning solution should've destroyed any DNA from Riley.

In the kitchen, cupboard doors are opened and someone's going through the garbage, laying it out piece by piece. In the living room, someone is dusting for prints. Kerry walks out of my office carrying blood bags in a large, gray container.

Kerry's face lights up when he sees me with an enormous grin. He's happy to see me, but not because he likes me. "Jack. Good of you to make it. Found your stash." He sets the bin on the counter. "We found some other things of interest too. You're going to need to come with us." He points to the men holding guns on me and with his finger, gives them a direction. "You're under arrest for aggravated assault, product tampering, and murder."

I'm placed in handcuffs and an hour and a half later, we arrive at the Pacific Northwest Regional Campus. It's a compound sprawling on five hundred acres, located east of Seattle, outside of a town called Carnation. The compound is the supernatural's version of a city hall and its various departments: Health and Safety, Security and Technology, Economic Development, courtrooms, and holding cells. Vampires and were-persons have their own sections in each department. There's some common understanding between them, but no one species governs another. On the day-to-day things, vampires deal with vampires.

The building I'm most acquainted with is Security and Technology. It's a gray, two-story concrete structure. Probably only ten thousand square feet on each level. The basement includes the Guard's headquarters, interrogation rooms, and holding cells. Two NISCU agents escort me from the vehicle to the door.

Jarvis opens the door from the inside. He's dressed in black and white camos, black steel boots, and a gun holster at his side. He glares at me. "Knew you couldn't be trusted."

I'm taken downstairs into an interrogation room. The agents walk out and lock the door. I'm still handcuffed. It's not like I could escape. There aren't any windows, and everything's made of steel and concrete, reinforced with rebar—a mix of carbon steel and silver. Cameras eye the hallways and lasers embedded in the walls are ready to incapacitate. All made to contain supernatural strength. The only things breakable, besides me, are the two metal folding chairs and a wooden table. A bottle of water sits on the table to pacify would-be victims of interrogation tactics.

All I can do is pace, or sit, and keep my eyes averted from the bright, blistering lights. It's not like this is my first time in one of these rooms. I've just never been on this side of the table and I always had my glasses.

For what seems like two hours, I pace and sit. And think. Not about the future, but about the past and how I got here. Where does that start exactly, the past? Whoever's trying to set me up, must know me, has studied me. My mind runs through the vampires I've known over the years and which ones would go to these extremes. Who dislikes me this much?

My mind grasps to understand it all. Bultrache—Blood Revenge written in Ester's blood. German. The letter, the postcard, the poems. Poems. My mind flashes to my wife's book of poems I've locked away. That's where I read those words *Sieh hin, sieh her! der Mond-scheint hell. Wir und die Todten reiten schnell.*

I sit down. This means something, but what? I reflect on my time in Germany during the war, but nothing stands out. Nothing to bring about all this. Fatigue washes over me and I drift back to the day that never leaves my mind in 1866, the day the monster took my wife and my child. The events are still vivid. I wish they weren't, but they're etched in like a deep scratch on glass. There's no getting rid of it.

In a daze of sorts, the words "Komm Zu Mir" slip from my mouth. "Come to me" in German. The words puzzle me until I remember my recurring nightmare. Those words are echoes of what happened, haunting me in my dreams.

My eyes widen in recognition, and my posture straightens. Can it be him? Is he the one behind all this? There's no reason for him to come after me, and according to Aron Johnson, he shouldn't exist anymore. I shake my head. No. It doesn't add up. There must be something else. I tap my forehead in frustration. *Think, Calloway.*

The door opens, interrupting my thoughts. Kerry and Simon enter. Kerry walks to the chair opposite from me and sits, folder in hand. Simon leans on the wall next to the door, arms folded. His face reveals discomfort, and I wonder who's going to be the good cop.

Kerry opens the folder, taking pictures out, and places them in front of me. A picture of Riley and the crime scene—my business card, the handkerchief, a strand of hair, the postcard. Other pictures include April Thompson, Nicole Leedy, a picture of the blood bags they confiscated, and the letter found in my office.

I scan the evidence. None of it points to me being the killer. It's loose at best. I slept with some of them and I lost control on Riley. I don't know if Kerry's aware of my involvement with Riley until he pulls out another picture. My bathroom garbage with what appears to be blood splatter. I threw the protective cloth I used for Riley's arm in it. But that doesn't mean they got any recognizable DNA.

The heat of Simon's gaze burns through me. I look at Kerry. His arms are folded, smug as he gloats. He's enjoying this. I suppose I would too if the tables were reversed.

"Why don't you tell me about your relationship with Riley. How do you know her?" Kerry asks.

I look at Simon. "Simon and I went for drinks at the Shipwreck a few weeks ago. I met her there. We ended up back at my place. Had a good time and sent her home in an Uber."

"Did you know her before that or talk to her afterward?"

I don't want to give any appearance that I'm nervous or have any reason to be. I lean back in my chair and prop my leg on the table. I shake my head. "No. One and done. That's how I roll."

Kerry glances at my leg but says nothing. He's going to take his time before he applies pressure. "We found your business card. How do you suppose she came about that?"

"Not something I know anything about."

"Who's William Thomas?"

I laugh. "That's a waste of a question. I thought they trained you better than that."

Kerry slams a fist on the desk. "You think this is funny. I ought to throw you in a cell. We can continue when you're ready to take this seriously."

Simon straightens his stance and steps forward. "Jack, you know we gotta ask. We need to sort this out. Don't make things worse than they already are." His eyes plead.

"It's my given name. And to your next question, No. I don't know how she got it. When I checked the drawer with my pocket squares, it was missing. Maybe she took it the night she came over. I never saw her before that night or since."

Kerry points to a picture. "We found this blood inside your bathroom garbage. Seems like an odd place, absent of any blood bags. What do you think the DNA analysis will reveal? Will it be a match to Ms. Jackson? Or will it match someone else?"

I want to look at Simon, but I won't take the risk. I hope I've covered my tracks, and he has said nothing about me losing control. "I don't have blood agreements with anyone. I only drink from a bag. Running down this trail won't get you anywhere useful in this investigation."

"I find your connections to these deaths quite damning. You've had some sort of intimate connection to all of them. You hang out at any other bars, Jack? Or do you like to take all your victims to the Shipwreck, like Riley Jackson and LeighAnne...?" He flips through his notes. "LeighAnne Grigsby."

"You can't be serious? I had nothing to do with LeighAnne, and I didn't kill any of these women. Open your eyes. Someone's setting me up. If you can't see that, then you're not good at your job."

I turn to Simon. "Doc has impressions of my teeth. Check the measurements. Call Meghan. I have alibis and video footage on my comings and goings that will show I can't be the killer. Simon, you know I'm not the killer."

Before Simon can reply, there's a knock at the door and it opens. Someone whispers something to Simon, and he leaves the room. I look at Kerry. "You're wasting your time focusing on me."

Simon steps back into the room. He holds my gaze and sighs. "No Vita-Life was found in your blood order. The letter found in your office, the note left with Nicole Leedy, and the paper in Riley's mouth, all the same as the paper found in your apartment. Along with the DNA match of Riley's blood."

Simon glances at Kerry and then at me. "You're charged with the murder of Nicole Leedy, product tampering, and the aggravated assault and murder of Riley Jackson."

"And when we're done with you, you'll face murder charges on these other victims." Kerry rises, walks to me, and leans in. I can feel his breath on my neck. "I'll personally make sure you meet True Death. You won't walk this earth any longer."

I look at Simon, trying to gauge his internal response. He squeezes his eyes shut when Kerry says the words True Death. Those aren't words vampires throw around easily and yet for Kerry, who lacks the finesse needed for these situations, the words roll off his tongue with a sharp bite.

Simon focuses his gaze on Kerry. Behind his eyes is a raging battle, a conflict between his obligation and duty to serve, protect, and maintain the balance between two worlds and his friend. The scales are tipping, and I'm not sure where he'll land. I'm counting on him to not give up on me.

Kerry stands, gathering the file. Simon walks to me, anchors his hand around my forearm, and pulls me to my feet. "Sorry, Jack. Got no choice." His gaze drops to the floor.

Simon escorts me through the corridor and down the stairs to my new home. He slides a steel door to the left, and I walk inside the stark room. The cell has the same protective elements as the interrogation room. I could be incapacitated with a push of a button.

I turn to Simon and he takes the handcuffs off and whispers, "In case anyone's watching." He slams his fist into my chest, knocking me back. He steps closer and continues talking just above a whisper. "I'll continue to work this and find out what's going on." His fist meets my jaw and I stagger back. He grabs my arm to steady me.

I yank my arm away. I understand what he's doing, but it wouldn't be normal for me to stand by and not act. I ball my hand into a fist and deliver a blow to his kidney. Simon doubles over.

"You don't think I'm guilty. Do you?"

He shakes his head. "Big holes in the evidence. As you said, alibis and timestamps don't account for it all. Someone's behind this."

He pauses." I don't think there's much I can do about the aggravated assault. You'll get a tribunal before they decide. You won't get transferred to Seattle PD until then."

"When will that be?"

"Three days, maybe four."

I need Simon to look at all the evidence and make sure he's looking in all the right places. Time isn't on my side. "Then you have little time to figure this out."

"I'll scour video footage, get the impressions from Doc. I'll work on it."

"Gather all the evidence on James Everly. It's clear he's involved. I think our vampire killed him and found another accomplice. Also, Brad Jensen. Shannon was dating him and there's something not right about him. He's the one who broke into her house. I have Paul Crandon tailing him. Check-in with Paul."

Simon's fists tighten and the muscles in his jaw flex. "She's dating Brad Jensen? The guy who broke into her house?"

Of course, that's what he hears. "Was, not anymore."

The display of care and concern he expresses angers me. "I don't know what's gotten into you or what's going on between you and Shannon, but let me remind you, you're a vampire. She's human. If I somehow get out of this, and you hurt her in any way, you'll meet your demise."

A threat. Stupid really, because Simon's my one chance to get free.

He takes a step toward me, grabs my shirt, and pulls me closer, baring his fangs. I don't flinch, and he says nothing. A few seconds lapse before he backs away, straightening his shirt.

I understand his reaction, and it tells me all I need to know. "Just make sure Shannon's safe. And Carla, too. I hired protective details for both. Paul knows to keep you informed. I've got a feeling this vampire isn't done and those close to me are at risk."

"Got it. You aren't the only competent detective in this town."

I smile. "Let's hope not. Oh, and one last thing. Have Nick get me an attorney."

CHAPTER 27

Carla Briggs

CARLA REFLECTED ON THE FACT that Jack Calloway had exited her life again. No return calls. Nothing. She thought about the other night being in his embrace. One evening closed the distance between the past and the present. It'd been three years, but to her, it was like time hadn't slipped between them.

It was a craving. An itch. And it was barely enough. Raw and intimate. An apology. But Jack was communicating something else. She couldn't be sure what it was, but she wanted to believe it was more than lust.

She got entangled in his orbit again. Carla had been pulled in like a magnet, and she couldn't have resisted if she tried. Why hasn't Jack called? Two days had passed with no communication.

She cursed at herself for being that girl. Yeah, the one who pines and waits for some guy to give her the time of day. Yet, she couldn't shake the feeling there was something more about their night together. A permanence to it. He not only communicated his regrets, but also his love. Jack disappearing made little sense. But didn't he disappear on her before?

Carla thought about Ted. He was the real deal. He was happily ever after. But ever since this case, ever since Jack's been in her space again, she couldn't see Ted as anything more than someone to have a pleasant conversation with. Sure, in bed Ted satisfied. He was tender and attentive, but never passionate. The chemistry she and Jack had was something entirely different. It was like an inferno, begging to be extinguished. Thinking about it stirred Carla's insides.

She knew something wasn't right the morning Jack left her house. It was in his eyes. He tried to reassure her with a hug and a kiss, but his eyes were pensive and distant. Jack was already somewhere else. More was going on with this case, and Carla needed to find out what it was.

As she drove to the South Precinct, the morning rain was pouring thick, making it hard to see through her windshield. She switched the wipers on high and let recall of the road guide her. Ed called and wanted to go over all the evidence with her, including the recent deaths of Emma Davis and James Everly.

Ed made his feelings clear when he accused Jack of murder, and Carla was angry about that. She wondered who was the suit at the table and why was he involved? The way Jack and he interacted, they were familiar with one another, but not in a friendly way. If it hadn't been for the chief, she knew Ed and the suit would have hauled Jack in. Maybe that's why Jack hadn't contacted her, he's sitting somewhere in a Seattle PD cell.

When Carla arrived at the precinct, she went straight to the conference room. The door was open. Ed had his back turned to the doorway, staring at the crime scene wall. A memory of Ed and Carla, when they were first married, flashed in her mind.

She had come home early and walked into the kitchen where he was standing over the sink, arranging flowers to put into a vase. When he heard her, he waved her out of the kitchen, his hand flapping over his shoulder, his back to her. Carla couldn't return until he finished. The vase with a bouquet of her favorite flowers— white lilies, was sitting on the kitchen table.

Her heart dropped at the memory. The distance between then and now was steep. At one time, they believed in a forever, but that time had long gone.

Carla cleared her throat. "Hey." Ed jerked his head, startled.

He smiled and pointed to the counter. "Coffee?"

"Sure." She went to the coffeepot and poured a cup, adding a splash of half and half. She turned to find Ed staring at her. She stirred her coffee as she focused on the crime wall. "You wanted to discuss the case?"

He glanced at the folder on the table. It was open and his notes were scattered. "Ah. Yeah." He scratched the back of his head.

A picture of Jack with strings running from his picture to Riley Jackson, April Thompson, and Nicole Leedy, had been added to the crime wall. Evidence tying Jack to those murders were pinned around his picture. Ed's gaze was on her the entire time, watching her reaction to the added evidence. Carla looked at him.

His eyes narrowed. "Carla. We have to look at this objectively. Whether or not we like it, Jack's involved."

She shrugged, trying to shake off his words. "I don't know. We need to keep an open mind, but Jack's worked for the Seattle PD for several years. He's practically one of us. He's never given me any reason to be suspicious."

Ed frowned and snorted dismissive laughter. Carla was sure he thought she was blindly defending Jack. She pointed to the crime wall. "Not in this way."

"Yeah, but what do you really know about him? When I investigated his background, there were inconsistencies. Strange things."

The muscles in her shoulders stiffened. Of course, he would dig into Jack's background, but it still surprised her. Carla could barely believe they were having this conversation. "What do you mean?"

Ed reached for the table, grabbing his notes. "What is he, thirty? No school records. No birth records. No family records. I found a private detective named Jack Calloway in the 1980s, would've been around the same age as Jack is now. There aren't any birth records for him either. Or death records. It's like he vanished." A single eyebrow lifted when Ed asked her pointedly, "How do you explain all that?"

Carla stepped back and glanced away momentarily. "Maybe it was his dad?"

The muscles in Ed's jaw ticked at her response. "Well, where's his dad now?"

She shrugged. Once, she'd asked Jack about his family and he told her they were dead. The forlorn look in his eyes when he said that was enough information for Carla. She dropped any further questions on the subject. She figured he would tell her what he wanted when he wanted to. What little she knew, Carla was going to keep to herself—for now.

Ed's hand raised in exasperation. "That's my point. You don't know. We don't know. It's like he's showed up out of thin air. And now all this." He pointed to the connections between Jack and the dead women.

Carla straightened her shoulders, swallowing her anger. "Ed, how objective can you be on this? You don't like Jack. Maybe you're looking for things that aren't there. Maybe it's become too personal for you. I may not have answers to your questions, but I know him. This isn't him."

Ed averted his gaze and stepped back. His voice softened. "I'm gathering evidence and looking at it. And the evidence is pointing to him. Maybe it's too personal for you."

She ignored his statement. She knew it was personal. But she also knew this conversation was dragging in the past that did not belong—betrayal and heartaches. Better left alone.

Carla loosened her shoulders, turned away from Ed, and walked to the head of the table. "Your theories are missing key evidence. The forensic evidence in the Hamilton crime scene, there was DNA found under the victim's nails. It belongs to a Brad Jensen, and the person who killed Emma Davis was right-handed. Jack's left-handed. Better add that to your crime wall and find out who Brad Jensen is. Stop wasting your time on Jack."

Ed frowned, silently cursing as he stared at the crime wall. He sighed. "My gut says Jack's connected. The paper left in Riley's mouth was the same paper found in Jack's apartment. And evidence of Riley's blood was found in his apartment too."

Her eyes narrowed. How would he know this? "Evidence from who? Not from my lab."

Ed reached to the table for another report. "When I was researching the case files this morning, I found this report."

She grabbed the report, studying it. Carla pushed out a deep breath. "From where?"

Ed shrugged. "Unknown. Not a lot of information on this, which is strange too." She handed the report to Ed.

Carla licked her lips and pressed them into a thin line, thoughts running through her head about Jack and Riley. "I agree there's a lot that doesn't add up, but what you have on Jack is circumstantial. We have scientific, verifiable evidence on James Everly and now Brad Jensen. What you should do is look for evidence that rules Jack out. Do you have video footage, witness statements, or other supporting evidence that places Jack at any of these crime scenes?"

Ed didn't answer that question. She knew he didn't have it. His focus had become tunneled, and he was grasping, trying to fit crooked pieces into a perfect mold.

His gaze landed on her. "You need to be careful." He stepped to her and his eyes softened. "I know you still…"

Carla waved a hand, cutting him off. "I'll be fine. I don't know what's going on, but I'm telling you you're looking in the wrong places." She gulped the last drink of her coffee, threw it in the trash, grabbed her things, and left. Carla briskly walked out of the precinct. The muscles in her jaw clenched, and her heart raced. She must talk to Jack and find out what's going on. But that's a problem, isn't it? She hadn't been able to get a hold of him.

Carla called Jack's office and cell phone again, but no one answered. She left another message, telling him it was urgent. She had a bad feeling.

She thought back on their night together. There was a sense of urgency to it. Carla wanted to believe it was the charge between them, but there was something else. Sure, it was unapologetic and tender and it was obvious Jack missed her. The call he received that morning changed his mood and, as much as he tried to cover it up, his eyes conveyed worry. She had to find him and figure out what was going on.

Carla pulled into the parking garage of Jack's building and took the elevator to the main floor. She stepped out to access Jack's penthouse elevator. *Penthouse.* She never asked Jack where he got all his money. It wasn't from his P.I. gig. Sure, he was in high demand, and well respected in the law enforcement community for his criminal profiles. But respect didn't pay for his penthouse.

When Carla taught Essentials in Toxicology class for the law enforcement agencies in San Francisco last year, Jack's name came up. It wasn't the first time his name was thrown around in one of her classes. He was well known for his uncanny ability to see what others missed.

Maybe that was the reason she couldn't cut ties with Jack, not emotionally anyway. He was always there in the atmosphere. She tried to block him out by working, teaching classes, and dating. Dating had been dismal.

Carla pressed a button on the keypad next to the elevator. A few seconds passed, and she pressed it again. No one answered. She turned to peer into Jack's office. The lights were off. Where could he be? Out of town? Other than Shannon, who's not around either, who else would know where Jack was or how she could get a hold of him?

Ed's words echoed in her mind. *What do you know about him?* What did she know? Carla thumbed through the files in her mind, trying to remember anything Jack said about the people close to him. She streamed through the images and conversations until she landed on one—Godson. That's right, she had been introduced to Jack's godson, Nick the owner of the Shipwreck. Maybe Nick knows where Jack is. Carla got back into her car and drove to work. On the way, she decided when her day was through, she'd stop by the Shipwreck. She needed to find Jack and nothing was going to stop her.

CHAPTER 28

Carla Briggs

BY THE TIME CARLA GOT away from work and went to the Shipwreck, it was four p.m. She walked through the double doors. The room was mostly dark, as most taverns are, but this one was unusually dark and lit by soft, warm lighting. It took a moment for her eyes to adjust, and when they did, Carla saw only a handful of people. Each one of them had stopped what they'd been doing and were staring at her. She felt self-conscious and looked behind her, hoping someone else had their attention. There wasn't anyone. She swallowed hard and continued to walk to the bar.

Carla looked around the bar area for Nick. When she saw him, he was walking out of his office talking to a server. He must have sensed her because he stopped in his tracks and stared at her. She shrugged it off as if his reaction meant nothing, but something told her it did.

Hurriedly, Nick walked toward Carla. As he did, she blinked hard twice, trying to clear her eyes. His body bristled, his posture stiffened, and his torso expanded. She was sure she had imagined it. Carla reasoned it was probably the nervousness she felt with everyone staring at her.

"Carla. What brings you here?" He barked, and she took a step back. His voice shook her, and she wondered if she had done something wrong. Carla straightened her posture and pushed forward with her inquiry.

"Jack's missing. Well, I don't know if he's missing, but something's not right and I can't get a hold of him."

Nick smiled and his cold eyes melted. He stepped to Carla and with an arm around her waist ushered her into his office. "What do you mean he's missing?" The hostility in his voice had been replaced with a gentleness that rolled through her. Nick pointed at the chair, signaling her to sit.

Carla didn't want him to dismiss her. She needed him to understand the urgency of the situation. However, she wasn't sure how much she could share with him, but since he was the only family she knew Jack had, she pressed on.

"We're working together on an important case. He was on to something, and now I think he's being accused of a crime he didn't commit. I've left messages and haven't heard from him. I'm worried something bad has happened or will happen."

Nick's face remained neutral. He was calm, which made her wonder if he knew more. "Do you have any idea where I can find him?"

Instead of answering her question, he excused himself, telling her he needed to make a call and to hang on. Five minutes later he returned. He leaned on his file cabinets and with a soft chuckle said, "I've known Jack a long time. He travels out of town for work often. Probably on a new case. I'm not surprised. I've learned if Jack doesn't want to be found, you won't find him."

Carla's teeth clenched as she resisted the urge to bite back at him. She shook her head. "This isn't that."

Another man, handsome and built, walked into the office. His shirt sleeves were rolled half-way up his forearm, revealing tattoos and strength. A brown, red-highlighted beard was neatly trimmed, unlike Nick's, whose beard was unkempt. The man's eyes were alert but narrowed as his gaze met hers. He wore black pants, black boots, and stood in the doorway. Something about him was familiar, but she couldn't put her finger on what it was.

Nick's posture straightened. "Simon. This here's Carla."

Simon extended his hand. His shake was firm. "Carla, nice to meet you."

She smiled. "We sort of met the other day."

Simon turned to Nick. "When you're done, Nick, I have some questions about the incident the other night."

"Okay. Hey. Carla's asking about Jack. She thinks he's missing."

"I talked to him a couple of hours ago. Sounded like he somewhere North," Simon said.

The two men towered over Carla and she felt caged in by their commanding presence. She stood to gain equal footing. "You talked to him. He's okay then?"

Simon's stance relaxed. "He's fine. I wouldn't worry about him. He'll resurface. He always does."

Nick laughed. "Like a bad penny. I'm sure he'll call you when he can."

Carla didn't buy their nonchalance. She knew they were placating and brushing her off. Most likely they thought she was overreacting. A woman pining over Jack, that's all.

She smiled softly. "If you're sure he's okay, I'll wait for him to call."

Simon stepped toward Carla. "Let me walk you out." She nodded, and he followed, walking her to her car. She told him thanks, got into her car, and drove away.

Their responses were odd, and she wondered what they were hiding. Their smiles and relaxed postures covered a thick tension and told her Jack wasn't okay. She gripped the steering wheel, opened her mouth wide to relax her clenched teeth.

Carla arrived at her house and pulled into the garage. Just as she stepped out of her car, her phone rang. Her jaw tensed when she saw who it was. She had enough male chauvinism for one day. "Ed."

His voice was sharp and blunt. "Do you know where Jack is?"

"It's not like Jack and I keep in touch."

"Did you know Brad Jensen dated Shannon Tieg, Jack's assistant?

She huffed out a breath. "No, Ed. Why would I know that?"

"Brad Jensen is dead."

CHAPTER 29

Jack Calloway

A KNOCK ON MY CELL door interrupts my thoughts, bringing me back to the present. Back to the cage, I find myself in. I sit up and roll my shoulders to release the kinks. The clanging sound of three steel bolts unlatching is jarring. The door slides open. A lanky man with thick black hair walks in. His rounded eyeglasses make his angular face pronounced.

"Jack. Long time. May I sit down?"

I point at the only chair in the room. It's plastic and uncomfortable. "Jeremiah. Thanks for coming. The luxury awaits."

There's a tightness in my chest that loosens. I'm relieved to see Jeremiah Jones. One because I desperately need a lawyer, and two, because Simon isn't giving up on me.

Jeremiah offers legal representation to many Were packs. I helped him on a case a few years ago, when the Seattle PD went after the wrong man. The profile I produced led to the arrest and conviction of a woman. For what I've fallen into, I need someone like him, part human and part Were, who can represent me in both worlds, human and supernatural.

Jeremiah opens a file. He briefly looks through it, and then his gaze lands on mine. "You've got yourself in a pickle, Jack. Simon filled me in some and I've reviewed the evidence." Jeremiah's breath draws deep. "Can you trust Simon on this, being that he's the head of the Guard? You know my fondness for vampires, company not included. You can't trust them. And I'd rather we'd met somewhere not surrounded by vampires, but here we are."

Jeremiah's thought processes aren't always tangential, but he makes his points clear. "I can trust Simon. He won't stop until all the evidence is on the table. He'll run down all leads and make the right connections. I trust him more on this than the Seattle PD." I pause. "Did you have trouble getting into the campus building?"

Jeremiah's eyes convey satisfaction with my answer, and he doesn't press the matter further. "I'm here, aren't I? Let's get to it. Your tribunal is tomorrow afternoon. That'll be at minimum a review of the evidence."

I stand, my gaze on the floor. I pace the length of the bed, which isn't many steps. It's a small cot, not even long enough to keep my feet from hanging over the end. "Minimum I can handle. What's the worst-case scenario?"

He crosses his legs and straightens his back. "I'm not going to shine you on, the evidence doesn't look good. Worst case, they find you're guilty of murder, vampire-on-human murder, and the cause of all those deaths. The fact that you've fed on blood without Vita-Life doesn't help your case. At least it wasn't in your last blood order. You get a ninety-day supply, correct?'

I nod. "I've never needed it. I only took it to preserve what little relationship I had with the Dracul. Just insurance. I've been in control of myself for over one hundred years."

Jeremiah looks over the tops of his glasses. "Then what happened with Riley Jackson?"

I avert my eyes. "I don't know what that was."

"The worst-case scenario is True Death."

An anxiousness strangles my chest and sets off desperation. "Jeremiah, I didn't do this. Someone's setting me up. The evidence isn't solid, the timing doesn't align, and Simon needs more time to find the truth."

Jeremiah stands. "That's what I'm going to ask for—time. I need more to put a defense together. Damn vampires. Always in a hurry. I'll try to push it out to Thursday."

My shoulders deflate. "Let's hope Simon has cleared my name by then."

"I'll see you tomorrow," he says and walks out.

The bolts latching echo in my cell. I'm alone with my thoughts and the concrete blocks again. I think about Carla and what she's doing. I wonder what she thinks of me now. I didn't intend to shut her out. The thought grips my chest. Now, I may never see her again.

True Death. It crosses a vampire's mind from time to time, but you think you're invincible. Well, we practically are. Beheading will kill a vampire. A stake to the heart will put a vampire into a grave for eternity until it's removed or unless it's made of silver. A silver object stuck in a vampire's heart, kills. Sunlight is a mild burn, a slow rise of heat warming from the outside in. A week of continuous exposure would only result in first-degree burns. With sustenance, vampires continuously heal. Like I said, practically invincible.

My heart's another matter and those wounds don't heal easily. It was selfish of me to go to Carla the other night, but I couldn't stay away, especially knowing it might be my last chance to hold her. These past three years, she's all I've wanted and I've hated myself for that. I've hated myself for not giving her what she needs. Now, I hate myself for letting her feel rejected. If I make it out of this, she probably won't talk to me ever again. I slump back onto the bed.

Sometime later, I realize I must've drifted off when the sound of the sliding door causes me to bolt upright. I'm in warrior mode, ready for action. But the action doesn't find me. Simon walks into my cell, closing the door behind him.

He hands me a bag of blood and grunts, "Dinner."

I have had little of an appetite since they have locked me up. And he must've known because he says, "you need your strength." Then he growls, "Don't make me force you."

I reach for the bag and slurp it down. Satisfied that I ate, he takes a seat. "I hope you have some good news for me," I say.

He reaches for the back of his head, rubbing it. His face contorts. I can tell there's something he doesn't want to say. "We know the WHC was broken into about three months ago. The blood bags marked with the Vita-Life were switched out. We've reviewed the video footage and the only person we've been able to identify is the delivery man. As you know, he was killed by a vampire about six weeks ago. We know at the time of his death, you were in San Francisco."

This news makes my chest expand and my posture straighten. "Well, that's good news, isn't it?"

Simon hesitates before responding. "Yes and no. Dennis Mathews is his name. Know him?"

The name's vaguely familiar, and I search my mind on where and why. Then I remember. "Last year, I got an email from Dennis Mathews. He wanted to hire me. He claimed his identity was stolen and feared he was being followed. He sounded like a nut job and I had Shannon respond to his email, suggesting another P.I."

"Another connection to you, but loosely at least. He started working for the WHC in January of this year. How do you receive your deliveries?"

"Meghan signs for them and takes them up to my apartment. She has strict instructions not to open the boxes."

Simon's eyebrows furrow. "Any reason to believe that Meghan's in on this?"

I wave this notion away with both hands. "Trust her explicitly."

He tilts his head and gives me a quizzical look. "All the same to you, I'm going to look into that."

I avert my gaze and wonder if I can trust anyone. "Anything else?"

He nods. "I checked your video footage on the night Riley was murdered. You left the Shipwreck at nine-forty p.m. and got home at eleven-fifteen p.m. You didn't leave your place until nine-thirty a.m. the next day."

"Yeah. That sounds about right. What's Riley's time of death?"

"Ten-thirty to eleven p.m. You could've killed her and made it home by then."

My eyes widen in surprise. How easy it was for him to suggest I killed her. "From the Shipwreck? Even for me, that's pushing it."

Simon crosses his legs, leaning back in his chair, exhibiting a non-threatening posture. A move to set the suspect at ease. "When you left the Shipwreck, where did you go?"

I shake my head reluctantly. "I don't remember." And I don't. It's completely blank.

He lifts an eyebrow, questioning me. "Come on, Jack, you don't remember? That will not help you."

I heat up inside and pull at my collar. "I know. I know. But I swear, it's blank. I remember leaving and I remember waking up the next morning."

Simon is quiet. When he speaks, his voice is low. "You know how that looks?"

I grimace. "Like bloodlust took over."

A loud exhale escapes his mouth. He shakes his head, averting his gaze from mine before saying, "Exactly. I think I'm able to rule out your direct involvement in the other murders, but you're not in the clear on Riley."

I think about the implications of the words 'direct involvement,' but more so, I wonder what indirect means. "Are you saying if I'm cleared of any direct involvement, I can still be implicated indirectly?"

"We want to make sure it doesn't look like you're the one pulling the strings. Clear evidence coupled with a good defense will help."

My stomach lurches. I lean over with my arms crossed, pressing in on my stomach. It isn't a hunger pang, I'm soothing. "That doesn't sound good."

"I'm still working on this. I haven't given up." He hesitates. "And Shannon's helping."

My breath hitches. My thoughts jumble with worry, and they come out in a string of chopped-up statements. "I don't want Shannon to know about us. I don't want something bad to happen to her because she's associated with me. It'd be my fault. My fault for not taking care of her. For having her near me."

"Jack, stop whatever you're thinking. She doesn't know about us. Her detail has been with her and I'm checking in on her. All she knows is that you went away on a case and could be gone for a week or two. She knows you asked for my help. I'm working with her on the digital footprints and I've asked her to keep me apprised on anything she finds." Simon stops and momentarily averts his eyes, staring at the wall. He smiles. "But she's curious, and I'm doing what I can to keep her distracted from this line of the investigation."

I frown. My imagination of what's keeping her distracted makes me uncomfortable. Shannon's an attractive young woman. Dark brown hair, an angled cut that follows her jawline, and warm hazel eyes. She has high cheekbones and a dainty nose. When she's mad, her face flushes and with one look she could drop you to your knees, figuratively speaking. Physically, she can too, with her training in Judo. She's smart and street savvy. Any man would be attracted to her, and that's what I want for her, a man. Not a vampire. I flex my hands and bring my fingers to my temples, rubbing the tension away. "I don't like what your smile is suggesting. I get it. She's attractive enough that you'd have to be blind not to notice, but what can you offer her, Simon? Not much. She's a good girl, smart. Our world isn't for her."

"I don't know, Jack, I…"

I hold up my hand. "Save it. You know how I feel." I also know by the look in his eye, he's smitten.

Simon shuffles his feet in nervousness. "I've tasked her to focus on the timelines of James Everly. She wants to stay involved in the investigation. She's safe and at your apartment now."

"What does she think your job is?"

"I told her I often work for you, that I'm a P.I. too."

"I guess that's a suitable cover, not too far from the truth. If it comes to her safety or sanity, compel her. I don't want her screwed up by this."

Simon goes quiet. His lips thin and his eyes dart. "Something you're not telling me?" I ask.

"Carla went to the Shipwreck a couple of hours ago looking for you."

My heart skips a beat. I stand abruptly, my mind racing. "She didn't. By herself? Is she all right? Was she hurt?"

Simon pats the air with his hands, signaling me to calm down. "She's fine. Nick was there and made sure no one else got to her. She too knows you're on a case and when you can, you'll resurface."

I should've been focused on the fact she went to the Shipwreck, and the danger she put herself in, but the moment he said she was looking for me, I couldn't stop my heart from flipping. "She went there asking about me?"

"Yes. And she seemed beyond concerned."

"What does that mean?"

He smirks and raises his eyebrows. "Like the concern you don't have for just a colleague."

I look away. This isn't a conversation I'm prepared to have. Especially since I've been trying to steer Simon away from a human. What would I say? I love her and I've been a stupid fool. No, I can't say that even if it's the truth.

"Didn't you place security on her?"

"Yeah, started last Friday."

"I didn't see anyone. Not in the Shipwreck and not in the parking lot."

I know there was one assigned. Hell, I saw him Friday morning before I left Hamilton Park. My instructions were to be a shadow, but Simon can spot shadows, and in this case, he would smell it. Panic rose in my throat. "There should be someone around her at all times. Contact Paul for me and find out what happened." He agrees with a nod.

"Did she buy it, that I'm out of town?"

With a mischievous look, Simon shakes his head. "Not for a second."

Simon stands. "I've got to get going. I'll see you tomorrow at the tribunal." Before he leaves, I thank him again.

My insides churn thinking about Carla's missing detail. I shake my head. What a mess this is. How do I protect her when I'm locked up? I've got to find a way out of this. If something happens to Carla, I don't think I'd come back from that.

I also know if she doesn't hear from me, she'll keep digging until she finds the answers she's seeking. And some answers aren't worth digging for. I better find a way to call her. Tonight.

I pound on the door, yelling for someone. At least thirty minutes pass before the small metal plate in the door slides open. It's big enough for me to know Jarvis is standing on the other side of the door. The last person I need right now.

He barks, "What do you want?"

I look up to the ceiling. If I believed in a God, I would silently pray for mercy. "Someone other than you. Who else is working?"

He grunts. If Jarvis spoke in complete sentences, you would know he's college-educated and his speech, believe it or not, is eloquent. But all I get are grunts and barks. "You got me. What d'you want?"

I take a deep breath, slowly releasing it. I need to convince him to help me. "I need to make a phone call. It's urgent."

"Not somethin' I care about," he says.

I clear my throat to not choke on my anger. "Jarvis. I need to let my human colleague know I'm okay. If she doesn't hear from me, she won't let it go and I don't want her to know about *us* or this." I point around the cell.

He's quiet and his eyes narrow. I can tell he's weighing whether or not he can trust me. He reaches for the latches and unlocks the door. He steps in and pulls out his phone, handing it to me. "Make it quick." He crosses his arms, standing like a statue, watching my every move.

I enter her number and push send. It rings. Rings. And rings again. I turn my back to Jarvis and walk to the corner of the room, listening to her message. Like a warm compress, the sound of her voice soothes the muscles in my shoulders.

"Carla. It's Jack. I'm sorry it's taken me this long to let you know what's going on. I'm on a case and I'll be out of town for a few days. I'll contact you when I get back." I linger. I want to say more. Tell her I'm thinking of her. Tell her I want to wake up with her every day. Tell her I love her. But Jarvis is listening, towering over my words, and I don't need him knowing any more than he already does.

I hang up and hand him the phone. "Thanks," I say. He grunts and walks out. The door slams shut and latches with a clunk, binding me to this solitary cell once again.

CHAPTER 30

Jack Calloway

A TRAY OF BLOOD BAGS sits on the floor. They're arranged in alphabetical order—A, AB, O. The blood is a rich, dark red. The bags are face up, and the tubes point toward me. They should beckon to me, but my unfocused gaze burns past them. Despite what Simon said about keeping up my strength, I've lost my appetite. I shift my position away from the tray to face the wall.

Time ticks away slowly, like a vampire's beating heart. Thump. Thump. Thump. The sound bangs in my ears. I've gone from pent-up energy, ready to bust through these walls to an unmovable malaise. I can only hope the tribunal will go in my favor.

At the sound of the door opening, I rise, inching to a sitting position. My legs hang over the bed. Someone I don't recognize—a vampire stands outside the doorway. "Time to go," he announces with finality to his words.

I stand, shaking out my arms and legs before they're shackled. He walks in, telling me to put my arms in front of me, and he snaps handcuffs over my wrists. Next, he locks chains around my ankles. A small fire burns inside, pushing me to test the handcuffs, pulling with my full strength. I know I can't escape, and if I tried, I'd be unconscious in no time.

He looks at me, his eyebrows raise. I shrug. "Just testing." They're impenetrable.

We walk through the basement corridor; the light is dim, and the potent smell of mildew wafts in the air. We reach a set of stairs and I hesitate. The thought of maneuvering them with my feet chained is daunting. A hand reaches my underarm and steadies my steps.

At the top, we walk through another set of doors. At the end of the hallway, two large maple doors, side by side, greet us. Two guards stand post, one on each side. Above the door written in Latin are the words "Sit iustitia videbunt lucem." May justice see the light. It's in this room where my fate will be determined.

One guard opens the door, and his gaze meets my eyes. There's a softness to them and he tips his head. I return the gesture with a smile.

The doors close behind me, and my eyes take in the room. A high ceiling is surrounded by maple-paneled walls. There's one window on the right side, extending from the floor to the ceiling. Soft ambient lights jut out from the side walls, giving the appearance of warmth.

Centered in the room are two small oval tables. A wide walkway separates them. At the tables, three blue leather chairs await their arriving guests. Several steps away, a large horseshoe-shaped table wraps the room. It's slightly elevated, giving the appearance of power and stature for those who sit there. The table's big enough to seat at least fifteen people, but only five chairs are in place. My shoulders slack and my chest caves inward. Five people will determine my fate today.

I'm ushered toward the center of the room and to the right, Jeremiah, my counsel sits, thumbing through a file. I join, taking a seat next to him.

He tilts his head, looking over his glasses at me. "Jack, you're looking paler than usual. Are they feeding you?"

I straighten my posture. "I haven't felt like eating."

I'm distracted by raised voices behind the entrance doors. I listen in. Low growls and heated discussion ensue. A familiar scent reaches me. I would recognize it anywhere, and I'm not sure how I feel about him being here. I whisper to Jeremiah, whose eyes are already on the door. "It's Nick." He nods as if he already knows.

Jeremiah stands, which is more like a leap, and walks through the doors. He's reasoning with the guards, letting them know Nick's family and he's here to support me. That takes more convincing because who would believe a were-person and a vampire are family. Not only is it dangerous, but it's also not natural.

I watch the door. Soon it opens and both Jeremiah and Nick walk through. My gaze meets Nick's. The look on his face is grim with worry. I nod and smile. He finds a chair along the back wall and sits.

Jeremiah returns to our table and as soon as he does, the door in the back-left corner of the room opens and several vampires walk in.

I recognize four of the five men, who are now finding their seats in front of us. Aron Johnson, Simon's father, Beau Whitmore from South Carolina, Philip Xavier from Spain, and Raul Rocha from Brazil. What's surprising is of the four I know, they are all members of the twelve original families. They are Dracul. This knowledge sounds off alarms in my head. I'm not sure what to make of it, but my stomach lurches and with an elbow on the table, my hand reaches my forehead. Tension creeps across my shoulders. I remember the last time I was in a room with at least three of these men.

These same men decided what level of involvement the Ascenders would have with the Department of Homeland. I wasn't their favorite choice for a representative, but I operated in both worlds, and choosing me made the most sense. They agreed to my involvement only because Aron vouched for me. He agreed to take responsibility for my actions, and I agreed to take the Vita-Life blood mix.

I nudge Jeremiah for the identity of the unknown man. He leans over and whispers, "Carl Schneider."

I recognize the name. "Schneider. From Germany?"

He nods. "The same."

I ask under my breath. "Why are the families in Seattle?"

Jeremiah answers, his gaze fixed on the men. "Who can ever really know the reasons vampires do what they do." He shifts his focus to me. "What I've heard is several of the families are in town. Why, I don't know. Obviously, some of them are joining us today as judges."

The confidence drains from my body and I notice concern in Jeremiah's narrowed eyes as he studies his file. Great, neither of us is confident.

I'm so focused on why they're in Seattle and calming the impending doom rising in my throat, I don't see Simon walk in. He sits at the table across from ours. I wonder if he knew the Dracul would be here today. Our gazes meet. He has a great poker face which is flat and other than his pursed lips, he doesn't reveal much. If Simon knew the families were overseeing today's proceedings, he would've told me.

Simon's purpose here is to answer questions the judges have on the charges and evidence against me. He'll do his best to provide facts and remain impartial. It needs to be clear he has done his job thoroughly and with integrity. He's in a precarious situation, working secretly on my behalf and needs to be careful. Now, his life is threaded with mine.

Aron clears his throat and scans the room. "I assume everyone who needs to be here is here, correct?" Jeremiah replies with a "yes sir."

"Then let's get started."

"Today's proceedings will include a review of the charges brought against Jack Calloway, evidence that supports those charges, and based on that evidence, the judges will determine how to proceed. Also, information on Jack's character and history of his behaviors may influence final decisions made by this panel. If charges are supported, a sentence up to True Death can be exacted. Jack, do you understand the nature of these proceedings?"

I nod. "Yes, sir."

"Counsel, how would you like to proceed?"

Jeremiah stands and steps around the table, addressing the panel. "Sirs, thank you. I'd like to start by asking for a two-day delay in these proceedings. I only met Jack yesterday, and we need additional time to review the charges and evidence he's facing and prepare a proper defense."

The panel pulls in together and talks in whispers. They open files in front of them. Philip points to a paper he pulls out. The discussion continues for five minutes.

They right themselves, straightening their postures, and Aron addresses Jeremiah. I can't tell if it was in my favor or not because his face is neutral, but when he says, "Denied," it's clear. "Let's move forward. Raul, please read the charges."

Jeremiah returns to the table, his face neutral, not revealing his feelings about the Dracul's denial. "Jack Calloway, you are charged with murder, aggravated assault, and product tampering. What do you say to these charges?"

"Sirs, I plead not guilty. I believe someone's trying to set me up. The evidence is circum…"

Jeremiah kicks my ankle, causing my face to contort into a grimace. He cuts me off. "Sorry sirs, Jack doesn't presume to know what all the evidence is, but he's stating he's not guilty."

For the next hour, I listen intently as they discuss the evidence and ask Simon questions. Many times, I want to add my explanations or theories, but when I open my mouth, Jeremiah is quick to kick my ankle, although softer than the first time.

Jeremiah points out when my alibis, video surveillance, or other evidence doesn't coincide with forensic evidence collected or the time of deaths. He was denied the added time to prepare, but he had been thorough in his understanding of all the details to date. He doesn't falter or miss anything important. I only hope it's enough.

I peer at Simon occasionally, wondering how he's holding up as his father asks him questions about me. He's asked about my character and work ethic. His position must be difficult, a member of one of the families, head of the Guard, and my friend. He remains stoic throughout, answering the questions directly. When the questions turn to Riley Jackson, at times his voice sounds strangled, as if caught in his throat. He testifies about the night I met her. What were my mood and behavior? They move to Riley's crime scene. They know I was there and they ask how I acted when I found out it was Riley's dead body.

Simon is prepared, his case notes in front of him. He looks over at me when they question him about the German notes and my dad's handkerchief. The inquiry on the items written in German prompts Carl Schneider to ask further questions. Jeremiah argues the killer planted evidence during the break-in at my place.

Beau Whitmore with his Southern drawl steers the conversation to the blood bank break-in and subsequent death of the delivery driver. "We have here that Mr. Calloway's current blood shipment which he received last February did not contain the Vita-Life mix. Mr. Calloway has taken Vita-Life for several years. On the night he took Riley Jackson home, we understand Mr. Calloway lost control, and she nearly died. We also understand it wasn't only Mr. Calloway's order that had been tampered with. Simon, please discuss your findings on this."

Before Simon answers, Jeremiah adds, "Sirs, Jack doesn't deny he lost control, but we want you to be aware Jack took advantage of the medical training he received in the Army and used that training to give her a blood transfusion. In addition, he made sure she got to the hospital. It was never his intention to harm Ms. Jackson. It's been well over one hundred years since he's had to contend with bloodlust."

Aron nods. "Thank you, Mr. Jones. We've taken note."

Simon puts forward the evidence on the break-in, the days, and times the product was tampered with, by who, and the behavior and status of the delivery man. He discusses separate case evidence from the three vampire-to-human deaths his team investigated. He emphasizes in those cases, the blood orders were altered. Each of them, including me, had a break-in, and if there was video footage, something was faulty with it.

I'm appreciative when Simon relays I was out of town when both the third victim in the Seattle PD investigation and the delivery driver were killed.

Simon stands, glances over at me, and as if he throws away the script he says, "There isn't conclusive evidence that Jack's involved in these killings. I've worked with Jack and have known him for many years. He's a good man. I'd trust him with my life." He sits, waiting for further questions from the panel.

Raul Rocha, who'd been quiet through most of the inquiry, speaks. His eyes narrow as he stares at me. "I wonder if Riley Jackson would feel the same, after a clear loss of control and a near-death on Mr. Calloway's part. And a subsequent death that has Mr. Calloway's name written all over it?"

Jeremiah stands. His voice matter of fact. "The flaw in that argument gentleman is the video footage recorded Mr. Calloway leaving the bar at nine-forty p.m."

Raul replies, his tone is condescending. "And not arriving home until eleven-fifteen. Plenty of time to kill Ms. Jackson. Can anyone tell us Mr. Calloway's whereabouts between leaving the bar and getting home?"

At the rear of the room, behind the closed doors, heated voices escalate. The men standing outside the door are blocking the entrance of someone. I hear the words "Homeland Security," and "National Inter-Species Crime Unit." Aron Johnson's face tightens, and he stands. "Simon, find out who it is."

I already know who it is, Kerry LaMoine. He's probably here to gloat at my demise, letting me take the fall for crimes I didn't commit. I watch Simon as he walks to the maple doors, closing them behind him. I hear Simon say to his men. "It's all right. He's on this case."

A few minutes later Kerry and Simon enter, walking to the oval table opposite me.

Simon speaks. "Sirs, additional evidence was brought to my attention. It has substantial weight in this case. May I present it?"

Aron glances to the panel members for confirmation. They all nod in agreement. "There's additional evidence supporting James Everly and Brad Jensen as the perps in the Seattle PD case. Mr. Calloway's office has been working on tracing the IP addresses from computers used to secure dates with the deceased women. Addresses were discovered, along with video footage of the perps. It's a café in the Queen Anne District. The time stamp on the IP address and video footage support other forensic evidence that those men were involved in the killings. Also, Brad Jensen was found dead early Monday morning, while Mr. Calloway was in custody. Since Jack was in custody, he couldn't have killed Brad Jensen. Dr. Ron Patterson has impressions of Mr. Calloway's teeth. The measurements don't match any of the victims in any of the cases. I have the reports here." Simon holds up a manila envelope.

Aron addresses Kerry. "For the record, please state your name and your affiliation with this case."

Kerry pushes his shoulders back and straightens his jacket. "My name's Kerry LaMoine. I work for the National Inter-Species Crime Unit as a lead investigator."

Aron points to the envelope sitting in front of Kerry and Simon. "This evidence, did you bring it here today? And if so, can you confirm that it's an accurate representation of the facts stated?"

Kerry nods. "We both have the reports on the teeth impressions, however, I brought forward the other evidence presented. The evidence we have doesn't place Mr. Calloway at any of the crime scenes."

I'm skeptical about Kerry's turn of character, but regardless, a flutter of hope rises in my chest. Shannon's work paid off, as did Doc's. I knew Doc would follow through on getting his reports to the right people.

Raul speaks. His voice is clipped. "What about Riley Jackson?"

Kerry answers. "Dr. Patterson found two different bite patterns on her neck. One is Mr. Calloway's and the other, unknown. The puncture wounds from Mr. Calloway's teeth were healed. However, the unknown wounds were made at the time near her death."

Jeremiah stands. "Sirs, considering the new evidence, my client's charges should be dropped."

Beau Whitmore replies. "There's still the matter of Mr. Calloway losing control and nearly killing a human. As you know, that's a punishable offense."

I stand and step around the table to address the panel, leaping around the foot launching for my ankle. "Sirs. Whoever the vampire is, has purposefully orchestrated all of this, to make it look like I'm the killer. I don't know who he is, and I don't know why, but I need to find that out. Any of my close associations," I glance at Simon, "are in danger until he's caught. Do whatever you want to do to me, but first, let me catch the killer. Let me make sure everyone's safe."

The panel quietly converses amongst themselves and I go back to my seat. Aron speaks first. His voice controlled. Exacting. "Does anyone have anything else to add before we deliberate on our decision?"

The room grows quiet. Only the sounds perceptible to vampires and were-persons can be heard. The slow beating of a vampire's heart. Throats bobbing up and down with each swallow. No one speaks.

Aron's commanding voice is decisive. "Very well. We'll take the new evidence, recess for thirty minutes, and come back with our decision."

They file out of the room through the side door. I lean back in my chair and look over to Kerry and Simon. They're immersed in a discussion while they flip through the reports in front of them. The muscles in my shoulders loosen and I let my head fall back, resting on top of the chair. I close my eyes. On one hand, I feel some relief and on the other, I worry about Carla.

Time takes on a different meaning when you've lived for as long as I have. There's no actual day or night. It all blends in a stream of activity. But it's in moments like this, where I feel the urgency of time, and it's inching along like a slug. I can hear the secondhand ticking around the clock.

The side door opens, jarring my attention, and I straighten my posture. The panel takes their seats. This time, it's Philip Xavier who speaks for them. "Mr. Calloway, we've reviewed the charges, the evidence in this case, and the testimonies presented today. It's clear to us there's a vampire in our community who doesn't hold to our mandates, and who's manipulating others to torture and kill for him. These aren't the codes set for us by the Dracul, and it isn't something this panel condones. As you know, we've set up our societies to live peacefully and in collaboration with humans. Not everyone has agreed with this, but we've been successful in our efforts over the last century. Actions as presented today threaten our very way of life— our existence. We cannot allow that. We've taken into consideration your history, your character, and the evidence presented and find that you are not guilty of the crimes brought here today."

"We emphasize caution, as it's clear you are being targeted. Because of this, your visibility puts us all in danger. We understand the desire for justice and even for revenge, but we cannot allow that. Therefore, although we're releasing you from custody, we require you to relinquish all your efforts in these cases. No checking in. No dropping by. Let the Guard, the Seattle PD, and NISCU handle this. Simon will keep you apprised of our efforts, but only because we know you well enough, to understand, you'll find a way to it if we don't. Better for us to control this than to lose control of you. Also, you're not to take on new cases. In other words, lie low for the next month. Go on a vacation. Understand?"

My shoulders release and a breath escapes my lungs. Do I like the terms? No. Can I live by them? Maybe. Will I agree because I don't want to hear what "or else" means? Yes. I have my life and at least I can protect Carla and Shannon. "Yes sirs, thank you."

The panel concludes and adjourns. Everyone stands. I shake Jeremiah's hand and murmur my appreciation. The response I get from him makes me laugh. "My bill will be in the mail." He smiles and winks. He gathers his things and leaves the room. Simon and Kerry walk over to me.

Simon places his hand on my shoulder. "We did it, Jack." I want to hug him, but we don't have that kind of relationship.

Instead, I extend my hand. "Thank you, Simon. You didn't let me down."

Simon points to Kerry. "Don't thank me, it's Kerry who rushed the new evidence over. I had a voice-mail about it but hadn't checked it."

I extend my hand to Kerry's. We shake. "I owe you for this."

"I wouldn't be doing my job if I ignored the evidence. I came after you hard. I will not apologize for doing my job. However, I could've listened to what you were saying. I'll enjoy you owing me. It'll be my calling card."

I chuckle. "One call, that's all. You're still not my favorite."

Kerry smiles. "Nor you, mine." He turns to Simon. "We need to get this bastard. You need intel, manpower, anything, let me know."

Nick approaches me, and with an enormous grin, throws his arms around me for a proper hug. "I don't know what I'd do without you." Tears well in his eyes.

I pat him on the back, reassuring him. "I'm not going anywhere."

Nick releases me.

Kerry leaves just as Aron Johnson approaches. "Boys. Outstanding work, Simon." Aron's three hundred and fifty years old, so I suppose we are boys to him, but being called so smarts a bit. "We'd like to speak to you both, let's go to the conference room in the back."

I smile at Nick and tell him I'll see him later.

We follow Aron through the side door into a small conference room. All panel members are sitting around a table. Aron motions for us to have a seat.

Carl Schneider addresses us. "Gentlemen. Recently, we got information we think relates to the vampire in these cases."

Aron clears his throat. "Before we share, Jack, this isn't meant for you to take any action, it's only to show we're working on this. I know how important it is to you."

Beau leans forward, placing his hands on the table. "We've information on the vampire we believe is perpetrating these crimes. We know he's of German descent and most likely originated from down south, like Georgia. We think he's been in the Seattle area for about six months."

My posture stiffens and I turn to Simon. "Did you know about this?" He shakes his head. For all the stoicism Simon portrays, his face looks as surprised as I feel.

Aron interjects, "We've been working on this behind the scenes."

"And for many years," Philip says.

The pitch in my voice matches my disbelief. "Years?"

Aron continues, "Yes, we've been following him for many years. His methods have remained the same, using humans to do his work. Over time and with technological advancements, patterns emerged."

"We first learned of him in the 1870s. The Dracul had existed only thirty years. It took time for vampires to assimilate to the changes. We thought he was a member of the VSL."

Raul shifts in his seat. "He was reckless like the others, but his actions stood out. It wasn't random. The next time he was on our radar was in the 1920s and then again in the 1950s.

At some point in this discussion, Philip stood. His arms clasped behind his back as he paced the room. "He's been manipulating others, finding humans to torture and kill for him for over a century. With all his victims, two distinct patterns exist—incremental torture over weeks and bite marks predating their deaths.

Aron lets out a breath. "We think your killer is the same guy."

My jaw slacks and my mouth slightly parts. "And you were going to let me take the fall?"

Aron met my gaze. His eyes softened. "No, son, we never were going to do that, but for several reasons, we had to follow through on the tribunal."

Beau slaps the table with a hand. "We're mandated too. We must do things by the book, politically, and for the best of our society. If we ignored the evidence, ignored the implications of you being involved, it would've put what we've worked for in jeopardy."

Aron's gaze hadn't left me. "By pulling you off the streets, we'd believed, given his patterns, another victim would arise, potentially clearing your name."

I stand and step away from the table, folding my arms. "Did you know about Brad Jensen's death?" The men nod. "What about the Seattle PD?"

"Kerry tied all the evidence together, absolving you from any suspicion. A call to the chief will be made," said Simon.

Aron spoke, his voice penetrating like electricity stinging my chest. The words resounded deep in my core. "Another word of warning, Jack. Do. Not. Take. Action. We're handling this."

I roll my eyes and tip my head. "So, what? Twiddle my thumbs, while a mass-murdering vampire is threatening those I love?"

"Exactly. Lie low for the next month. We're close to catching him," Aron says.

I mutter in defeat. "I'll try."

"Do more than try," Aron scolds.

I stand to leave, but remember I'm without a vehicle. I turn to Simon. "Can you give me a ride home? I've got a hiatus to get to."

CHAPTER 31

Jack Calloway

ON THE WAY TO MY building, Simon and I discuss what his father and the Dracul revealed this afternoon. I tell him about the German book of poems my wife had and where she got it—from the German immigrant who helped my family during the Civil War. Although I never met him, he was human, I'm sure of that. I decide it's time to tell him about Ester and what they wrote on the wall of our home.

"Blood Revenge. In German?"

I nod and explain my thinking at the time. "Her death was in the 1920s. It was twenty years from when I destroyed the nest in New Orleans and I figured someone was exacting revenge for it."

We both agree the German angle fits, especially considering the Dracul investigation, but we still don't know how I'm tied to it.

Simon scans the road as he drives. "Do you think this same vampire killed Ester?"

Rather than answer, I shrug. It's not something I want to consider because if that's true, he's been after me for some time.

"Anything like this happened to you in the 1950s?" He asks.

I think back and it didn't take long before my memory settled on my service in WWII and where I landed afterward.

In the 1940s, I traded the printing press for a gun and found myself in the Army again. Most of my time in Germany was post-WWII, during the occupation, and lasted until 1946. I completed my military service in San Francisco at a POW camp that housed Italians. I remained in San Francisco until the early 1960s.

I'd gone into business with Antonio Favero, an Italian I met while serving at the POW camp. After reparations, he returned to Italy. Eventually, Antonio immigrated back to San Francisco where we started a business.

In Italy, his family were well-known tailors. During the encampment, he'd fix tears, sew buttons, and take in sleeves for the other POWs and stationed servicemen. During the day he worked at the cannery and at night, a sewing machine and thread were his companions. It was the night shift where we became friends.

I handled the business end, staying behind the scenes, and he was the face of our tailoring business. Given my lifestyle, this arrangement worked perfectly. He was creative, and I was practical. Within five years, his skill set and fashion-savvy became known, and our little shop was in high demand.

He was doing well. He had gotten married, had a baby, a home–the whole human package. One-night tragedy struck while he and his family were sleeping. A fire started in the attic, accelerating and engulfing his home in flames, taking him and his family with it.

I've had a few moments of joy in my life, but most of it has been wrought with tragedy and pain. If not my life directly, then indirectly to someone I know, someone close to me. It never occurred to me these tragedies were connected. I'd chalked it up to being an unlucky bastard.

Antonio and I weren't confidants, but we were partners and I had a deep respect for him. He worked hard and made something for himself and his family. The memory of his death, and my father and mother losing their lives in a fire, haunted me then as it does now. His death was too close to all my ghosts, and I became angry and adrift once again. I had to get out of San Francisco.

I don't know how long I'm quiet in thought before I answer Simon's question. "Yes. Lost a business partner in a fire. Same as my parents."

Parking near my building, Simon asks, "Is there anyone in the last one-hundred-fifty years, of German descent, that stands out?"

When I reply, there's a hint of desperation in my voice. "That's just it, Simon. I've gone over it hundreds of times. No. No one. Not in my time in Germany, not anytime. Any vampires I know from Germany, wouldn't do something like this."

Simon drops me off and I walk into my building, heading toward my office. It's after four p.m. and the lights are off. I enter, look around, and go to my desk. Since leaving the campus, I haven't checked my phone messages.

The first four messages are from Carla. Rather than listen to the rest of my messages, I call her. It goes straight to voicemail. "Hmmm." The last message said it was urgent and to call her. That was Monday morning, and I called her Monday night, leaving her a message. I haven't received a call from her since. Whatever the problem, it must be resolved.

I restart my messages. The police chief is next. "Jack. I'm calling to let you know the department no longer considers you a person of interest. I told Ed to back off. You're in the clear, but it still isn't a good idea for you to come back to this. Give me a ring when you can. We'll talk."

I don't know how everyone expects me to lie low, and I wish they would stop telling me to. Especially when they know I can't do that. I don't do vacations.

The next message is from Ed, left this morning. "Jack. Call me as soon as you get this." He demands and ends the call. First, he accuses me of murder, and next, he wants me to call him. Screw him. He can wait.

There isn't anything pressing at my office and I leave to go upstairs. When the elevator doors open to my apartment, a sigh of relief releases in my chest. Home. Jasper's head pops up from the couch. He stretches, yawns, and struts over to me. "Hey, buddy. Miss me?" I pick him up and hug him, nuzzling my head into his. He's purring but pulls his head away from mine. "All right, I'll put you down."

Shannon's detail sits in the living room, flipping through a magazine. I nod to him and he points, "She's in her room."

"Have there been any problems?"

He shakes his head and another wave of relief washes over me. What I need is a swim, dinner, and to find Carla. Not necessarily in that order. I decide while Shannon's in her room to go into my office and grab a bite.

I close the office door behind me and grab three bags from the refrigerator. I don't bother with a glass, drinking the blood straight from the bag. As I finish, a knock on the door grabs my attention.

I quickly discard the bags and open the door. When I do, a high-pitch squeal rings in my ears and Shannon wraps her arms around me in a tight bear hug. I stumble, but steady myself and chuckle. "Glad to see you too."

She peeks her head around my shoulder. "What's in here?"

I step us through the doorway and close the door. "My office and nothing for you to worry about."

Concern shadows her eyes. She reaches with her finger to wipe off a corner of my mouth. "Are you bleeding?"

I step around her and wipe my mouth with my hand. "Ah. I cut myself shaving."

The Were in my home looks at me and raises his eyebrows. The mirth in his eyes relays the ridiculousness of my answer. I admit it wasn't the best response, but maybe it's enough to where she won't detect the lie.

I change the focus away from me. "What have you been up to the last few days? Simon tells me you tracked the IP addresses to a café. You know, digital forensics is a valuable field. Have you thought about what you'll specialize in when you finish school?"

Shannon's eyes glaze over dreamily, and I don't believe it has anything to do with forensics. My eyebrows narrow and my jaw tenses. I step away from her and walk into the kitchen. She follows.

I lean on the kitchen counter, crossing my arms. "I've known Simon for a long time. He's a good guy." I don't know what to say next. How do I warn her without pushing her to him or making him look bad?

I meet her gaze and smile. "I don't want you to get hurt. He's not known to settle with one woman, and you're still young with so much ahead of you. I want you to find the right man."

She pushes her shoulders back, straightening her posture. "Who says I'm looking for Mr. Right or want to settle down? After Brad…" She trails off, looking downward. She clears her throat and smiles. "You worry too much about me."

My stomach turns. I don't want to hear about her love life, and I forgot about Brad. I reach for her arm. "Brad's death. You okay?"

Her eyes pool and she nods. I pull her in. "That's why the security? You knew?"

"I had a feeling he wasn't safe." I release her and she wipes the tears from her eyes. Her face takes on a seriousness, wiping away any sadness. She's been through a lot and experienced things a young girl should never. When I first met her, she was homeless and doing whatever it took to survive. Fortunately, her short criminal career in hacking afforded her a bit of a living.

I tip her chin up and grin. "See. You give me much to worry about." She laughs, punching me in the arm.

I rub my arm where she hit me, pretending I'm in pain. "I'm going to head for the pool, maybe we can get dinner afterward?"

She takes a step and grins a sly smile. Mischief dances in her eyes. "I've dinner plans." She turns and rushes away from me.

"Are you having dinner with Simon?" I yell after her as she disappears down the hallway. She doesn't answer and before I can call out to her again, my phone rings.

"Paul. You were my next call. Simon told me Carla's detail wasn't with her the other day."

Paul pauses before he speaks. His voice is somber. "Yeah. I talked to Simon. That's why I'm calling. We found him."

"Good. What did he say? Do I need someone else for this job?"

"Jack. He's dead. It's why he wasn't with her."

A flush of heat rushes through me, my stomach twists, and my throat dries. I freeze in place and my breathing speeds up. I'm not sure I can stop the panic from knocking me down. In the distance, the detail's voice is calling my name. I know he's only a few feet away, but the tunnel I'm in reverberates his voice and I've difficulty grasping it. *Focus on the voice,* I tell myself. I grab hold and it pulls me into this moment.

I choke out. "Where's Carla?"

He answers hesitantly, "We don't know."

I end the call and rush to the garage. I call Ed. A lump forms in my throat and when I speak my voice is thick. "Ed, where's Carla? Have you seen her? Has she been at work?"

"I was…" he stumbles, "hoping she was with you. She never made it to work yesterday or today. No one's been able to get a hold of her and I was waiting to hear from you. I thought maybe she was with you."

On the other end of the phone, I hear keys rattling and a door slam.

"I'm on my way to her house now," I say.

"Okay, I'll meet you there."

CHAPTER 32

UNSUB

SHE'S A FIGHTER. I'LL GIVE her that. I can see why Jack's particularly interested in that lovely creature. I rub my jaw where the force of her foot struck. The struggle was advantageous to me, as she underestimated the monster she was fighting. It fanned the flames of the predator within. The hunt and the rapture that pumps through my body when my prey gives in is a victory I savor.

This woman has had an unusual effect on me. Something about her excites me, and I can see why Jack likes to play with her. There's a beauty about her—narrow face, blue eyes, thick blonde hair. And curves. In my tunnel vision pursuit to ruin Jack, I almost missed her beauty. I've taken a lover here and there, but they all became food. Humans aren't much more than cattle. They're easy to dominate, to manipulate, and own.

She has sparked a new interest and I've come up with an alternative plan. A brilliant plan. It'll be the ultimate revenge. Shame I hadn't thought of this before. If I had, her punishments would've been less severe. The terror in her eyes when I'd pinned her down and elongated my teeth was priceless. I had to drain her to unconsciousness to wrangle her into the car.

The control I've wielded over Jack this past century has been satisfying. Vindication for my family, and for the life I lost.

I bring my fingers to my lips. I can taste her blood just thinking about it.

When she awoke chained in my basement, I'd been sitting on the edge of the bed admiring my prey. Her face paled as she realized her situation. If she wanted to scream, she couldn't. I bound her mouth. I leaned into her ear and whispered, "You, lovely, are mine," and kissed her neck. Her reaction surprised me. She didn't cower or tremble with fear. She didn't pull away. Instead, she met my eyes in defiance, holding back the tears when they pooled in her eyes. It struck me as funny and I laughed. She faced the predator head-on. That was her mistake.

Had I noticed the power her actions had over me, I wouldn't have hit her in the face for the outright defiance she displayed or threatened the lives of those she loves. I wouldn't have stripped her of her clothes, or fed on the inside of her thigh, while I watched her writhe in fear. That was my mistake. No, I would've made sure she enjoyed herself. And I, would've enjoyed the whimper she made when she succumbed to the pleasure.

Yes, had I known; I would've planned differently. No matter. My new plan will work.

Early on I compelled her and now, no longer bound, she willingly sits on my lap as I drape kisses along her neck. I intertwine my fingers in her hair and yank her head back. Her gaze meets mine. Lust fills her eyes and my mouth crashes onto hers. Her body's responsive, and now I own her.

CHAPTER 33

Jack Calloway

GIVEN IT'S WEDNESDAY EVENING AT five forty-five p.m., traffic will be a problem. And there aren't any shortcuts or straightforward routes to West Seattle. The one supernatural ability I could use right now, I don't have. My motorcycle will have to do.

I zig-zag through traffic, going in between and around the rows of stopped cars. My erratic driving gets me a finger and a shout from a few motorists. All thoughts of injury or death are far from my mind. Carla's hurt or worse, and I just need to get to her.

I make it across the bridge, exit, and head along Harbor Avenue. I pull up to Carla's. Barely putting the gear into park, I flip the kickstand and jump off the bike. I hop the steps, taking two at a time, and break through her front door.

Frantic to get to her, I call out Carla's name, but no answer returns. I skim the area. It's mayhem. A flipped chair lies on its side. A lampshade is separated from its broken base, scattered on the floor. Framed photos that were once on a side table, the glass shattered. A pizza slice with cold, hard cheese sits in an open pizza box on the dining room table. By the appearance of the living room, I can tell she fought her attacker.

I scan the floor and see drops of blood trailing to the door. I focus my senses and breathe deep. The blood's at least a day old.

I hear a car pull up outside, quick steps, and an accelerated heartbeat, fear coursing through its blood. I turn to the door as Ed pushes his way inside and stops, standing silently. His face pales, taking in the scene.

Ed takes off his shoes and points to mine, and I do the same. He pulls out pairs of blue latex gloves and hands me a pair. He surveys the ground, looking for a clear path to walk.

At least one of us can think clearly because right now my body's weighted and my thinking's muddy. My heartbeat is in my throat and a wave of guilt makes me nauseous. I point to the broken lamp. "There was a struggle."

Ed, with determination in his eyes, heads down the sky lit hallway, like a man on a mission, surveying each bedroom. When he returns, I'm standing in the same place. "The bedrooms and the bathroom are intact. Her gun's still in her nightstand."

I glance around the living room and my gaze lands on a silver object. It's slightly protruding from under the couch. Recognizing it, I point. "Her phone."

The phone is snapped in two and the battery is separated. Ed pulls from his pocket a plastic bag, reaches for it, and places all the parts inside. "Unanswered calls. Straight to voicemail," he says as if it's why she didn't answer. Better than the alternative—she's missing.

The muscles in my legs twitch, prompting me to move. My slow and steady stride carries me to the kitchen. I look around and nothing seems out of place here either. Out of the corner of my eye, on the refrigerator, I see a postcard-size note with my name. It reads,

> *Jack. Come alone and she won't be harmed. Only you. Anyone else and I'll slice her from top to bottom. No phones.*

An address on Queen Anne is written on the paper.

My stomach lurches and a pit forms in my throat. I look over my shoulder. Ed's taking pictures of the brokenness, which was once her living room. I fold the note in half, putting it into my pocket. I hear Ed calling for a unit. I walk into the living room, along the path Ed created.

Ed frowns as he surveys the scene. "What do you think?"

I stuff my hands into my pockets. "I think our UNSUB has her." A truth that squeezes my chest.

Ed sighs. "If we follow the pattern, we know we have at least a week, maybe two. Either way, time isn't on our side. We need to do whatever it takes to find her."

I'm at the door when I say, "That's exactly what I'm going to do."

"Not alone, you're not. I'll call the chief. We need every resource we can get."

I reach into my jacket pocket, grabbing my sunglasses to shield my eyes from the setting sun. I dash to my motorcycle. Before I start it, I call Simon. He answers and I blurt out, "He has her."

"Who has who?" Simon asks.

The words stream out from my panicked mind. "The vampire. He left me a note. He has Carla. Told me to come alone. I'm leaving now."

"Jack. No. You don't know what you're walking into. Let's plan. Be smart about this."

"He could kill her. I've got to go."

"Jack, I think…" I end the call before Simon can finish. I look around the neighborhood for a garbage can, spot one, and walk to it, tossing my phone. Then I take off.

As I get near the house I was sent to, I slightly ease off the gas. I don't want to give myself away. I scan the area as I pass by the house. I loop around the block and drive by once more. The house is nestled between two larger craftsman style homes. It's narrow and like most of the houses on this block, there's a garage in the back accessible by the alley. The house is dusty gray with white accents. A deep porch greets the street.

It's a quiet neighborhood, across from a park. A good cover, hiding in plain sight, and I wonder what secrets the park could tell with a killer living in its midst. Are bodies hidden among the shrubs and trees?

This isn't the image most people have of a serial killer, but even the darkest of killers have families, work regular jobs, and are upstanding members of their communities.

I drive around the block, park, and go on foot, walking in the alley that separates the row of houses. Unattached garages and fences shape distinct boundaries between each home. I take cover behind a garage. I peer around, searching the home I've been summoned.

A painted wooden fence wraps the backyard and an archway at the gate's entrance welcomes. A maple tree provides shade from a morning's rising sun, and the ornamental grasses and shrubbery are symmetrically planted, giving space for growth. *A bit too normal,* I think.

Minutes tick by as I observe the house, watching for motion and noticing all the potential entrances. My gaze lands on a basement window on the backside of the house. It's large enough for me to slip into. I tune my senses, listening for voices inside the house. A male voice, smooth and playful, dances in the air. A feminine voice drawls syllables out, lazily forming words.

I zero in on their playful conversation, and what I hear doesn't seem right. My other senses pick up an uptick in heart rate and hear her words, "I'm yours," along with a moan. I stumble back and catch myself, holding onto the side of the garage. I know that voice, but not the words she's saying. I shake my head in disbelief and my stomach flips. It's Carla and something's wrong.

My hands clench into fists and the muscles in my face strain. A volcano of rage erupts in my chest and I rush into the yard. Any thoughts of a covert sneak attack leave my mind and all that exists is a primal need to kill him, whoever he is. I rush the stairs, but before I get to the last step, there's a sharp pinch in my neck which halts my movements. I reach my hand to rub the pained skin and understand what's happened. A dart has pierced my flesh. I stumble, steadying myself on the porch railing. My gaze searches for the person who took the shot. I look up and in a tree, a man crouches. *How didn't I know he was there?* My vision blurs and I try to find solid footing, anchoring my legs, but the muscles in my legs are stiff and unmoving. I fall, landing on my back, a numbing sensation expanding over my body, and before I lose complete consciousness, I see his face. The man in my nightmares. The monster who took my family and made me what I am. I hear him say, "Willkommen, Jack." *Son of a bitch*, I think before it goes dark.

CHAPTER 34

Jack Calloway

MY EYES WINCE WITH PAIN as my awareness returns. The pounding in my head is deafening. My muscles burn like acid is eating them away. I look at my legs, expecting to find my flesh disintegrating, but see they're intact. The dart must've carried a toxin and the effects are slowly waning, but in its wake a residue persists, leaving me groggy and weak.

I lift my arm, but a weightiness pulls it down. The sound of iron scraping cement rustles with any movement I make. I'm chained and I muster all the strength I can and tug, barely moving.

From somewhere in the room, menacing laughter erupts. "Heavy-duty, fifteen-thousand-pound pure silver encased in iron. You won't be going anywhere, Jack."

I attempt to say, "Where's Carla" but the words are slurred and garbled.

The monster laughs. "What's that, Jack? You're not making any sense."

I shake my head. *Wake up, Jack.* My eyes narrow as I search to find the vampire I'm talking to. My eyes slowly sweep the room, taking everything in, at least the best I can in my current state. The walls are gray and concrete. *Is this a cell?* No. The size of this room is larger and furnishings fill its space.

To my right, close to me, is a double bed that's exceptionally made. This strikes me as odd, and my gaze lingers. The corners of the bedcovers are tucked, and not a wrinkle is seen. On a table, placed next to the bed, sits a tiffany lamp and a wooden rocking chair. My head bobs and dips to my left. A small room with the door slightly ajar lets me glimpse inside—a bathroom. A metallic smell reaches my nose and I stare at the surrounding floor. Bloodstains and not all mine.

The man walks to me, standing a few feet away. My gaze moves from the floor to his eyes, slowly taking him in. I've been searching for this man for so many years. He's haunted my dreams and given me a will to survive. I need to know him, understand what drives him, and use it to my advantage. One way or another, for all that he took from me that cold December day, I'm going to kill him.

He appears as an ordinary man. He's casually dressed, wearing cotton pants, like sleepwear and a blue t-shirt, with a black hooded zipper jacket. He wears blue and white tennis shoes which look new—no scruffs or creases mar the surfaces.

He's tall, and his face is narrow. Thin, light brown hair recedes, giving his forehead prominence. An unassuming look, except for his eyes. Those are dark, almost black, and an emptiness and hatred fill them. This is no ordinary man. There's an organization and purpose about him. It's in his eyes and around this room. He has carried out this sinister plan, maybe not all the steps, but he's known, whether by appetite or perversion, what he's doing.

I'd asked the wrong question. The way to know him is to play on his narcissism. If I admire him and show him respect, I can draw him out.

I lift my head, meeting his gaze. "You've gone to a great deal of planning."

He sits in a chair a few feet away. He doesn't hide his satisfaction. His smile brightens his face. "How long have you've been asking why, Jack? How long have you cursed the man who enjoyed your wife? Burned down your home? Did you ever wonder who was always there? Taking your family, friends, and lovers?"

"For over one hundred and fifty years, I've been in the shadows, ruining you." He leans in, knowing that even if I want to grab him, I'm too weak. I won't give him any more satisfaction over the control he has. I keep my gaze locked on him.

He pulls out a blade from his pocket and slices my cheek, angling downward. "Well, let me introduce myself." He addresses me eye to eye. "My name is Arnold Wainwright. And the pleasure is all mine."

Wetness runs down my cheek and drops of blood land on my shirt. In this state, bound by silver, I won't heal as quickly. I don't flinch at the cut, but I blink hard at his name. Recognition hits me. "When I was away at war, you were there for my family." It wasn't a question. My wife had written to me about him.

A glimmer shines in his eye. Internally congratulating himself for a well-executed plan. I take advantage of his gloating. "You did, in fact, play me well, but why…?" My gaze falls to the floor in thought. "My family was only ever kind to you."

He jerks away from me and rises from his chair. His face hardens. "That's where you're mistaken. Your father took everything from me. He killed my boy, watching as he drowned, laughing as he slipped away. The cruelty of youth caused my boy's death and your father got away with it."

I shake my head. None of this makes sense to me. My father was a respected man. He was generous and charitable, always willing to give a helping hand. Even the slaves he had were treated fairly. I can't imagine he'd have taken any pleasure in someone drowning, let alone luring them to their death. "You're confused."

He sneers. "I worked for your grandfather a season, and my boy Judson would come with me. Your grandfather was a good man, helping us that summer. Judson was a couple of years younger than your father. The kids, however, made fun of my boy. We were poor. Our clothes were tattered and dirty. It wasn't his fault we had nothing. All he wanted was to be liked by your father and his friends."

"One day, they led Judson to the river, urging him to go in. They promised him, if he could swim across the river, he could hang out. He didn't know how to swim but went, eager to have friends. A fast current swept him away while your father gleefully laughed. That's what they told me. A few hours later, Judson's body was found. They said it was your father's idea."

"The prominence of your family and their word stood over anyone else's in the county. It was determined as an accident. We were nobodies. We were barely recognized as humans. Your father got to have a full life, but he robbed my boy of his."

The anger in his eyes had boiled over, and his fangs were bare. I thought back. Once, as a child, I complained to my uncle, when my father took a particular stern tone with me. I commented on a family who was begging for food on the side of the road. My uncle said, "Your father is shaping your character. The character of a man is his only true currency." He also shared the man who became my father, wasn't always so. At six years old, I didn't understand any of it, but I learned to treat others with respect regardless of their station.

I thought about the river where my father was raised, near to our plantation. My father cautioned about the river currents. He'd hired someone to teach me how to swim, and although I proved to be an excellent swimmer, he hated the idea. "I have nothing to do with what my father did or didn't do."

Arnold angles his knife and slashes the other cheek. "I swore I'd get my revenge. I'd take from him what he took from me. And when this happened to me," Arnold points to his fangs, "I knew I had lifetimes to do so. I've made it a point to take from your family. I'll take everything you care about Jack. No matter where you've gone, I've been right there."

An image of Ester's lifeless body enters my awareness and I understand what he's telling me. "You killed Ester. You were behind the fire in San Francisco. And the deaths of all these women here in Seattle."

He looks at me through hooded eyes. The corners of his lips curl. "Everything, Jack. I'll take everything."

Footsteps descending the stairs interrupt our conversation. I look past him to the entrance. Carla steps in from around the corner and my eyes go wide. On one hand, I'm relieved to see her and on the other, the shock has jarred my mouth open.

She's dressed in an oversized t-shirt, nothing covering her legs. As she comes nearer, I see the bite marks on her neck and wrist. She's carrying a glass of blood and when she sees Arnold, she smiles and hands him the glass. "I wondered where you ran off to. I'm getting lonely. Come back to bed."

She steps in closer, and he brings her into an embrace, kissing her. She doesn't deny him or struggle to get away. Her hands run down the sides of his torso. My mouth, still agape, closes and my jaw tightens.

"Carla. What are you doing?"

She glances briefly toward me. Her head tilts like she doesn't register who I am. Arnold speaks low in her ear and points to me. "Carla, sweet pea. I'm entertaining our guest."

Carla's eyes widen in delight and she smiles. "Oh. How good of you to stop by."

A growl erupts, and I crawl to my knees, yanking at the chains. There's no give to them. "What have you done to her?"

"Like I said, everything, Jack." He turns to her, sliding his hand up her thigh, and grabs her ass. "You go on back to bed, I won't be much longer."

She walks out of the room. I hear her footsteps reach the top of the stairs. My insides are boiling. I yank at the chains again to free myself and he laughs. "No point Jack." He swirls the blood around his glass. "You're my prisoner. I'm going to slowly drain your life away." He downs the blood, licking his lips. "You'll die in agony as you listen to me ravage her."

He walks to the bed table and picks up a different blade. He comes toward me. "When I'm done with you, the last memories you'll have will be the screams of Carla's ecstasy." He walks toward me and with a burst of speed, he stabs my chest, nearly missing my heart. The pain's so intense I cry out. It burns and the pain seeps deeper.

Delight dances in his eyes. "It's a silver blade, made especially for you. Too bad I missed your heart. Next time, I'll be better practiced." The words are both a tease and a threat. He laughs and walks away. I hear the basement door shut and lock. My head hangs.

Any energy I have is draining from my body. I widen my eyes and shake my head, trying to pull myself out of this stupor, but it's no use. It will be just a matter of minutes before I'm unconscious. I've got to think of a way out of this. A way to escape. A way to save Carla.

My throat constricts and my body slumps with heaviness. Disappointment colors my vision. I failed Carla, just like I've failed everyone else. I'm tired and my struggle is slipping away.

CHAPTER 35

Simon Johnson

SIMON PULLED THE SHEETS OVER her and slid out of her bed. She released a breath but didn't wake. What she stirred in him took Simon by surprise. He found her intriguing, and a tinge of regret and guilt squeezed his chest.

He'd gone over to Jack's place to check on Shannon, liked he promised he would. Simon stayed longer than he intended. They drank, talked, and laughed. It had been a while since he enjoyed the company of a woman. She started flirting with him. Her hands playfully touched his arms and her eyes lured Simon in. It was obvious where the night was heading, and he should have left. Instead, Simon told her detail to take a hike and before he knew it, they were tearing each other's clothes off. He knew Jack wouldn't be happy about these turns of events.

Simon gazed at Shannon. She was beautiful, and he couldn't deny there was a charge between them. When was the last time he felt that way about someone?

Trina. And she broke his heart. They had been together for seven years and Simon thought it would last forever. They had agreed when she reached thirty, they would consider turning her. Trina was twenty-nine when she told Simon there wasn't a forever between them. That was two years ago when he found her with another man—another vampire in her bed. Simon was heartbroken.

He'd sworn off humans, just vampires from then on out. However, vampires are fickle, moody, and unpredictable. He had secretly longed for something constant and long-lasting.

Simon walked out of the bedroom to find his jeans. Their clothes littered the floor from the living room to the bedroom. He pulled his phone from his jeans pocket and checked his messages. Nothing from Jack. His shoulders sunk.

It was two a.m. and Simon knew he needed to call Nick. Nick and Simon weren't particularly close. They knew each other from the bar, talked in passing, and a few times, Jack, Nick, and he hung out. But Nick and Simon didn't go out of their way to talk with one another. After all, Simon had little to do with were-persons. Not socially, anyway. But Nick was close to Jack, and Simon knew he could count on him. Nick would close the bar soon, and maybe he had heard from Jack.

Simon typed in Nick's number and he picked up on the second ring. "Nick."

"Simon, a bit of a surprise. And late. What's up?"

"It's Jack."

"Did something happen? Is he okay?" The concern in Nick's voice was clear.

Simon's voice was tight and strangled. "I don't know."

Simon updated Nick on the evidence they had, the status of Carla, the note Jack found, and where Jack went last night.

Since their last conversation, Simon had tried calling Jack a few times, but there had been no answer. Which most likely meant Jack got rid of his phone. "I haven't heard from him since yesterday. I think he's in trouble."

"Do you know the address he went to?"

Simon ran his hand through his hair. "No clue. If he doesn't contact us today, we'll need to act. In the meantime, I suggest we get a team together and meet later. I'll talk with my father, see what he knows. A NISCU investigator is in town working on Jack's case. I'll call him too."

"Okay, I'll contact Paul and ask him to put trackers on Jack and Carla. I can close the bar down and we can meet here. What time?"

Simon thought about his day and what needed to be done at work—mostly paperwork. "Let's meet at 7:00 p.m. Maybe we'll hear from him before then."

"Okay, I'll see you tonight," he said and hung up.

Simon was so engrossed in his conversation; he didn't hear Shannon walk into the room. She cleared her throat, and he jerked his head. Simon met her gaze. She stood by the couch, naked. She didn't hide from him, and her confidence warmed Simon's insides. The regret and guilt faded away.

Simon wrapped his arms around her, his hands drifted down her body, and his lips caressed her neck. He breathed in the smell of her skin, vanilla, and cinnamon. "Did I wake you?"

"What happened to Jack?" Simon lifted his head from her neck, and she pulled out of his arms, turning to face him. "I heard you talking about Jack. Something's wrong." His gaze held her eyes, filled with concern and worry. Shannon's naked body distracted him. He wanted to pull her back to him, but she was needing reassurance, not his hands on her body. He breathed in and refocused his attention.

He was in a precarious situation. He didn't like to lie, but he didn't know how much truth to tell either. And he didn't want her investigating Jack's disappearance. She would not accept the words like "don't worry." He needed to give her enough, but not too much.

Simon's gaze dropped to the floor. He answered, "I don't know. Carla was taken. We think the Seattle PD's Triple M Killer's involved. Jack went after her. And before you ask, I don't know where he went. He called me on his way and then discarded his phone. I think he's in trouble."

She jerked her hand to her mouth and Simon could hear her pulse accelerating. "No." She stepped back, arms across her chest, and her hands rubbed her forearms. "What are we going to do?"

He reached for her and pulled her back into his arms. Her head rested on Simon's chest. "I've got a team working on it. If we don't hear from Jack today, we're going to find him."

She looked up, her eyes wide. "I've got digital access to the victim's online profiles, their hard drives, and the delivery driver's hard drive. I've hacked into Brad Jensen and James Everly's digital footprints, too. I've been thinking maybe I'll find another IP address or some other footprint revealing the third killer. I've been searching all those files this week looking for a link."

Shannon continued to fill him in on the work she'd been doing, and for whatever reason, it turned Simon on. His lips met hers, his hands cupped her ass, and he pulled her into him. "This talk's turning me on," he whispered in her ear.

Simon's fingers reached between her legs and their kiss deepened. "I don't want to work right now." He picked her up and carried her into the bedroom.

After a couple more rounds of having his way with her and drifting in and out of sleep, the warmth of the sun pressed upon him, signaling it was time to go to work.

Simon threw his legs over the edge of the bed and stood to get dressed. Shannon stirred and opened her eyes. "Work," he said. The regret returned, and he was torn between the need to get out of there, and staying in bed. Unfortunately, work and finding Jack was his priority.

She opened a dresser drawer and put on a shirt and a pair of shorts. "Tracing." She said mocking him. The smile left her face and determination set in. "Maybe I can find Jack's location."

They walked to the living room, and Simon collected the rest of his things. Before they could say anything more, the elevator opened and the Were-dog returned. His presence cut through the awkwardness and added to it.

Simon walked to the elevator. He was uncomfortable and unsure of how he felt. He turned to Shannon who was in the kitchen pouring a glass of orange juice. "I will find Jack," he promised. She said nothing, only smiled and drank her juice. "I'll stop by before my meeting tonight and check in on you." He thought, almost aloud, *Next time, we won't fall into bed.*

She nodded, and they said goodbye. When the door closed, Simon's throat constricted, strangling the rising ache in his chest. He can't get attached. He won't let himself, for her sake and his.

He called Kerry and filled him in. Kerry agreed to join them and gather any resources he could. He'd contact his supervisor, Angela Channing, who could provide intel they wouldn't have otherwise. She had pull with Seattle PD, and they'd need all the help they could get to retrieve Jack and Carla. Simon's phone rang, and he glanced to see who it was.

Simon answered, "Jarvis."

"Boss. We have a situation. That vampire who was breaking into houses… we picked him up last night. It was reported he'd nearly killed a Were a couple of weeks ago and well, he's here in detention and the word must've got out because there's a group of Weres down here demanding justice. Old law justice."

Simon didn't want to hear this, let alone have to deal with a mob of Weres. Demanding Old law meant not recognizing the treaties between Vamps and Weres. Old law allows a pack to hunt a vampire, and that has a lot of political implications. "Shit. Does Donovan know?"

"Yeah. He reached out to someone in the Lycaon."

"I'm on my way." Simon hung up and cursed aloud. This wasn't what he needed. Vampire and Were politics were tenuous in the best of times. The Dracul and the Lycaon had forged peace treaties, and their alliance was relatively workable. Still, it was hard to erase a six-hundred-year history of being mortal enemies. After all, they were born to annihilate each other.

With a deep sigh, Simon pulled out his keys and headed to the campus.

CHAPTER 36

Simon Johnson

SIMON SPENT THE LAST few hours working with his werewolf counterpart. They scheduled a community meeting with a representative from both the Dracul and the Lycaon. It provided a forum for their voices to be heard. Satisfied with this, the crowd dispersed.

He was five minutes late for his meeting with his father, Aron Johnson. Simon's father was extremely busy and on a day like today, normally Aron would have canceled. However, with Jack missing, and the capture of a vampire as a foremost priority for the Dracul, he wanted an update. If only Jack had laid low, none of this would've happened. As he thought this, he knew it wasn't true. Events were set in motion some time ago. He just didn't know how long ago or what any of it meant.

Simon walked into his father's office. Aron Johnson was one of the world's most powerful people, yet his surroundings were simple, minus the heavy security systems and guards that enveloped his life. He stayed humble and valued his role in stewardship. Aron was unassuming, and it worked to his advantage. He was a master at diplomacy and had powerful allies. Aron garnered respect even from those he considered enemies. He didn't get angry too often, but when he did, his actions were swift and exacting.

When Aron was human, he was a great warrior and chieftain in the Scottish Highlands. It was there in the 1600s, where he met a man who took a special interest in his battle skills. Had Simon's father known, perhaps he wouldn't have invited that unlikely creature into his clan. In doing so, most of his people were slaughtered. Whether or not he wanted it, Aron became the next generation of ruling vampires.

Donovan and Simon were actual brothers, born from his father and mother. A rare gift for vampires, and it elevated their father's status. It also elevated Simon and Donavan's statuses, and Donovan used that to his advantage. Their mother died a century ago, and her death devastated Simon's father. She was his father's rock and to this day, he deeply missed her. Behind closed doors, Aron was simply a loving and doting father. "Hey pops."

"Simon, my dear boy." He hugged Simon with a quick embrace. "Come, sit. Tell me what's going on with Jack."

Aron paced the room, frowning the entire time Simon filled him in. "Nick's contacted his cousin to put trackers on Jack and Carla. I've looped in Kerry and he's brought his command up to speed." Simon's pocket started vibrating. "Hold on, I need to check this."

It was a text from Shannon. Just seeing her name put a grin on Simon's face. He didn't think about his father's gaze upon him as he read the text.

"Someone new in your life, boy?" When Simon looked up and met his father's gaze, there was a twinkle in his eye. "No. It's nothing." Simon's neck felt warm, and he shifted in his seat. His father was none too happy when his relationship with Trina turned serious. It was one thing to have an occasional fling with a human or have a drudge. Vampires can control both. It was another to forge a committed relationship.

When Simon told Aron he was in love with Trina, Aron grew quiet and paced for what seemed like hours before he voiced his concerns. "You're the descendant of one of the most powerful vampire families in the world. As such, you have a greater responsibility than most. A relationship with a human could affect your responsibilities to our family and our society." Simon had responded by telling Aron he loved her, and he couldn't help his feelings. Simon reasoned that Donovan was the eldest. He would be the one in their family to become the next Dracul. Simon wasn't interested in the position or politics. Aron didn't like Simon's answer, but he didn't argue it. He could have forbidden it. He had the authority. Maybe the love he had with Simon's mother kept him from doing so. After all, she was human when they met.

Simon raised his phone. "My text. Looks like we got a lead on the killer's address." He stood, put the phone back into his pocket, and walked to the door.

"Simon." His father snapped, halting his steps. "What's the address?" Simon relayed the address, and Aron wrote it down. "What time and where are you meeting tonight?"

Simon released a breath and turned to him. He didn't understand his father's interest in this information. It wasn't like him to be involved in law enforcement activities. "Dad, I need to make several calls. I need to find out if this is the right place. If Jack's, there. If they're alive." Simon released his frustrations in a rant, while his father tapped his fingers on his desk, waiting for an answer. His laser-focused stare stopped Simon's commentary from continuing. Simon realized he shouldn't have been so quick to shut him out. A phone call from his father could move mountains. "Shipwreck at seven p.m."

"I've got resources. Might come in handy. You may go," he said.

Simon exited and walked toward his office building, twenty-five yards away. He was so lost in thought, he didn't hear his name called until the voice was on his heels. Donovan shouted, "Simon, get your head out of your arse."

"Yeah, sorry. Got things on my mind. Do you need anything?"

He looked at Simon, puzzled. Incredulity in his eyes. "You have a Were protest and demands for death at your doors this morning and you're asking me if I need something?"

They stopped outside Simon's building. "Well?" He asked impatiently.

"All right, what's going on?"

Donovan and Simon had always been close. They were competitive as kids, but always had each other's backs. There was little they wouldn't do for one another. And even though Simon didn't expect Donovan to have a care about Jack, he filled him in.

"That's where my mind's at. I'll have Jarvis follow up on the events of this morning while I focus on this Jack thing."

Once in his office, he called Nick and gave him the address Shannon sent. If Paul's trackers pick up Jack's or Carla's scent, it'll be clear where they need to go. Simon texted Kerry with their meeting time and place.

He got another text from Shannon asking to go to the meeting tonight. He hadn't responded. He needed to give a plausible reason why she couldn't go. One that didn't sound like he was hiding something. Simon needed to end this thing between them sooner rather than later. He hated lying, and that's all a relationship with him would be—lies. Simon rubbed his temples, releasing the tension in his face.

An hour of desk duty passed when Simon's cell phone rang. A number came up as *City Building*. His experience told him it was an office connected to the City of Seattle.

"Simon Johnson," he commanded. Simon thought a firm voice would hide any signs of worry. He was trying to push aside doubts he had about finding Jack and Carla in time.

"Simon. This is Ed Halstead with the Seattle PD. We met before. Kerry LaMoine contacted me today. He said you might have information on Carla Briggs's disappearance." Ed's voice was authoritative and direct until he said the word disappearance. His voice shakily trailed.

Simon had only met Ed one time, and it wasn't planned. Jack, Nick, and he went to a car show and Ed was admiring the same car they were. Jack introduced Nick and Simon. They all chatted a bit about the show. Nick talked to him about the bar and Simon said nothing about being a private investigator. That's how Jack explained his connection with him to his human counterparts.

The tension between Ed and Jack was thick and eventually they pulled him away citing "Nick's dream car's over there."

"Kerry, huh?"

"Well, yeah, anyway, we've been frantic over here trying to track her. We're on a case, one where I think she's got mixed up in and now she's in danger. I'll do whatever it takes to find her. This guy... this guy doesn't play nice."

Shit. Simon wondered what Kerry told Ed. The last thing they needed was the Seattle PD mucking this up. Another lie he had to dream up.

Simon paused, maybe too long before he said, "Lead fell through. We thought we had a beat. Turned out to be nothing. I'm sorry. I'm working on it. Jack's missing too." He closed his eyes, shaking his head. Why did he say Jack was missing?

"If you come across something, anything, please call me."

"I will." His insides turned at the promise he wouldn't keep. As he was growing up, his mother and father emphasized the importance of telling the truth. They believed words could build or tear apart, especially someone's character. And here he was making promises and covering up truths. Sometimes, Simon thought, the truth could hurt more.

Simon ended the call quickly before he said anything else that could be incriminating. Lying made him uncomfortable. Anyone perceptive enough would see the heat blushing his neck when he lied. Simon pulled at his collar, letting the heat escape.

When Simon finished what he could, what his mind allowed him to focus on, it was four p.m. He was tired. He'd slept little this week, and a weariness blanketed his body. He shifted the focus from his fatigue to finding Jack, and a renewed energy moved through him.

He checked out for the day, giving his deputy an order. "Jarvis, I won't be on the job this weekend, but if you need me, call." Simon would work, but not for the Guard, and Jarvis didn't need to know that. He could count on Jarvis's help and discretion under normal circumstances, but this rescue mission wasn't exactly by the book. Plus, Jarvis didn't like Jack.

Simon got into his car and headed to Jack's place. He promised to check in on Shannon, and he both dreaded and longed to see her. He created a weird situation, having slept with her, and he needed to give her a reason she couldn't go to the meeting tonight.

He stepped into the elevator and rode to Jack's apartment. He started pacing and uttered, "I need you here, in case Jack shows up." True. "Jack would kill me if I put you in danger." That was true. "You're safer here." Yes. All true. Simon reassured himself.

He entered Jack's apartment and saw his office door standing open. An alarm triggered in his head. "Shannon?" He called out as he walked toward the office. Shannon burst through the door, eyes-wide, carrying bags of blood.

"What the hell is this? Why does Jack have a refrigerator full of blood?"

Crap, it was restocked. He thought. Wait. How did Shannon get in there? And wow, she was sexy as hell with bags of blood in her hands. Simon could feel his eyes pulse as his pupils dilated. An instinct born in a vampire.

He looked away momentarily to gain composure. "Shannon, how did you get access to the office?"

She emphasized her filled hands, jerking them. "That's your question? How I got into the office." She pushed her hands forward. "What about these?"

The conversation Jack had about compelling Shannon, if necessary, flashed in Simon's mind. Was this the time? Only if he couldn't dissuade her interest. Erasing someone's memory was a delicate matter.

Simon swiped his hand through his hair and breathed out. "Shannon. I… I'm sure there's a logical explanation. When we find Jack, you can ask him."

"Why are you so calm about this? This isn't normal."

He squared his shoulders and folded his arms. "Look, I don't have time to deal with whatever this is. I only came by to make sure you're okay." His voice was gruff and impatient. His gaze swept the apartment. "Where's your detail?" At the very least, her detail should have stopped her from going in there. He thought Jack would have left those instructions.

She snapped "He's in the bathroom. Not that it's any of your business."

Simon didn't respond to her comment, he was focused on wanting to strangle her detail. It was a far better fate than what Jack would do to him. Anger welled in his chest and his hands balled into a fist. Shannon stepped back.

Simon walked to her, took the bags out of her hands, and placed them on the counter. He would've put them in the fridge, but that might look suspicious. *Damn.* Deception didn't come easily. Should he tell her? If she reacted badly, he could compel her.

"I'm sorry. Everything's going to be fine." Simon lifted her chin and their gazes met. Her eyes pooled with tears.

"I'm scared for Jack."

He grabbed her hand and led her to the couch. The Were-dog came into the living room and Simon's sharp glare sent him a message. He picked up a book, scurrying outside to the balcony.

"Let me get you something to drink."

Simon went to the kitchen, grabbed a glass, and filled it with water. He handed it to her and their fingers collided. Electricity passed through him and he withdrew from her touch. Simon moved away, putting distance between them.

"When we find Jack, you can ask him. He's affiliated with the World Hematology Center. It probably has something to do with that."

Her gaze softened, and her shoulders relaxed. "Oh, well, that would make sense, I suppose."

Simon stuffed his hands into his jacket pockets. "Look. About last night."

"You don't need to say anything. It happened. We're both adults."

"No, listen. I like you and last night was fun. It's just my work—my life doesn't have room for relationships." Not human relationships and not Jack's assistant, but he didn't say that. "I don't have space for them."

"I get it. It's not a big deal." Shannon looked away, hiding her injured pride.

He smiled. "Shannon. I don't want you to think you're not a big deal. You are." He wanted to say more like she was someone he could fall for. Or their relationship would only be based on lies and that's why it couldn't happen. Instead, he remained quiet. It was simple he was a vampire and it couldn't work.

She looked at him through hooded eyes. "The ole it's not you, it's me bit."

"No. It's not like that at all." But it was that, for other reasons, because what he wanted to do was hold her hand, caress her skin, and wake up next to her.

Simon kissed her on the cheek. "Thank you." He headed towards the elevator and said, "Now, I've got to figure out how to rescue Jack and Carla from a psychopathic monster."

CHAPTER 37

Shannon Tieg

"I'M GOING INTO THE OFFICE, I've some work to do," Shannon yelled to her detail, pointing to Jack's office door. She was annoyed, having a babysitter, but she knew it made Jack feel better. Her detail glanced up from his book and gave her a nod.

Monday morning, when Shannon was at the office, a messenger from Boyd, Leighton, and Zirkle delivered a small, four-by-three-inch clasped envelope. Inside was a piece of paper and on it was a digital code. With no other instructions, she wasn't sure what it meant. Immediately, she began connecting any dots she could think of. There weren't many.

Shannon remembered a conversation she had with Jack two years ago. She thought it was nothing more than him sharing industry knowledge. "In this business, you always need to be prepared. It can be dangerous. You never know who you're dealing with or who might get upset with what you're doing. Take measures to protect yourself. Always have a plan B, an escape route, and never let one person have access to what you know. Set up an emergency plan in layers," he'd told her.

When Simon left this morning, Shannon went downstairs to the office, continuing her digital search for the third killer. Once she traced the IP addresses in Queen Anne, she searched the building. She discovered the digital code bypassed required fingerprint and eye scans, including giving her access to Jack's home office. There was only one problem. She didn't know what she was looking for.

Earlier, when she first entered Jack's office, she was surprised. She stepped into a fully furnished apartment with an exit door leading to a stairwell. She'd taken the stairs and when she reached the garage, she thought *this must be Jack's escape route.* She was also surprised by the state-of-the-art video surveillance system in his office. He had eyes on the entire building.

When she approached the floor-to-ceiling bookcase, her fingers skimmed the edges until she came across a button underneath one shelf. She pushed it and from the rear, a drawer slid out. In it, she found passports, cash, and other personal items. At this, she thought, *Jack's plan B,* and Shannon understood the digital code was part of Jack's emergency layers.

Next, she had scanned the room for anything personal. It'd occurred to Shannon the items, locked away in Jack's office, must hold some significance. On the bookshelf, she saw a picture of a man with an uncanny resemblance to Jack. She'd taken the picture out of the frame and written on the back, were the names William, Caroline, and Julia Thomas, dated 1861.

Shannon's gaze landed on a family album. Thumbing through it, she found birth and death certificates for William, Caroline, and Julia, a marriage certificate, and various pictures of people she'd never seen. By the age of the photos, they hadn't been alive for decades.

After an hour of searching, nothing stood out. Shannon was thirsty when she opened the door to Jack's refrigerator. She was alarmed when she found the refrigerator full of blood bags and hoped Jack had a plausible reason for them, like the explanation Simon gave her—Jack's work at the WHC.

Since her earlier efforts didn't yield any leads, she wondered if Jack's emergency layers included something stored in his computer. If he wanted her to find something, it made sense he'd place it there. She didn't want to invade his privacy, but decided his life was more important than his privacy. Now, back in his office, she sat at his computer and logged into her network analyzer and password cracking software. Fifteen minutes later she was searching his files.

First, she accessed his phone and email records. She entered keywords, narrowing her search to people's names—Carla, Simon, Nick, and Ed. She found a file Simon sent Jack a few weeks ago and opened it. It contained investigation notes on a murder and a break-in at the WHC. Simon's email attachment and strings of text messages gave her access to his computer and phone.

Shannon had a passion for everything about computers. She was in middle school when she took her first computer programming class. After that, any computer science book she could get her hands on, she devoured. So by the age of sixteen, she could program and hack almost anything. It was her exceptional computer skills that got her expelled from high school. She hacked the school database and altered grades. School was the only structure in her life.

Shannon wondered where Simon was meeting tonight. She knew Jack often went to the Shipwreck tavern and had met Simon there a few times over the years. She searched for any phone or text messages that referenced the Shipwreck and found one, a text message sent today from Simon to Kerry, "Shipwreck 7 p.m." She guessed they'd be there.

She thought about the modern-day crime shows where detectives focused on following the money and turned her attention to Jack's bank accounts, quickly scanning activity over the last week. She discovered Jack was a millionaire with diversified investments.

Shannon deeply exhaled. Her investigation hadn't given her any more leads on Jack. Because he was a private person, she knew little about him. She didn't know where he was born or anything about his childhood. Heck, she'd never been to his apartment. Now, she had access to everything. Why? Did he want her to have access? Did he know he was walking into danger? The questions worried her because for Shannon it meant Jack might not return.

Shannon glanced at the clock. Six p.m.

She shut off the computer and placed the picture and family album back on the shelf. Other than knowing the meeting place and time, nothing else stood out.

In the time she had known Jack, he hadn't mentioned his family. She asked once, and he said, "they're all dead," and left it at that. For Shannon, Jack was all the family she had. He was a pain in the ass acting like an overprotective big brother, but she needed him. Drugs took her father when she was fifteen and Shannon didn't know where her mother was anymore. The last time she saw her, she was walking Aurora avenue, selling her body to feed her habit. For all she knew, her mother could be dead.

Shannon couldn't lose Jack too. She wouldn't. Simon didn't think she had much to offer to their rescue mission, but he was mistaken. What he didn't understand was she'd survived the streets for two years, in and out of shelters. She learned how to protect herself against predators, how to keep her possessions safe, how to make money, and how to go unseen. She'd witnessed overdoses and stabbings. She knew what starvation felt like and the best con's for getting what she needed.

In the time Shannon had known Jack, she'd gotten a black belt in Judo, and for the past two years, she's spent every week at the shooting range. Jack made her take classes. He told her, "If you're going into this business, you need to know how to protect yourself with your hands and a gun." Now, a Taurus TX 22 with two magazines was in her purse at all times.

Which is what Shannon's detail didn't see when she went inside the office. She'd grabbed her purse and jacket. He also didn't know she'd disabled the security systems. Shannon stepped into the stairwell and entered the garage where she got into her car and exited.

When Shannon got to the Shipwreck, it was six-forty. Several people hung around outside the perimeter, most engaged in conversation, but when she walked toward the doors, their conversations grew quiet and all eyes were on her. An alarm triggered inside her head and Shannon became as vigilant of them as they were of her. She wasn't sure why she felt a sense of danger, but she did and knew to trust her instincts.

The tavern was dark inside, and a low light illuminated the tables. Her eyes adjusted to find twenty or thirty people milling about. A server carried tabs instead of drinks, dropping them off at the tables. Another was at the bar, cashing people out. Several people glanced at her, some staring. It was strange and reminded Shannon of an all too familiar feeling that warned her of danger. The tiny pricks of tension along her shoulders signaled her to pay attention. Shannon brought her purse in tighter, touching her gun for reassurance, and preparing to use it if necessary. She scanned the room, looking for a familiar face.

"Whatever you're looking for, sweetheart, look no further, I'm here." A deep, melodious voice soothed her ears, reaching from behind. However intriguing the voice was, she jerked her head and stepped away to the side.

A beautiful smile with deep green eyes greeted her. He was attractive, and his beauty nearly stole her breath away.

He picked up Shannon's hand and kissed the back of it. "You are a vision of perfection. Let me introduce myself. I'm Gerard Bisset and I'm all yours tonight." He ran the back of his hand down her arm.

"Sorry." She pulled her arm back. "I'm Shannon. Looking for Simon Johnson. Have you seen him?"

"No. Thank goodness. He's stuffy and a bore. A pretty thing like yourself would surely enjoy someone more entertaining like myself."

Half the room emptied, and more patrons walked past them to exit through the doors. "Why's everyone leaving?"

"A private party." He put his arm around her waist. "Let's find somewhere else to continue our conversation."

Shannon tried to step out of his grasp, but he held on tight. That was when she realized how strong he was and what little room she had to maneuver. "Sir. Please let me go." He pulled Shannon closer, their gazes meeting. Shannon's hand locked onto her gun, but it was all she could do. He began whispering something, and she felt her muscles loosen. She jolted when he was jerked from behind, releasing her as he was thrown back.

Gerard righted himself, hands balled in a fist. His eyes changed to a reddish hue. Next, his face slipped into something slightly different. It was him, but his features were sharper. A growl erupted from him. "How dare you?" His near-perfect teeth were angular and uneven.

It was Simon's voice that cut through her confusion. "Never go near her again." They stood face to face with fury in their eyes. Shannon got a glimpse of Simon's eyes and they had the same reddish hue.

Another man, slightly taller than Simon, got between them. "Simon. Not here. Gerard leave." Gerard backed away, composing himself. His face and eyes returned to the handsome man she saw minutes before. He straightened his clothes and smiled at Shannon, approaching her. His teeth were in perfect alignment again. She took a step back. "Sorry, darling. Next time."

Gerard walked past Shannon, leaving the tavern. She didn't move. Shock froze her limbs. What happened? Her mind reeled. His transformation was familiar and haunting. It reminded Shannon of something, but she couldn't place it.

She felt pressure and a tug on her arm. Shannon didn't fully realize Simon was dragging her outside until the evening's sunset pierced her eyes.

"You need to leave."

"What… was that? She stammered.

"Doesn't matter. You can't be here."

Indignantly, she said, "You don't get to tell me what I can or can't do."

A growl erupted from his chest. "Yes. I. Do." His voice was elevated and stern. "When it comes to your safety, I do. Where's your detail?"

Shannon yanked her arm from his grip, stomped off toward her car, turned around, and flipped him off. She muttered to herself, "I don't need you. I know where Jack is."

CHAPTER 38

Simon Johnson

"GODDAMN WOMAN," SIMON SAID ALOUD and walked into the Shipwreck. She doesn't have a clue how close she came to being Gerard's plaything. What was she thinking coming here?

Inside, Simon saw Donovan shaking hands with a man. Donovan was always the consummate diplomat, and to others his smiles granted promises. He took his role as a community leader seriously. He worked tirelessly to secure our futures for generations to come. However, Simon was the one person who could see past Donovan's smiles and smooth words. And right now, as Donovan headed in Simon's direction, his face wasn't in a diplomatic mood. "What woman makes you forget not only where you are but also your position?"

"Jack's assistant. I don't know why she was here, but I promised him I'd keep her safe."

"Try again. I know you better than that. A human? Again?"

"No. It's not like that," Simon said in a low voice.

"We don't have the luxury to let emotion get the better of us. Our roles are too valuable."

Simon scanned the empty room and found Kerry, Paul, and Nick staring at them. "Let's go sit down."

They joined the group. Nick looked to Simon and then to Donovan, his brow raised. Donovan gave him a nod and Nick let out a breath, shoulders relaxing. The lack of confidence in Nick's eyes irritated Simon. "I'm okay. Can we focus on why we're here?"

The group spent the next hour discussing what they knew. Paul's trackers found Jack and Carla's scent. That confirmed the address Shannon found belongs to the killer. Kerry had the house blueprints, and they were reviewing the layout, noting entrances and blind spots. He discovered a couple of other facts. The house owner's name was Arnold Wainwright, and the crime scene at the storage unit was owned by Arnolt Wagenmacher. "Other than the storage unit, Arnolt Wagenmacher doesn't exist," said Kerry. "My office tells me it's German for Arnold Wainwright." His office passed this information to the Seattle PD. It was probably how Ed came to call Simon.

Donovan leaned back in his chair. "This Arnold Wainwright is the same guy the Dracul have been following for a century."

"So, wait. The guy the Dracul has been tracking is the Triple M Killer?" Nick asked.

"Looks like it," said Simon.

Paul said, "My guys found three vampires guarding the area around the house. I've assigned two Weres to standby waiting for our command. They're in the park."

"We must immobilize those vamps to get to the house," Simon said, and all the men nodded in agreement.

Simon turned to Paul. "What do we know about the neighborhood?"

Paul shrugged. "Quiet. Human. Family-oriented."

Donovan cleared his throat. "Whatever we do, we need to minimize the damage. We don't want a diplomatic nightmare on our hands."

Simon picked up his phone. "I'll have Sandpiper put a field around the house and the block. That'll keep the neighbors unaware of the activity and away from the neighborhood."

Simon recruited Sandpiper to the Guard five years ago for this unique ability. To humans, looking at an area surrounded by this protective field was like wearing rose-colored glasses. This talent came in handy when protecting a crime scene involving the supernatural.

With a plan in place, reinforcements called, and directions given, they exited the tavern, walking toward their cars. Outside, leaning on Kerry's car, was Ed Halstead.

Ed smirked. "Not much of a crowd for a Friday night and with your somber faces, I wouldn't hire you for marketing. By your appearances, you're headed for trouble. What's the mission?"

Simon stepped toward Ed. "What brings you here?"

"Same reason you're all here. You need to fill me in, or I'll arrest you for obstruction of justice."

Kerry jumped in. "Ed. For reasons I can't discuss, Homeland's taking the lead. Your chief's been informed."

That wasn't exactly true. Yes. Homeland knew what was going on and they were in communication with the chief, and they provided them intel, but this was a semi-rogue op, and Simon could tell by Ed's stance, he would not back down.

Ed folded his arms. "I'm not going anywhere. I'll do whatever it takes to recover Carla."

The deserted parking lot and the clear dusk sky didn't release any of the tension surrounding them. The atmosphere vibrated with electricity. "We don't have time for arguing," Simon communicated to the group.

"Ed, this is an undercover mission. It's dangerous. We have a plan and the people to execute it. We've got it covered. If we need back up, we'll contact you," Nick said.

Ed flashed a phone. "I've got Jack's phone. He was with me when he tossed it. Our IT guy got into it and I put it all together. You." He pointed at the group. "Here." He paused. "I know about Jack. I know," he emphasized. "So, if that's what you're worried about, don't. I'm not new to the idea."

The men glanced at each other. They thought they knew what *idea* he was talking about. *Do we include him?* They were silently asking each other with their eyes. He was here for Carla and maybe including him would be to their advantage, especially with the police department. But at what cost to the rest of them? Simon gave the group a nod as a sign to move forward.

Nick cleared his throat. "Have you ever gone against them?" He asked before he went inside the Shipwreck.

"Look, I'm here and ready to help."

When Nick came out, he walked to Ed and handed him a gun with a couple of magazines. "This will be your only defense for where we're going. Defense only." Nick emphasized defense.

Ed snapped. "I have a weapon."

"Not like this and not with bullets designed to render vampires or... others, immobile." Ed's movements stopped. He stared at Nick, his expression flat. He sighed and reached for the gun.

Simon shifted the conversation. "Kerry, you and Ed ride together. Fill him in on the plan. Nick, you and Paul, and Donovan and I will ride together. We'll meet where discussed."

And then Simon thought to himself, *I hope they're still alive.*

CHAPTER 39

Jack Calloway

I GROGGILY COME TO NOT knowing how long I've been out. Minutes. Hours. The dim light emanating from the lamp painfully pierces my eyes and I struggle to open them. I lick my lips. My mouth is so dry, it's like rubbing my tongue over sandpaper.

I'm on the floor, laying against the wall, and my head hangs over my body, too weak to lift. My clothes are soaked with blood. My blood. My skin stings where Arnold stabbed my chest. Again. Millimeters from my heart. I don't know what's more painful, being stabbed or hearing Carla's laughter, or her begging for more.

I know better than to put her in danger. If she makes it out alive, her world will be broken, and she'll be scarred. And for what? Because I couldn't stay away from her. I'll never forgive myself for what I've done.

The tap of a drum beat and the deep sorrow of a string quartet ring in my ears. The sound of Chopin's Funeral March draws closer. *Am I hallucinating?* I shake my head to stop the noise. I hear footsteps plodding closer. A whistling pierces my haze. I lift my eyes and feel him towering over me, his shoes point toward me like daggers. My captor has returned.

"Ha, Jack. I see you're awake. You're doing an outstanding job dying slowly. I'm quite enjoying this."

He steps back and sits in a chair. I dig deep within to access the strength to lift my head. My head wobbles as I strain to face him.

However small the gesture may be, I don't want to give him the satisfaction of defeat.

"I've quite enjoyed your woman too. She's a wildcat, that one. I think I'll keep her."

I swallow, making a way in my throat for words to form. "You have me. Let her go. She's not a part of this."

"I can't do that, Jack. Let's call it collateral damage. But I promise you, however long her life is, she'll enjoy it." He grins and licks his lips.

In the distance, soft steps brush against the stairs. Carla enters the room wearing barely enough and revealing too much. Her hair's disheveled, and a vacancy overcasts her eyes. My stomach dips and my muscles tighten.

She walks to Arnold, offering her wrist. "Breakfast." He smiles, telling her she's a good girl and feeds on her wrist. He pulls her closer and sits her on his lap, continuing to feed. Her other hand twirls his hair.

This is madness and there isn't a damn thing I can do about it. "Carla," I squeak out. "Stop."

Arnold lifts his gaze to me and pulls away from her wrist. "Carla, baby. I've made my decision. I want you to be mine forever." She giggles with excitement.

My stomach lurches. "No." I will my leg muscles to move, twitches nudge my thighs, but nothing happens. His cruel laughter bangs in my head.

He pricks his finger with his incisors and droplets of blood pool. He lifts his finger to Carla's mouth. "My love. This will bind us together forever. Drink."

Carla suckles his finger and moans. He kisses her neck while sliding his hand across her thigh. My head drops. Any amount of energy I have slips away. It's that moment the will to survive leaves my body. I can't live with what I have done. I welcome death. I hope for it.

Feet shuffle. Pitter-patter sounds sweep the floor and the stairs creak. Carla's light steps drift away. I feel the energy of his suffocating presence. I don't move. I can't.

A yank of my hair thrusts my head up. The monster and I are face-to-face. He's so close the smell of his breath impairs my senses. He whispers, "Everything, Jack." A piercing, sharp object stabs me, and a blistering pain lances my shoulder, above my heart. The next one I know will kill me.

I'm left, laying on the floor, with no will to care. Waiting for death to come.

***

Thunder rumbles in the distance. I count the seconds between. Boom-one. Boom-two. Boom-three, waiting for the crackle of lightning and a light to illuminate the night sky. There's nothing like a summer rain in Georgia. A brewing storm silences the world, preparing for its symphony of roars and whips, heralding a cleanse the rain brings.

The smell of wet dog penetrates my nostrils. Otis, my lab must be around here somewhere. "Come here boy," I mumble.

Wait. I pause my thinking. Otis. What's he doing here? He's dead. Died when I was a boy. I can't be in Georgia. I strain to listen. Another shot of thunder rolls through the air, but it's not thunder.

It is the ominous sound of a gun. A woman screams, and I hear men shouting. *Growling?*

I listen for heartbeats. At least ten distinct rhythms, some slow like a vampire's heartbeat. Most of the beats are outside the house. Others are human. Heart rates accelerate and a guttural cry rips out, slicing the air. The muffled sound of fists hitting bone and the cries of agony and death tenses my muscles.

Minutes tick by and my awareness pushes past the fog. Enough to know someone's getting slaughtered. Is that good or bad? Do I care?

A crash at the basement door sounds like an ax slicing through wood. I struggle to open my eyes. Friend or foe is the question that lingers, but it's all the energy I can muster.

I hear my name and a small sound escapes my lips. More of a whimper and not loud enough to get anyone's attention. Hands tug and pull at me.

"Shit. Silver. Donovan. Get Kerry or Ed. We can't directly touch this. And have Nick search for keys in case we can't find something to cut these."

"Carla?" Her name slurs from my mouth.

"They're not here. Paul's team found a scent trail and is tracking them. We'll find her," Simon says.

"Ed has bolt cutters in his car. He'll be here in a minute," says Donovan. *Donovan's here?*

"Simon, I got blood." I hear Nick's voice.

"Here, let me through." *Ed Halstead. What's he doing here?* No way Ed's here. I must be hallucinating. "Kerry. Help me get these cuffs cut." The man who's not Ed says.

A couple of loud snaps and my body falls over with a thud. The heaviness wanes in my arms and legs. I'm hoisted to the bed. I feel something wet touch my lips.

"Jack. Drink," says Nick. His voice firm and demanding. Someone tips my head back and the liquid trickles down my throat and warms my body. Energy rushes from my torso out. I flex my fingers and widen my eyes. Instinct takes over and I grab the bag, finishing it. "More," I grunt. I drink four more bags and with each bag, my body heals bit by bit.

My eyes scan and see five men staring at me. Their clothing torn, remnants of gashes lance their faces, and fatigue fills their eyes.

"What's with all the commotion?" I ask.

"It's called saving your ass," Donovan barks.

"Carla." My movements are jerky but swift. I stand and take a few steps before I'm face to face with Kerry, Simon, and Nick, standing in my way.

"No. Paul's tracking them. When they land in a spot, we'll go. We're not going in blind." Simon's forceful tone stops my movements.

"We think he's heading to another property he owns. A warehouse in Ballard," Ed says.

Ed's eye is black and blue. Jagged, torn flesh opens to a gaping wound on his right forearm. Blood oozes from it.

My gaze meets Ed's. "I'm not sure why you're here, not saying I don't appreciate it, but it's confusing. That tear…" I point to Ed's arm and turn to Nick. "Tell me it's not a full moon, and that tear isn't from a Were?"

Nick shakes his head and Simon fills me in on their band of misfits, and what they've learned in the past twenty-four hours.

My gaze falls to Donovan and Simon, who are standing side by side. My heart drops. "He bound Carla to him." I look away. I don't need to explain what this means. Carla's inextricably tied to Arnold Wainwright. The only way to break the bond is if one of them dies.

"Let's go upstairs and see what else we can find out about him," I say.

"Kerry's upstairs searching, but I agree, let's get out of this basement," Simon replies.

Upstairs in the kitchen, Kerry's flipping through paper files. He has found nothing new and continues to thumb through, pulling papers out. Nick places a bandage around Ed's arm, and Simon and Donovan are whispering.

A palpable tension fills the air as we wait for Paul's call. Each of us paces different parts of the house. Simon reaches out to Shannon, letting her know we're okay. I overhear him apologizing and I'm curious what for, but that question can wait.

I peer outside. A couple of Weres stand guard at the perimeter of the property. When Simon gets off the phone, Donovan calls their father, giving him a status report. Simon calls Jarvis requesting help with cleanup. Apparently, they killed three vampires to get to the house.

As we wait, I pace the gray laminate flooring in the living room. The blue leather couch, mahogany tables, and accent rugs tie the space together, creating a sense of balance. It's a strange contrast to a killer's mindset.

I think about what it takes to pull off what they've done, and the level of clearances they had to get. I'm surprised they could orchestrate it all in such a short time. "You cleared this op with Homeland, Seattle PD, and the Dracul?"

The room goes quiet. The only answers are gazes hitting the floor and others scanning the room looking for an out. "But you couldn't have pulled this all off without some help?" I ask.

Simon clears his throat. "Yeah, we had some." He doesn't offer anymore. Hopefully, no one's head will be on the chopping block when this rogue mission comes to light.

My mind trails to Carla. I try to push thoughts of her away because my throat constricts, and my chest tightens when I think about the danger she's in. Breathing in and out slowly calms the anxiety, but it's not enough. "Any alcohol in there?" I say to those in the kitchen. Nick brings me a glass of wine. I take it from him and gulp it down in one drink. He's the only one who knows about my anxiety.

Simon, who had stepped outside a few minutes ago to take a phone call, comes back inside. He shakes his head, waving anticipation off the faces staring at him. He walks toward me and in a low voice, he says, "Something you need to know. Shannon got into your home office. She found the blood. I did my best to calm the situation. I used the excuse of your affiliation with the blood bank. Seemed like she bought it."

The muscles in my jaw tick. "Shannon and her damn hacking skills."

Simon admonishes me. "Those skills saved your life."

Sarcastically, I say, "You're saying my investment in her digital forensic and security software was well worth it?"

"What I'm saying is be prepared. Also, I don't know for sure it was her, but I saw a car like hers parked down the block. It's not there anymore."

I sigh. "I'll deal with whatever comes up."

Simon's phone rings and we all stop what we're doing. It's Paul, and he's found them at a warehouse. This time I listen to Simon as a plan's formulated. These men have risked their lives to save me, and none of them show signs of hesitation about our next steps.

Simon addresses the group. "There aren't any guards at the warehouse. We won't need the same manpower."

Kerry has the blueprints to the warehouse and uploads them to our phones.

Ed hands me my phone. "Found this. Thought you'd want it."

"You were watching?"

"I was detecting. Knew you were up to something."

We agree that Simon, Nick, and I will enter the warehouse first. Kerry and Ed will hang back, giving us ten minutes before they come. Simon asks Jarvis to have the Guard surround the building. He turns to me. "This time we won't let him escape."

I don't want to sound like an ass, but I ask, "How did he escape?"

"They weren't here. On the other side of the basement is a hidden door. It leads to outside access two blocks down. They left through that."

"Jack." He places a hand on my shoulder. "Carla won't come out of this in a good place, not after what she knows and what she's experienced. Are you prepared to deal with that?"

"He has to die. That's the only way she'll survive this."

Simon says nothing. Instead, he calls out to the group. "Let's go."

Thirty minutes later, everyone is standing in their assigned areas around the perimeter of the warehouse. Simon, Nick, and I take our positions at different insertion points.

The two-story building is made from sheet metal and wood. Inside are several offices and separate extensive storage areas. My entry access is an outside window on the second floor. It's one of the few that opens directly into an office. The drop from the window to the floor won't be steep. Several alcoves with low-hanging eaves make my climb to the second floor easy.

Within seconds, I'm inside the building. The dark warms my senses and I listen for sounds. A muffled whimper leads me out of the office to a set of stairs. The sound echoes, like the hollow banging of a steel drum. The reverberations make it difficult to know the exact location. As I move through, the whimper turns to sniffles. I hear a woman whisper for help, but I can't be swayed. I know Carla's under his power and even though I want to run to her at once; I need to be careful.

I search, looking for any movement. He's around here somewhere and I won't be caught off guard. I remain alert, stalking, and stopping every few moments to watch and listen.

On the other side of the building, something falls with a crash. A loud pop, yelp, and an oomph ring through the building. In the distance a low light flickers, casting shadows. I push it all away. My focus is Carla, and once I get her out of harm's way, I'll find him.

I move around rows and stacks of boxes, following the sounds. I inch around a corner and find a five by ten metal shipping container, where the cries rattle throughout.

"Carla?" I call out.

"Oh my god, Jack." She bangs on the inside. "You gotta get me out of here. Please hurry before he comes back."

I whisper, "Carla, you're safer where you are. Hang tight. I'll be back."

"No. You stupid fool. Get me out now." Her voice is harsh and the frosty edge slices through me. I briefly hesitate, but I don't let this dissuade my efforts. I start to leave, but before I turn, a movement of swift air brushes past me, and something cold wraps around my throat and presses inward.

A metal wire burns my skin and a wave of weakness passes over me. I don't let it take hold. I push through the pain, grabbing the wire with one hand, pulling.

With no immediate backup, I dig deeper. I slam the back of my head into my assailant. He stumbles, loosening the wire enough for me to get my arm around his neck, putting him into a chokehold. He struggles to gain control, throwing a punch to my side. He steps a leg through mine, aiming to take me down. He does, and we both topple over. We both scamper to our feet, ready to pounce.

I hear Carla's echo cheering him on. "Arnold, be careful, baby." Who she's become, under his influence, taunts, and fuels me.

He steps to me, swinging. We're both moving fast, but his punch slams into my jaw and the force throws me into a floor beam. He comes at me again, throwing punches. I duck, grab his legs, and flip him over. He rushes to his feet, pulls out a gun, and shoots. Normally, bullets wouldn't stop, but these burn. I feel the sting in multiple places where silver pierces my flesh. I drop to the ground on my knees, doubling over. The tip of his boot kicks me in the side with a force that knocks me two feet across the floor. The silver weakens my energy, but I can feel my body working to push the bullets out. It's slow and painful.

I rise to a knee and hear a clink from a bullet landing on the concrete floor. Once again, he wraps a wire around my throat, twisting while pulling. Two more bullets fall to the floor. Little by little, my strength returns. With one hand, I grab the chain behind my neck, pulling toward me. I angle the leg I'm crouched on toward my reach and pull out the silver sheathed blade I took from his house. The last two bullets drop to the floor and I'm able to leap to my feet, dig in, and pull him toward me. I throw off the sheath and jab the knife into his heart, applying pressure.

His eyes widen as he drops to his knees, releasing the chain. Blood gurgles from his mouth and unrecognizable words choke out. I whisper in his ear, "Spiel ist aus." We both fall to the floor. *Game over.*

He heaves and sputters blood. His flesh sinks in, his bones crumble, and he disintegrates into ash, leaving only his clothes behind.

I rush over to the shipping container, unlocking it, and hoist Carla out, setting her on her feet. Her gaze lands on where Arnold once was, tears pool in her eyes, and she passes out. I catch her, carrying her to the floor in my arms.

Kerry and Ed burst in with their weapons raised, ready to shoot. They clear the area and lower their guns.

Kerry calls out, "Where's Simon and Nick? They came in twenty minutes ago."

"Haven't seen them." Alarm enters their eyes, and they begin searching the warehouse.

Carla stirs. "Carla. Carla, sweetheart," I soothingly say.

She struggles to open her eyes and when she does, recognition flashes across her face. She trembles and flails pushing her way out of my arms. I release her and she shrinks away in fear.

"Carla. It's me, Jack. I'm here. You're okay."

Revulsion fills her eyes. "Don't touch me. You monster," she yells.

"No, it's Jack. I love you."

"Don't come near me." She shouts, tears forming in her eyes.

Ed walks into view and Carla rushes to him. He places his arms around her as she sobs. "The paramedics are on their way," he calls out to me. "I'll make sure she gets to the hospital. I'll make sure she's all right."

I nod and watch him carry Carla away.

My gaze hits the floor and my insides crumble.

CHAPTER 40

A MONTH HAS PASSED SINCE the day I watched Ed leave the warehouse with Carla. The day I killed my maker. When I ended his life, a heavy burden was lifted from mine—I'm not sorry for that. But when I think about all the death and destruction he caused over the years and how my anguish kept me locked away, revenge came at a steep price. I didn't realize how constricting my resentment for Arnold Wainwright was. The anger and guilt I'd carried handcuffed me. I can see that now.

Losing Carla was the ultimate price I paid. She won't have anything to do with me.

The first couple of weeks were unbearable. She spent three days in the hospital and for the next two weeks; she locked herself away in her house. Every night, I stood outside. I listened to her tears and watched her pace in her living room when she couldn't sleep. I wanted to go to her, hold her, and tell her I won't let anything bad happen to her again.

I couldn't make that promise. I hadn't protected her and look how that ended. Everything she knew to be true is a lie. Nick tells me to give her some time, but time doesn't heal all wounds. I've learned that much.

When Ed was younger, he'd learned a good friend of his was a vampire. It wasn't something he believed, but when he found out about me it confirmed his experience. His knowledge of vampires and his presence that day became a refuge for Carla. He's still coming around about were-persons.

Ed providing Carla comfort pangs me with jealousy, but her well-being's more important. He checks on her daily and tells me she's coming around day by day. She got dressed last week, started running, and began eating regularly. Her body has healed and next week, she will go back to work.

He tells me she's still having nightmares. With something so horrific, she may have nightmares for many years. She was experiencing anger and shame over her vulnerability and failing as an officer. Every time she looked at her wounds, she faced those feelings. I told Ed I can take it all away—erase the pain and horror. It's the least I can do.

The day after our ordeal, I conferenced with Chief Phipps, Ed, Kerry's boss, Angela Channing, and Donovan. Together, we reviewed the events and shared our information. We also formed a story the public could accept. Ed led the news conference and got the credit for taking down the "Triple M Killer." A man who tortured and manipulated his victims, including his accomplices, who were casualties to his madness. All the perpetrators of these crimes were dead. Case closed. Justice for the victims and closure for their families.

Shannon and I had a long talk. She'd gotten the code I left for her in case I didn't return. She's the closest I've to an heir. If something were to happen to me, I'd make sure she's taken care of for life. Had she kept searching my office, she would've found the hidden compartment in my desk with my will. Of course, my lawyer has the original.

She had questions about the blood in my office, for which I replied, "I've served on the board of the World Hematology Center, and although not on the board currently, I take platelet blood to underserved community cancer clinics." It was enough to quell her curiosity.

"Who are the people on your bookcase? And how come I can't find you anywhere? You don't exist." She had asked.

I was a bit surprised she hadn't researched me sooner. I told her, "I've got a history I can't share. Maybe there'll be a time when I can, but it's not now. I need you to trust me and not dig any further. It's for everyone's safety." Her gaze drifted to the floor, and she was quiet. Eventually, her gaze met mine, and she studied me. I got a nod and an okay.

Shannon returned home three weeks ago and overall, everything's back to normal.

I say hello to Jim and Stan as I walk into the Shipwreck. Nick's behind the bar, I catch his eye, he smiles and nods toward the back center of the room. On my way to the table, a petite redhead briefly catches my eye when she smiles at me. I smile back to be polite. A couple of months ago, I would've talked to her, sent her a beer, and thought nothing of taking her back to my place, but instead, I keep walking. Shannon follows my steps as I walk between the tables.

We have been meeting every Friday night since this misfit of characters came together. Unlike other times, we agreed Shannon could join us tonight. She was integral to our success, and tonight we're celebrating. Kerry's in town and will join us too. We are the last of our group to arrive.

Nick, with the authority of Simon and Donovan, announced to all the patrons—directed more toward the supernatural ones, "be on your best behavior between now and ten p.m."

Three pitchers of beer and six full glasses sit around the table. In front of an empty chair is a beer and a shot of hard liquor. *Must be my seat.* Nick knows what I need.

Shannon and I take a seat. Simon, who's sitting directly across from us, catches Shannon's eye. They hold each other's gaze, and something passes between them. She clears her throat and looks away. I haven't asked if something is going on. I guess I've been too caught up in my own stuff. I've seen her in the office scanning her text messages and smiling. I only hope it's some boy she met at school.

Donovan sits on Simon's left. He's talking to Ed, who sits next to him, and Kerry leans into Donovan's and Ed's discussion about last night's Mariner's game. I'm happy to see them and not hiding a smile, I say hello. We catch each other up on our week. Laughter and camaraderie are shared between us. A little later, Nick slides into a chair and joins.

A special bond was formed between us on that day. I've seen that happen during a military operation or in war with a squad or platoon. When you're in a battle, your survival depends on those around you and the bond becomes tight. The differences among us are vast, but we all share some commonalities. Oaths were taken to serve and protect. To uphold truth and justice. And a secret that depends on our discretion and protection.

It's here where Ed catches me up on Carla's progress. "How's Carla doing?"

"She's managing. It's a lot to come to terms with. I think she's sleeping better." I know he stays at her house, on the couch, and when he does, she sleeps better. For that, I'm glad.

Shannon turns to me. "She called the other day asking questions about you. Like what do I know about you, your family, and your past? I know little in that regard and suggested she ask you directly."

I search out Simon and Ed and they understand the meaning of my glance. Ed says, "I'll speak to her." All I can do is nod. With Shannon present, we can't talk about *it.*

A small flutter of hope swirls in my chest, but I don't get to feel it for too long. A server comes over and hands me a scotch on the rocks. "From the girl over there, the redhead." She sits a few tables away and I can see her from my angle. Donovan and Ed turn to find her.

I hand the drink back to the server. "Tell her thank you. She's beautiful, but I'm not interested."

"Don't waste a good shot, Jack. Here, give it to me." The server hands Donovan the drink. He raises it to the girl and smiles. She looks to me and then to him. The server walks over to her and says something in her ear. It's too loud in the tavern for me to catch the words.

I don't realize they're all staring at me until I take a drink of my beer. "What?"

"When have you ever turned down a woman?" Simon asks.

Simon's taunting me. I know it's in good nature, but of all people, he should know what I'm going through. "I do. I have." I take another drink.

Nick rushes to my defense, patting me on my shoulder. "Let Jack be, guys."

"Kerry, you're heading to Los Angeles tomorrow?" I ask, quickly changing the subject.

"Yeah. I got a call to work with the Federal Bureau of Investigation." Kerry sighs. I can tell he isn't looking forward to it. "You have any connections there?" He asks.

"In the Bureau or in general?"

"Law enforcement."

"A few. I worked a serial arsonist case in LA a few years back."

"Anything I should know about the landscape?"

We all spend the next hour sharing tricks of the trade, one-upping each other, and laughing. At ten p.m., Shannon arranged for an Uber to take her home and I leave shortly thereafter.

I get into my car, reach for my phone, and listen to the one message I have. It's from Carla. "I can't sleep. I have questions." I text her with an invitation to come over. With my breath held, I wait for her response. She agrees and I rush home.

When I get home, I jump into the shower. My stomach flips thinking about Carla. I don't want to get my hopes up, but my heartbeat speeds up a little. I towel off and throw on a black t-shirt and blue jeans.

I nearly trip on Jasper rushing out of my bedroom. "Sorry, boy." I pat his head. Our relationship has improved in the last few weeks. He's back to sleeping on the corner of my bed. I think he trusts me again.

In the kitchen, I pull out a bottle of red wine and a couple of glasses. The intercom buzzes and my heart stops. Through the camera, I see it's Carla and buzz her up.

The elevator opens and I walk to the entrance, meeting her. She steps out and freezes upon seeing me.

"Carla. It's okay. You're safe. I promise." She smiles and steps inside tentatively.

I remove her jacket and drape it on a bar stool. "Let me get you some wine and we can sit and talk."

I fill our glasses with wine and walk into the living room where she's sitting on the couch. I hand her a glass and she quickly pulls back, her eyes wide.

"I'm sorry." I take it away. "It's red wine. Can I get you something else?" I silently curse. "I'm really sorry, I didn't think…"

"No, it's okay. I'll take the wine. I'm sorry. I just…" Her voice trails and her gaze is distant.

"You don't need to explain. It's okay. Can I sit down on the couch?" I ask.

She smiles and nods. I sit and for a moment silence fills the space. I gaze at her. She's beautiful and I've missed her. She's wearing a black, cotton, pencil skirt and a light pink, short-sleeved blouse that hangs just off her soft shoulders. Her hair's an inch longer since the last time I saw her. Physically, there isn't any evidence of what happened to her a month ago, but she's paler and there's a shadow behind her eyes.

"You look beautiful. I'm glad you came over." I sip my wine. "You have some questions for me?"

For the next two hours, I answer questions about my age, being a vampire who I was before I got turned. We talked about my wife and daughter, which wasn't easy for me, but I wanted her to know all of it.

We talked about the professions I've had, the wars I've been through, the monster I'd become after I was turned, and how I broke free from that. She didn't have many questions about Arnold Wainwright. Ed filled her in on that.

We sit on the couch, my leg on one side of her, and her back against me. She rests her head on my chest. By the end of the two hours, her defenses are lowered enough to where she lets me hold her when she cries.

I smooth her hair. "I'm sorry I let this happen to you. I tried to keep you away." We talk about that too—why I pushed her away. "This past month I've gone crazy not knowing if you were okay, not being able to hold you."

Carla tips her head, peering at me with a smile. With warm eyes staring at me, her hand grazes my jawline. "Jack, take me to bed," she whispers.

My arms stiffen and a lump forms in my throat. "Carla. There's nothing more I'd like than to have you in my bed, but with all you've been through, now isn't the right time. There's no hurry."

"I want you to. I want to know all of you."

"Are you sure?" She nods and shifts her body, straddling my lap.

My lips brush hers and I tell her, "I love you and always will."

I pick her up and carry her to my room, kicking Jasper out. I set her down, my hands sliding down her body. I kiss her deeply, madly, and she returns my kiss. Her hands are under my shirt, caressing my torso. She tugs my shirt up and I throw it off. My desire for her is intense. I want to rip her clothes off and sink deep into her, but I restrain myself, for her sake.

I remove her blouse, unclasp her bra, and kiss her breasts. She moans. I'm nearly undone by the sounds she makes. I lay her on the bed, my knees spreading her legs, and continue kissing her. We remove the rest of our clothes. I get on my knees, grab her legs, and pull her down to me. With my touch, her breathing becomes heavy, and her hand tugs at my hair. She erupts, calling out my name. I kiss her thighs, giving her a moment to come down.

"Jack, I want you to bite me." I freeze and pull away. She sits up. "What's wrong?"

My hands caress her legs and I look up at her. "Carla, I can't bite you."

She reaches for my face and slides off the bed, straddling my lap. "Why not? I want you to." Her mouth kisses my neck and I moan.

"I watched another man bite you and it nearly killed me. That wasn't what I wanted for you." I say through clenched teeth. The thought alone knots my stomach.

In a sultry voice, Carla whispers. "Jack, tonight I want all of you. Everything you are. Everything you have to give."

A low growl rolls in my chest. "Are you sure?"

She nods.

"I…" My mouth finds hers and I kiss her hungrily, lifting us, I toss her onto the bed. Her legs part for me and I climb on top of her, kiss her breasts, and find her mouth again. I lift my head. "I'll let you know before I bite, but you need to tell me if it hurts too much."

I position myself. Her legs wrap around me and hungrily we lose ourselves in desire and ecstasy. I feel her getting close. My eyes dilate, filling with a red hunger. "Now," I whisper in her ear.

"Now…" Her words strangle underneath my teeth, sinking into her neck. She cries out, writhing, while I keep thrusting. I let out a groan as I send both of us over the edge, enjoying the waves of pleasure ripping through our bodies.

My lips caress her body and I whisper, "I love you." Our gazes meet and she smiles. I roll to my side and pull her into me. When our breathing stabilizes, I ask if she's okay.

"Yes. You do that well." Her fingers glide down my forearm. "Our bodies fit."

My chest warms and I kiss the back of her head. "I'm glad you're here," I say and drift off into a deep sleep.

Later, I wake to Carla caressing my arm. We fell asleep entangled. Now she's facing me. I pull her in closer and kiss her. "Good morning." It must be because I feel the room warming.

She smiles at first, then her eyes narrow and her lips become thin. She gazes at me with an intensity that clutches my breath.

"What's wrong?"

"You said you can make me forget. Compel me."

I draw my head slightly back. "Yeah, sure. I can." I stumble over the words. "I will if you want me to. What part?" I ask flatly.

She sits up. Her eyes darting. "All of it. I can't live in this world, Jack. It's too much for me. I want to go back to knowing there's only one world I fit in. No vampires. No Were-things. I need concrete. Logic. I'm a scientist and I need plausibility." She trembles as she speaks. She slides her legs over the edge of the bed to stand.

"Wait," I say, my voice commanding. I stand, walk to her side, and sit next to her, putting my arm around her. "What's this all about?" She relaxes into me.

"Jack, I just can't do it. I had to know. Had to know what it'd be like, you and me. All of it. If I could live this way and I can't. I'm sorry."

I stand up, looking for my jeans to pull on. "So, you thought you'd come over here and use me? Get one more thrill and leave my life for good?"

She stands and reaches for my arm. "No. I... This is hard for me. Everything I've gone through it... it's changed me. I wanted us. I love you, but I can't. I mean," she trails off before speaking again. "I want a family. Children. Family vacations. Normal. You shouldn't exist. This shouldn't be real."

Her words stab. "You want to forget me too?"

"I want to go back to the way things were."

I go quiet, thinking about the implications of this. "That means erasing your feelings for me, knowing we dated in the past, but it didn't go anywhere. That you only regard me as a colleague. It couldn't be any other way. Otherwise, you'd always have a pull toward me, and it'd lead you back to where you are now." I want to be selfish, tell her we can work through all these things, but the reality is I can't give her normal. As much as I want to, I can't.

"I'm sorry," she sobs.

I bring her into me, embracing her. "It's okay. I don't like it. It hurts. Deep. But if that's what you want... I want you to be happy, you understand. I'd do anything for your happiness."

Carla's tears subside. I kiss the top of her head. For this to work, I must consider anyone else it may affect. "What does Amy know?"

"Nothing. My team thinks the chief arranged for me to attend a conference in Boston, and afterward, I flew to Florida to aid in an investigation. It's not outside my job duties, so it's believable. I guess I've taken some vacation time to while in Florida. I've kept in communication with my team through email and talked to Amy twice."

"Anyone else know, outside of the chief and Ed?"

She shakes her head. "Who'd believe me?"

We get dressed and make a clear plan on what suggestions to use. I'll enhance her cover story with some memories—places she's been to in Boston and Florida, flying into SeaTac airport, what day she got home and unpacked. She'll know that she went to the doctor a few weeks ago because she fell down the stairs at her house and got banged up. A fact her hospital records already state. We make sure the suggestions are plausible and can be supported by others or evidence. Since few people know the truth, managing this story won't be difficult.

This was one of the most painful conversations I've ever had and through it, my stomach clenches. I don't want to do it, and probably Simon should be the one to compel her, but it's the one gift I can give her. It's the normal I can give.

After we come up with the plan, I hold her. She cries and my heart breaks. "I don't want to do this. I don't want to let you go."

She touches my face and whispers, "Thank you." We share a deep kiss. One, which says it all.

"You ready?" I say just above a whisper.

When the elevator doors close, I hoped she'd come back, telling me she'd made a mistake, but I know she won't. She was resolute in her decision. Once she gets into her car, her feelings for me will disappear and all the horror that occurred a month ago will be nonexistent.

I need to let Ed know. After all, he's been her confidant throughout. He'll need to know the new story so he can corroborate it. Later I'll call the chief, but for now, I only text Ed and Simon with a brief, "I compelled Carla."

My breathing stops. I feel my body sway and the room spins. The walls are closing in and I'm unable to escape the freight train barreling toward me. I drop the phone, willing my legs to move, and make my way to the bedroom, dropping onto the bed. It's here I wait for these feelings to pass.

Unfortunately, this time I don't think they will.

CHAPTER 41

SUMMERS IN SEATTLE ARE GORGEOUS. The air's crisp and clean and the mountains are green with only a tuft of snow on their tops. Sailboats glide across the Sound. People flock to the beaches, grilling and playing volleyball. The water sparkles, dispersing the sun's rays. I take it all in, standing behind the U.V.-protected glass that surrounds my apartment. In another month, the rain will return. "I can't believe it's September already," I say to Jasper, who's sitting on the windowsill looking out. I sigh. Time to get a move on it.

I grab my keys and head downstairs to my office. I walk out of the elevator into the foyer and to my office. The lights are on.

"Shannon, I'm surprised to see you this early." I tease.

She rolls her eyes. "It's not that early. I'm in between gigs."

She's interning for the Seattle PD in their evidence lab. She doesn't talk to me about it, other than her hours. I know it's because she's working with Carla and she's trying to spare my feelings.

May was a rough month for me. I wallowed in self-pity and regret. I didn't eat. I didn't take phone calls, and I hardly left the couch. It pained me to lose Carla, and I rationalized it was for the best, and for her it was. But for me, my insides were ripped apart.

Unfortunately, Nick, Simon, and Shannon had access to my apartment. If I had the energy, I would've told Meghan to erase their access. However, in my state, I don't think she would've. I tried to get rid of my housekeeper too. I told her to take paid time off until I called her. She didn't listen either. She continued to show up to straighten the apartment and feed Jasper.

Nick, Simon, and Shannon took turns checking on me every day. After six weeks of watching my misery, they must've gotten desperate because Aron Johnson walked through my elevator one day. He had, after all, lost his wife of two hundred years. I'm sure they reasoned if he couldn't talk any sense into me, no one could. And it worked because, comparatively, my loss didn't come close. Although, I think I was mourning the cumulative losses I'd experienced and hadn't properly grieved. I realized it was time to move forward. However, that would work and a new case was perfect timing.

A couple of months ago, I was hired by an influential family who suspected a family member of stealing some of their prized possessions. They thought if they involved the police, their reputations would suffer. It didn't take long for me to have enough evidence pointing to their nephew as the culprit. It was an easy five grand and a good distraction.

In my absence, Shannon spruced up the office with new front office furniture. She placed plants in the corners and got a TV installed. I'm not sure how she works with the news running all the time. She told me it's the background noise that helps her focus. I glance at the television and back to her and sigh. It's noise to me, much like the music she listens to.

I open my office door and enter, leaving the door ajar. On my desk is the Sunday copy of the Seattle Times. *Ugh, more news.* I pick it up to toss it in the garbage can when the front-page article catches my attention. "Seattle Times Reporter Found Dead—Circumstances Suspicious." I sit down and read the first paragraph.

"Keith Daniels, an investigative reporter, was found dead on Sunday, August 30, 2019. Daniels died of asphyxiation caused by paralysis from a toxin called Tetrodotoxin. Tetrodotoxin is found in marine creatures—blue ring octopus, the pufferfish, and the Pacific Newt. Death ruled a homicide."

I stop reading, but I'm stuck on the name. Keith Daniels. Where have I come across his name before?

The television noise interrupts my thoughts and I get up to close the door. Before I do, Shannon says, "Have you heard about this case?" She points to the television. "I went to middle school with her. She's missing." She turns up the volume.

I stare at the face shown as Jennifer Shultz and listen. "Jennifer Shultz, daughter of the prominent Seattle defense attorney, Hick Bradley, has been reported missing. Bradley is currently running for a U.S. Senate position. It is rumored that Shultz was involved in sex trafficking. She's been missing since Saturday."

"They got that wrong," Shannon says. "Bradley was her stepfather. And her mom died, I think. I remember her. She was a year older, but we rode the same bus to school. She was a good student, smart, and involved in school clubs. She was nice enough. I mean, we ran in different circles, but... then I stopped seeing her around."

"Hope they find her. It's not likely though, especially if she's involved in sex trafficking. The life expectancy for trafficked persons is seven years. She either angered a John or angered her pimp. Or a drug overdose took her life. Either way, it's not a good end."

I close the door and return to my chair. It's mid-week and I haven't got through all my mail. No better time than the present.

I go through the envelopes, sorting bills from the letters requesting my services. At the bottom of the pile is a large manila envelope. There isn't a return address. I hesitate before opening it. After the last letter I received with no return address, I'm not sure I want to know what's inside. But curiosity gets the better of me, and I open it and shake out its contents. A police report dated September 23, 2008, falls out. I read through it.

> *A thirteen-year-old female reportedly raped. A man entered her home at approximately 9:30 p.m. No forced entry. Parents - Pam and Hick Bradley were away. No one else was in the home. Medical tests show evidence of vaginal and anal tears. Pregnancy test negative. The accused, a pizza delivery man, Caucasian, 5'8 in height, and brown hair. No other marks or identification known.*

Interesting. I wonder if the thirteen-year-old in this police report is the missing Jennifer Shultz? I look at the envelope, searching for any markings that would give me a hint where it came from. Who would send this to me? And why?

My mind drifts to the reporter found dead. Jennifer was declared missing on Saturday. Daniels was found dead on Sunday, and I was mailed a police report about Hick Bradley. Coincidence? I lean back into my chair and tap my fingers on my desk. Keith Daniels. Jennifer Shultz. Why are those names familiar?

I turn on my computer, open my email, and scroll through between February and May. An email I'd received a few months ago lingers in my mind. I'm not sure I read it, but something's prompting me to find it.

After fifteen minutes of scrolling and deleting unnecessary mail, I come across an email from Jennifer D. Shultz. It's marked priority. I remember glancing through it, however, I probably didn't respond. I read it.

> Mr. Calloway,
>
> I have sensitive information. If it gets into the wrong hands, my life will be in jeopardy. If that should be the case, I'd like to hire you, in advance, to find out what happened to me. I can pay whatever your fee is, and I'll cover all your expenses.

I continue scrolling through my emails, searching for her name. I find another one sent to me in July.

> Mr. Calloway,
>
> I haven't heard from you. I'm in trouble. Please, I need your help. I have fifty thousand dollars set aside in your name at Bank of the West. I've signed a power of attorney authorizing you these funds should anything happen to me. I sent information about illegal activities my stepfather is engaged in to Keith Daniels with the Seattle Times. If something happens to me, I have permitted him to get that information to you.

I jump out of my chair, open my door, and shout at Shannon. "Find me everything you can on Jennifer Shultz, Hick Bradley, and a reporter who was recently found dead, Keith Daniels. Everything."

Shannon startles at my voice. "Jennifer Shultz, why?"

"We have a new case."

If you enjoyed Jack's story, please leave a review. It really helps, and I would greatly appreciate it.

For newsletters, promotions, and book information: Subscribe

ACKNOWLEDGMENTS

Writing Jack's story came from a motivation I couldn't ignore. In the process, a whole new world opened, which has forever changed me. I appreciate everyone who took a chance and read his story. I hope you've enjoyed it as much as I have.

It took a whole bunch of people to complete this book and I wholeheartedly thank all of them. I couldn't have done this without some incredible people. Editor and author extraordinaire DeeAnna Galbraith, whose house and I were fated to collide. Without her guidance, Jack wouldn't have a story loudly to tell, and to James Feldkamp, who helped tighten the story and made sure the investigative procedural story was told correctly.

A big thanks to Vikki at VCBOOKCOVERS.COM for the wonderful book design and Ava Mallory for an awesome Blurb. Go team! And to my writing group Wordherders, your knowledge has been invaluable.

To my fantastic book reviewers who, out of their own time and generosity, helped get Jack's story right. Susan, Kurt, Ann, and Crystal – THANK YOU!

And thank you to everyone who listened to me go on and on about my writing journey, struggles, and achievements.

ABOUT THE AUTHOR

Carmen Cady holds two master's degrees, one in psychology and the other in business. In her past incarnation (a few years ago), she spent her days fascinated by the human psyche and understanding what motivates behaviors. Currently, she spends her days crunching numbers and crafting suspense and romance novels. But when she's not studying the human condition, crunching the numbers, or crafting new stories to share with the world, she enjoys spending time with her family, being in nature, and as a visitor in her cat's home which is in the beautiful Pacific Northwest.

For more information about her, visit her at:
Website: https://carmencady.com/
Facebook: https://www.facebook.com/carmen.cady.104
Twitter: https://twitter.com/cadypublishing